ADVANCE PRAISE FOR *WISHES COME TRUE !*

"Witty, wise, and sensuous–Kathleen Nance delivers a timeless story of magical love!"
— Nikki Holiday, author of *Heaven Loves a Hero* and *Bedroom Eyes*

"Remember the name Kathleen Nance, because this shining star is destined to burn brightly in the firmament of contemporary fantasy romance. In her sparkling debut novel, *Wishes Come True*, Ms. Nance spins a delightful tale of love, magic, and wishes gone awry. her clever humor and quirky, heartwarming characters will enchant you, and I guarantee you'll fall in love with her yummy out-of-this-world djinni hero!"
— Pam McCutcheon, author of *Quicksilver* and *A Reluctant Rogue*

FURY'S PASSION

"You know nothing about me, Zoe Calderone. You know nothing of my people or what my life should be beyond these." He lifted his wrists and struck the copper bands together. A bolt of blue energy passed from his wrist to the bands on his upper arms. "Like all humans, you condemn what you do not comprehend. You live your tiny, separate lives, filled with your petty concerns."

He wanted to stay angry, but as he noticed her flushed cheeks and bright eyes, another emotion unfurled inside. Desire, never dormant when he was with her, grabbed him with its hot, sweet grip.

She wanted prim and proper, arguments, control.

He would give her passion, wildness, no choices.

The door slammed shut and locked with a click. He stepped forward. She stepped back, swallowing. She had finally realized he would no longer allow sway over him.

"I shall show you the capabilities of *ma-at*," he said, "the effort and imagination it demands. Show you what I have wanted to do from the moment I laid eyes on you."

Wishes Come True

Kathleen Nance

LOVE SPELL BOOKS NEW YORK CITY

For my Dad.
You taught me that knowledge is understanding, that any
door was open to me, and that hard work and learning are
necessities. I hope you can read this and be proud.

LOVE SPELL®

February 1998

Published by

Dorchester Publishing Co., Inc.
276 Fifth Avenue
New York, NY 10001

ISBN 0-505-52248-9

The name "Love Spell" and its logo are trademarks of Dorchester Publishing Co., Inc.

Printed in the United States of America.

Chapter One

"No, Mary, you may not conduct a seance."

"But, Mom," the little girl wailed, "Elvina says—"

"Her name is Ellen, and *you* should call her Miss Ellen."

"It's rude to call someone a name they don't like." Mary parroted back one of her mother's admonitions.

Zoe Calderone saved the computer file she was working on, rubbed her eyes, then rotated her desk chair to look at her nine-year-old daughter. Her ex-husband had done one thing absolutely right during his brief fling with married life. He'd given her Mary.

Fortunately, he'd also passed on to Mary his looks and coloring. She had to admit, with Mary's fine blond hair and hazel eyes, the girl looked like the fairy she professed to have as a friend. Especially now, dressed in a pink chiffon skirt Mary had found at a garage sale, pink ballet slippers, and a hair wreath of dried flower buds. The Wonder Woman T-shirt was a distinctly modern touch, however, as were the smudges of charcoals and paints on Mary's face.

"You're right," Zoe acknowledged. Ellen DeVries, her friend, who shared the other half of the duplex, had asked to be called Elvina. The name was more compatible with her spirit guides, Ellen—oops, Elvina—had explained. Zoe hadn't understood the explanation; she had enough trouble remembering the name. "Call her Miss Elvina." She licked her thumb, and then wiped a smear of green paint from Mary's chin.

"E-e-e-w, spit. That's gross."

"Sorry." Zoe ruffled Mary's hair.

"*Miss* Elvina says tonight's the best night," Mary continued, "because it's the summer solstice. And it's not a seance, it's a conjuring."

"Do you know what a solstice is?"

Mary shifted impatiently on slippered feet. "It's the start of summer, the day when there's the most daylight. Quit being a teacher, this is important. If you let me, I'll . . . I'll study my math flash cards, just like you've been nagging me to. Every Monday, all summer."

Zoe leaned back in her chair and studied her daughter. Like all parents, she'd learned the value of compromise and a good bribe. "What exactly do you want to do? And I think you need to study the cards daily. You almost failed math last year."

"We're going to conjure up a genie! Besides, I didn't almost fail; I got a C. How about twice a week? After all, I'm doing a lot of dog-sitting this summer."

"A genie?"

"Yeah. When Miss Elvina and me—"

"When Miss Elvina and *I*."

"—When Miss Elvina and I went to the flea market last month there was this guy there we'd never seen before, and he had the neatest things in his booth. You should have seen them! Real pretty crystals, red and yellow and blue ones, and cool pictures and lots of super old books." Mary bobbed from the computer to the window and back, her hands punctuating her enthusiasm. She stopped and wrinkled her nose. "Most of the books were falling apart and made me sneeze when I opened them."

Zoe relaxed in her chair. Mary's stories were seldom brief.

"There was this one book," Mary continued, clasping her hands together. "Miss Elvina got kind of a weird look on her face when she touched it. She said her spirit guide told her to buy it. When I asked her what that meant, she laughed and said she just had a hunch that she should buy it. You know how you're always telling me to trust my instincts, that if something doesn't feel right I shouldn't do it? Like that time Jocy gave me a can of beer. Did I ever tell you about that? Well, I figured it was something like that—"

"Mary, get to the point." She'd find out about Joey and the beer later.

"I *am*. Miss Elvina couldn't read much of the book—it was too faded and had words I never heard before—but this one section she could."

"And what did the book say?" Zoe couldn't hide her skepticism.

Mary bounced up and down on the balls of her feet. "It told how to conjure up a spellbound genie. It said 'between' times are best for working the magic. The solstice is a 'between' time, so it's gotta be tonight, even if we haven't done all the preparations, and Miss Elvina needs another person to do the magic right." She paused to take a deep breath.

"I don't like you involved in this, Mary. I'm going to have a talk with Ellen—Elvina—about filling your head with nonsense."

"Ple-e-ease, Mom. This is important. I really wish you'd let me."

Something in the tone of Mary's voice caught Zoe's attention.

Her daughter had always been a beautiful, beloved mystery to her. Where Zoe's world was factual and pragmatic, Mary's was full of creative fantasy. Her room was papered with bright pictures she'd drawn of fairies, elves, and other creatures from her imagination. She slept with a stuffed unicorn. At the end of a school day she raced home to shed her plaid uniform and don the airy clothes she favored. Since they were practical in the hot New Orleans climate, Zoe indulged her daughter's tastes.

Mary understood finances were tight. She rarely asked for things. Only once before had Zoe heard that tone in her daughter's voice. At the age of five, Mary had wanted to take art lessons. Zoe had scrimped, cutting down on her noon lunch to find the funds. To this day, the lessons were the light of Mary's life.

Now Zoe heard that same tone. "Why is it so important to you?"

"For you."

"What?" Zoe sat up straighter.

"You're so serious all the time. You don't laugh much. You don't see anyone. Face it, Mom, you need a genie."

"I see lots of people."

"I *meant* like a date."

10

"I date. Sometimes."

"Your last date was in April," Mary drawled. "He patted me on the head like a baby and brought you home before ten. Genies can't make you fall in love, but I can wish for you to meet someone you'd love anyway. That way you get a new husband and I get a dad."

Zoe let out a breath. "Wishing won't get you what you want in this life," she said, sounding harsher than she'd intended.

"Sure it does, and this will show you."

Her daughter was losing sight of the barrier between reality and fantasy. It was time to end this nonsense.

"No. You can't do the conjuring. It's a waste of time." She swiveled her chair back to face the computer screen.

"Prove it."

Zoe turned back. "What did you say?"

"I said, 'Prove it.' Let me do this magic, and if it doesn't work, I'll shut up forever about genies and wishes." Mary jabbed her fists into her waist, looking as determined as when she'd prepared for her first art display.

"Do you mean that?"

"Yes."

Zoe didn't believe they'd conjure up a genie, didn't believe it for an instant. Genies didn't exist. Magic didn't exist. Wishing just screwed things up.

She worried about Mary's fascination with magical solutions and didn't like the idea of her daughter dabbling in spells and rituals. Perhaps this was an opportunity to prove magic held no answers. "All right." She stopped her daughter's jubilant dance with a raised hand. "But I don't want you 'doing magic.' I'll help Elvina, and you can watch."

"No. You'll just go through the steps. You'll make

11

fun and not believe. It won't work, then you'll tell me 'I told you so.' "

Zoe considered Mary's objections. "I won't promise to believe, because I don't. But I will do whatever Elvina tells me to do, and I'll do it reverently and sincerely."

"Promise?"

"I promise."

Mary studied her for a moment, then nodded. "You're careful with promises. All right."

The wind chimes outside her window clinked in a soft melody, though Zoe could see no breeze in the bushes. "In return, you have to do the math cards three times a week."

"Deal." Mary stuck out her hand. Zoe gave it a firm shake and wondered what she had agreed to.

She'd agreed to insanity, that's what she'd agreed to. Why else would she be barefoot, sitting on her hardwood floor between a yellow tablecloth weighted with seven stones and the fireplace she never used?

What had Elvina said? The fireplace, which opened into both halves of the duplex, also represented a "between" spot. As did now, dusk, with the laughter of children drifting through the open window, a light sound surrounded by lazy, sultry air.

The blasted candle wouldn't light! Zoe shook out the match with an impatient snap before it could singe her fingers. She should be working, putting the finishing touches on two new project proposals from ZEVA, her fledgling multimedia business. Instead, following the ancient book's instructions, she was trying to light three candles with a single match, but the one shaped like a frog refused to ignite. She'd used three matches and twice burned her fingers.

Striking another match, she glared at the white wax frog. "Light, dammit," she commanded. When it blazed, she lit the blue dragon and yellow unicorn. She blew out the match and wiped her damp forehead on her T-shirt sleeve. It wasn't nerves, it was New Orleans in June, but Elvina had insisted the windows be open. Zoe's stomach rumbled. Elvina had also said they couldn't eat until afterward.

"Genies like music," Elvina said. "Mary, pick out a tape."

What in their limited selection of tapes might be considered appropriate for genie-conjuring? Zoe couldn't think of a thing, but apparently Mary had no such qualms. A strong guitar beat boomed into the room, followed by Mary-Chapin Carpenter's voice commanding them to show a little inspiration and spark.

Zoe raised her brows in question. "Mary-Chapin Carpenter?"

Mary, wearing a white school shirt and white gym shorts, her hair drawn back with a white, lace ribbon, plopped down beside Zoe. Elvina had insisted that only the colors blue, white, and yellow could be present in the ritual area. She'd given explicit instructions: no shoes, Mary in white, Elvina in yellow, Zoe in blue. Zoe had complied with a solid blue T-shirt and a pair of frayed cutoffs.

"I don't want to conjure up a genie who won't like country music," Mary explained. She leaned her head against Zoe's arm, an innocent, trusting gesture. "Thanks, Mom, for doing this."

She ruffled Mary's bangs. "You're welcome."

Zoe watched Elvina finish the preparations, noting that she'd carried her yellow theme to the max. A saffron yellow gauze skirt softened her ample behind. She wore a yellow T-shirt that had gotten too tight, the one with the words *I'm elf-friendly* in fancy

13

script below a picture of a strange creature in a bower of leaves. Right now, the picture was covered by at least two dozen strands of Mardi Gras beads in varying shades of yellow and gold.

Elvina bustled about, laying out plastic cups filled with—Zoe leaned over, dabbed a finger into one, and sniffed. Honey. Dirt in another. A third contained stiff brown hairs.

Zoe looked at them suspiciously. "Elvina, where did these hairs come from?"

"Abby's dog."

"The Cartiers' mutt? What did you do to Wolvie?"

Elvina sank to the floor, her skirt swirling about her legs. "We just snipped a few hairs from his tail. It didn't hurt. It's supposed to be goat's hair, but the volunteer at the petting park kept watching me, so I couldn't get any."

No wonder Elvina and Mary had been so willing to go to the Audubon Zoo and leave her alone to work last weekend. "If I didn't love Mary, and if you weren't my best friend and partner, and if you weren't offering me free baby-sitting . . ." Zoe muttered.

"You'd still be doing this because you promised Mary," Elvina retorted.

"Then let's get started."

Head tilted, Elvina assessed her readiness for the ceremony. "At least you wore blue like I told you."

Zoe tapped her earrings. "Even these are blue. I only had white underwear, however."

Elvina drummed her fingers against her chin, and then nodded. "I guess that's okay." She placed a piece of white paper in front of Zoe. A series of interlocking squares drawn in blue bordered the paper. In the middle were some incomprehensible words. "You're going to read the spell."

"I can't read that!"

"Just sound out the words when I tell you to. Stop before you get to the English. Now, join hands."

Above the flickering flames, Elvina grasped hands with Zoe, while Mary watched. The room darkened, as the shadows of twilight crept from the corners. The children must have gone inside, for outdoors was quiet, and stillness pervaded the room, except for Mary-Chapin singing about passionate kisses. Oz, their tabby, strolled into the room, tail high, ears flicking. He rubbed against Zoe, renewing his claim on his humans, then curled himself against Mary's bare leg. Zoe realized she'd been holding her breath and slowly released it.

"Start reading, Zoe," Elvina whispered.

"*Ashadu inna la illaha.*" Zoe stumbled over the unfamiliar words. The hairs on her arms rose, as though a faint electric charge coursed through her. The darkness grew until only the flicker of the candle flames softly lit the room, making Elvina's face a mask of yellow and charcoal. Zoe swallowed; sweating on the outside, arid on the inside. Her voice grew slower, deeper. "*Audubillahi min ash-Shaitan er-Rajim!*" She almost shouted the last word.

"Now close your eyes and visualize." Elvina's voice grated across her nerves. "Visualize the form you wish the genie to appear in. Visualize, hold the image, say the image aloud."

This was ridiculous! She didn't believe any of it. Zoe tensed her muscles to rise, to leave, then subsided. No, she couldn't. She'd promised Mary.

"Make him look like Brad Pitt," Mary whispered.

Zoe closed her eyes. Brad Pitt? Nah. She liked clean-cut, like Keanu Reeves in *Speed*. Of course, there were all the Superman comics she'd read as a kid. Muscles, dark hair, and a tush to die for.

Pierce Brosnan? Those "Remington Steele" reruns, *Goldeneye*—

"Pick an image, Zoe!" Elvina's impatience cut across her daydreams.

"Jimmy Smits," Zoe blurted out, opening her eyes. Mary groaned. "I'm visualizing Jimmy Smits," Zoe insisted and pulled her thoughts in line. Thick, dark hair. Strong hands. Smooth skin. Black eyes. Bedroom eyes. The vivid image brought heat to her face.

"Say the last words," Elvina said. "Say them three times."

Zoe dragged her focus from the image to the words. The time had come to finish this. "In the name of Solomon, the great magician, I do tie thee! In the name of Solomon, the great son, I do command thee come to me. In the name of Solomon, the great builder, I do compel thy obedience."

She repeated the phrases twice more. Louder, more forceful, adding her heart.

Then . . . nothing. The music tape fell silent. The flame in the dragon guttered, extinguishing itself in its own wax; and a thin line of smoke wafted up, carrying the scent of dying candle. Zoe slumped, heard Mary's restless rustle beside her. Hadn't she learned long ago that wishing just made things worse? Now, Mary, too, would learn.

So why did she feel so sad?

"Look, Mom."

Zoe followed her daughter's pointing finger. Smoke from the dragon entwined with smoke tendrils from the other two candles, also now extinguished. The three strands rose, braiding themselves into a single column, thicker, more substantial. As the smoke grew taller and wider, it also grew more solid.

Oz rose from his lazy sprawl and stared at the

smoke as if he eyed a bird on the back porch. He didn't hiss or arch, merely stood at alert attention. Waiting.

The smoke formed appendages. Arms, legs, a head. Color swirled in the depths, changing gray into warm honey.

What was happening? What kind of elaborate trick was this?

She couldn't tear her gaze away. Every instinct screamed that she should get up, should run from this smoke, but she couldn't budge. Zoe grabbed Mary and hugged her tightly, burying Mary's face in her shoulder.

"Mom, I want to see."

"No." Zoe hardly recognized her own harsh tones. "You shouldn't be watching."

"Mom," Mary complained in a muffled voice.

"No," Zoe whispered. The smoke became a man. He wasn't Jimmy Smits, but the conjuring had lost nothing in the translation. Tall, he towered over her sitting cross-legged at his feet. Dark eyes blazed with an undefined emotion. A strong nose. Firm, frowning lips. Smooth golden skin pulled tautly over impressive muscles. Dark, wavy hair. Not just on his head, but also—

Zoe's glance shot back to his face. Other than the metal bands around his wrists and upper arms, the man was totally naked!

Chapter Two

"Who dares summon a sleeping djinni?"

Feet spread, arms akimbo, breath harsh, the man radiated both power and annoyance. The rich glow surrounding him bathed the sparsely furnished room in mellow gold, banishing the shadows of evening. The three candles flared to life again.

His gaze narrowed on Zoe. "What are your wishes, Summoner?" he asked, his voice echoing against the walls.

"Oh, be quiet!" Zoe snapped at the glowering man. She rounded on Elvina, refusing to believe this was anything but a joke that had gone too far. "Ellen DeVries, how did you do this? Whatever you did, the trick is no longer funny. Mary's here, and you dare to bring a naked man—"

"Naked man? Mom, let me go!"

Elvina's mouth hung open, and her eyes were wide and bright. One hand clutched the Mardi Gras beads and twisted them into knots. A smidgen of doubt colored Zoe's surety that her friend had snuck this stranger into their house. Practical jokes weren't Elvina's style, especially one like this, with Mary in the room.

"Look, Zoe," Elvina whispered, pointing at him. "Believe what your eyes and heart tell you. He *is* a genie."

The glow surrounding him faded, replaced by sharp silver sparks encircling his dark hair. "I am not a *genie*," the man retorted, making the word sound obscene, "I am a djinni." He enunciated clearly: *d-jh-ihn'-ee.* "Djinni," he repeated, turning his back on Zoe to address Elvina. "You will say it correctly."

"Djinni," Zoe found herself echoing along with Elvina, bemused at the sight he presented. Bless the saints, he was as magnificent from the back as from the front. Broad shoulders tapered to a sleek muscled back that led to one of the finest derrieres she'd ever seen. Better even than her ex's, and his had been his best feature. A derriere she could fully appreciate since it was near eye-level from her sitting position.

She shook her head. Wherever Elvina had found this guy, he was good. Fantastic, exotic looks, and he had the haughty genie—no, djinni—act down cold.

Mary stirred against her. "Mom, let go. I can't breathe."

Zoe snapped back to reality. "Oh, for Pete's sake, put some clothes on, mister, or I'm calling the police."

How dare a mortal, a woman, speak to him in that tone? He whirled around, the papers at his feet fluttering from the motion, and faced the human who had called him. Since she hadn't phrased her command as a wish he had no obligation to obey, certainly not for the unknown Pete. Curious; there appeared to be no male in the home. Then he saw the young one she cradled protectively. A true home absorbed the personalities of its residents, so he concentrated a moment and picked out the child's name: Mary.

"Not for Pete's sake, but for Mary's sake, will I."

He drew a loose thread from the cloth beneath his feet, for transformation was easier than creation, and then intoned the words of weaving and color. His hands tracked from shoulder to hip, the energy of *ma-at* shimmering beneath his palm. The thread became loose, lightweight, red pants and a yellow shirt with orange sleeves. He studied the sleeve a moment, made it a brighter orange, a little more billowy and softer, and then turned his attention to the woman who had summoned him, starting with her properly bared feet.

From the expanse of leg she showed, and a very pleasant view it was, he judged she'd about come to his chin. She was rounded where a woman should be rounded, not overly so, but enough for a bountiful handful. He paused at her face. Not beautiful, her face was pleasant: thick brows above dark eyes, straight, brown hair that brushed the curve of her jaw, a full mouth. No, he decided, she was beyond pleasant. Her face was intriguing, full of character.

Right now those eyes were wide and the mouth open, as though she were surprised. She squeezed her eyes shut, shook her head once, and then opened her eyes. "If you're a genie—djinni," she said, "and not some elaborate joke, then how do you know my daughter's name?" Her arms tightened around the girl, who had twisted and now stared at him with a delighted, bemused expression.

He owed no explanation, but it amused him to give one, for she would not understand. "You have lived here for many years. Your house speaks of you."

"My house speaks? Yeah, right."

He frowned at the interruption. "The woman behind me is Ellen. Or Elvina."

"Call me Elvina." The woman stood and moved to face him. At first glance she seemed rough, with a too-tight shirt, a chest covered with gaudy beads, hair of an unnatural blond shade, and coloring on her eyelids. Then he saw her face, an older, lined face, a face that had known both kindness and sorrow.

"Elvina it shall be," he said, inclining his head. "And you, woman who summoned me, are Zoe Calderone."

She eyed him through narrowed lids. "What are you called?"

"You may call me Simon." No djinni *ever* gave a true name.

"Are you really a djinni?" Mary breathed.

"I am."

Mary broke into a grin, then jumped up. "We did it, Miss Elvina! We conjured up a djinni!" She began dancing, her feet moving in tiny, excited steps. At her enthusiasm, a tension in Simon eased. These wishes would be ordinary, easy to grant, not twisted or loathsome.

Zoe rose, then began to circle him. "There's a trick to this," she muttered. "There's got to be. Lights? Video?"

He had been right. The top of her head came to just above his chin and, when she moved, the bared expanse of leg was even more intriguing. Hesitantly, she touched his arm. Her palm was slightly rough. No pampered lady, this: she had done honest work in her life.

How long had it been since he'd known the gentle touch of a female? With the warm contact, softer feelings—feelings he'd long ago abandoned—stirred.

Simon stared at her hand, its skin fairer than his, lying just above his hated wristbands. She moved, and her shadow fell over the copper band, dulling the shine and turning it the color of old blood. Had he forgotten a human had placed those bands upon him? Sudden anger deepened his voice. "I am not required to grant access to my person unless you wish it."

"Access to your—?" She snatched back her hand. "Don't be silly."

"You might think about that one, Zoe," Elvina said dryly.

The woman who'd summoned him ignored her friend. "You're not a hologram. You're real." She resumed her circling study, an intent, puzzled look upon her face. "How did you get in here? And those clothes. There's got to be a rational explanation."

"We get wishes, right?" Mary burst in. "Three wishes? Oh, boy, what will I wish for first? I know what the last one will be, that's for Mom, but I've got two others." She grabbed his hand. "Could I get some new paints or the full set of the Girls' Club books or fairy ambrosia? Can you make me smart in math, so I don't have to study flash cards all summer? No, no, first I want that beautiful glass unicorn I saw at the mall. I wish—"

"Wait, little one." He stopped her with his voice, then crouched down to her eye level. Withdrawing his hand from her clasp, he held her gaze with solemnity. "You cannot wish. Your mother called me. Only she can wish."

What would she wish for? he wondered. Probably money or some material benefit, judging by the shabby interior of this house. Humans were so predictable. Numerous wishes he had granted, but very few had been unique.

He rose and turned to Zoe, who now peered out the window, her face reflected in the single wide pane. "Chris," he heard her say, "I bet Chris did this."

This time it would be easy. Three quick, simple wishes, and he'd be only seven summonings away from release from his thousand-year exile. Maybe the other two females would call him after Zoe had used her wishes. He'd be almost free. *Free.*

"What are your wishes, Summoner? I can do anything but bring the dead to life or foretell the future."

The woman turned from the window, her hands planted at her waist. Her lips tightened, but she said nothing. Why did she not state her wishes? Uneasiness crept in.

"Can you do love spells?" Mary asked. "The djinni in the movie said you couldn't."

What was a movie? Simon refused to ask. Instead, his blood raced, turning wariness into the more familiar feeling of anger. Solomon's beard, would they compel him to perform one of those detestable rituals? "Love spells are a crutch of the pitiful," he said and pointedly swept a haughty glare past each of the three females.

In the ensuing silence, the cat's meow was a jarring note.

Elvina cleared her throat. "Do you need a place for your lamp?"

Must humans persist in believing that idiocy of

the lamp? Did they expect him to be *grateful* for the summoning, thinking they'd released him from a cramped, gloomy prison?

"I do not live in a lamp," he said deliberately, "and may the next person who asks become the tongue of an anteater. The djinn do not abide for long on Terra. We have homes—on another plane of existence—but *homes*." Sharp longing for his people and his homeland, Kaf, knifed through him.

"Don't yell at them," Zoe said in a tight voice.

He was tired, tired of this woman's commands, tired of being bound. He tapped his wristbands together with a reverberating ring. "Is that your first wish?"

"No."

"Tell me your three wishes, so I may grant them. What will you have? Gold? Power over your enemies? Forbidden knowledge? A sweet spring of water? A pleasant-dispositioned camel?"

Taking a deep breath, she dusted her hands on her shorts. The woman did have nice legs. He might have enjoyed tarrying a trifle longer to appreciate them, but she would use her wishes and he would be gone. She strolled forward, until she was close enough for him to feel her soft breath on his chest. She looked up, and then smiled.

Simon frowned. That sweet look worried him. So far this summoner had not reacted as all the others had, with anticipation and glee, with eagerness to use the wishes they had so desperately sought.

"A pleasant camel? Now there's an item even Neiman-Marcus hasn't come up with. So, I'm supposed to believe that whatever I wish, you'll grant it like that?" She snapped her fingers.

"Zoe, you'd better watch what you say," Elvina warned. "These wishes are for real."

Zoe pivoted on one foot to face her friend. Her

hair whirled past Simon in a soft wave, and one strand caught on his chest. He smoothed it down, distracted by its sleekness.

"For real?" Zoe said. "Puff the Magic Dragon is as real as genies—"

"Djinn is plural," Simon interrupted.

"Excuse me, *djinn*," she threw over her shoulder. She turned to Elvina, but her thumb jabbed back and poked Simon. "He is a trick of some kind." Her voice rose. "I don't believe in magic or wishes. I don't believe if I say, 'I wish I had a new car,' that, with a poof, one will replace the heap in my driveway."

The powers of *ma-at*, of magic, exploded from the etheric realm and flowed through Simon, energizing him, increasing his strength. He drew from the primal fires of Terra, melding them with the essence of Kaf.

What was a car? From Terra, he pulled the knowledge he sought. A car was a mode of transportation. Many kinds of cars there were, yet the summoner had not set any parameters. He could question her, or he could fulfill as he chose.

He held his hands above his head, wristbands touching. "Your first wish is granted, Summoner."

"My first wish? What wish? I didn't wish!"

"Oh, Zoe!" Elvina rested her forehead on her fist. "What have you done?"

What had he done?

Shaking her head, Zoe walked around the car. "I can't believe he did this."

"Great car, huh, Mom?" Mary skipped beside her, running a hand across the gilt dragon painted on the trunk.

"Great?" Great wouldn't have been her first choice. Flamboyant, maybe. Gaudy monstrosity would be the most accurate. "It's so red, my eyes hurt." Zoe peered in the driver side window. "Is that a steering wheel? Rainbows surrounded by a cloud?" She walked to the front and popped the hood.

"Take a look at these doors!" Mary said. "They look like wings. How fast do you think it goes?"

"Not very," Zoe answered, resting her hands on the frame and staring at the empty engine compartment before her.

Mary looked with her. "Cool, it must run on magic."

"It will go whatever speed you think," interjected Simon.

Zoe threw an irritated glance at the djinni lounging against one of the redbud trees lining her driveway. The night wind ruffled his hair. He watched her, his face an impassive mask.

"Fix the car," Zoe told Simon, proud of her calm tone.

"Only if you wish it."

Zoe gritted her teeth. "You didn't do it correctly the first time. Contractually, it's up to you to set it right."

His brows lifted, and he crossed his arms at his chest. "Contractually? *Ma-at*, magic, does not follow your Terran concepts. What displeases you about the car?"

Besides being a horror to anyone with a modicum of taste? Zoe settled for the practical. "How am I supposed to take it to the brake tag station for inspection? Look at it! It's big. It's . . . red."

Simon shrugged one shoulder. "You did not specify your preferences. I was forced to choose without knowledge of the summoner's desires."

"If you didn't want a new car, then why'd you

wish for it?" Mary asked, with a hint of her mother's practicality.

"I didn't think Simon was real," Zoe grudgingly admitted.

Mary gave her an incredulous look "You saw him materialize. What'd you think he was?"

"Not a djinni, that's for sure," Zoe muttered. She hadn't wanted to believe; any explanation had been more acceptable than that. "I thought he was one of Chris Cartier's jokes. You know Chris wants a career making special effects for the movies." Zoe hated the defensiveness in her voice, hated having to explain herself.

"Chris is good, but not that good," Mary retorted.

Never one to run from reality, Zoe had to believe in the unbelievable. She, Zoe Calderone, the pragmatic woman who turned off David Copperfield specials, had undeniably conjured up an honest-to-God djinni. Not the wisecracking blue giant of the movies, nor the sweet, mischievous blonde of television.

No, she had to get one who was a combination of Jimmy Smits and Yul Brynner with an attitude.

Zoe strode over to Simon, stopping a yard away to draw in a deep breath and clench her fists. She prided herself on her control, on her calm in the face of crisis. Yet something about this man, this djinni, loosened her tongue and made her say things she never intended. She would not give in to annoyance again.

At her approach, he straightened, and his dark eyes narrowed. The shifting wind molded his silky shirt to his chest, outlining the play of muscles as he breathed deeply. He uncrossed his arms to rest his hands on his hips. The streetlamp's yellow glow reflected off the metal bands on his wrists.

Tension and power radiated from him and shot

through her. For a brief moment, her breath jerked to a halt, then resumed with a whoosh.

She took an unobtrusive step back, not liking the fact that she had to look up at him, not liking the effect his closeness had on her nerves. She forced herself to relax her hands and shifted her shoulders to ease their tension.

"It doesn't have an engine," she said between clenched teeth.

"You did not specify an engine. It will provide transportation. Is that not the function of a car?"

"Does it use gas?"

He frowned, his eyes unfocusing for a moment, a foreigner deciphering an unknown word. "Your noxious human fuels pollute your air, waste the richness of Terra, your earth. This vehicle diverts Terran energy streams, then replaces them to their proper flow, eternally renewing itself."

It was an environmentalist's dream and Chevron's worst nightmare. Zoe rubbed the bridge of her nose. "In other words, it runs on magic."

He lifted his chin and sniffed. A scowl marred his smooth features. "You did not specify it should run on *gas*. I provided a superior vehicle. I thought the summoner would be pleased."

The summoner was not pleased. Resolutely, Zoe ignored the little voice reminding her that she'd always thought Detroit and Japan could do a better job of emissions control. She shook her hand at the car. "It doesn't have a license plate, and I can't apply for one, since I don't have registration papers. I'll be arrested if I drive it."

"You did not specify—"

"I know, I know. Couldn't you have thought of a few of those things yourself?"

"Cars were not part of this world when I was last here."

"Then perhaps you should learn more about our world before you go around granting wishes."

Rubbing his thumb against his lips, he eyed her. His intent look enveloped her, stealing her breath as surely as the languid, muggy air did. "Perhaps I shall," he murmured.

Suddenly, he was a blur, a whirlwind of energy, throwing dust. She shielded her eyes with her palm.

Someone named Abigail approaches. His disembodied voice echoed through her.

His voice? In her mind? How did he do that? Aw hell, could he read her mind? Zoe's hand dropped. She spun around, fists clenched, but Simon had disappeared.

I shall return. Should you desire to wish, just speak aloud, and I will hear you. His voice faded on the wind.

Zoe glared at the car filling her driveway. She'd be damned before she'd use another wish. Long ago she'd learned there was only one dependable thing about her wishes. They always made matters worse.

Chapter Three

Simon found the environment he needed south of town. Humans had destroyed and covered up so much of their natural habitat, it was difficult to locate an isolated place of peace and simplicity. However, at least one visionary had recognized essential needs and set aside a refuge. Humans called it—he searched for a name—Jean Lafitte National Park. Deep in the bayous of Barataria, Simon emerged on a wooden bridge in the middle of a swamp.

No humans were near to see his sudden appearance for it was deep night. A lazy alligator raised one drowsy eyelid, but Simon soothed it with a low croon. A faint ruffling of air followed by an arrested squeak told of a hunting owl. Insects chittered, their noise magnified in the thick, hot air. Heavy odors of rotting vegetation overlaid the delicate floral and musky animal scents. After studying the area, he shifted to a small island of loam and leaves hidden from the path.

With a wave of his hand, Simon divested himself of his clothes, preferring oneness with nature. He knelt beside the bayou's murky waters and lifted two huge fuzzy leaves. Cupping them in his hands, he intoned the necessary words to weave them. When he pulled his hands apart, the leaves stretched into a narrow, soft rug that he lowered and sat upon.

A mosquito landed on the nape of his neck. He did not brush it away, nor did it bite. A tiny garter snake slithered through the grass to inspect the unthreatening invader. Simon gave it a brief stroke before he crossed his arms in front of his chest. His hands rested on the copper bands encircling his upper arms, the symbols of his djinn status. The bands at his wrists, the bands that bound him, he kept carefully apart, for they were unnatural, not of djinni making.

Simon gazed out into the bayou, looking first at the surface of the dark water and the shiny leaves floating within, and then looking beyond, into the soul of the place. He concentrated, slowing his breathing and his heart rate, and let his spirit open, seeking the turquoise tablet that had been stolen from him.

Stolen by Minau, that faithless human female, and her sorcerer father.

Without the tablet, he could not live among the djinn, free. Without the tablet, he was an exile in his own land.

At each summoning, Simon had sought his tablet. Thrice, over the centuries, he had caught traces of it, faint hints of that missing piece of him. He'd learned, however, that to seek actively those wisps of feeling caused them to evaporate like mist before the morning sun. He sought not a physical location, but a site of magic.

With a spell fueled by rage, Minau's father, the sorcerer, had concealed Simon's turquoise tablet and replaced it with the copper wristbands of a bound djinni, compelling Simon to serve 101 masters before the tablet's return. For a while, Simon had thought his harsh sentence would be served quickly. Then, the books of spells were hidden or lost, machines took the place of magic, and few humans called him from his exile.

Zoe's had been his ninety-fourth summoning.

If the enchantment had weakened, however, if he could sense the tablet on his own, he could reclaim it now. He need not await the whims of summoners and the fulfillment of the binding.

He would be free. He could live with his own kind again.

Simon wandered through the accumulated ancient memories that surrounded him and bared himself to the tide of emotions. Untamed nature entwined with his soul. The emptiness inside him spread through the winds and energies of Terra, seeking the sweet song of his tablet.

Yet, all he sensed was Terran, only Terran.

Bitter disappointment knifed into his gut, though he had not expected success. The sorcerer had been strong.

So, he must resume his hunt for books of Terran magic. In them, he might find an incantation, a ritual, another means to regain his tablet before the terms of the binding were fulfilled.

He had found, early in his binding, that he could not be freed by a simple wish. He had tricked one summoner into uttering those very words, but nothing had happened—except the summoner becoming quite angry. Something more was needed, and only Terran magic could provide the answer.

Simon turned to learning about the world where

he now found himself. Pink sunrise had turned to yellow noon before he finished. Sweat coated his body, and he shook with exhaustion. He needed to return to his home, Kaf.

First, however, he would see his new summoner, Zoe.

Zoe studied the cramped office that overflowed with floppy disks, repair manuals, and computer-generated bills and invoices. Elvina had been right. This appliance repair company was a prime candidate for ZEVA's services.

"I'm Zoe Calderone." She shook the office manager's hand.

"Deborah Martinez. I understand ZEVA has a product that might interest us."

Yes, a prime candidate, and Elvina had discovered it while getting her sewing machine repaired. Six months ago Elvina had taken over the sales position at ZEVA, but Zoe still didn't know how her friend did it. Elvina scheduled no visits, developed no marketing strategies, made few phone calls, and eschewed high-pressure tactics. Yet she'd brought in as much business in half a year as Zoe had generated the eighteen months prior.

Call it luck, call it serendipity, call it cosmic awareness, but for Elvina it worked.

Zoe pulled out a compact disk. A wave of her hand encompassed the mishmash of files. "All that fits on this one disk. ZEVA can archive your data, now stored on floppies, to a CD. No more lost data from spilled coffee or fading tapes or misplaced papers. With a push of a button, your repairmen can access whatever schematics they wish. Want," Zoe hastily corrected, hoping a djinni wasn't nearby.

Deborah nodded encouragement. "Show me how it works."

Zoe slipped the CD into her laptop and called up the demo. On screen, colorful block letters spelling ZEVA shifted from a line into a circle, then spun and morphed into a woman's smiling face.

"Welcome to ZEVA Multimedia Data Storage and Retrieval System," said the animated woman. "Please press enter to begin the demonstration."

Zoe sat back and watched Deborah work her way through the vivid demonstration, exploring the possibilities for retrieval and display. Multimedia—an entrancing meld of graphics and animation, sounds and song, video and text—was the future, as far as Zoe was concerned.

What would a djinni think of this twentieth-century version of magic?

"How long has ZEVA been in business?" Deborah asked.

Zoe brought her attention back to her customer. "We've done desktop publishing for five years and expanded to multimedia two years ago."

"Is it just you and Ms. DeVries?"

Zoe shook her head. "I oversee the creative and technical aspects." Well, she *did* oversee then, since she was the only one working on them. "You'll also deal with Abby Cartier, our head"—*head and only*—"accountant. We have support personnel and additional financial backing." *Vivian was responsible for the sound, and each woman had contributed what few monies she could.* "ZEVA is small but solid, with the flexibility to respond to your changing needs."

Nodding, Deborah returned her full attention to the monitor.

Zoe relaxed, until her thoughts threatened to drift to the irritating djinni again. Instead, she concentrated on ZEVA.

ZEVA was her dream.

At the age of twenty—divorced, pregnant, and with no marketable skills—Zoe had sworn she'd never again allow herself to be left helpless. Running her own business, beholden to no one, answerable to no one but herself, had seemed the solution.

It hadn't quite worked out that way, but she didn't regret taking Elvina, Vivian, and Abby as partners.

She'd worked hard for her teaching certificate and then started desktop publishing as a supplemental source of income. When she'd developed an interactive tutorial for her computer class, however, she'd loved the versatility of multimedia to teach, entertain, and serve. She'd known that was her niche, and she'd started ZEVA to explore the possibilities of multimedia.

Last year, wary of hoping for success but buoyed by the positive response to the jobs she'd completed, Zoe had quit teaching to devote her energies to ZEVA. Four months ago, she'd won a contract to produce tutorials for the school where she'd formerly worked.

ZEVA was poised for success and that success rested on *her*. Abby, Vivian, and Elvina were depending on her. Zoe gripped her briefcase. She wouldn't let them down.

Certainly she'd never risk ZEVA on anything as precarious and undependable as wishes.

Deborah had finished the demonstration. She leaned back in her chair and looked at Zoe. "I'm impressed. The ability to include repair schematics for our service techs would be a big plus. Can you write me a proposal to present to the owner?"

After clarifying details about the services of interest, Zoe promised, "I'll have it for you next week."

Outside, the summer heat of New Orleans

slammed into her. Zoe unbuttoned the top button of her white blouse and lifted her hair off her sweaty neck. If only she could take off her panty hose. No one should have to wear panty hose in ninety-degree heat and 90 percent humidity! She shifted her laptop computer from hand to hand and trudged down the sidewalk to the bus stop, swearing she'd find the funds to replace the red monstrosity Simon had left with her.

Zoe leaned against the sign, while cars roared by and poured their smelly exhaust over her. The hot wind from their passage made her feel gritty, not cool.

A Lincoln pulled up beside the bus stop. The passenger window rolled down, teasing her with a blast of cool air, and the driver leaned across the seat.

"Car in the shop, Zoe?"

Aw hell, it was Roger Broussard, looking refreshed and natty in a three-piece suit.

"Just a little problem," she answered. "I'm working on it."

He glanced at her laptop. "Got any new prospects?"

"As if I'd give you a clue after that stunt you pulled with the law firm."

Roger smoothed a hand across his silver hair. "Now, Zoe, I had the lowest bid. It was simply a little healthy competition."

"You wouldn't have thought of approaching them if you hadn't seen me in their offices," she said mildly. "How's the work coming?"

His lips tightened. "We're almost done."

Zoe resisted the urge to snicker. Apparently Roger hadn't realized the amount of grunt work involved in scanning old records onto CD when he'd undercut her. She'd bet her one bottle of nail polish he was far from done.

"I've hired a crew to speed the process," Roger said.

Interesting. She didn't know he had those kinds of resources to fall back on. Might he be stretching himself a bit thin?

"I also have a new animator working on the Dillards' sales training program," Roger offered. "I think you know him."

The smirk on his face irritated her. Roger's company was bigger—he had employees—and the department store chain had elected to go with flash, rather than her smaller company. Roger could talk a good line. He had polish and poise, but he was surface only, no depth. She'd establish herself with solid service and products. After all, she'd won the contract for the school tutorials from him.

When Roger paused, waiting for her to ask about the animator, she smiled at him. "Are we playing Twenty Questions?"

A faint flush stained Roger's cheeks. "He just got into town, so I was lucky to sign him. Dustyn Calderone is quite talented."

Damn and blast! What was her ex-husband doing back after all these years? Zoe gripped the laptop handle with aching fingers. She stared at Roger, refusing to let him rattle her.

"He is talented," Zoe agreed. Mary had gotten her artistic skills from her father. "Friendly word of warning, Roger. Beyond his art, don't depend on him." She broke her glance away. "Looks like my bus is coming."

When she ignored him further, Roger rolled up the window and drove away. Pulling correct change from her pocket, Zoe scowled at the retreating car. Dustyn and Roger Broussard working together. Her shoulders and neck tensed at the mere thought. She didn't like the sound of that, but she couldn't do one damn thing to stop it.

An irresponsible ex-husband, a pesky competitor, and a haughty djinni all intruding on her well-ordered life. This was shaping up to be one lousy week.

On the bus ride home, Zoe put together a proposal for the appliance repair shop. Wanting to run the figures by ZEVA's accountant first, she stopped at Abby Cartier's house, a small square of brick on the corner of the block.

As Zoe went up the front steps, the screen door crashed open. Chris Cartier, Abby's grandson, stomped out. "Stop nagging," he shouted over his shoulder. "I'm fifteen. I don't need you telling me what to do." Long blond hair flying, silver cross earring waving, Chris flung himself down the steps. Zoe stepped aside.

"Oh, sorry, Ms. Calderone, I didn't see you."

"Anger has a way of clouding the vision."

Chris rubbed a hand across his black Nine Inch Nails T-shirt. "She shouldn't be so nosy. I'm old enough to decide when to come home."

"Like last night?"

"What'd she say?" He kicked a toe against the steps.

"Not much. She came by the house, wondering if you were there since it was an hour past your curfew. She was worried."

"I wasn't getting in any trouble." Chris rubbed his shirt again. "I was with friends. We're trying to create a hologram. Haven't quite got it yet, but we will."

"What are you going to do with a hologram?"

Chris shrugged.

They probably planned on scaring the wits out of

someone with the images, Zoe decided, but resisted the urge to delve further, knowing he'd just clam up. "What'd you get on that video you made for your communications class final?" she asked instead.

"An A." Trying for nonchalance, he couldn't keep the pride from his voice. "It brought my average up to a 3.8."

"It deserved an A-plus. The computer-generated illusions were superb."

Chris shrugged again, his current mode of body language, but Zoe could tell he was pleased with the deserved praise.

"That teacher never gives pluses or minuses," he said. "And . . . thanks for letting me use your equipment."

"I've incorporated that exploding volcano image you created in my tutorial. So, what time did you get home last night?"

"Two A.M.," Chris mumbled.

At least he'd come home, though she knew Abby wouldn't see it that way. "How long you grounded for?"

"This weekend."

"It could have been worse."

Chris shot her a glance, the sullen look settling back on his face. "I got busy, lost track of time."

He needed something to do besides hang out with teens who spent their days figuring out ways to pull elaborate pranks. Maybe she could provide him with that something. "Would you be interested in doing some work for me? Like an internship, since I couldn't pay a lot. Most of it would be routine, but there is some animation I think would enhance the tutorial. You could work on that, too."

"Yeah, I'd be interested."

"I run a business. How can I trust you not to

break our verbal contract like you did your agreed-on curfew with Abby?"

Chris thought for a moment and then flashed her a grin. "Because I'd get to use your new 3-D modeling program?"

"I'd expect you to put in at least two hours a day," Zoe said, smiling. Once he got going, Chris would spend more time than that. "You can start tomorrow. Agreed?" She held out her hand.

He gave her hand a firm shake. "Agreed."

The strength of his grip surprised her, and Zoe realized he had gotten taller than she. He was no longer a boy, but a man in the making, trying to find his path.

Zoe watched Chris lope down the sidewalk.

Except for a little brother, Chris was surrounded by women, three of them several decades older than he. What did they know about the changes a near-man was undergoing, about the pressures, inside and out, he felt? He needed a man to confide in. Unbidden, Simon's image rose in her mind. Zoe shook her head. No way!

Inside, she found Abby frowning at her computer screen, a pen balanced precariously behind her ear. Zoe greeted her, then opened her laptop and called up the report. Abby studied the figures, her hand running through her cropped salt-and-pepper hair, and made an occasional correction.

Five years ago, when Chris and Joey came to live with her after their parents' deaths, Abby hadn't known how to turn on a computer. A fifty-year-old woman who'd never worked outside the home, she said she didn't need to learn. When her husband sued her for divorce two years later and started living with his secretary, Abby had been thrust into an intolerant job market to support herself and two growing boys. Most prospective employers didn't count home management skills or an occasional stint in a husband's construction company office experience. She'd lost all hope until Zoe started ZEVA and offered her the position of accountant.

A few courses, a lot of self-study, the confidence of her partners, and Abby had bloomed into a savvy financial manager who made sure not a penny was wasted.

"Looks good," Abby said, the lines around her lips relaxing as she finished her intent study. "Will you have the time? The first tutorial's due next month."

"It shouldn't be that intensive. I've got the program already, so it's just a matter of scanning the records. I thought maybe Chris could do it. I told him I'd offer him an internship, if you have no objection."

"Of course not. Thanks. You didn't have to do that."

Zoe dismissed the gratitude with a wave of her hand. "He's got an agile mind and more technical skills than most of his teachers. He needs a challenge besides concocting special-effects tricks with his friends."

Abby's stiff posture slumped. "I don't know what to do with that boy. He's like a different person these days."

"He's a teenager. It's a lousy time for him and for the people who care about him."

"Yoo-hoo, Abby." Vivian Winslow peeked around the door. A feather drifted from the arrangement in her hair to Abby's polished floor. "Oh, hi, Zoe, I'm glad you're here."

Abby groaned.

Oh, dear, thought Zoe, what's the argument this time?

Vivian Winslow, as flighty as Abby was stolid, had joined ZEVA's team at the same time as Abby, having been left alone and without support when her adored, feckless husband died. "I must have that new synthesizer," Vivian announced, settling into a chair with ladylike grace, gauze skirt floating down on a cushion of sultry air.

"I told you," Abby said, "only if the old one broke."

Vivian ignored her. "Zoe, you know I'm trying for a new sound with this tutorial, but my synthesizer won't do what I want. *Abby* says we can't afford it."

"A new synthesizer is fifteen-hundred dollars," Zoe said gently.

Vivian made a moue of disappointment. "That much?"

" 'Fraid so."

"ZEVA can't squeeze that out?"

"No," said Abby. Zoe nodded in agreement.

"Then I shall just have to go back and rework my composition." Vivian gave a long-suffering sigh, rose, then drifted toward the door. "Fortunately, I have an idea." She was humming as she left.

"She'll probably come up with something brilliant," Abby admitted.

"She will," Zoe agreed.

Back at home, Zoe exchanged power suit and panty hose for summer comfort, then went into her computer room. She closed the door with a firm click as her signal not to be disturbed, put on her headphones, turned up the music, then got to work.

"What is it you do with that machine?"

The unexpected question echoed in her headphones above the Cajun melodies of BeauSoleil. Zoe's hands flattened on the keyboard, printing a line of *F*s across the computer screen. Her head and shoulders jerked backward, only to be stopped by a solid, masculine chest. The headphones slid forward until the headband rested on her nose.

Zoe counted to ten, then added another five when that didn't work. She picked the headphones off her ears and dangled them around her neck. Only then did she rotate in her chair to glare up at a grinning djinni. "Didn't you see the closed door? Don't startle me when I'm concentrating. I wish—" She stopped.

"Complete your sentence. You wish what?"

"Never mind, just an expression." It was her turn to smile when he frowned at her. Zoe listened in one earphone; the music continued, undisturbed by disembodied voices. "How did you make your voice come through the headphones?"

"Throwing one's voice is a simple trick we learn as children."

Zoe turned back to her computer, trying to remember what she was doing. She toyed with the headphones, then laid them on her desk. A child's trick? One shock from that trick with the voice was sufficient. And Simon didn't seem inclined to leave. She saved her work and rotated her chair.

Simon prowled around the room, reading a paper from the top of a stack, stroking the back of the chintz-covered sofa, ringing the belled wind chimes in the window, crushing a leaf of the potpourri. He drew in the clean scent with obvious relish.

"What have you been doing?" she asked.

"I found there is much that is new in your world." Simon sprawled on the sofa, his arms resting on the back.

"When were you here last?"

"Over one hundred years ago, by your time, in Asia."

"Not many people doing the conjuring bit these days?"

"No." His reply was terse.

Wondering what she'd said to set him off, Zoe

scrutinized him. He'd certainly adapted to today's lack of dress code.

He was barefoot now, though he'd left a pair of sandals on the floor. His yellow tank top exposed a hint of curly hair on his chest and left bare his firmly muscled arms. A couple more washings and his frayed denim shorts would be indecent instead of breath-stopping sexy. As he leaned back, they rode dangerously low on his hips because the zipper was three-fourths undone.

"When was the zipper invented?" she asked, wondering if he didn't know how to work one.

"The what?"

She gestured toward his pants.

Simon looked down. "Ah, so that is what it's called. We do not use them. It has proven uncommonly difficult to shut."

"Well, you have to make sure the teeth are lined up." Zoe tried to gesture the movements.

"Perhaps you could demonstrate."

Zoe scooted her chair forward. Simon leaned back, smiling.

He couldn't be wearing anything beneath, not with that expanse of skin showing. The image of her first view of him, the memory of his physical perfection intruded, splintering her tenuous calm. Her fingers trembled from an elemental urge to find out if his skin felt as smooth as it looked. Zoe jerked her hands back. "You can do it."

Turning her gaze back to the computer screen, Zoe started to type. Soon she heard the rasp of the zipper, a pause, an unintelligible word whose meaning was all too clear, then the rasp again.

She felt a sudden breeze, then Simon was beside her.

With a careless wave, he moved her stacked papers aside to float cross-legged just above the desk.

He smiled as he studied the photo tacked beside her computer, a picture of Mary dressed as a fairy and holding her first art-show ribbon. Attached to the wall beside the picture was an article from the *New Orleans* magazine about local up-and-coming women. He flipped through the article, read the paragraphs about her, then turned an intent gaze on her.

"Have you decided what your wishes will be?"

"Haven't thought about them since your whirl-wind disappearance last night."

"Have you an enemy? I can send him nude to Ant-arctica in the dead of winter."

Roger Broussard maybe? Nah, not even Roger deserved that fate. Dustyn? He hadn't done any-thing yet. Zoe shook her head.

"No enemies? Such an exemplary life you've led, Zoe Calderone." He picked up one of the daisies gracing the table beside her desk. One long, lean finger caressed the petals, before he reached out and stroked the flower across her cheek in a soft, tickling touch.

Zoe forgot to breathe.

"You enjoy flowers, I can see. Your garden can be perpetually filled with exotic, perfumed blooms of jasmine, orange blossom, and hyacinth. You need never weed, yet the soil will remain dark and rich, the scent fragrant, and the sight pleasing."

Zoe rubbed her cheek. He sure knew how to tempt.

"Weeding the garden is relaxing," she answered. "Besides, I'd probably develop allergies."

Simon's lips tightened, and he dropped the daisy onto her keyboard. There was a sudden breeze, then, instead of floating beside her, he stood a foot away, arms crossed, head tilted.

"What is it you do with that machine?" he repeated.

Zoe sighed. She leaned back in her chair and crossed her arms. "Go away, Simon. I have to work."

"What work do you do?"

He *was* persistent. "I teach adult-ed computer classes during summer, and I have to prepare an outline for tomorrow's class."

"What else?"

"I own a computer business, a freelance multimedia services provider." Let him mull over that for awhile.

Simon rubbed a thumb against his lip, thinking.

Aw hell, that simple action shouldn't tangle her insides.

"Freelance?" he mused. "A knight who hires out?" Then he smiled. "I see. You do independent work for hire?"

"That's about it."

"So this is a computer." Suddenly, Simon was beside her again. He laid a hand on the monitor casing and stroked it, as though learning the workings by touch. "I have heard about these. How do they work?"

When Simon leaned in front of her, studying the computer screen and blocking her view, she saw a string of tiny gold beads braided through the hair at the nape of his neck. His very nearness stole the air from her lungs. She breathed deep, drawing in the faint scent of sandalwood, as her gaze drifted down his body. The metal bands around his upper arms and wrists looked copper. She touched one of the hieroglyphics etched in the soft metal. "What does this mean?"

Before she could blink, Simon had retreated a yard away. He stood, arms akimbo, eyes glaring.

"Don't touch that." His voice echoed, as though he spoke from deep in a tunnel.

Zoe snatched back her hand. "Sorry." *How do you handle a belligerent djinni?* "You're damn touchy."

"It's not attractive when a female uses profanity."

"It's not appealing in men either." No way would she admit that she usually watched her language, but he had a way of riling her, disturbing her, so the words she'd heard too often as a child slipped out.

"Ah, but I'm not the one using such language. Why does your man not correct you? Where is your man that you must work so?"

Zoe glared up at him, refusing to feel intimidated because he was towering above her, standing when she was sitting. "You have been away for a while. Women are no longer chattel. We have careers and take care of ourselves."

"It is so hard to assimilate local conventions. Your females are free? I didn't believe humans would progress so far." His brows knit in thought as he stared at her. "There was a man; you have a child."

"Yeah, well, he found married life wasn't for him. He skipped out years ago." And was he planning on skipping back in?

"So, humans have not changed that much." Suddenly Simon was right beside her again. Really, his habit of instant movement was disconcerting. Head tilted, he studied her. "You are independent? Free to choose?"

His gaze started at her spotless white Keds, ran up her bare legs, encompassed the shorts and cotton shirt she wore in deference to the heat, then settled on her face, first eyes then mouth. The back of her neck prickled with the spread of blushing warmth. The way he looked at her, she felt like she'd sprouted antlers in the middle of deer season.

The computer sparked and snapped, as if drawing electricity from the surrounding air. Zoe spun toward the screen, breaking the sensuous spell. Had the computer overloaded the wiring in her old house? "Oh, blast, if I've lost my work—" As she hit the save key and exited the program, she looked over her shoulder at Simon. "Why should I use my wishes? Give me a good reason."

The next thing she knew he had whirled her chair until she faced him. He leaned over her, placing his hands on the arms of the chair, trapping her. Zoe pressed back against the chair.

He tilted her chin with his forefinger. His eyes widened and darkened, until that was all she could see. She felt light-headed, as if she were floating. Musk, oranges, and sandalwood, his unique scent enveloped her. He surrounded her, held her, overwhelmed her, all with a single point of contact.

"Everyone has needs, desires, impossible goals," he intoned. "What do you wish for, hope for, Zoe? What dreams do you have that seem beyond your reach? What do you yearn for, yet fear you have no hope of attaining? Financial reward? Comfort? Success, in whatever form you measure it? Or are your yearnings darker and more dangerous? For revenge, for power? That is what I can provide."

Zoe stared into his black pupils. ZEVA, her dream. The business she wanted so much to succeed. She could visualize it to the last detail but feared to voice her vision aloud, afraid it would disappear like all her other dreams. The school tutorial. The work. Elvina, Abby, Vivian, Mary, Joey, and Chris. All of them relying on her. She wanted— Zoe blinked and shook the muzziness from her head. "Simon, are you trying to hypnotize me into wishing?"

A surprised look crossed his face. His eyes narrowed in speculation, then Simon straightened and shrugged. "How is this for a reason? If you use your wishes, I'll go away."

Zoe considered. Now that was a definite temptation.

"You needn't look so pleased," Simon grumbled.

"How about if I wish for things like world peace and no more disease? Could you do that?"

"Yes." He hesitated, then blew out a breath. "But not in the manner you might expect. For example, man is so aggressive, the only way I could assure world peace is to create an absolute dictator who would have everyone too terrified to commit a crime. With no disease, you're going to have to think about ways to combat the resulting overpopulation and increased demands for food and resources." He shook his head. "When you try to force global changes, when you alter natural forces, you interfere with powers beyond comprehension. You should listen to and respect these forces, not attempt to combat the natural order and cycle. Your wishes should be used for personal impact only."

Zoe chewed on her lip. Global good was out and personal things, like cars, got screwed up, too. "Can I transfer the wishes to someone else?"

"No."

"Can I wish you to go away?"

He rested his fists at his waist. "That would not be a good thing to try."

His wavy hair shone as with a supernatural light. The cords in his neck tightened. Menace emanated from him, as though anger were a physical entity. Maybe in a djinni it was. Maybe it wasn't a good idea to anger a djinni.

"Why?" she asked.

"Say the words and see, if you dare."

"I wish," she began, testing what he'd do, "you would go—" Her tongue twisted in a painful cramp.

The phrase *tongue-tied* suddenly acquired a whole new meaning.

Zoe struggled with the words but couldn't force them out. She waved a hand in frustrated surrender. Her tongue relaxed.

"I told you not—" Simon began.

"I wish you would go—" She tried to spit the words out before he even finished speaking, but the same thing happened. She couldn't wish him away. "Tha ha a uhee ick," she growled. He muttered a strange word; her tongue loosened again. "That was a dirty trick," she repeated.

"What makes you think I did that?" he asked, not smiling, chin up, very much the pose of a haughty djinni.

"I just assumed—"

"Don't assume."

"Sorry."

"I told you it would not a be a good thing. That happens, and I alone can loosen your tongue. The cramping grows exquisitely painful if I don't. Do not make that wish. Ever."

For now, she was out of arguments. "I guess I'm stuck with you."

He nodded. "Until you use your wishes."

"Then I have the feeling this is the beginning of a beautiful friendship, sweetheart." She tried her best Bogie imitation.

From the puzzled look on his face, Simon had apparently never seen *Casablanca*. He crouched down until his face was level with hers. "Why won't you ask for what your heart desires, Zoe?"

Back to the infernal wishes! The first time Zoe remembered wishing for her heart's desire she'd been seven. She'd believed Santa truly answered dreams when, at the Toys for Tots Christmas give-away, she'd gotten the magic set she wanted. When she'd put on her small magic show, her father had ridiculed her efforts. The next day he'd walked out, leaving Zoe and her mother. Thinking her lack of magic skill had made him leave, she'd wished hard for her father to come back. Oh, he came back, all right, and spent the following six months drunk and unpleasant. When he'd left, this time for good, he'd taken the tiny bit of cash her mother had accumulated for groceries, and given Zoe a split lip when she protested.

Zoe had never wished for him again.

Ten years later she'd wished to escape from her mother. Dustyn, her ex-husband, had been the answer to that wish. He'd stayed for three years, until she'd told him she was pregnant.

After Mary was born, she'd given up wishing. Instead, she'd put all her energy into surviving and making the best life she could for her daughter. She'd trusted in nothing and nobody but herself.

Zoe's lips tightened. She refused to expose pain she'd long ago dealt with. *Why won't you ask for your heart's desires?* he had asked. She rose abruptly, sending her chair careening across the room, and stalked over to the window. "Why won't I wish? Because the cost is too high."

"There is no cost."

She whirled to face the djinni standing beside her.

"No?" She shoved her hand toward the window. "A simple wish and now I've got neighbors coming to gawk at my new car, a car I can't drive. But the real cost is higher than you can imagine; the real cost is dependence. I'm trying to instill self-reliance and self-esteem in Mary. Now, thanks to you, she's off in a fantasy world, imagining how she'd use three wishes."

Zoe took a step forward. "A woman can only rely on herself and her abilities, Simon. No one else, nothing else. So you can just forget about us and go back where you came from. Wishes are a useless crutch, and I don't intend to use mine. Ever."

He stared at her, his dark eyes sparkling with repressed emotion, seeming to grow with every passing moment, and his black hair once again took on an unearthly glow. "We shall see, Zoe Calderone. Prepare, for when I return I shall be living with you until you use your wishes."

He stepped back and began to whirl until he was a blur of shadow, then disappeared. The papers on her desk flew to the floor. A stack of manuals tumbled off a shelf.

"I just got those straightened up," she yelled to the air. "You'd better not make a habit of that if you're going to—Oh, no." Zoe sunk into her chair and pounded her forehead on her fist. Did he say he was going to be living here?

What was she going to do with a clever, haughty, magic-wielding, whirlwind-producing, heart-stoppingly attractive djinni around the house?

Chapter Four

The dry heat of Kaf enveloped Simon like a comfortable blanket. Behind him, a small fountain of scarlet-tinted water sprayed into the air and splashed down tiers of rock in a pleasant tinkling sound. He sat upright and cross-legged on a lounge in the courtyard of his home, a pile of tiny pieces of wood before him. His hands arranged the wood into intricate patterns, while he regained his strength and considered his problem.

He could not allow Zoe Calderone to refuse to wish.

One of the pieces wouldn't fit. As Simon shaved off a sliver of wood with a knife, the blade slipped and nicked his thumb. He sucked on the injury, soothing the pain, and frowned at his creation. The grain on the carved bits of wood created a mixture of shadow and light that resembled a powerful river. He squinted at it. A Terran river—the one they called the Mississippi—not a Kafian one. Impatiently, he began shifting the pieces.

By the blowing sands, he had been apart from his own kind for too long. He was in danger of forgetting himself.

Djinn normally stood above the foolishness of humans, and were indulgent of their frailties. Too many times, however, he'd experienced Terran ignorance, greed, and hatred to have any sympathy left. He had buried his soft feelings for humans, and he could not allow them to resurface. Not even for an independent woman whose defiance made her eyes snap and whose wariness was fueled by an agile mind.

Someone's feet scraped on the sand blown across the open entryway to his courtyard. A tall, dark djinni, dressed in flowing robes of midnight blue, strode in.

Pleased by the interruption, Simon set aside the small box he had made. "Welcome, Darius," he called. "So, once again you brave the wrath of King Taranushi to come to me in my exile." With a wave of his hand, he moved tart barberries, sweet melon, and chilled fruit juice from inside the house to the courtyard.

"He has long given up trying to stop me. Besides, he wants to know what you're doing. I'm his best source." Without invitation, Darius reclined on the other lounge and picked up a slice of melon. He surveyed the denim and yellow Simon wore. "I see you've been called again. An easy summoning?"

Simon shook his head. "Already I've needed the stop-speak spell to keep her from wishing me away. I'm too close to freedom to lose even one summoner."

"So, you made mush of her tongue instead. Why would she call you, then, just to wish you away?"

"She didn't believe it would work."

"And you were so charming, she was ready to send you away immediately?" Darius shook his head, amusement curving his lips. "You've lost your touch, Simon. What did you do to make this woman angry?"

"She accidentally wished for a car."

"A car?"

"Their current means of transportation, and a wasteful, foul-smelling thing it is. I made a few improvements."

Darius laughed. "Changes she did not like, I gather. Every other summoner simply crafted their wishes with more care after one of your tricks. This time your cleverness has turned against you, my friend."

Unfortunately, Darius was right. Zoe Calderone was different. Simon shifted uneasily on the chaise. His reactions to her—a desire to study the emotions flitting across her revealing face, an urge to run his hands down her curved sides, a heat that filled him like sun-warmed sand—also were unique. And unwanted.

Darius chewed his fruit and then swallowed. His eyes narrowed in thought. "Why, then, if she has not wished, are you here? I thought you preferred to remain on Terra until the wishes were granted."

"I needed to revitalize." Simon shifted his hand and another piece of melon drifted toward Darius.

Darius nabbed the fruit and frowned. "You only need return to Kaf every twelve Terran days for revitalization. Has that time passed?"

"Vanishings, whirlwinds, a light truth-speak trance. I even tried hypnotism." *And seeking.* Simon shrugged, making light of his weakness. "I used so much magical energy, I had to return early."

"You never were one for moderation." After a moment's silence, Darius frowned again. "Perhaps if you were to tell her—"

"I will beg from no human."

"You are much too harsh on them, my friend."

"You have not been granting their wishes for a thousand years because a human female betrayed you to her sorcerer father!" That sorcerer had been his first summoner. Simon ruthlessly thrust away memories of what the man had obliged him to do.

"There have been a few amusing times." Darius waved his half slice of fruit. "Do you remember the man who wanted to turn everything in his home into gold?"

Simon chuckled, grateful for the change of subject. "I felt no obligation to tell him that the sand beneath his dwelling was not strong enough to hold so much weight."

Darius gave a bark of laughter. "I was glad you called me to watch his face as his entire treasure sank into the desert. And what about that dungpile despot who wished for new weapons for every member of his personal army?"

"He was a vicious, stupid man. The wish was fulfilled. Slings were new to his people."

"None of them knew how to use them," Darius answered, echoing Simon's laughter. "And they grew so angry with the loss of their anticipated plunder, they turned against the man."

"He deserved his fate."

"Have the wishes ever been used for good?"

Simon shook his head. "Not all have been evil, but none have been selfless. If someone goes to the trouble of calling a djinni, they do so for a reason, because they want something."

The two friends continued to converse while they watched the shadows grow longer in the courtyard, the peace of companionship blunting the years of separation. At last, a chill in the air forced Simon to lengthen the legs of his denim shorts and add a sweatshirt. One thing he liked about this new Terran time—once he'd mastered zippers—was the comfort of the fashions.

He picked up the wooden box. The marquetry now depicted the meandering fire streams in the Tower Lands of Kaf. A wave of his hand across the lid sealed the wooden pattern to the box. He would give it to Mary.

"Are you rested?" Darius asked, watching the transformation.

"Yes, and your company has helped. Tell King Taranushi I do well." Simon looked into the distance, but the encircling mountains blocked the view of his beloved city. His hand stretched toward it, tightened, then lowered. He turned back to Darius.

Darius fixed his gaze on Simon. "Keep strong and true. We all look forward to the time you can rejoin us."

A sensation, like a tiny mosquito buzzing through him, alerted Simon. Guarding his worrisome thoughts, he waggled a finger at Darius. "No telepathy, my friend. Have you forgotten the many lectures about not abusing your rare gift?"

Darius gave him a wry grin. "You always were more attentive to the tutors than I. I shall respect your privacy, my friend, but know that I will do aught I can to help."

"Your friendship is a precious boon to me."

The two djinn rose and clasped right hands around each other's elbows. "May the desert heat fill you," they said together. "May the skies above and the sands below guide you. May peace surround you." They embraced, then Darius tightened his robe about him and left in a column of dust.

Alone, Simon gazed at the distant mountains. Would he ever rejoin the community of djinn? His hand grazed his chest where his turquoise tablet should be. "The power of *ma-at* must be tended with care." Softly he quoted the credo, the words of passage, instilled in him since birth. "Forces unleashed cannot be recalled. Heedless rendering upsets the delicate balances. Wise and wary, shall I yield my knowledge. This I swear by the blessed dictates of Solomon, by the eternal unity with Kaf." His fist clenched around empty air. "This I hold close to my heart." The words faded on the rising wind.

He must never forget. He was djinn. The years of exile could not change that fact.

Simon shook the sand off his feet and made a swift circle about his waist with his hand. A soft, woven belt with a leather pouch dangling from it appeared. He tucked Mary's box into the pouch. It was time to return to Terra.

The thought of seeing Zoe sent a strange gust of exhilaration through him. She had made him feel again, had looked at him as though he were bone and blood and not simply a conduit for the *ma-at*.

She had surprised him, when he had thought no summoner could. Didn't want her wishes? No one had refused wishes before and, by Solomon's beard, she would not be the first. He had no doubt he could induce her to use them in time, but the battle joined should prove interesting, for he had a hunch Zoe would be a clever opponent.

Zoe. With the single word, his imagination created vivid images of her, how her curves might fit in his hands, how she might taste. Her scent, fresh as the tang of a juicy pear, teased his memory. His fingertips tingled with an urge to learn the textures of her.

Perhaps he would find other compensations during his short stay. Simon smiled in anticipation.

Zoe dumped the plastic bags onto the kitchen table, pulled a brown bag filled with boiled crawfish from her load, and stowed it in the refrigerator. What did she need a car for? There was a grocery and fish market nearby. The parish bus system was reliable. Walking was one of the best forms of exercise.

Yeah, and who did she think she was kidding? Eventually she'd have to either drive the monstrosity or buy another car and, truth was, she couldn't afford a new car. Even with her teacher's discount, it had taken all her savings and all her partners could contribute to buy the equipment and supplies needed for ZEVA. After grimacing at the vehicle in the driveway, she grabbed a sack of dry cat food from her bags and deposited it on the floor of the pantry.

The groceries were nearly put away when Elvina and Mary came in. Zoe leaned a hip against the counter and eyed Elvina's bulging shopping bag. Blazoned across the side were the words CRESCENT CITY CURIOS, in a mishmash of styles and colors, followed by the logo—entwined triple Cs. What had they bought this time? The last shopping trip had yielded glow-in-the-dark plastic jewelry.

Mary hopped onto the counter and opened a bag of pretzels. "Can I have some, Mom?"

Zoe laid a light kiss on the top of her head. "You can have ten."

While Mary counted out her pretzels, Elvina plunked the bag on the counter and asked, "Have you seen Simon again?"

"No, bless the saints," Zoe answered. It had been

twenty-four hours since his last dramatic departure. With luck, he'd given up.

"Mary and I fixed up my spare room for when he returns."

"*If* he returns."

"He will. Do you think he'll mind sleeping on a futon? What sort of focal points or energy aids would be best, do you suppose?"

Zoe threw her a you're-asking-me? look.

"We put in candles, of course," Mary said.

"But we couldn't decide if there is some native crystal or elemental material he will need," Elvina added.

"New Orleans doesn't have rocks and crystals," Zoe answered, reaching for a pretzel. "Just shells."

Elvina shook her head. "Shells don't have the proper harmonies." She snapped her fingers and gave Zoe a sidelong glance. "I know, a glass prism, like the one you have in your window."

"Uh-uh, you can't have mine." Zoe shoved the pretzel in her mouth.

Elvina shrugged one shoulder. "I'll find something else. Oh, by the way, we used up your potpourri, Zoe."

A headache sprouted behind her eyes. Zoe massaged the bridge of her nose. Her daughter and her friend were determined to welcome the stranger in their midst, regardless of her opinions.

Which meant they'd have to explain his presence. "I don't think we should tell anyone about Simon. About him being a genie and all." She braced herself for an argument.

Mary stopped sucking the salt off her pretzel stick. "Of course not."

Zoe stared back in surprise. She had expected Mary would want to tell the world.

"If they believed us, people would be bugging him

all the time to do his magic. Me and Miss Elvina talked about it. He's going to be her cousin, Simon James."

Zoe let the lapse in grammar slide. "I didn't know you had a cousin, Elvina."

"She doesn't. It's pretend," Mary answered, and then tilted her head to eye Elvina. "Are you sure I can't tell Joey and Chris? Or Miss Vivian and Miss Abby?"

"No," said Zoe, wondering how long Mary could keep the secret.

Elvina seconded the response with a shake of her head. Mary shrugged and stuffed her remaining pretzels in her mouth.

"What's in the bag?" Zoe gestured toward the Triple C logo.

"We got the neatest things," Mary said around the mouthful of pretzels. "Look." She pulled a plastic headband from the bag. Attached to it were two springs topped with gold, glitter-covered balls. Mary put it on and waggled her head back and forth. The balls waved in a mad dance while bells inside tinkled merrily. "Isn't this cool?"

"Mary," Elvina said before Zoe could reply, "I just remembered I've got some prisms hanging from the shade on the lamp next to my bed. Why don't you string them on the gold braid from my sewing kit and hang them in Simon's room?"

"Those will be perfect!" Mary hopped down from the counter. "I can't wait for Simon to come back." She flung the words over her shoulder on her race out the door.

When Mary had left, Elvina dumped the contents of the shopping bag onto the countertop. "I got these for you, Zoe."

Zoe stared in amazement. A plastic replica of the King of the Krewe of Barkus dog parade. A deck of cards featuring caricatures of local notables. A visor with a row of blinking lights along the bill. A T-shirt that read MARINATED AT MARDI GRAS. She picked up a toothbrush with a handle shaped like a naked man. "For me?"

"Don't worry, Mary didn't see me slip that one in." Elvina wound up a six-inch figure dressed in chartreuse satin and wearing the mask of a Mardi Gras float rider. Its arm moved back and forth, as if throwing the tiny string of beads.

Scowling, Zoe stopped it. "You bought these for me? Why?"

"You're going to use them to produce a sales catalog."

"What?"

Elvina smiled at her. "Mary and I were browsing, like we do, and talking to Leo."

"The Triple C owner?"

"Right. He wants to expand his market share. There are so many places that sell this type of thing that I think he'll do well."

Zoe looked at the array heaped on her counter. Elvina was right; the products were an in-your-face tacky that would probably sell very well indeed. She just didn't understand what people saw in them.

"This is cute." Elvina stroked a small, furry mound that emitted a fake purr. "When Leo said he'd been kicking around ideas to promote the products, including mailing out videotapes, I suggested ZEVA might have some innovative suggestions. Leo said to give him a call tomorrow."

Her heart beating more quickly, Zoe picked up a small box and wound the key on the bottom. To the tinny sounds of "The Stripper," the top popped open. Zoe dropped the box in surprise. Instead of a jack-in-the-box clown, a well-endowed plastic female dressed in a G-string burst out.

"Novelties?" she questioned, more to herself than to Elvina. "I have no idea why these things appeal to people. How could I design a catalog to entice them to buy?"

"Do you have the time to do it?"

Zoe mentally arranged her work schedule. "Yes."

"Question is, will you?"

Zoe tapped a fingernail on the counter. This type of creative, commercial commission was important. If she wanted to make a success of ZEVA, wanted to break out of the pack, she couldn't be content with typing dissertations and scanning old records on to CD. She had to take a few chances.

Could she do it? She picked up the erotic music box. How could she make a professional presentation with things like this?

Zoe grimaced. She could not afford to pass up the opportunity.

Elvina stroked the crystal pendant she always wore and eyed Zoe with a mixture of fondness and exasperation. "For once in your life, honey," she said softly, "let loose."

The alarm on Zoe's watch beeped. Grateful for the interruption, she glanced at the time. "I've got to get changed or I'll be late for class." She laid a hand on Elvina's shoulder. "I'm being an ungrateful wretch, I know. I'll call Leo tomorrow."

"One more thing."

Zoe paused in the doorway.

"Dustyn Calderone is back in town. He followed us into the store."

Anxiety clutched her gut. "I know. Did he say anything to Mary?"

Elvina shook her head. "He didn't approach, just hung back, watching and listening. Mary didn't notice him, but then, she's never seen her father before."

63

Zoe let out a short breath. "Did he hear about the job?"

Elvina nodded.

And if Dustyn knew, Roger knew. Roger and Dustyn. Dustyn and Mary. Aw hell, all she needed now was for Simon to return.

"Zoe, I deleted the whole page! How do I get it back?"

Zoe suppressed a sigh. Of all the students in her adult-ed class, Barbra could be counted on to find a way to mess up the exercise and to refuse to figure out the solution herself. At least this time the problem should be easy to fix. "Pull up the edit menu, Barbra. See the undelete—" She stopped.

Simon had reappeared and was levitating above the bank of computers. Her students, all working diligently, didn't seem to notice.

"What are you doing here?" she hissed.

"I'm taking your class," Barbra replied, indignant.

After mouthing, "Go away," toward Simon, Zoe turned back to her student. "Sorry, I didn't mean you, Barbra. Did you get the page back?"

Zoe barely listened to Barbra's litany of errors. Instead, she watched Simon move from student to student, studying their work. What was he planning? She wiped her unexpectedly sweaty palms on her skirt. Over the shoulder of one student, Simon reached toward the keyboard.

"Don't bother them," she snapped.

Barbra peered in the direction Zoe was looking. "Bubby Remoulliard?" she asked. "He always hums while he works."

If Zoe had had any doubts about whether her students could see Simon, they'd just been removed.

"Hey, Bubby," Barbra shouted, "knock off the tunes. You're bothering Zoe."

"Was I humming again?" Bubby, who had not progressed beyond hunt and peck, looked up from his intent perusal of the keyboard.

"Not him," Zoe said, "the man—Oh, never mind."

"Man? What man, Zoe?"

"I'm not a man, I'm a djinni," Simon said.

"There is no man," Zoe said firmly.

Bubby spun around. "Is someone watching my work? I hate it when someone watches my work."

Simon did another of his impossibly quick moves to get out of Bubby's spin. "His words are pure drivel," the djinni informed her. He leaned over Bubby's shoulder and peered at the screen. "The quick brown foxes jumped over the naked, wheezing lady."

"That sentence uses all—" Zoe started to explain. "Wait a minute, what did he write?"

"You promised not to look unless I asked," Bubby said. The djinni poked a key. "Hey, what happened to my screen?" Bubby hunched back over his keyboard.

"Simon," Zoe warned.

"Who's Simon?" Barbra asked, looking around.

Simon shook his finger at her.

"Must have been a trick of the light," Zoe muttered. Fortunately, Barbra accepted the weak explanation.

"Zoe," Simon called.

When she glanced over, he blew her a light kiss over Bubby's head. Something soft grazed her cheek. Startled, Zoe cupped her hand to her face. Bubby brushed down his hair in an absent gesture but didn't budge from his one-fingered pecking.

"They can't see me. Right now I'm invisible to all but you."

"Invisible? Yeah, I'd figured that out."

"There's an invisible code?" Barbra asked.

Zoe dropped her hand and looked at the screen. "What? Oh, no, just pull up the edit menu again."

"Yes, invisible." Simon nodded. "They can't hear me either. Just you."

"How did I get so lucky?" Zoe muttered.

"Zoe?" Barbra looked up, puzzled.

"Click on undelete, Barbra!"

Simon burst out laughing. No one in the class noticed.

Zoe stalked to the door, motioning Simon to follow her with a jerk of her head. "Keep working, I'll be right back," she told her class. "We'll learn how to set up tables during the last hour."

Outside, in the hall, Zoe crossed her arms and tapped one foot. "Go away, Simon. I'm trying to teach."

"Only if you wish it. Distracting you, am I?"

At least he'd stopped levitating. He lounged with one shoulder against the wall, feet crossed in front of him. He'd changed into jeans that looked as if they'd been molded around him—in his case they might have been—a bright blue sweatshirt dusted with a random sprinkle of glitter, and boots.

Blast, why did he have to look so good?

"How did you find out where I was?"

Simon gave a negligent shrug. "A djinni can always find the one who summoned him."

"You knew I was teaching a class?"

"I returned to your house first, to give Mary a small present. Your partners, Abby and Vivian, were there, listening to something Vivian had composed. Delightful women. I was pleased to meet them."

Zoe squeezed her eyes shut against the returning

headache, and then opened them. "What did you tell them?"

"Elvina came in with her friend Lucky and introduced me as her cousin." He crossed his arms and raised one brow. A faint silver glow emanated from him. "You think to keep me a secret?"

"It seemed easiest."

"You thought, if they knew, they would press you to use your wishes? You thought they would want their own desires fulfilled?"

"I thought, if word got out, we'd have every kook in New Orleans beating down our door."

After a moment, Simon inclined his head. "I shall comply for the moment. You should be grateful to Elvina. If she hadn't told me you were teaching, I would have materialized in your class in full view, not invisible. How would you have explained that?"

"I'd have pretended I didn't know you."

"Even when I did this?" He straightened and moved to her side. He wrapped his arms around her, trapping her hands between them, and kissed her.

Djinn must have had years of practice at kissing, because Simon sure was good at it. He held her close, one hand cradling her head, the other splayed on her back, and he took his time.

His lips coaxed, enticed, promised delights. They slid from her mouth to her cheek to the corner of her eye before returning to her mouth.

Zoe opened to the alluring invitation when his tongue traced the seam of her lips. He tasted sweet, like dates and ripe oranges. His hand began a lazy exploration of her spine, matching the slow exploration of his tongue, sending bytes of pleasure across every one of her nerves. Her palms flattened on his warm chest. She leaned into him, no longer sure of the strength in her legs. He wove a sensuous spell over her.

Spell. Zoe opened one eye, then the other. She drew her mouth back a scant inch. "Are you casting a love spell on me?"

Simon moved away so fast that Zoe stumbled forward. His hand shot out and braced her until she regained her balance, and then he dropped her arm.

With shaking hands, Zoe straightened her narrow skirt and tugged down the edge of her jacket, gaining time until her pounding heart slowed. She willed herself to calm dignity. Only then did she find the courage to look at Simon.

His dark eyes glared at her; one lock of black hair fell across his forehead. He stood with feet apart and fists on hips.

"Don't ever believe I would resort to *love spells*," he spat. "These I do not need. These I do not do."

"I didn't know there was an etiquette about these things," she answered, struggling to banish the tremor from her voice. That kiss had shaken her more than she cared to admit. She smoothed her mussed hair.

Simon relaxed and a slow grin, full of male satisfaction, took possession. "For a mortal, you have a powerful kiss. You may be wearing a prim suit, Zoe Calderone, but underneath is silk."

She flushed. How did he know that? Zoe fussed with the top button of her blouse, making sure it was still properly fastened.

Simon laughed deeply, full of rich mirth. "We're going to have fun."

"In a pig's eye," Zoe muttered, then reached to open the classroom door. She froze. She'd forgotten that earlier she'd pulled up the window shade in the upper half of the door. Zoe squeezed her eyes shut, then opened them to an unchanged scene. Her entire class was staring at her, some amused, some shocked, some puzzled, but each one eager to see what their teacher would do next.

They hadn't been able to see Simon. She didn't want to even think about what she must have looked like to them.

Zoe rubbed the bridge of her nose, her headache in full bloom. She almost broke her own rule and dismissed class early.

Zoe was a good teacher, Simon reluctantly admitted. She was attentive to her students' needs, polite, if somewhat reserved. She answered questions with unfailing courtesy, never exhibiting exasperation when that one woman—Barbra—asked the same question five different ways. By now, Simon figured even he could have answered it.

Zoe. Round and soft and warm, she was a nicer handful than he first had imagined. He'd started the kiss more out of curiosity, and because he knew it would annoy her, than for any other reason.

He'd continued the kiss, made it better, because he'd wanted to, because she made him feel alive again. There was hidden passion in her, passion he seemed to release, passion that radiated back to him.

Passion, exuberance, life, they excited him. Isolated during his exile, separated from the female as well as the male of his own kind, he'd gradually numbed himself to wanting the pleasures of the flesh. It had been centuries since he'd felt the tugs of desire, especially for a human female.

Blowing sands of Kaf, he wanted this one!

He'd denied his nature for too long, and now his innate sensuality was reawakening because of Zoe

Calderone. He found himself whistling in accompaniment to Bubby's humming.

When not watching Zoe—who was doing a good job pretending to ignore him—Simon amused himself by helping Bubby press the keys faster, by rotating the pictures on the screens, and by reading Zoe's notes.

Eventually, he sat down before a computer not in use. All machines, he'd learned, needed to be activated by some method. He could have used *ma-at*, but he preferred to use devices in the manner their creator had intended.

Simon ran his hands across the unyielding plastic box. How did one order this machine to start? There were wires coming from the back. Maybe one of those . . .

Zoe sidled over to him. "What are you doing?" she whispered, her eyes trained on her students.

"Turning on the computer."

"Pull those wires and no one will turn on that machine again."

"Then show me."

Her jaw tightened. Simon moved a hand toward the wires. Zoe shot a glance at her students. "Use that monitor," she said in a low voice and nodded to a computer facing in the opposite direction. No one would be able to see him working there, Simon realized.

"I thought you didn't care if they saw me." Smiling, he shifted chairs.

Zoe gave an indignant huff and snapped up a tab on the machine's side. It started humming. She looked at her students again, but Simon could see that none were paying attention to their teacher. Zoe took a silver disk and plopped it into a drawer she'd opened with a push of a button. Her fingers danced over the keys until Simon found himself looking at a picture of a fair-haired girl with a remarkable resemblance to Mary.

"Hi," the girl said. "I'm Computer Kate. Call me C. K. I'm gonna take you on a tour through the computer. Man, you won't believe what this thing can do."

"Hello," Simon responded.

"It's a computer simulation," Zoe whispered. "Don't talk back, just do what it says, and keep the volume down." She pointed to an arrow.

Simon nodded absently, for C. K. was pointing to the parts of the computer. New words—monitor, keyboard, CD—and old words with new meaning—memory, mouse, stroke—claimed his attention as Zoe went back to her class. The sounds of his rapid keystrokes were drowned out by the activities of the other students. Fascinated with the colorful pictures, the bits of musical background, the "mouse" that moved him from topic to topic and place to place on the screen, Simon explored the wondrous amusement and knowledge these computers offered.

There was something they couldn't duplicate, however—the warmth of the connection to a living being. He looked up, wanting to tell Zoe he'd completed the tutorials.

That woman, Barbra, was squinting in his direction, as though trying to bring something into focus.

Simon looked down and saw a harder outline around his hands. He was starting to materialize. Selective invisibility took a lot of effort. Between the length of time he'd spent in the class and his lack of concentration, his control was waning. Simon transported into the hall, away from that door window, and removed the aura that made him invisible.

His knees buckled. He braced himself against the wall, nauseous fatigue coming over him. The walls around him rushed in with dizzying speed. He closed his eyes and drew in a slow, steady breath, let it out, repeated the action. Only when he felt the spinning in his head settle did he open his eyes again and take another deep breath.

Gradually, the dizziness, the nausea, the weakness faded.

How could he need the rejuvenating air of his homeland so soon? Until he revitalized, complex magic would be impossible, although he could still do little things.

Tonight, while Zoe slept, he would return, for he had to establish himself as a part of her life now. Give her no room to doubt he would be there. If he was always around, there would be opportunities to persuade her to wish, opportunities he could create, opportunities he could take advantage of.

Simon's mouth tightened.

Zoe must use her wishes and soon! He had straddled two worlds for too long.

Yet he would have to be subtle, restrained, when he maneuvered her to wish, otherwise her partners, Elvina and Abby and Vivian, would not summon him.

A rare surge of hope coursed through Simon, energizing him. Here, with the three partners, was a chance to halve the remaining seven summonings—if he proceeded cautiously, wasn't bullying or cruel.

Using force had never appealed to him.

That, he told himself, was why he did not bring the full measure of his abilities to bear upon Zoe, not because she intrigued him or because of the cozy welcome of her partners.

Tonight he'd begin the campaign. Tonight he would become part of Zoe's life.

The thought sent a thrill through him.

He straightened his shoulders and, smiling, strolled into the classroom.

At his entrance, Zoe cast a wary glance at her students, obviously wondering if they saw him.

He made sure they could.

"Zoe, I came to walk you home." He wrapped an arm about her waist and gave her a solid kiss.

"Oh, Zoe," Barbra cooed, "you didn't tell us about him."

Simon gave Barbra a gracious nod. "I live with her."

Zoe stiffened and moved away. "Let's call it a night, everyone. I'll see you Thursday."

The students turned off machines, gathered notes, then left one by one, giving the two of them amused or interested glances. Only Barbra delayed. "Zoe, I still don't get how to set tabs. I'm such a computer illiterate." She cast a coy glance at Simon. "I bet you understand all this."

"I'm still a novice. Zoe is the expert."

"Here, Barbra, I'll show you again," Zoe offered.

For twenty minutes, she went over the material, giving Barbra the benefit of one-on-one tutoring. Simon leaned against the table and waited.

Finally the woman smiled. "Oh, I see, I get it. Thanks, Zoe. My boss said I had to learn this or I'd be fired." Barbra collected her belongings and left.

Zoe started to turn off the computer Simon had been using, then stopped and stared at the screen. "You got through the senior level? I started you on the beginning tutorial that my first-graders use."

"I am a fast learner."

"That's amazing. I've never known anyone to go that fast."

She stared at the machine in a bemused fashion.

When he reached across her to turn it off, his arm brushed her breast.

Zoe shied back, her eyes blinking as though she was emerging from a dream. Without another word, she yanked a clear cover over each computer, piled her notes into a neat stack, and shoved the papers into a battered briefcase. Her heels clicked on the tiled floor as she strode to the door, turned out the lights, and then turned the lock in the doorknob. Only then did she look at him. "I need to lock up. Either come with me now or do that whirlwind trick of yours."

Simon walked out, puzzled by her frigid tone. He stopped outside the door and raised his brows. "You are angry," he stated.

Zoe flushed and moved her briefcase from one hand to the other. "Don't ever do that again, Simon."

"What?"

"Kiss me in front of a student or a client."

"Why not? You enjoyed it." He slid one finger along her jaw, aiming for her mouth. She stepped away, still not smiling, but her cheeks were flushed.

She slammed the door shut, rattling the knob, making sure it was locked. "It was unprofessional."

He started to tell her to wish for it but stopped. He didn't want her wishing for him not to kiss her.

Her jaw tightened for a moment. She swallowed, and then straightened her shoulders. "I need the money this job brings. I also need to maintain teaching credentials to afford the equipment I use. Don't mess it up for me." She started down the hall.

Simon followed her. "Wish for the money, Zoe." He was, for once, serious, finding he wanted to help her.

"And have the IRS and FBI thinking I'm a drug dealer or Mafia queen because of the unexpected funds?" She shook her head. "No way."

"They need not know." He could arrange that once he figured out who IRS and FBI were.

"You never give up, do you?"

Simon subsided into insulted silence. The woman was impossible.

Zoe locked the door of the school, pocketed the key, and then checked the door again. She looked at the sky and took a deep breath. "I'm always surprised when I go in during daylight and come out to darkness. If you don't have a magic carpet to spirit us home, I'm afraid we're walking. At least I am."

"I shall walk with you."

In Zoe's neighborhood, small, neat houses and duplexes shared tree-lined streets with beauty parlors, home-based day-care centers, and corner seafood markets. The mix gave the place a congeniality Simon found pleasing.

The night was cooler than daytime, although temperatures in the seventies could not be called cool. Simon transformed his sweatshirt to a T-shirt, as warm, humid air closed around him, bringing the scents and sounds of evening. Sweetly scented flowers perfumed their path. Bugs banged against the streetlights with sharp clicks. A dog rushed up to the fence surrounding the house they passed, barking enthusiastically until Simon quelled him with a soft command.

"We don't use flying carpets," Simon said, finally. "We don't need them. Djinn can travel in a step and a thought, taking along whatever or whomever we hold."

"That's convenient. Your people must have an easy life. Doesn't it get boring?"

Before Simon could answer, he noticed a human leaning against a tree ahead, watching their progress. The human must have selected the spot with care, Simon realized, for the streetlight in this block was out, leaving the area dark. Zoe didn't yet see the danger. She walked with her head down, watching where she stepped on the uneven concrete.

Simon tensed, shifting closer to Zoe. An odd feeling rose in him, a need to see that no harm came to the woman beside him.

They neared, and the lurking man straightened.

"I been waiting for you," he growled. His fist lifted. In it, he held something long and narrow.

Chapter Five

During his seeking, Simon had seen the violence of this time, the guns, the knives, the fights. He did not need *ma-at* to move in a blur, grab the man's wrist, and slam it against the tree, dislodging the weapon. The human swore with pithy crudity. In one twist, Simon backed him against the tree and pressed his arm against his throat.

"You shall not have breath to say those words."

Zoe grabbed his arm and tried to pull it away. "Let him go. You're choking him."

"I know," Simon said flatly, without relenting. "He had a weapon. He was going to hurt you."

"No, he wasn't. Were you, Mr. Knox?"

The man glared at them, his scalp dark with anger under the thin strands of white hair.

"Simon, I'll handle this." Zoe set down her briefcase and lifted what Knox had dropped. "See, no weapon."

Simon glanced down at the object Zoe held. A

newspaper. He lifted the pressure on the man's throat.

Knox gave a harsh cough and looked pointedly at the wrist Simon still held. "Call your watchdog off, Calderone, or I'll sue for assault."

"Please, Simon, let him go."

Simon had seen too much treachery to trust the human. Yet without one of their weapons of destruction to aid him, the man would be as a toothless tiger. Simon released his hold, deciding to indulge Zoe in this.

Knox shook his arm, and then hitched his sagging, stained pants higher on his bony hips. He snatched the paper from Zoe and stabbed it with one finger. "Isaiah Junior got sentenced yesterday."

Zoe rubbed the bridge of her nose. "I saw the article."

"They're sending my boy away for five years. His mother's crying her eyes out. The neighbors don't come round no more. Don't you care?"

"I am sorry for you and your wife, Mr. Knox."

"If you're so sorry, why'd you blow the whistle? Why'd you testify?"

"I couldn't just forget the theft, or lie about it in my testimony."

"He'd have put the money back. He just had some bad luck."

"Bad luck with the ponies."

"With Isaiah Junior gone, what am I supposed to do now?"

"Mr. Somerset didn't fire you, did he?"

Knox grunted. "He said you told him I didn't have nothing to do with it. You expect me to be grateful?"

"No." Zoe shifted her shoulders and picked up her briefcase. "Why did you stop me tonight? What do you want?"

"I wanted to watch your face when you heard

78

about Isaiah Junior. See if you had any more emotions than those damn computers you work with. Well, I got my answers. You're a damn heartless bitch."

Zoe flinched. Simon took a warning step closer to the man.

Isaiah Knox shook a grimy finger at him. "And don't you be threatening me again. I ain't laid a hand on her, and I ain't going to. I just wanted her to know how real people feel." He thrust his hands into his pockets and slouched away.

Only Zoe's light touch on his arm restrained Simon from teaching the human a proper measure of respect. He glanced down at her and decided Isaiah Knox could wait.

The moon cast a glow on part of Zoe's face but left the other half in shadow, hiding her thoughts, while she watched Knox disappear. She let out a slow breath and rubbed the arm holding her briefcase. "That was unpleasant."

"What was he talking about?" Simon asked.

"His son was the purchasing agent for the school system where I used to teach. During some periodic file maintenance I did on the computers, I found he'd been defrauding the schools to the tune of several thousand dollars. That money should have gone to the kids. Isaiah Junior's only regret was getting caught."

Shoulders hunched and faintly trembling, she started down the last block toward her home. Simon caught up to her, and she looked up at him, frowning. "You didn't need to get violent, Simon. I had the situation under control. Isaiah Knox is the school custodian. I've known him for years. He was angry, but he wouldn't have hurt me."

Simon's view of humans wasn't so benign. Knox wouldn't be content with tonight's confrontation, he believed. He started to say as much but stopped when the streetlights illuminated the white lines around her mouth.

Knox had been decidedly wrong about one thing: Zoe was not without emotions, just good at concealing them. Except with him. Deciding to distract her, he snuck a hand around her waist.

She looked at the lights coming from the windows of her neighbors' house and walked a little faster. "Take your hand off."

"Only if you wish it."

"I suppose I should be grateful you didn't use your magic to zap Isaiah into a puddle of mud or freeze his hand in ice."

"I couldn't," Simon muttered.

"What?" Zoe halted at the foot of the walk leading to her house.

Simon used the pause to kiss the side of her mouth.

She brushed her palm across her cheek. "Stop that. What did you mean you couldn't use your magic? Is there some limit to the number of times you can use it?"

Finding he enjoyed the sensation, he kissed her again, on the nose. Zoe batted him away.

"If I tell you," Simon said, "will you let me give you a proper kiss?" He wanted her willing.

She eyed him warily. "Just a kiss?"

"Yes."

"Will you tell the truth? The whole truth? No tricks?"

Simon had to consider that a moment. "What I say will be the truth."

She paused, and then said, "All right."

Simon reached for her. "Kiss first."

Zoe braced her hands on him. "Facts first. Kiss second."

He wouldn't have to cut his kiss short to answer her question then. "One restriction on djinn ensorcelling—"

"There are limits governing these things?"

"Of course! Magic is not anarchy. Under these limits, I could not use my magic when I thought he was threatening you."

"Come again?"

"For the one who summoned me, I can do no directly beneficial magic unless it is wished for."

"Let me get this straight. Unless I wish it, you can't do anything that will *help* me."

"That's right."

Her lips pursed. "Does that mean you can do things that will annoy me?"

"Certainly."

"You can help others who haven't called you?"

"Yes, as long as it doesn't benefit you." He waved a hand. "Of course, this can be somewhat ambiguous. Some acts are more neutral than beneficial."

She shook her head. "Seems like this wish business is not all it's cracked up to be. What's the benefit to me?"

"You get your wishes fulfilled. And this." He leaned against her and settled her into a comfortable embrace, enjoying the soft feel of her in his arms.

She squirmed away, and then stood on tiptoe to give him a light kiss on his cheek. "There's your forfeit kiss."

That had not been satisfactory in the least.

"Ah, no. Remember? I said I get to kiss you. Will you be like most humans and renege on your promises?"

"You don't have a good opinion of the human race, do you?"

"My experiences with humans have been most enlightening."

"Don't any of your people live here full time, djinn who could give you a more balanced view?"

"Djinn cannot live permanently on Terra."

"Why not?"

Simon looked into the distance, at the faint yellow lights outlining the bridge across the river. "Our strengths derive from the world of Kaf. We must revitalize there." He glanced back at her. He had promised truth, not the *entire* truth. The weakness was none of her concern.

Zoe tilted her head and studied him, until Simon grew uncomfortable with her steady perusal.

"Do you keep your promise?" he challenged.

She stepped forward. "I don't think you fight fair."

He gathered her up again. "Djinn are noted for their trickery."

Once he overcame her initial hesitation, the kiss was better than the one in the hall. She made tiny, breathy moans with each caress of his hand or stroke of his tongue, the movement of her lips an arousing motion. Her breasts pressed into his chest, burning him with their soft touch. He filled his hands with her round bottom and pressed her against his growing hardness. Her hips slipped across him in a slow rotation, sending his every thought and sense into roaring chaos.

If djinn were creatures of air and fire, she was the fan and the tinder.

With *ma-at*, he removed her jacket and flung it on a tree branch, allowing him greater access to the soft skin on her throat. While he stroked and kneaded her back, his talent slipped the blouse's buttons from their fastenings. He wanted to feel the silky lingerie she wore beneath. She arched against him, while her hands stroked the length of his arms. A word murmured against her ear, and her shoes were on the grass beside her. His mouth followed hers as he lowered her slowly from her tiptoes to her feet.

"Ouch!" Zoe stilled, broke away from the kiss, then picked up one foot and shook it. "A rock cut my heel." She looked down. "Hey, what happened to my shoes? Where's my jacket? My *blouse!*" Her arm came between them and clutched the edges of the blouse together. "Blast it, Simon, this is a public street. This kiss is no longer *proper.*"

She glanced around. Simon felt her skin warm further when she noticed Elvina and Lucky watching them from the front porch swing.

He reluctantly let her go, and then found himself annoyed at his own reluctance. She was human! Humans were unreliable, deceitful, self-centered. These things he could not allow himself to forget.

If only his need did not call out to him—to gather her again into his embrace, to never let go until her passion matched his, to find respite in her arms.

Zoe shoved her feet into her shoes and righted her blouse with jerky movements. "You're worse than a guy I dated in high school. I thought he was all hands, but you've done him several better." She glanced at the jacket in the tree. "How—?" She shook her head and snagged the jacket. "Never mind. I don't want to know. And no more undressing me in public!" The last she threw over her shoulder as she stomped up the steps.

Lucky stopped the swing's lazy motion.

"Evening, Elvina, Lucky. Warm night, isn't it?" Zoe greeted them without stopping her flight inside.

The door shook with the force of her slam.

* * *

The cat jumped on the keyboard and swished his tail in Zoe's face. "Out mousing, Oz?" she asked and set him on the floor.

He meowed at her, the only sound in the still, deep hours of the night. Zoe stretched her hands overhead and rotated her shoulders. Nights were often her most productive times, but tonight she was having trouble concentrating.

Simon was a distraction she couldn't afford.

That walk home after class tonight had been distinctly unsettling. The unpleasant scene with Isaiah Knox was minor, however, compared to the effect Simon had on her.

Why, when all her attention had to be focused on her work, did her libido decide to come out of its years-long dormancy? After Dustyn, she'd decided the dubious pleasures of sex weren't worth the trouble of catering to a man's ego. Then, with a few not-so-brief kisses, Simon had showed her exactly what she'd never gotten in the years of her marriage.

Damn, she'd missed a lot.

She touched a finger to lips that tingled in memory. Tonight's walk home had been a mere sample. If they ever went to bed together, were naked together . . . The man conjured from the smoke of three candles would be a potent lover; she knew that as surely as she knew that Oz was rubbing against her legs.

She settled the cat into her lap and petted his soft fur. "I have too much at stake, Oz," she whispered. "The next few months are too important for me to risk a brief, distracting fling with someone who'll be gone as soon as I give him what he wants." She stroked under the cat's chin. Oz lifted his head and purred loudly. "Feels good, huh, Oz? That's how I feel when he kisses me. Oh, how I wish—" A tiny rustling sound caused the words to catch in her throat. She whirled, her arms tightening around Oz. The cat gave a meow of protest and jumped to the floor.

Simon lounged against the doorjamb, but his eyes belied his casual stance.

Zoe glanced at Oz as he stalked from the room, at the cat who'd gotten through a door that should have been closed.

Simon had been listening all along, waiting for her whispered wish. How could she have been softening toward him? She wasn't even sure she liked the djinni. She simply lusted after him, and lust could be buried in work.

"Close the door when you leave," she said coldly and turned to the screen.

A thick cloud settled around her computer.

"What?" Her hands fell from the keyboard. *Oh, no. Not a fire!* She shot from her chair and started hunting for flames. It didn't smell like fire, more like a damp, cool fog. Nothing felt hot. Everything else was normal.

Suspicion eating at her, she sank into her chair. "Simon," she called through gritted teeth.

"Yes?" He stood next to her, dressed only in those faded cutoffs.

His masculine grace jolted her. Blast, the man knew how to wear denim. But she was still furious.

"Get rid of that." She sliced a hand through the fog.

"Only if you wish it."

"I have to work!"

"Only if you wish it." He folded his arms and returned her glare.

She didn't flinch from his gaze. "You expect me to work with that cloud obliterating the screen?"

"I expect you to wish it away."

"So, that's it." The gloves had come off. What the

85

djinni didn't know was that pressuring her only made her more determined not to give in. She rose from her chair, reached up, and turned the ceiling fan on high; then she sat back down. Resolutely she turned her back on him. "Good thing I learned to touch type."

Eventually Simon, and the fog, left.

For two days, Simon lurked, alert and knowing, and tried to catch her unaware, to get her to say phrases people used with blithe casualness. "I wish you'd leave me alone." "I wish I could do that." "I wish I had a nickel for every . . ."

In frustration, Zoe buried herself in her work. She delivered the proposal to Deborah Martinez at the appliance repair store and met with Leo at Crescent City Curios. That meeting had been productive. Leo had been thinking of equipping his salesmen with portable TV-VCR players, but the idea of a multimedia sales catalog appealed to him as he envisioned his salesmen toting laptops and touting dribble glasses. Zoe promised to work up a sample listing for a couple of products with her final bid proposal. She had to have money in hand before she'd develop the entire catalog and burn the master CD.

While ideas for the catalog simmered, she worked on the tutorials.

"They just don't move right," Zoe muttered to herself, trying to morph math problem numbers into karate figures. "Maybe Chris can film a Tae Kwon Do class while I'm waiting for Martinez to get back to me." She leaned back, frowned, and drew in a frustrated breath.

The warm, lush scent of home-baked bread brought her attention from her monitor to her surroundings. She blinked to refresh her tired eyes and glanced around. Scraps of paper covered with pencil scratchings littered the floor. A couple of floppies balanced precariously at the edge of her desk. A slash from a purple marker decorated her arm. The items Elvina had purchased from Triple C were strewn across every surface. Her normally tidy room looked like Simon had just left in one of his whirlwinds.

Her stomach grumbled, reminding her that she'd skipped lunch. That bread sure smelled good. She glanced toward the window and saw sunlight streaming in. Since it hadn't rained, she'd thought Mary and Elvina were going down to the levee, but Elvina must have decided to show Mary how to make the crusty loaves of whole-wheat bread that were the hit of every school bake sale.

Maybe she could take a break, Zoe decided, find Chris, and have a thick slice of bread slathered with butter. Zoe's stomach growled.

She shoved back her chair and went in search of sustenance. As she burst into the kitchen she called out, "That smells so good. I wish you'd cut—"

She pulled up abruptly. The kitchen, redolent with the tang of yeast, was empty. Zoe surveyed the counters. No bread. She opened the oven door. No bread. The oven wasn't even warm.

"Blast you, Simon, I'm hungry."

He appeared before her, close enough for her to feel the heat from his skin and catch the elusive scent of sandalwood that surrounded him. She stepped back.

He laughed but didn't follow her. "What would you like? Fruit? Strawberries? Melon? Guava?" The scent changed to the fruity, sweet aroma of guava juice and a glass of the pink liquid appeared in his hand. Droplets of moisture slid down the frosty glass. "It never becomes empty. You can drink your

87

fill forever. Cold, a hint of sweetness." He smacked his lips in a small kiss.

Blast, how had he learned about her rarely indulged passion for guava juice?

"Elvina," Simon said, answering her unasked question.

"Elvina should keep her help to herself." The glass disappeared. Zoe strode to the pantry. Everything she searched for, everything she thought might taste good, everything she craved, seemed to vanish even as she reached for it. She contemplated a bag of noodles. Maybe if she boiled them up, put lots butter on them, a sprinkling of Parmesan cheese . . . ?

The noodles became iridescent green. She turned from the shelves in disgust.

"Taco chips and salsa," Simon whispered. "Chicken, spicy with red pepper." He paused. "Frozen Snickers."

Blast, Elvina! Zoe stomped to the kitchen door, trying to quell her clamoring stomach even as she drooled over the thought of frozen Snickers candy bars.

"Where are you going?" Simon asked.

"To eat dirt," she grumbled, hoping he didn't realize she had a stash of mini Snickers in her desk. As she pounded around her workroom, devouring the bag of candy, she blasted Simon, djinn, wishes, and magic in a glorious explosion of emotions.

Finally, temper released, Zoe flung herself down on her sofa and propped her feet on the arm, assuming one of her favorite thinking positions. She tapped her fingers together. *Logic, Zoe; think it through.*

Railing at Simon was counterproductive. It spoiled her work time, and it did nothing to solve the problem of his presence, for she had no power over him. He was a djinni, for Pete's sake!

The simplest thing to do would be to use her last two wishes. Not for anything big or important. No way! Trouble was, even with small wishes, she could see ways Simon could turn them bad, and she had no doubt his imagination was more creative than hers.

Beyond that, there were other considerations. If she used her wishes, Mary would want to follow her example and summon Simon. She didn't want Mary thinking that wishing away one's problems, even small ones, was acceptable. She wanted her daughter to grow up confident in her abilities to solve her own problems.

Mary and Elvina would wish, and then maybe they'd let Vivian and Abby know so they could share in the wishes. After that, who? Chris? Joey? Too many people, too many wishes. Too much potential for disaster.

Also, Zoe had learned not to back down from a challenge. She hadn't gotten where she was by giving up. Simon's actions were almost a dare, and she found herself reluctant to give in.

Besides, wasn't granting wishes part of the job description of being a genie? Maybe Simon would be glad for a little break. It'd be like a vacation. She'd be doing him a service.

Logic forced her to face one other reason she didn't want to wish. Mary had said she didn't laugh much and Knox had compared her to her computers, yet, with Simon, she *felt*. Frustrating as he was, irritating as he was, Simon excited her. Around him, her breath quickened, places inside her tingled to life, her skin tightened and glowed. Simply put, she didn't want him to leave just yet.

So far, he hadn't done anything harmful. The car had been simply a mistake. He hadn't done anything to Isaiah Knox, though she'd felt the tension in his arm and seen the sparks surrounding him. Unless he did otherwise, she would just wait on the wishes. Maybe there was a statute of limitations on these things.

Zoe had always told Mary you could not control other people's actions, but you could control your own reaction. With Simon, Zoe decided, she could fret or she could have fun.

She opted for fun.

And fun she had over the next days.

When her sun catcher rotated wildly, flashing her face and monitor with red and blue, she merely thanked him for giving her inspiration for a color scheme.

When she'd commented that the lawn needed water and the rain that fell during the next hour avoided her grass, Zoe set out a sprinkler, told Mary she could play in the spray, and ignored the questioning looks from the neighbors.

In the teasing game of cat and mouse they played, the mouse was winning for once.

Half a week later, Zoe decided Simon was enjoying their skirmishes when every song coming across her headphones referred to wishing. The tactic had been so subliminal, and sneaky, she hadn't even been aware of it until he'd resorted to "When You Wish Upon a Star." Zoe bit her lip not to laugh aloud and began humming the tune, off key.

She was still humming when she went into the kitchen for a cold drink and jerked to a halt. The one man she'd hoped never to see again leaned against the counter. With unwarranted familiarity, he held Mary's painting, the one displayed on the refrigerator, his head tilted in intent study.

When he caught sight of her, he turned. The whip-lean silhouette, shaggy blond hair, and firm butt hadn't changed; however there were more lines in his face and a harder edge to his mouth than there had been ten years before.

"Hello, Zoe. It's been a long time. Mary inherited my talent, didn't she?"

"Yes, she did, Dustyn. Now, get out of my house."

Chapter Six

"This is my house, too, Zoe." The painting fluttered to the counter.

"Not anymore. The judge awarded it to me—lock, stock, and mortgage—in lieu of child support." Fury, sweet and hot, added insolence to her words.

"Why didn't you change the locks?" He dangled a key fished from one khaki pocket. "Hoping I'd come back?"

"Hoping you'd stay away was my nightly prayer." God, she'd been an insecure fool when she'd married him.

His lips tightened at the insult. Dustyn never could tolerate criticism.

"Why did you come back? What do you want?"

"I missed you and wanted to see my daughter. Is that so strange? I made mistakes during my foolish youth, but I've learned from them." He opened the banded collar of his white cotton shirt with a quick flick of his hand.

Oh, damn, he was good. He could still lie and look absolutely innocent. If she didn't know him so well, she might have been fooled. "We both know better than to believe that. What do you really want?"

"I must admit, I expected a warmer welcome from my wife."

When he reached for her, she stepped back and crossed her arms. "Ex-wife."

The sad look he gave her would have brought tears to her eyes if she hadn't shed them all ten years before.

"We had some good times, though." Dustyn glanced around the room. "What happened to the flower vase I gave you for our first anniversary? You said you'd always keep it there, on the windowsill."

He'd made the vase during his pottery phase. He'd given it to her instead of the new blouse she wanted because he'd spent all their money on a potter's wheel. "Elvina—Ellen—is using it to hold her incense."

"So, that oddball witch still lives next door?" From the derision in his voice, apparently Dustyn hadn't changed his opinion about Elvina's eccentricities. Even when she'd been called Ellen, he hadn't liked her, perhaps because he knew Zoe had found strength in her friend's nonjudgmental support.

"Don't say one word against her," Zoe grated. "Just cut to the chase."

Dustyn's nostrils flared as he sucked in a breath. "I didn't come here to argue. At least, not if you're cooperative." He pulled some papers from a shoulder satchel and slapped them on the counter. "According to these divorce papers, the judge granted me visitation rights. I want to see Mary."

It hadn't taken long for the repentant husband act

to fade. Fearful of what he really wanted, she folded her icy hands across her chest. "You've had those rights for the past nine years and couldn't be bothered. Why now?"

"People change, my dear." He ran a critical glance over her. "Even you. When we were married you were a bit chunky, but now you've lost some of that excess."

Zoe tightened her stomach muscles but said nothing. Dustyn was good at making her feel inadequate. The less she said, the less emotion she showed, the less ammunition he had.

The lines around his mouth deepened. "I want to see Mary, and the papers are still valid. Are you going to drag this through the court?"

She wanted to say yes. She wanted to tell him to get the hell out and never see Mary, but she couldn't. He was serious about this, and a nasty court battle would serve no one, least of all Mary, who would be caught between feuding parents.

"Just give me a couple of days to tell her," Zoe replied, conceding him this.

One corner of his mouth lifted in satisfaction. "What have you told her about me?"

"Very little. That she gets her artistic talent from you. That you felt you had to live apart from us."

Dustyn trailed one finger down her arm. "You never could deliberately hurt someone," he said. "I've missed you, Zoe."

Zoe heard a low sound, like a growl, but she couldn't determine the source. The hairs on her arm stood up, and a shiver ran down her spine.

Dustyn's gaze focused behind her shoulder, and all color left his pale face. His eyes squeezed shut, and then opened wide. "What's that?" he croaked.

Zoe looked over her shoulder.

The creature was huge, reaching from ceiling to

floor, and shaped like a salamander. Its green body shimmered with flames of red and orange, flames that reached out with deadly fingers only to snap back before touching Dustyn.

Aw hell, why hadn't Simon let her handle this? She didn't need any help.

Then she turned back to Dustyn. For her, the unexpected had lost its power to startle, but Dustyn hadn't been living with a djinni the past week. He scrambled back until the countertop stopped his escape. A sheen of sweat coated his brow.

She couldn't resist. "What's what?"

His finger shook as he pointed. "That, that lizard. It's huge, monstrous. You must see it!"

"A lizard?" Pressing her lips to curb a smile, Zoe looked again at the fearsome apparition, and shook her head. "Maybe Chris is pulling one of his pranks again. Or maybe you've been working too hard. Roger Broussard can be a tough boss."

The kitchen grew warmer, and a bead of sweat dripped in her eye. She ignored it. "Or maybe—" she lowered her voice to a rough whisper and leaned closer—"it's magic."

Dustyn wiped his face on his sleeve, shook his head, and began backing out the door. "Later, Zoe. We'll talk later."

Zoe waited until the sound of his footsteps had faded, until the salamander disappeared and the kitchen temperature returned to normal, before she called out, "Simon, that was truly wicked."

Simon materialized beside her, staring at the door, his powerful presence filling the confines of the kitchen. "She is mine, popinjay," he murmured. "Until she uses her wishes, no one touches her." The air around him shimmered. A sharp brightness surrounded his head, turning the soft black of his hair to the star-kissed darkness of space.

Zoe took a step away from him. She hadn't been afraid of the salamander, but Simon, like this—dominating, possessive, nonhuman—was another matter.

Only when he turned back to her did he seem to draw in, to become more mortal than magic. "Childish pranks," he said mildly, and grinned.

Her heart did another flip-flop, and then settled to a steadier beat. The rush of apprehension lifted. His humor, his smiles, always made her feel . . . lighter, somehow. "I thought your magic couldn't benefit me," was all she could think to say.

"The *ma-at* was a benefit for me." He sent her another devilish grin. "Was there not a possibility you might have feared, too, and wished the creature away?"

Zoe relaxed. "Not unless he mysteriously appeared in one of my work files."

"Always the work with you, hmmm?" Simon touched the uptilted corner of her mouth. "It is rare to see you smile. You never laugh."

Mary had said that. Isaiah Knox had intimated the same thing. Had she lost the joy of life in the work of existence?

"Am I really that humorless?"

"Since you did not scream at my little salamander, I would say there is hope."

Zoe smiled again. His finger brushed along the lower edge of her lip to the other corner, making her feel soft and inviting. She looked away and cleared her throat. "Would you like some iced tea?"

Without waiting for an answer, she retrieved the pitcher from the refrigerator and poured two glasses. Simon tilted his head, watching her movements a moment, and then got ice cubes from the freezer.

"Do your people drink tea?" she asked when he

scooped three spoonsful of sugar into his glass.

"We have a similar steeped drink. Serving it is an honored tradition with my people," he said, rotating the glass between his palms to dissolve the sugar, "but we usually drink it hot."

"I'll make you some." She reached for the teakettle.

"This is fine." He looked up and grinned at her. "If you were to follow the formalized tea ceremony, it would be an hour before I got my drink."

"An hour? What does the ceremony entail?"

"Among other things, the water must be heated slowly to just simmering, then steeped until it is dark and strong, almost bitter. The glasses must be as clear as sunshine and of a thickness that the heat cannot escape. Words of blessing and sharing are spoken and answered. The tea is presented like so." He bowed over his outstretched hands.

"It sounds like a beautiful ceremony."

He looked at her, his eyes crinkled in humor. "And we do not use tea bags or instant tea."

Zoe's smile grew wider. Simon's gaze slipped from her eyes to her mouth. The humor shifted to something more primal. He opened his hand, and the glass, instead of falling, drifted to the counter. Hers floated from her lax fingers and joined it.

He ran a lazy glance from her head to her bare feet.

Dustyn's look had made her feel inadequate. Simon's look made her feel infinitely desirable. Zoe swallowed. During their lighthearted skirmishes these past days, Simon had made no sexual moves toward her. As she had grown more accustomed to him, she'd found she missed his kisses.

"He touched you like this," Simon said. Giving her every chance to pull away, he stroked her bare arm with just the tips of his fingers, a slow touch between sleeve hem and wrist. "My touch is more welcome, no?"

"No, I mean yes," she whispered.

Her eyes drifted shut under his soothing caress and sleek voice. His hand drifted across her abdomen to repeat the caress on her other arm. Muscles fluttered in expectation. A warmth deep inside her flared to life.

He did not draw her to him by clasping her and pulling her near. Instead his drugging strokes grew fainter, until she found herself moving forward to renew the touch. The faint scent of sandalwood teased her, the scent that was as much a part of him as his expressive face, his infectious humor, and his magic.

His magic. Simon was a being from another plane of existence who would never be a part of her world. When he was blatantly exotic, she had no trouble remembering that, but when he was companionable and sympathetic, like now, it was dangerously easy to forget.

Zoe opened her eyes and ran the back of her hand down his cheek, across his smooth, firm skin. A muscle twitched beneath her fingertips, a telltale sign. To have this effect on him was sobering. It was too much, too fast, too ethereal, too real.

She moved that all-important inch away from his touch.

Simon stopped her with his dark, fathomless gaze. "Do you never want pleasures for yourself, Zoe?"

"Enough to know they can only bring pain," she said, in a rare admittance of vulnerability.

His hand clenched, and then lowered. "Tonight, your caution shall rule," he said, his voice rough-edged. "But Isaiah Knox was quite wrong about you, and together, very soon, we shall find out how wrong."

He disappeared. The whirlwind blew a lock of hair in her eyes. She smoothed it behind her ear, knowing his words echoed her thoughts.

Nearly a week later, Simon patted the dirt around the plant he'd brought back from his latest revitalizing trip to Kaf. Since the plant lived on the banks of the Oxus River, he thought it would do well in the warm, moist climate of New Orleans. Planted at the front of Elvina's herb garden, it would be a bit of home visible from his window.

He sat back on his heels and turned to the towheaded boy at his side. "Would you like to water it?"

"Sure!" Joey Cartier, Abby's grandson, picked up the plastic can and poured a thin stream around the plant.

Simon stroked one of the fuzzy, pink-tinted leaves. A faint cloud of white puffed from the underside of the leaf, bringing with it a sweet, complex scent.

"I never seen a plant do that. Can I try?" Joey dropped the watering can and reached out a grubby finger.

"You must wait for the plant to give permission. We have a story about a woman who loved the scent, but did not honor the plant. She grew greedy, wanting its fragrance to herself, wanting it always. She uprooted the plant and took it home, where she lay, stroking it, releasing the scent until it filled her room. The plant was angry to be so mistreated but could not escape, for she had potted it in a small jar. Instead, as her strokes grew harder and more frequent, the plant released all its stored scent in one burst and died. The power of the fragrance burned the woman's nose. Never again would she abuse one of the plant's brothers, for she could no longer smell."

"Wow." Joey stared at him, his eyes wide. "Did you get permission from the plant to move it?"

"Of course."

The boy looked back at the pink leaves. "How will I know?"

"Put your hands around it, without touching." Joey complied. "Now wait."

In a few seconds, a grin burst across the child's face. "My hands tingle!"

"That is your permission."

As Joey patted the plant, Mary came running down the sidewalk, carrying the box Simon had made for her. Dustyn trailed behind her. "Hi, Simon, hey, Joey," she called. "Did you know my dad is back? We spent the whole day together. He's an artist, just like me. Says he's going to let me see some of his work and maybe we can have a show together. Can you believe it? Me with a real show, with a real artist."

Dustyn joined them and surveyed Simon like a wary tomcat.

Dusting his hands on his shorts, Simon rose. "Slow down, little one. I have not met your father." *At least not when I was visible.*

"I forgot. Simon, this is Dustyn. *My dad.* Dad, this is Simon."

Dustyn nodded but did not extend his hand. Simon's eyes narrowed at the insult, but he said nothing for Mary's sake.

"Simon, look what he gave me." She opened the box. Inside was a set of charcoal pencils. "Aren't they fabulous? Just the kind I wanted."

"Then they are a special gift."

"Hey, Mary, you gotta see this!" Joey called. Mary

plopped down beside him, and soon the two fair heads were bent toward the Kafian plant.

"Are you staying with Zoe?" Dustyn asked, glancing toward Mary.

"With Elvina."

"In what, ah, capacity?"

"In the capacity of cousin."

"I didn't know she had any cousins."

"I am from a distant land. This is my first visit to New Orleans."

Dustyn nodded toward the box Mary had laid on the grass. "Are you the one who made that for her?"

Simon inclined his head in acknowledgment.

"I'm not sure I want strange men giving my daughter presents."

"In fact, I have known her longer than you."

Dustyn's lips tightened.

Whatever had Zoe seen in Dustyn? Human females might call the fair hair and lean features handsome, but Simon found the man disquieting. His speech and attitude bore a strong resemblance to the many summoners who had used their wishes to give themselves false strengths and courage.

Mary, who'd been talking to Joey and missed the exchange, looked up. "Neat plant, Simon. Hey, Dad, come on in, while I let Mom know I'm back."

"Sure, honey."

As they walked away, Simon heard Mary ask, "You're not going away again, are you?"

"Of course not. Let's ask your mom if she'd like to join us for an ice cream."

Simon's eyes narrowed as he watched them disappear, and he crossed his arms, prepared to follow them. Zoe was a determined woman, but he'd caught glimpses of her vulnerable core. Surely she wouldn't respond to Dustyn, even if they had once been intimate?

Then, he stopped. Her antipathy to Dustyn in the kitchen had been strong, but her attraction to him, Simon, had been stronger. He smiled. He could allow some distance.

But not too much.

A movement caught his attention. Chris slouched into the yard. Simon had met the young man several times over the past two weeks. The first time, Chris had been arguing with Abby about having to take the bus when he'd just got his beginner's license, whatever that was. The last time, Chris had regaled Simon with a tale about putting plastic explosive on an unpopular teacher's desk, so each time she'd closed a drawer, she'd been rewarded with a noisy bang.

"Hey, squirt," Chris called to Joey, "Grandma wants you."

Joey, plucking weeds from around the plant, ignored him.

"Joey!" Chris moved closer, his hand in his pocket. Joey turned his head.

Chris's arm tensed. A sharp crack stopped his motion with a jerk, and an astonished look came over his face. He clapped his hand to his chest. Red liquid spurted between his fingers and dripped down his arm. He collapsed with a load groan.

Simon was at his side in an instant, kneeling, pulling his hand away, gathering healing powers, looking for the wound.

There was no injury.

Joey ambled over and looked down at his brother. "The sound was good, but the blood's still too runny."

Chris gave a hoot of laughter and jerked his head toward Simon. "It was realistic enough for him."

Simon rose before the words were finished. He glared down at the sprawling young man.

Chris gave him a curious look. "Man, you sure move fast."

"You amuse yourself at my expense?" Simon lifted one hand. What would be fitting retribution for trifling with a djinni?

Chris popped to his feet and brushed off the dirt, smearing the red splotches on his shirt. "Grandma says I take five years off her life." He eyed Simon, oblivious to his imminent brush with djinn anger. "Don't tell me you're gonna be uptight. How will I know if an effect works if I don't try it out?"

Joey tugged Simon's hand. Simon glanced down and saw his wide, guileless eyes. "Chris is gonna make special effects for the movies. He's really good at it."

"That's because I try out different stuff and have you to tell me what doesn't work, squirt." Chris gave Joey an affectionate cuff, leaving a streak of red in his hair. "Go on, Grandma wants to talk to you."

When Joey left, Simon's fury abated as his curiosity rose. He touched the sticky liquid on Chris's shirt. "What was it you did?"

Chris tossed his head, throwing a lock of hair out of his eyes, and pulled a small device from his pocket. "I planted the flash earlier and detonated it with this. The blood?" He slapped his hand to his chest and groaned dramatically, then opened his shirt. "Burst the blood sac when I did that." He peeled plastic from his skin, wincing when the tape came off.

Simon laughed. "You suffer for your art."

"No pain, no gain." Chris rested his weight on one foot. "You want to come see the hologram the guys and I are working on?" His eyes narrowed thoughtfully. "You know, if we videoed you and used you as a model, it'd stop the argument about who was gonna have to do it. You interested?"

Simon found he was curious about what their technology could do. "I'd be honored to accompany you."

Chris blinked. "Yeah, right. You got a driver's license? I can drive if there's a licensed adult in the car."

So that was what a beginner's license was. "I can produce one if required. Be warned, I will ride in no car except Zoe's."

"That thing!" Chris looked at him in horror. "I wouldn't be caught dead in it."

There was no accounting for human preferences. Simon shrugged. "Nonetheless, that is my condition."

Chris sized him up with a long look. "You ever played *Doom*?"

"That would be a new experience for me."

"How about a competition, winner picks the car? I'll even take Nightmare level and you can have Wuss."

Simon was intrigued. "A competition it shall be."

The creative writing teacher dismissed the evening class, but Elvina barely listened to next week's optional assignment, her thoughts elsewhere tonight. If she could get Zoe to use that car, it would be a first, conciliatory step toward accepting Simon and his magic.

Elvina gave a snort and stuffed her notes in her backpack. Zoe, ever practical, wouldn't get behind the wheel if there was no license plate on the car. Well, if they couldn't get the plate by legal means or by magic, then they had to find an alternate method, and Elvina had a plan.

She would ask Lucky tonight. Lucky had once told her he'd spent time in prison, though he'd never told her what for. Maybe he knew some-one. . . .

"Would you like to go out for coffee, Elvina?" Lucky St. Cyr asked, shoving his papers into his back pocket. Though they went out for coffee every Friday after class, he still asked as if he expected her to refuse.

"Sure, Lucky," Elvina agreed, as she had since that first night when she'd asked him about the disturbing, intense imagery in his poems. When she hefted her backpack, Lucky gave the pack a boost with his hand, and Elvina smiled her thanks. Their fellow students might give Lucky a wide berth, but he always treated her with chivalrous kindness.

"I liked your story," he said as they slid into a booth at the fast-food franchise, steam curling from the paper cups they held. "How'd you get the idea of highlighting today's problems through the observations of a genie bonded to an ancient sorcerer who refused to die?"

"Something happened recently that gave me inspiration."

She left it at that, and Lucky didn't press her for further explanation. They often talked of things others might find strange or disturbing or private, and no question was forbidden. They had an unwritten rule, however, that a barrier of silence was never probed.

"I saw this." Lucky reached into his backpack and pulled out a black candle shaped like a horse. "I thought you might like it. Isn't your spirit guide a horse?"

His hands, covered with thin white scars, handed the horse to her with delicate care.

"Yes, it is." Elvina stroked the smooth surface of the candle, wondering how the maker had carved the nuances of the steed's movement into wax. She sniffed it, and the scent of balsam overcame the hot, greasy odors of burgers and fries.

Lucky, cracking his knuckles, watched her intently.

"Oh, Lucky, thank you. It's beautiful!"

His rough features relaxed. "It's nothin'. Just a little something in exchange for the bread you brought me last week." Over the Formica-topped table he enfolded her hand in his. "I like you an awful lot, Elvina. It was nice being at your house the other night and swingin' on the front porch. I'd like to do that again sometime."

"I'd like that, too." Inexplicably shy, she found she couldn't ask him the favor. A pile of trays clattered to the floor in the corner. Elvina started, whirling in her seat.

Lucky turned her face back to his. "Elvina, you've been jumpier tonight than a cat headed out a closing door. What's eatin' at you? Something to do with that woman and girl you live with, I reckon." His voice turned harsh.

"I need a favor."

"Anything for you."

Elvina shook her head. "Wait until you hear before making promises." She took a deep breath. "Do you know where I could find a forger?"

Zoe studied the screen and frowned. She'd scanned in images of half a dozen Triple C novelties, input the data about them, and developed a search strategy with the authoring system. Point and click; she ran it through the premastering system, then did a trial search of the products. The program ran well, but it needed something to coordinate the images as the patron clicked through the catalog. She added a tiny, blinking arrow.

While waiting for the premastering system to incorporate the new data, she picked up a pair of black-framed glasses and donned them. The lenses diffracted light, giving a rainbow aura to whatever she looked at. She bobbed her head in time to the music coming through her headphones, watching the changing colors, listening to the sultry sounds of Evangeline's "Hurricane."

Suddenly, the image of Simon's conjured salamander came to mind. Zoe yanked off the glasses, stopped the program, and pulled up clip art images until she found one close to what she wanted. Could she manipulate it to match her mental picture?

She played with the capabilities of her animation software. Add flames, make the skin iridescent, change the size. She tried for a scamper, settled for a bounce. There! Now put it in the pointer, save copies, run the sample.

Yes, it worked! The little salamander danced from product to product, snapped his fingers to bring a closer image, made faces when the browser exited. She shook one fist in jubilation. What Simon could do with magic, she could do as well, or better, with technology.

Then she looked at the images through the harsh eyes of pragmatism. Triple C was a business, even if they did sell ridiculous novelties. They couldn't send dancing salamanders across the country and expect to get orders for their products. Reluctantly, Zoe sat back down at the computer, locked the salamander into the computer's memory, and reinserted the arrow.

Maybe she could add some glittering edges to it.

When the sample was finished, a staid shadow of its first incarnation, she ran it through the premastering program again. It looked crisp and professional, it had the information in clear text, and the graphics were discreet. Yes, this would do.

While the program saved on a disk, Zoe took off her headphones and walked around the room, using muscles that had been motionless for too long. A car door slammed nearby. Elvina must be getting home late from her class. She stretched up her locked hands and took a deep, cleansing breath, enjoying the faint scent of honeysuckle that came from the vase of flowers near her desk.

The music tape cycled to the beginning and Evangeline started "Bayou Boy," singing about the dark-haired boy with the red-hot heart. Giving in to impulse, Zoe started a free-form dance to the rocking beat. Her voice low, she sang accompaniment with more enthusiasm than tune. Her shoulders dipped, her feet shuffled, her hips swayed. The breeze from the ceiling fan ran cool fingers across her and ruffled her hair.

"Is that a native dance?"

Zoe froze, hips shifted left, toe pointed down, neck and face suffused with warmth. A glance over her shoulder showed her Simon leaning against the door. She planted her foot and straightened, dropping her arm to her side. Evangeline faded into the background. Zoe put her hand to her cheek, hoping her palm would be cooler. It wasn't. She smoothed down her hair.

"Don't you ever knock? I thought you were asleep."

"Djinn do not require much sleep. And I was out, not asleep."

She moved to the desk and began straightening, not looking at him. "Where were you?"

"With Chris." His breath tickled her ear.

She looked up, startled, for she hadn't heard him move closer.

He laid a hand on the papers she fussed over. "Do

not be embarrassed. Dancing is a time-honored tradition with my people."

She straightened her shoulders. "I was celebrat-
ing because I finished a project. At least the demo."

"Then you should celebrate by dancing. You are
very graceful." The teasing grin that had been with
him during their past few encounters was gone. He
seemed serious, contemplative even. The door
swung shut. He made a motion with his hand, and
the music changed to a flute and harp melody never
before heard on her tape player. He laid his palms
against hers and laced their fingers. "This is a dance
the djinn do at celebrations. Shall I show you?"

"I don't dance very well." Graceful? Dustyn had
called her a klutz.

"I will teach you."

"Does it take wishes?"

"No."

"Magic?"

"Only the magic of movement, two djinn in harmony."

"Will a djinni and a human do?"

"We shall make adjustments."

The dance started slow, for which Zoe, already
too warm and breathless, was grateful. Only their
hands touched. Simon danced in a graceful circle,
urging Zoe to follow with the ease of his motions.
She felt awkward at first, until she saw the look of
pure pleasure on Simon's face. He was concentrating on the joys of the dance, not the hesitation of
his partner. The foot movement was similar to one
she'd done in aerobics. Step, cross, step, glide, stop.
She grew more confident with each measure of music.

Flute and harp soared. The intricate harmony
and cadence pushed the instruments beyond their
normal range. The tempo of the music increased,

until Zoe felt as if she were flying around the room, anchored by her palms instead of her feet.

Two moved as one, each oblivious to everything but the other.

She was as fluid as precious water trickling down a mountain, Simon decided. Whoever had convinced her otherwise was wrong and blind.

Simon had watched her. To his surprise, he had enjoyed their games of cat and mouse, and he thought Zoe had, too, though she rarely smiled and never laughed. There was an intriguing vulnerability about her—pregnable weaknesses she kept well hidden behind a calm, serious exterior and an instant willingness to help others without ever asking for a hand herself. She seemed very different from the other humans who had summoned him.

That, as much as the desire for Elvina, Vivian, and Abby to summon him, had kept him from using the full powers of which he was capable. He found he wanted to know more about Zoe Calderone, not just to find the key that would make her wish, but to understand her.

He wanted to hear her laugh in joyous abandon.

So, he had watched. And in the watching, desire had grown until it was an ever-present ache that only hours of lusty, sweaty, sensual play could assuage.

He moved faster, and she stumbled a bit. Using that as an excuse, he shifted his hold from her hands to her waist, then brought her close and let her feel his arousal. Her muscles tightened beneath his palms. With each rapid breath she took, her breasts brushed against his chest, and with each touch his skin tightened, sending a dazzling shower of need through him.

"I want to come together with you, Zoe Calderone," he said in a voice no louder than a summer wind. "You have been with a man; you know what this means." He lowered his head and kissed her, deep and passionate.

She made a small sound—protest, surrender, and desire all blended into one—but she made no effort to turn from his questing lips. A wave of his hand, and the bright work lights dimmed. He floated down to the sofa, turning at the last minute so she lay beneath him.

Lifting himself on one elbow, he gazed down at her. The soft lights reflected off her sable-brown hair. One strand caught on her cheek until he brushed it behind her ear. Her lips were open, moist, rosy from his kisses. Her eyes were wide and bright with tears.

"Do I hurt you?" he asked, leaning down to kiss the corners of her eyes. The soft, delicate skin tasted of the salt from sweat and tears.

"No," she whispered, "but I should not want you so much. It can't come to any good."

Those self-doubts, those insecurities; he wanted to wipe them from her. He slipped his hand beneath her shirt until he cupped her breast in his palm. His thumb stroked across her nipple, making her gasp and press against him. Taking advantage of her movement, he slid between her legs and resumed the kisses, dragging his lips from her mouth to her neck to her breasts.

The air around them sparkled with the elemental forces of desire and sensuality, crackling with the charged energy arcing from him to her and back.

"What's that?" she whispered against his hair.

"Intense djinn emotions," he murmured. "Do they frighten you?"

"No."

"Good," he breathed and stifled further questions with a kiss.

Simon was making the first motions to have them both the way he wanted, naked and joined, when a beam of light from the hall intruded.

"Mom?" Mary's sleepy voice drifted into the room. "Are you there?"

Beneath him, Zoe stilled. Her hands scrabbled at her unfastened blouse. Simon sprang away and cloaked himself in invisibility.

"Is Simon there, too?" Mary asked. "That wind . . ."

Zoe looked around the room. "He's not here. Something the matter, baby?"

Simon shook with the effort to bring his fires under control, wondering why Mary and Zoe could not see the shimmering energy surrounding him. Djinn emotions were not so easily controlled and quenched as human ones seemed to be.

"I thought I heard something outside and it scared me."

Zoe wrapped her arm around Mary and dropped a light kiss on her hair. "You probably heard me working, or the wind, but I'll check after I get you tucked back in bed." They left, but Simon heard Zoe add in a low tone, "I'm here for you, Mary. I'll protect you."

While he was here, he, too, would protect the child.

Simon rematerialized, then went outside and circled the house. At the rear of the red car, he discovered a pen, its outer covering shattered under a careless heel. He touched it, and his finger came away blue from fresh ink.

He stood and examined the area around him. The wind blew his hair in his eyes. As Simon shoved it back, a white fluttering caught his eye. Something was caught in the upper branch of the redbud tree.

Nabbing the unreachable debris was not difficult

for a djinni. His brow furrowed as he read the words scrawled on the piece of notebook paper. "Door. Music. Sparks. Invisible." The last was underlined several times. The fading of the lines gave mute testimony to the broken pen.

Frowning, he looked up from the paper and froze. Someone standing here had a direct view into Zoe's workroom. Everything that had just transpired would have been easily seen, and probably heard, through the window.

Chapter Seven

"Where are you going?" Zoe asked the three in the kitchen the next morning. She rubbed sleep from her eyes and shoved tangled hair behind her ears. When she saw Simon eyeing her exposed leg, she jerked down the hem of her nightshirt and blushed from the vivid remembrance of him seeing, and touching, that very spot.

"We're going to Brechtel Park for a picnic," Mary answered.

Elvina held up a basket in mute testimony.

"No one thought to ask me if I wanted to go?"

Mary shrugged. "You were asleep."

Pain slapped into Zoe at her daughter's indifference. Past times, she had grabbed Zoe's hand and dragged her to the car, eager to explore some new site they had heard about or anxious to revisit an old favorite. Now, Mary looked at her with impatience. God, the hurt that look caused, as if someone had stomped her stomach flatter than a CD.

114

Zoe raised a protective hand, fluttering it against her belly.

"You worked late last night," Elvina said gently. "It's early still, and you've never been a morning person."

The accuracy of the logic did nothing to blunt the feeling that she was losing her daughter. "Give me a few minutes to get ready."

"But, M-o-o-m, Simon said we have to get there early if we're to find fairies for me to draw." Mary held up a sketchpad.

Fairies! Bless the saints, what nonsense had Simon been filling her head with? What was his presence doing to her family?

"Don't you want me to go with you?" Zoe asked.

"Of course we do," Elvina soothed.

"Waiting is so boring," Mary said with a huff, crossing her arms and putting her weight on one leg, the picture of disgust.

Zoe's eyes narrowed. "Perhaps I can find something for you to do for twenty minutes. Have you studied your math?"

Mary hesitated, and then lifted her chin. "Of course."

"Don't lie to your mother, little one," Simon said in soft admonishment.

"Don't interfere," Zoe snapped. "This is between Mary and me. I'd prefer to speak with her alone."

Simon glared at her, the sparks starting. "You order me?"

Zoe glared back.

"Let's let them hash it out in private," Elvina urged.

Simon glanced at Elvina, then relaxed and followed her out.

Zoe eyed her defiant daughter. Mary was growing up. Already, the first baby fat had melted from her and she had sprouted over the last months, becoming all legs. She'd always known Mary would grow up, known they'd have to go through the strains of adolescence like all mothers and daughters. She just wasn't prepared for it to start now, precipitated by a djinni.

"This isn't about whether you have to wait for me," Zoe said, striving for calm. "It's about whether you're willing to hold up your end of a promise, Mary. It's about whether you just lied to me." Zoe lifted Mary's chin so they looked in each other's eyes. "I will always love you, no matter what you do, never doubt that for an instant. Trust is another matter. Trust can't grow in doubts and lies. Trust is believing someone won't let you down."

Mary's eyes filled with tears, and Zoe gave her a hug.

"I'm sorry, Mom. I haven't been studying, like I promised. It's just . . . Math is so stupid, and there's been so much going on. Dad coming back and taking me out and talking about a show. And it's been so much fun having Simon here. He tells wonderful stories. Things are more fun with him. He's never boring."

The ache caused by Mary's innocent words froze Zoe. Her hand, which had been stroking her daughter's hair, stilled. Had all their pleasures been boring? Was joy in simplicity lost behind the dazzle of magic?

She didn't let the hurt out. "I understand, honey. It wasn't that you didn't study, but that you lied about it."

"I won't do it again."

"Then work on your math while I get dressed, and we'll consider it forgotten."

After all, could she fault Mary when she had felt the dazzle as well?

*　　*　　*

The trees on both sides of the road ended, letting Simon see the park proper, with its playground, picnic tables, and grass-covered mounds that New Orleanians considered hills. Geese and ducks honked at the side of a reed-edged, dark green pond. Zoe pulled off the side of the road and parked.

Mary raced to the pond, sketchpad in hand, the scarf tied around her waist streaming behind her. "C'mon, Simon, let's hunt for fairies. If I see one, I want to draw it."

Simon took a step, and then stopped. "After I help your mother unload."

Mary jumped onto a white wooden bridge leading to a tiny island in the fish pond. She leaned over the side, her hands cupped on either side of her face, and stared down at the water.

Zoe paused in pulling the picnic basket from the trunk and watched Mary with a fond look. "She does that every time we come. Says she's bidding hello to the denizens of the pond." When Simon reached for the basket, she waved him away. "There's not much to carry."

Mary came skipping back. "Come on, Simon, Elvina."

"Come with us, Zoe," Elvina urged.

"She doesn't believe." Mary frowned. "They won't come out if she comes."

Simon winced at Zoe's slight recoil. Though the words had been said in honesty rather than with intent to wound, nonetheless Zoe had been hurt.

"Your mother has a good heart," he said, softening Mary's rejection. "That they would acknowledge."

Zoe had a too-bright smile on her face, in odd contrast to the pinched look about her eyes. "No, that's okay. She's right, I'm a non-believer. Go with her. You, too, Elvina. Make sure she doesn't fall in the water. I brought a magazine to read."

"We would like to have you with us." Simon tried to overcome her rush of excuses.

Zoe shooed them with a wave of her hand. "I'd just scare the little critters away." She turned and headed at an angle to a picnic table.

As Simon followed Elvina and Mary over the white bridge to the island's tangle of undergrowth, he looked back. Midday in New Orleans in early July was hot and humid, yet Simon suddenly found his mouth as dry as the sands on Kaf while he watched Zoe smooth a colorful plastic tablecloth over the wooden table.

Sweat had formed a damp patch on the back of her shirt and molded the fabric to her front. When she stretched across the tabletop, her shorts rode up, exposing more of her long, trim legs. Simon gripped the handrail on the old bridge.

A faint breeze caught the edge of the tablecloth, so she set the picnic basket on one end to anchor it. When she'd finished, she took a plastic cup Mary had told him they'd gotten at a local celebration called Mardi Gras and stuck it under the cooler spout.

Elvina had made something she called lemonade. In Simon's mind water, sugar, and yolk-yellow powder weren't lemonade. He watched Zoe take a sip and run her tongue around her lips to catch an errant drop. Perhaps he should just take his portion from her. It wouldn't taste so bad if it was flavored first with Zoe.

Holding the drink in one hand, she picked up her computer magazine with the other and began an earnest perusal of the contents, her foot moving in time to the music on the small radio she'd brought.

Simon smiled, and then directed his attention to the cup and cooler. Transformation would be difficult without touching the drink, but possible. He whispered the needed words. Now it was true lemonade.

"Simon, come on!" Mary called again.

Zoe took a drink, then pursed her lips and stared at her cup. She sipped again, then smiled and looked up at him. "A bit tangy, but very tasty," she called. A goose honked at her.

Good, the smile was back in her eyes. He blew her a kiss and transported to Elvina's side.

Although the center of the island was a tangle of vines and brambles, Simon could tell there were no fairies in the area. He shook his head. "It's a pretty place, Mary, but it doesn't have the feel of Faerie."

She took Elvina's hand and briefly closed her eyes. "It doesn't, does it? Let me show you around before we go back to Mom."

At the far side they came across a young boy fishing. From the frown on his face, it appeared he wasn't having much luck.

"Catch anything?" Mary asked.

"A couple of little ones," the boy replied. "I don't keep any of them, but I wish I could hook a big one."

"Are there big ones in there?" Mary peered into the weedy water. "There are trolls, you know. They eat the fish."

"I don't know about trolls, but I'm sure there's a granddad fish. A big'un. I've seen his shadow." Suddenly the boy's fishing pole bent in an arc. "I've got him!"

The two children squealed while the boy fought the fish. He struggled, reeled it in, and then held up a nine-inch fish for Mary to admire. In a moment, they threw it back. The boy handed the pole to Mary to try her luck. Mary handed him her sketchbook to look at.

Elvina glanced at Simon. "It was nice of you to let him work for it. He enjoyed it more."

"The fish wanted it that way."

Mary took her turn at the pole. When she caught a fish, she jumped in excitement; then she handed the pole to her newfound friend. He rescued the fish and tossed it back into the water.

Simon understood why Zoe was so fiercely protective of Mary. Blowing sands, he had started to feel the same way, though he had no right, and certainly no desire, to feel so.

"I know neither you nor Zoe will appreciate this," Elvina said, "but as your elder, I'm going to give you a bit of advice, Simon."

Startled, he turned to Elvina. "Elder? By your time, I have passed a thousand years."

"Human years, not djinn years. To your people, you're still a youngster, I bet. I figure it's like dog years, in reverse."

Simon thought he might have been very subtly insulted. He studied Elvina. Her blond hair stuck up in untidy spikes. The T-shirt over her chest was stretched thin. She wore a crystal on a chain around her neck. She'd thrown off her sandals, and her toes burrowed into the grass while she leaned against a tree.

To what purpose did she give the advice? Simon's deep-rooted distrust of humans kept him from believing Elvina might care about his needs. He leaned against another tree, crossed his arms, and waited.

The silence didn't seem to faze Elvina. "Zoe's been locked into herself for a long time, yet you seem to get a rise out of her." Her glance flicked down his body. "And I think she does the same to you."

His faint blush of embarrassment annoyed Simon.

"I'll be blunt," she continued. "Are you trying to seduce her into using her wishes?"

Seduction. Simon suppressed a slight shudder. There had been one summoner, a sorceress, six centuries ago. With her, seduction had been part of her wishes. Try as he might he could never forget her evil, nor her insatiable and twisted appetites.

"That is not your concern," he replied, cold seeping into his voice.

"Oh, but it is. I want Zoe to have some fun, some excitement. I think you can do that. You'd benefit, too. When she's relaxed, when she likes you, when she *trusts* you, she'll do anything for you. Like use her wishes. I want her to wish for something she really wants." She crossed her arms, in imitation of his pose. "Just don't you dare let her fall in love with you. I don't want her hurt again. *Comprende?*"

Simon wasn't impressed by her threat, for there wasn't an ounce of evil in Elvina. He knew—he'd met evil before. Yet, since he had no wish for a human to love him, had no wish to love a human again, he nodded. "Love is not something I desire."

"Why don't you go talk to Zoe? I'll watch Mary for awhile."

Deep in thought, he made his way toward the picnic table. How could he get Zoe to trust him? The tricks and subterfuge, the half-truths he had used with other summoners, did not work with Zoe, were counterproductive even.

Without being aware of it, he had made progress, Simon realized with a start. Like that night in her kitchen, after the salamander. And last night. He had been content simply to be with her during their fruitless discussion about the paper he'd found. He had wanted to help, and she had relaxed with him. Her friends and the children had welcomed him.

He already *was* a part of Zoe's life, the first step toward trust and caring.

Simon shook his head, not liking the maelstrom of confusion nor the warm promise of belonging that thought brought. One thing was important, only one thing could be. Zoe had to use her wishes.

He was just emerging from the undergrowth when he heard Zoe.

"Get back, you beast! Ouch! Stop that!"

That sour-sweet taste of real lemonade could grow on one. Zoe leaned over to refill her plastic cup. A stinging nip on her hip brought her sharply around.

"Ouch!"

A three-foot-tall goose was aiming for their sandwiches. And her hip was still in the way.

"Get back, you beast." She shooed the goose with her fingers.

Such minor distractions did nothing to deter a goose that had honed its technique on hundreds of picnickers. It aimed for the fingers. Zoe retreated, scrambling onto the picnic table and pulling their basket to safety. Deprived of its booty, the goose honked and went for her bare toes.

"Ow. Stop that!" She retreated to the middle of the tabletop, clutching the basket to her chest. "Go away. Shoo!"

The bird circled the table, honking and flapping its wings. Zoe went around after it, trying to scare it away without hurting it, but nothing she did deterred the beast. It wanted a sandwich!

"What a fetching sight you are!" She heard

Simon's amusement. Zoe glared at him standing at the foot of the bridge.

"It's the goose that's fetching. Fetching our lunch," she told him, irritated, and waved her hands again at the persistent beast. She had to do something. There was a fallen branch, still full of leaves, about a foot from the table. If she could get to it . . .

Simon strolled toward her. "If you wish it, I can send it away."

"Well, I won't." Zoe studied the goose for a moment before reaching into the picnic basket. She pulled out a sandwich half, tore it in two, and then flung the pieces, one after the other, as far as she could. The goose hurried to the prize, his orange feet skimming the grass, ready to protect his fare from the other ducks and geese that came quacking at the sight of bread.

Zoe scrambled down from the picnic table and hefted the branch. "That was your sandwich, Simon," she told him.

The goose, having finished the sandwich in two bites, waddled back toward the table. Zoe rattled the leafy branch at it. Simon gave it a warning look. Honking sadly, the goose retreated to the edge of the pond.

Simon turned back to her, a smile lighting his face. "If you could have seen yourself, Zoe. Standing on the top of the table, yelling at a goose, holding that picnic basket as if it were your precious child." He imitated her mincing steps, his shoulders shaking with quiet laughter.

Zoe crossed her arms and scowled.

Simon threw his hands wide. "You're delightful!"

He wasn't laughing at her, Zoe realized, wasn't being mean-spirited. He'd found genuine amusement in the sight. Her lips twitched. From his view, it must have been funny. She was twice the height and three times the weight of the goose, yet she'd been the one trapped on a picnic tabletop, fighting a dumb animal for peanut butter sandwiches. Come to think of it, it was pretty funny from her point of view, too.

Laughter bubbled up in her. She broke into a wide grin. A hearty chuckle, then another, followed. She burst out laughing.

Simon's smile widened. "And that is a delightful sound."

When their laughter quieted, she shifted and felt an ache in her hip. "I wasn't laughing when the blasted bird nipped me."

Simon was at her side in an instant, suddenly serious. "You are hurt?"

I'm getting used to those sudden moves, she realized, bemused. Zoe rubbed the sore spot on her hip. "I think it's just a bruise."

He lifted the hem of her loose shorts. The skin was starting to darken around the red slash from the goose's beak. He covered it with his palm. "With a wish, I can take away the pain and the bruise."

Her heart skipped a beat, a second, then resumed. "It'll heal soon." She cleared her husky throat. "I'll just use some antibiotic cream. To make sure there's no infection."

He wasn't listening to her. She wasn't listening to herself. His warm hand circled gently on the bruise. The soreness was lost in a spreading sensation of tingling comfort. His head was bent, so he looked at her leg, not her face. His skin was smooth and golden. The sun glinted off the tiny row of gold balls at his nape. She touched one. The strong cords in his neck tightened as he angled his head a little.

"No magic, hmmm?" he murmured. "Should I just kiss it and make it better then?"

He didn't move. She knew he hadn't moved, yet

she could swear she could feel his lips at her hip, giving her gentle kisses. Her hand flattened on his neck. Beneath her fingers, she felt a blaze of warmth, as though she touched the sun. The inferno flared through her.

I shouldn't be doing this, she thought.

The kisses moved higher. Zoe's eyes unfocused. The world became a blur, but feeling sharpened. She felt the muscles in his back shifting beneath her arm, the heat of his skin beneath her hand, the wisps of a cool breeze on the leg he bared, his tender soothing motion at her hip, the phantom lips touching her.

No, that couldn't be a tongue, trailing along the lacy edge of her panties. He was standing beside her. He wasn't, couldn't be dipping beneath the silk.

"I don't . . . I never . . ."

Never? The word sounded deep within her mind. "I think it's better now."

Passionate kisses moved to her belly. Zoe's hand tightened on Simon's shoulder, her legs too weak to hold her.

This is better? The lush words seemed to come from inside her head. Yet it was Simon's voice.

"Can you read my mind?" she whispered.

Nay, just give you my thoughts. A definitely naughty thought slid neatly into her. She flushed.

A goose honked, and a duck answered in angry reply. Zoe blinked and looked around. They were right in the middle of Brechtel Park. And, though the only place he physically had touched her was at her hip . . . they were in a very public place. "Simon, we can't, we mustn't." Her protest was thready, weak. "Stop." She put all her determination in that single word and was grateful that he didn't tell her "only if you wish it," for she might have wished the runaway feelings gone. Or wished them never to stop. Instead, his hand dropped to his side, though his ragged breathing gave proof to the difficulty of his action.

For a moment, Zoe buried her face in her palm. "Will we never be private when you choose to make love to me?"

He stepped away, and his hands settled on his hips in a familiar pose. "I was not making love to you. I was making love *with* you. I felt the desire, too." He sounded thoroughly disgruntled.

Her gaze flew to his tight cutoffs. He was as aroused as she was. Embarrassed by her automatic response to his arousal, she looked back at his face. His brows lowered in a frown. She hoped he never played poker, for his face was one of the most expressive she'd seen in a man. Right now arrogance warred with anger and frustration.

She couldn't help it. Nervous laughter billowed from her.

"You laugh at me, woman?"

She looked again at the spread stance, the fists at his hips, and started laughing for real. "If you were bald, you'd look like Yul Brynner." Another peal of laughter burst from her. "You even sound like him sometimes."

He stared at her as though he didn't have a clue what she was talking about. He probably didn't.

"Sometimes we'll rent the video of *The King and I*," she explained. Then, in a spurt of atypical spontaneity, she lifted one hand and started humming. "Shall we dance?"

Simon smiled and caught her hand. The radio she'd brought switched to the tune she had hummed. He whirled with her in a circle, and then spun her away. Another twirl and she faced him, her hands resting in his. She felt out of breath and dizzy, not from the dance, but from his nearness, his male scent, his smooth touch.

He planted kisses on her knuckles. "Are you sure you won't wish us to a place of privacy?" he breathed. "I know of a beach, with cool blue sand and flowers that perfume the air with exquisite, lust-inducing fragrances."

"You don't need anything lust-inducing."

"They're not for me, they are for you."

"I don't need anything lust-inducing, either. Those shorts of yours are enough," she admitted.

He gave her a very masculine, very satisfied grin. "Come, I want to show you something." He tugged her hand. She followed him to an isolated spot on the pond's far side. A soft breeze fanned across her damp skin, leaving cool comfort in its wake.

"Watch," he said, pointing toward the water's edge, while he wrapped one arm around her waist in a loose embrace.

Zoe leaned back, feeling Simon's warmth and solidity behind her. At first she didn't see anything but tall weeds, a dirt ledge, and green water. She shook her head. "I don't ―" she began over her shoulder.

Simon pushed gently against her cheek until she faced forward again. "Hush, just watch."

She watched until her eyes turned dry, listening as Simon murmured hypnotically, urging her to see deeply, to open completely, to believe freely. A bee zoomed past her ear. A tiny snake slid across her sandal, tickling her toes. So relaxed, so attuned to her surroundings was she, the touch did not startle her. There was a rightness to the small creature that curled itself between her feet.

Many different shades of green blended at the water's edge. Delicate waves stirred by duck feet lapped against the soil. The weeds danced in the light wind, which carried the scent of leafy moisture.

Then, light—made of countless points of crystal—surrounded the spikes of the weeds. It glistened with a brilliance almost too sharp to bear. Zoe stared, awestruck, at the beauty, and then blinked. When her eyes opened, the light was gone.

"Did you do that?"

"You saw it, didn't you?" Simon whispered against her ear. "I felt you tremble."

"Saw what?"

"The *ma-at*. The magic."

Zoe shook her head. "No, I couldn't have. I didn't. It was a reflection off the water. It had to be."

Simon sighed. "You saw, but you are not ready to believe."

Zoe could feel his disappointment, but she couldn't accept what she'd seen. A genie from another dimension, that she had to believe. But to see magic in the earth surrounding her? Did that mean she had to believe in elves and trolls, witches and fairies? It was too much. She offered a crumb of conciliation. "I don't think I ever looked at the pond that closely before, appreciated the beauty of my surroundings in such detail."

"Then we make progress." His hand, which crossed her chest to cradle her hip, tightened. Glittering colors radiated from his touch, and then disappeared. The small snake at her feet slithered quickly into the brush.

"Even that little guy seemed a natural, nonthreatening piece of the whole," she said with a small laugh, the sense of magic fading. "If Roger Broussard had been here, you'd have heard cursing to make a sailor blush. He detests snakes."

Simon pressed one finger against her lips. "Uh-uh. No work talk."

"No work talk," Zoe agreed. Work, ZEVA, the note they'd found last night, all seemed distant. Simon had insisted he could cope with any difficulties that arose from someone knowing he was djinn. They had agreed that further speculation about the note was pointless and had decided to wait and see what happened. All that could be dealt with tomorrow.

Today was not for fretting. Today was for relaxing.

"Do you realize," she asked, "how many different kinds of plants there are, just in this tiny area? How many there must be in the whole world?"

"A world of them?"

She laughed. "You make me feel so good, Simon."

At once, Zoe found herself pulled tighter against him, cradled between powerful, denim-clad thighs, her back pressed against his chest. Simon nibbled on her neck, brushing aside the collar of her blouse with his nose. Shards of exquisite pleasure shot through her.

"Do you know what it does to me when you say things like that?" he asked.

"I think I've got some hard evidence," she replied lightly, trying to keep from falling into his sensuality.

He rocked against her. Oh, Lord, when he did that she tended to forget that they came from different dimensions. His dimensions seemed more than adequate.

She must have said it aloud, for he lifted his head and laughed. Zoe flushed and, in a blink, found herself facing him.

She rested her hands on his cheat. Not here, not now. Much as she wanted to start kneading the smooth skin beneath her fingertips, she used the leverage to push herself back.

"Tell me about your world," she said, anxious for any distraction, afraid of the intense emotions he aroused in her. "Tell me about Kaf."

So, she retreats again, Simon thought. Still wary, still uncomfortable with the emotions. He studied her a moment, and then stepped back to give her the peace of distance between them. Unwilling to relinquish the soft feel of her, though, he kept one arm at her waist, holding her in the cradle of his embrace, while they ambled to the picnic table.

He told her of a land of soft white sands and green, fertile valleys, of rivers that ran from rugged mountains and emptied into bays teeming with aquatic life, of winds that whistled songs of loneliness, strength, and vast horizons, of strange things that had no parallel on her world. He told of his people, their oneness with their world that allowed them to tap into the powers of their minds, giving them *ma-at*, or magic in her vernacular.

His hand tightened on her waist, the aching longing for his home and his people catching him by surprise, though it shouldn't have.

"It sounds . . . lovely doesn't seem an adequate word."

"Perhaps one day I will show it to you." The idea took hold, appealing even after reconsideration.

He wanted Zoe to see his home. It would be tricky getting her there, because the *ma-at* wouldn't work if she wanted to go, and he sensed she would be eager to see Kaf. Yet nothing was impossible.

Zoe interrupted his pleasurable ruminations. "Can humans go there?"

"Yes, humans can even live there."

"You said djinn couldn't live on Terra."

"They can't, not permanently."

"But humans can live on Kaf? Why is that?"

"The djinn need strong bonds to nature, to each

other. That makes us who we are, that gives us our *ma-at*. Take it away and we wither." He waved one hand, scattering imaginary dust to the wind. "We die. To live here, we would have to dissolve our bonds with Kaf and form new ones with Terra. No djinni has ever successfully completed the transference. Most humans, however, do not seem to have that connection and thus can transplant."

"Why, do you suppose, is travel possible between our two worlds, or dimensions, or whatever they are?"

He lifted one brow. "Magic?"

Zoe snorted. "There's more to it than that. There has to be a reason."

"According to djinn legend, we were once part of Terra, higher than the humans, but lower than the angels."

"I'm surprised your legend doesn't put you at the top of the heap," she teased.

He accepted her observation with a grin. "Azazel, our leader at the time, thought that was an oversight, too. Rather than accept domination on earth, he and his followers chose to live in Kaf. They wove their souls in the air and took the fire at the core into their blood. Because we had once been of earth, however, travel between the two was still possible."

"See, I knew you could come up with a logical explanation."

If she thought that was a logical explanation, she was making more progress toward the acceptance of magic than he'd realized.

Chapter Eight

The wooden leg was smooth and sturdy. Sitting cross-legged on the floor, Simon stroked it, pleased with the inherent beauty of the grain that had emerged when he lathed the curves into it. With a twist of his wrist, Simon joined the leg and then set the table upright. An experimental push verified that the table no longer wobbled.

Simon smiled, feeling content. He and Zoe had established a truce during their time at Brechtel Park three days earlier, and soon she would trust him enough to use her wishes.

After all, he had evidence of her growing ease with him. She had not complained when he had improved her flower gardens. She had accepted the neighborhood Garden of the Month award with grace. True, she had scolded when Simon had not left her alone with Dustyn last evening, but she had not been angry.

And after Zoe? He needed seven more summoners. Elvina, Vivian, Abby, Chris. Perhaps the two children. Lucky, maybe?

His fist clenched. Then, he'd be free, free at long last.

If they summoned him soon, he could attend the celebrations of Baharshan, the sacred djinn feast days, for the first time in so many years. Already he could taste the honey-sweetened dates, hear the lilting flutes, see the djinn children as they displayed their new proficiency with *ma-at*.

Once free, he could still visit Terra, still be part of the lives he found himself intertwined with, but on his own terms and in his own time.

A wave of dizziness came over him. He braced himself with the flat of his hand against the table. *Not now! It should not be this soon!*

Mary came in and dropped a pile of boxes on the floor. "You want to watch videos with me? It's Two-Dollar Tuesday at Blockbuster, so I got a bunch. I thought we could have a djinni fest."

Simon, fighting the nausea, did not answer. His bonds with Kaf felt like faded elastic, stretched by the weight of his numerous stays on Terra.

"Please, Simon. I finished my math cards, and everyone else is busy. Chris and Mom are working on the computers. Miss Vivian said not to disturb her until she figures out what's wrong with her sound. Miss Abby's sending out bills, and Miss Elvina said she had to visit some prospects after she took me to the store." She gave a huff. "Even Joey is cleaning his room."

Only the pressure of his fingers against the table kept him upright. He had to find Kaf, get away from Terra. "In a moment. First, there is something I must do."

"Okay. I'll go make popcorn."

Simon transported to Kaf for revitalization, then

lingered, savoring the returning strength and the renewal of his *ma-at*. He returned just as Mary came in holding a steaming paper sack. She stuck a black plastic rectangle from one box into a machine and pushed buttons, then bounced onto the sofa and offered him the paper sack.

It seemed a strange way to tell their tales.

Simon leaned against the stuffed cushions of the sofa and tried the popcorn. Light and salty, it was delicious.

At first, the colorful pictures and rich sounds on the television screen fascinated Simon. Humans had almost mastered the technique of storytelling in three dimensions. If the pictures weren't small and separate but a part of one's vision, if they had scent and touch, they would seem like djinn stories.

Then, in increasing horror, he understood the tales being told. Numbly he stared as each box told a different, but essentially similar, story.

Was this how humans viewed his people? Joke-cracking buffoons who lived in a lamp and fell for blatant tricks? Cruel, capricious demons?

In one, the magician did true magic, creation, and the humans just laughed. Simon's head throbbed from the racing pressure of his blood. Did humans not realize the magnificence of *ma-at?* That *ma-at* was a part of all living? Did they not realize that wielding a force of nature required great skill and greater energy to control?

The cold sickness of understanding twisted in his belly. Despair replaced hope. He had tempered his *ma-at*, seeing only the possibility of the final summoners. His unusual weakness had forced him to rely on energy-conserving manipulations. His exploding desire and fascination with the human female had distracted him.

Zoe must view him as an amusing annoyance, an

impotent buffoon, a minor challenge to overcome. Was that why she refused to wish? She thought him powerless?

Unless compelled by the humans who had called him, Simon had never twisted the power of *ma-at* into something dark and malevolent. He had been unwilling to enter that pitched path, for the decision was irrevocable.

To be free, must that be his ultimate choice?

The chill grew in him as video followed video, as memory of human failing followed memory.

With controlled fury, Zoe replaced the phone in its cradle and swore at the inoffensive instrument. First the copy shop had claimed to lose the order for the brochures, and then they said she wasn't due any money back. Fortunately, the invoice they'd given her stated otherwise. Faced with returning a significant sum of money, they'd miraculously found the order but had the gall to act as if they were doing her a favor.

It would be the last time that place got her business.

Zoe rubbed her hand over her weary eyes. She'd been working too hard. Things always went wrong in groups, as the past days had proved. Little things, but they added up in lost time and increased tension.

If she believed in those things, she'd say she was cursed.

Her stomach, now that her attention was off her work, grumbled. She'd gotten right to work this morning and had forgotten breakfast. When had she last eaten? Last night when she'd filched the remains of Mary's popcorn. Maybe it was time to remedy that lack.

The rhythmic clacking of Elvina's sewing machine was the only sound in the quiet house. She waited until the noise stopped before she knocked. When Elvina called, "Come in," Zoe tugged at the sewing-room door, a recalcitrant fixture with a tendency to stick, only to stagger back when the door glided open. Giving it a surprised look, she entered.

"When did you fix the door?" Zoe moved a stack of patterns to the floor and settled onto a brocade-covered hassock.

"Simon did it over the weekend. He's quite a talented woodworker, you know, even without using his magic."

Zoe felt a faint flush of embarrassment that she hadn't known.

Elvina snipped her threads, then pulled the brilliant mass of color from the machine. She ran a hand through her hair, making it stand up in blond spikes. Her peasant blouse sagged down one arm. Elvina resettled it with an impatient shrug as she held up a skirt made of alternating fuchsia and emerald panels, each panel coming to a point at the hem. She twisted her hands, causing the skirt to float out in a circle. "Do you think Mary will like it?"

The colors were so bright they made Zoe's eyes hurt. "Mary will love it," she answered truthfully. "Where'd you get the fabric?"

"Remember that bag of scrap clothes I bought at Goodwill? There were some curtains in there I cut up."

"Someone had curtains those colors?"

"Yeah, those sure must have brightened up the house."

Zoe kept silent. Elvina had a remarkable talent for taking old clothes and refashioning them to make something wearable, altering them to remove tears and stains. However, some of her creations were . . . well, unique.

Elvina began pinning on the waistband. "I saw Mary's art teacher yesterday, and he asked if you could type his dissertation."

Zoe rubbed the bridge of her nose. "Tell him yes." Where she'd find the time she didn't know.

"I did, then asked Vivian to do it, now that she's solved her music problems. She's a decent typist."

When Zoe started to protest, Elvina quelled her with a look. "It's done, Zoe. You don't need another responsibility. What you do need is to realign your balance."

She rose and lit a pink votive candle resting on a smoky mirror. The faint scent of carnations wafted into the room. She perused her selection of tapes and chose one before handing Zoe a deep purple stone. "Rub this with your thumbs like so," she commanded, demonstrating the stroke on her crystal.

Zoe shook her head. She never—well, rarely—argued with Elvina about her beliefs, but she didn't agree with them.

"You didn't believe in djinn, either."

"Can you read my mind?" Zoe grumbled, but started rubbing.

"I know you very well, Zoe Calderone. Now, take deep, cleansing breaths and concentrate on the stone's patterns."

Sitting beside her friend, with the rock warm in her hand, the pleasing fragrance of flowers, and the ceiling fan's faint whirr beneath the clear tones of gong and bell, Zoe did relax. The annoying clerk, the fruitless phone calls for appointments, the lack of response to her questions about the tutorials, the failure of one account to deliver a promised check, all faded beneath the peaceful power in the room.

"You look better now." Elvina took the stone from Zoe, and then picked up her sewing. Her needle moved rhythmically through the fabric, tacking down the waistband. "Are you going to tell me what's wrong?"

Business setbacks, a Peeping Tom, a tenacious ex-husband, a nagging sense of things going wrong. The list seemed endless, but she'd manage. She always did. "Nothing I can't handle," Zoe answered.

Elvina sighed. "Why not ask for help, if not from your partners, then from something beyond?"

"Like your spirit guides? No way."

Elvina shrugged. "Or magic."

That also led down paths she wasn't prepared to tread. "Speaking of magic, where's our resident djinni?"

"He took the children to the library. Everyone else was busy."

"He took them to the library? How? By transporting?"

"Chris drove your car."

"My car!" Zoe's voice rose an octave. "What about a little thing called a license plate?"

Without looking at Zoe, Elvina started sewing on a button. "The car's drivable now. A friend took care of the missing paperwork and got you a license."

Zoe didn't ask which friend. Elvina had a lot of friends, many with strange tastes and stranger abilities. "Illegally, I'm sure."

"Untraceable."

"No thanks."

Elvina looked up then. Her jaw jutted out. "For once, Zoe, stop being a mule and let me help *you*. Do you know what it's like to always be on the receiving end?"

Zoe was speechless, never having realized her friend felt that way. Uncomfortable, she changed the subject. "Chris has a beginner's permit. He needs a licensed driver. Simon isn't."

"I'm sure he can manage."

Zoe was sure, too. That was what worried her.

"We're here."

The car jerked to a halt, startling Simon from his brooding silence. A day had passed since he had seen the damning videos, and his anger had not lessened.

Chris Cartier threw open the door. "I have to get out of this before someone sees me. This is one weird car." He scowled at Simon. "I want a *Doom* rematch."

Simon, indignant when he'd found out what "wuss level" meant and appalled at a game whose sole purpose was to kill, had used his powers to defeat Chris at *Doom*. Simon didn't consider it cheating; he considered it using all his skills. When Chris tried to negate the deal, Simon had pointed out that, at fifteen, Chris was considered a man in Simon's culture, and a man stood by his agreements.

Simon hadn't relented on his preference for Zoe's car, but he had let Chris film him for the hologram and introduce him to *Myst*. It was a game he preferred, and Chris reveled in teasing him with clues to solving the puzzles.

"You figure out how to raise the ship yet?" Chris asked as they followed Joey and Mary into the cool, dusty library. He fingered the tiny silver cross dangling from one ear.

"Not yet."

"Let me know when you need a hint." Chris plopped down in front of a computer terminal. Joey and Mary huddled over another terminal, whispering and giggling.

"What is the purpose of these computers?" Simon asked, his interest rising despite his anger.

"It's the on-line card catalog." Chris scooted over his chair. "Pull up a seat, I'll show you." He fastened his long blond hair out of his eyes with a rubber band, and then hunched over the keyboard. "See, you can find out what books the library has, and if they're in. If they're at another branch, you can ask to have them sent to you." Chris's fingers flew over the keys.

"Are there books of magic?"

"I'll check as soon as I find out—Good, the new Effinger book's in. Magic, you said?"

In a moment, a short list of books appeared on the screen. "Any of those what you want?" Chris asked.

Simon scanned the listing. The publication dates were all recent; the subject matter all about tricks. He sought the ancient tomes, the books of lost spells, not these pallid replicas of true *ma-at*. He shook his head. "These will not serve."

"You ought to check the Web. I bet someone there will have what you want."

"Check the web?" The words were familiar, but Simon couldn't understand the meaning.

"The World Wide Web. The Internet. You know, surf the net. Don't they have anything on computers where you're from?"

"My village seems to be a bit backward," Simon answered dryly.

"The Internet is a network of computers all over the world. Ms. Calderone has access. Heck, I've got it through AOL. I'm doing our school Web page. Maybe you could find some group into black magic or something that could help."

Simon drew himself up, anger returning. Did no one on this plane know the old truths? *Ma-at* was not evil. It was a force of nature, a connection to soil, rock, flora, and fauna.

"I do not deal in black magic," he said, his voice hard.

Chris swallowed and stared at him with wide eyes, eyes filled with disbelief as he watched the efflorescence of djinn anger. "I just meant there's a lot out there."

The youth had intended no disrespect. Simon inclined his head. "I thank you for the information. You have given me—" he searched for some current slang—"a lead."

"Hey, Simon, which book looks the best?" Mary shoved four volumes into his lap.

Simon rose, holding the books. "Why don't we read a few pages of each, little one, and see."

In the library, Zoe followed a soft murmur of voices and soon located Mary, Simon, Chris, Joey, and at least two dozen other children. Simon sat cross-legged on the floor, the children spread in a semicircle in front, their enthralled gazes fixed on him. His hands moved in elegant gestures.

"The young prince despaired of finding the treasure promised him by the mighty djinn," he said, his voice low and rich. His face mirrored the despair of the fictional prince. "The gold had not brought him happiness." There was a soft clinking sound, coming from everywhere, but coming from nowhere. "Neither had the delicate fabrics." Zoe could have sworn a piece of velvet caressed her face. Several children raised their hands to their cheeks. "Nor had the many desserts." He smacked his lips together and Zoe could taste chocolate, dark and slightly bitter. She ran a tongue across her lips.

Simon looked at her, holding her motionless with

his gaze. Electricity arced between them, sharp and piercing.

"It was the mysteries of the night and the earth he sought, though he knew it not."

The story, the sensations, the magic that Simon created swirled around her. She softened, the hard core of disbelief unable to withstand the gentle sorcery weaving about her. He held her rapt, as entranced as his tiny audience, who recognized the magic they listened to, even if their parents thought of him as just a gifted storyteller.

Though he spoke to the children, Zoe could almost feel his touch on her. His eyes glittered with dark promises. His hair seemed to take on the glow of candles set against black velvet. A shadow crossed his face, giving him the look of Lucifer rather than a djinni. She thought she felt the brush of lips on her cheek, and when she raised her hand to the phantom touch, his lips lifted in a slow smile.

Fair warning, dear Zoe, you shall soon see of what I am capable. Simon's voice echoed in her mind.

She jerked at the foreign sound, still not used to this talent. *Aw hell, I think I'm in trouble.*

"It was the magic of the soil he needed." Simon concluded his story with the touch of a warm breeze and the scent of fresh-turned earth. "Without the healing powers of his Terra, he could not survive. He vowed to tend her carefully, and he always did."

There was a moment of awed silence when he finished, and then the children started chattering. Mary leaped up to hug him.

"Did you get some books?" Zoe asked, coming to Mary's side.

"Yeah." Mary spared her a brief glance before telling Simon, "That was the best story I've ever heard."

Zoe tried to ignore the pang of hurt Mary's words caused. She'd always read Mary bedtime stories, and the two of them had giggled over the way she'd done the voices. Together, they were working through *Anne of Green Gables*, though, Zoe admitted, she hadn't read it to Mary lately.

The librarian hurried over, suggesting a regularly scheduled story time. Simon politely refused. Mary tugged at his hand. "C'mon, Simon, let's check out my books. Joey, Chris, we're going."

Zoe tagged after the quartet, feeling superfluous until they got outside and she saw the car. "Simon, I want a word with you." She grabbed his arm.

Simon glared at her hand, until she let go and stepped back, swallowing hard against the chill that invaded her. Something was different about Simon. Something was happening that she couldn't understand. Something was very wrong.

Unable to unravel the mystery with the children nearby, she focused instead on her immediate purpose. "Chris isn't supposed to drive without a licensed adult in the car."

"I have a license."

"Let me see it."

He gave her a haughty glance and ignored her request.

"How'd you get here, Ms. Calderone?" Chris asked.

"The bus."

"You want a ride home?"

"Yes." At least *she* had a license. Zoe climbed into the back beside Mary and leaned her head against the window, afraid in ways she couldn't name.

The teasing humor she'd come to associate with Simon had changed subtly and acquired a hard edge. The way he looked at her still made her feel hot streaks of desire, but now icy apprehension mixed in, for his look held a promise of ruthless menace as well. Though the interior of the car had heated to sauna conditions while parked, Zoe shivered.

Elvina emerged from the channeling, fading the glow of contact by slow degrees. She got to her feet and paced around her room, releasing muscles held motionless, regrounding herself in the physical world.

A frown creased her face. She couldn't fully interpret the messages her spirit guide had shown her. Perhaps she was not ready to understand, for they troubled her deeply. Ominous energies were directed toward her home, though from what source and to what target, she did not know.

She would have to watch very carefully.

Chapter Nine

Still in a black mood, Simon spent the next twenty-four Terran hours transporting from place to place, always invisible, always observing.

In the past days, with Zoe, he had come to question his opinions of humans, opinions he'd formed over the long years of his servitude. For the first time, he'd seen goodness and caring and innocence in humans. He'd even felt a part of Zoe's extended family. Alone for so many bleak years, he had grabbed the feeling, held it close, believed it made a difference.

The videos had reminded him of reality.

He was djinn. They were human.

Now, everywhere he went, Simon saw human callousness and disregard for beauty and majesty. The air was befouled, the grasses were covered with cement, and the rivers were clogged with debris. Here he saw a knifing, there a drug deal. He heard an abandoned child crying, watched a scrawny dog scramble through rusted trash cans looking for a scrap of food.

Every part of him ached in despair and loneliness. He wanted to be gone from this place.

He could no longer tolerate awaiting the human female's whim. The camaraderie, the warmth, the kisses they'd shared in the past week faded behind one memory.

The whim of another human female had bound him.

Minau. With time, her looks had faded in his memory until he remembered only that she had been beautiful, but he would never forget her name, nor her faithlessness.

Minau had captured his heart. They had made plans to marry and live in Kaf as they must, for he could not reside on Terra, but Simon had expected she would make periodic visits home. Before the bonds were sealed, he'd foolishly told Minau his true name.

Her father, a powerful mage, had discovered their intent. Furious at what he considered a betrayal by his only child, he threatened to cast her off, to bar her from ever returning to Terra. Distraught, faced with the loss of everything familiar, everything human, Minau had claimed that Simon had cast a love spell on her and bartered his name for her father's forgiveness.

With that power, the mage had bound Simon in a sentence that seemed destined to last an eternity.

Simon pounded the copper wristbands together in impotent rage. He had loved, trusted, desired Minau, and she had proved to be as duplicitous as every human since her. He had been wrong about Minau, at a cost no djinni should have to pay.

It was wrong to have hoped this summoning would be different, better than the others. Humans were deceitful. It had been a mere fancy to see goodness in Zoe Calderone.

His fists clenched as he raised his arms above his head. The sky rattled, echoing his desolation. No longer would he wait or hope. He must act.

The reverberating clap of thunder sent a brisk breeze whipping across the river. Zoe, sitting in an open café, shivered and wished she had a sweater, though outer coverings in July-baked New Orleans were most useful indoors, where air-conditioning made it feel like December in Canada. She tilted her head to look at the sky. Distant gathering clouds foretold the routine afternoon shower. With luck, the storm wouldn't force cancellation of the neighborhood picnic to be held that evening.

Zoe took another sip of coffee and made a face. Cold chicory coffee was the one thing worse than warm beer. She glanced at her watch. If Roger didn't show up in five minutes, she was leaving. In a fit of domestic insanity, she'd volunteered to bring a dessert to the picnic in addition to her usual contribution of iced tea. A dessert she hadn't made yet.

Maybe she could wish for one.

Zoe frowned again, and not because of the coffee. After the library, Simon had disappeared for most of the past twenty-four hours, popping in and out, looking more dangerous and on edge each time. Twice she'd heard him mutter, "Humans!" She ran a finger around the top of her cup. Simon was a djinni, and thus, by definition, unpredictable. She didn't like feeling that a part of her life was beyond her control.

But it wasn't beyond her control. All she had to do was wish, and Simon would be gone from her life forever. That thought sat as uncomfortably in her stomach as the cold coffee and the McKenzie's buttermilk drops she'd eaten.

A small measure of trust had developed between herself and Simon over the past few days. The important things in her life—her business, her friendships, Mary—she couldn't relinquish control of, but maybe she could trust Simon to grant a tiny, inconsequential wish without tying her life in knots.

Like the car?

Okay, so the car had been a problem, but the problem had been solved. That unending glass of guava juice he'd once suggested was pretty appealing. What could he do with a glass of guava juice?

Provide an unceasing flow that filled the house with sticky, sweet, bug-attracting juice, argued her doubting voice.

No, Simon wouldn't do that.

Would he?

Trouble was, every time she thought about wishing, she remembered—oh so clearly—the last time she'd made a wish. It had been her twentieth birthday, and Dustyn's extravagant promises had filled her with joy and hope. That top-of-the-world feeling had just made the gut-wrenching disappointment that followed worse. Dustyn's abandonment a short time later had been almost anticlimactic.

Yet having Simon around made her feel very different. She felt lighter, more carefree, filled with possibilities when she was with him. He warmed and excited places inside her that had withered when Dustyn walked out.

Simon was different. He had never used his strength to harm her.

"You look as if you've worked through a problem, Zoe."

She looked up at Roger Broussard towering above her and motioned to the seat across the table.

"I did—a minor domestic problem. You're late, Roger. I was about to leave."

"Stay. I think you'll find my suggestion interesting." He ordered a refill on Zoe's coffee and a Mimosa for himself. They sat in guarded silence until the waitress had set cup and glass before them. "I'll get to the point," Roger began. "I propose we start negotiations to explore the feasibility of merging our two companies."

Zoe started to hoot with laughter, but then thought better of it. Roger had to have some reason for his ridiculous proposal. It would behoove her to find out what it was.

She leaned back in her chair and took a sip from her coffee to give herself thinking time. The fresh brew burned her tongue. Holding the hot cup in front of her, she asked, "What brought you to that conclusion?"

"We're wasting a lot of time competing against each other. We're cutting into both our profits when we underbid in an attempt to get a job."

She must be hurting him more than she realized. Zoe shook her head. "I don't underbid. I offer my work at a fair price."

"Then you might find yourself losing contracts." He took a sip of his drink. "Could cause you some financial difficulties. After all, a small company like ZEVA can't have a lot of reserve built up yet."

Zoe's eyes narrowed. Did he know that the appliance repair store had called yesterday afternoon with a distant, polite, but firm refusal to engage ZEVA?

Another question followed close behind the first. Could Roger have had a hand in her recent business difficulties? The thought was chilling. They were rivals, yes, but she'd believed they'd kept the competition honest. Until now, she hadn't considered her problems as pieces of a pattern. Zoe found she couldn't ignore the possibility.

The coffee provided an excuse for delay again. "Are you threatening me, Roger?"

He drew back in his chair, offended. "Of course not. I thought, since my company is bigger and better staffed, with a dedicated sales force, you might consider a buyout. Consider coming to work for me."

Zoe's hands tightened on the cup until the china burned her palms. "I started ZEVA so I could be my own boss. That hasn't changed."

"It might. Your husband is very talented. He put together quite a creative package for Crescent City Curios. You did know we'd also submitted a proposal?"

Blast, she hadn't known.

Roger paused in dusting a piece of lint from his lapel and peered at the collar of her shirt. "Are you wearing that hideous pin of Leo's?"

Zoe's hand flew to the one-inch pin. It was a snake with ruby-red eyes, cleverly fastened on the pin so it writhed sinuously every time she moved. She'd put it on because it reminded her of the park, forgetting Roger's aversion to snakes. "It's not hideous," she insisted. "I like it."

Roger got up with a look of disgust and motioned to the waitress. "I'll get the check. Think about my offer."

She would think, and she would investigate.

When Zoe got up, she looked again toward the sky. Ink black clouds thickened on the southern horizon. The heavy air made breathing difficult and moving a sweaty chore. An edginess, like electricity charging the atmosphere, quivered through her.

If someone was behind her business setbacks, who could it be? Roger, or Roger and Dustyn, seemed the likeliest possibility. She still didn't know all that her ex wanted, but he had an agenda. Of that, she was certain.

Then, there was that unpleasant scene with Isaiah Knox. Had he held more of a grudge then she'd realized?

She also couldn't rule out her unknown voyeur.

Oblivious to her surroundings, she strode to her car, got in the red monstrosity, and pressed her hand against the dash. A low hum followed.

Could Simon be behind the troubles? Zoe shook her head. No, his tricks had been gentle and amusing, not malicious. She couldn't believe he would be so cruel.

Before she got home, the threatening skies fulfilled their promise. Zoe raced from the car to the house but got drenched anyway. Inside, she detoured to the bathroom for a towel to dry her hair and bumped into a distracted Elvina.

Elvina gripped her arm. "Have you seen the book where we found the summoning spell?"

"No. I didn't know you still had it."

Elvina shivered. "I hid it. It's too dangerous for the unwise or the unscrupulous."

"Maybe you moved it, or maybe Mary took it to read and left it somewhere."

"I'll ask her." Elvina bustled off.

Zoe moved down the hall, and then stood silent in the doorway to the front room while she toweled dry. Simon was staring at an old movie on television, *The Seven Faces of Dr. Lao*. He filled the chair, as though he'd collapsed and spread across it. There was a fine, almost imperceptible, trembling in one hand. The quick-moving storm cast the room in shades of yellow, making his golden-tinted skin look sallow.

Was he ill? Perhaps, not being of this world, he didn't have immunity to some earth diseases, like the Martians in *War of the Worlds*. She knelt beside

151

him and rested the back of her hand on his cheek, feeling for fever. Although Simon always seemed warm to her touch, today he burned. Energy, swift and sparking, shot through her, leaving her as breathless as one of Simon's kisses.

"Are you all right?" she asked.

A muscle beneath her hand bunched. His eyes and hair glittered when he turned his head. "I am quite healthy," he said. "Your concern is unneeded, unless you will wish me well."

Zoe's hand dropped as though a surge of electricity had short-circuited every nerve pulse.

Simon inclined his head toward the screen. His face remained impassive. "There is a magician in this story. He does wondrous feats, creating beauty from nothingness, yet the townspeople just laugh and call him boring. They do not believe. Is this true of people today? Would they recognize *ma-at?*"

Zoe swallowed hard. He was in a strange, unpredictable mood, and she wasn't sure what answer he wanted. "Cars, space flight, television," she told him, "most of us don't understand how they work. We just know they do and not by magic. We see special effects in movies and TV. We tend to believe there's a rational, understandable answer for the inexplicable."

"What should the magician have done to prove himself?" Simon's voice was still low and measured.

"Maybe he didn't need to prove himself. Maybe he should have accepted that their disbelief was their loss."

"Perhaps. Perhaps other concerns would not allow him to accept." Simon snapped off the television, and then leaned against the box, feet and arms crossed. "I told Elvina I would provide a dessert for the festivities this afternoon. She was worried you would not return in time. Where were you?"

"A business meeting." Zoe got to her feet.

"Always business. Only a camel is a beast of burden in the desert, and even they stop to drink."

Zoe stopped pushing back a strand of wet hair to stare at him. "What's that supposed to mean?"

He shrugged. "It means you should find things to enjoy in this life. It is important to celebrate and give your family a sense of continuity."

"I can't neglect business. I'm the main support of this family."

"That doesn't preclude pleasure."

He had a lot of nerve, denigrating the hard work she put in, making light of the pressures. Zoe threw the towel to the floor. "What do you know about burdens and responsibilities, Simon? You've got magic. A wave of your hand or a wrinkle of your nose and you've got whatever you want. No effort, no sweat. I don't have magic to fulfill my needs. I have to work for them. If I don't, Mary starves and Elvina loses the roof over her head."

She closed the gap between them and matched his crossed-arm pose. "I feel sorry for you with your way. With no effort and no sweat, there's also no accomplishment. I'm proud of what I do. I'm proud when someone understands what I've taught them. I'm proud when a client likes the work I've done. Can you say that? It's all so easy for you, you and your bag of tricks."

"Bag of tricks?" Suddenly, the air around Simon crackled. Sparks shot from the tips of his dark hair. He was unmoving, frozen in his anger.

Had he grown a few inches taller? Had his face gotten harsher?

"Oh, stop it," she commanded. "That's just the sort of thing I'm talking about, intimidation with magic. Try fighting normally, like a man."

"I am not a man. I am a djinni."

153

"Now we're back to the voice in the tunnel."

"I get angry like a djinni," he boomed.

"Are you telling me all djinn ignite the air and grow bigger when they're angry?"

"Yes!"

Simon was beyond angry, he was furious. He welcomed it, nourished it, for it hid the weakness that once more challenged him.

She had no idea! No idea of the training and effort to safely wield *ma-at*. No idea of the pride his people took in their art, their handicrafts, their other skills.

"You know nothing about me, Zoe Calderone. You know nothing of my people or what my life should be beyond these." He lifted his wrists and struck the copper bands together. A bolt of blue energy passed from his wrist to the bands on his upper arms. "Like all humans, you condemn what you do not comprehend. You live your tiny, separate lives, filled with your petty concerns."

She didn't understand. She didn't believe. He had been her friend. He had been nice, but still Zoe avoided her wishes.

He wanted to stay angry, but as he noticed her flushed cheeks and bright eyes, another emotion unfurled inside. Desire, never dormant when he was with her, grabbed him with its hot, sweet grip.

She wanted prim and proper, arguments, control.

He would give her passion, wildness, no choices.

The door slammed shut and locked with a click. He stepped forward. She stepped back, swallowing. She had finally realized he would no longer allow her to sway him.

"I shall show you the capabilities of *ma-at*," he said, "the effort and imagination it demands. Show you what I have wanted to do from the moment I laid eyes upon you." He changed the Terran clothes he wore to a scarlet robe, and then grabbed a curtain in his fist. Fighting the aching weakness in his arm, he replaced the threadbare fabric with silk and chiffon drapes. He expanded them until the soft fabrics surrounded them both, floating without visible support, swaying from invisible puffs of air that caressed them with sandalwood-scented breezes.

Candles were the only illumination, their flames casting dancing shadows on the edges of the enclosure, hiding what lay beyond. Musky incense replaced the kitchen odors of bread and butter. The rugs beneath them, he transformed to a thick carpet of vines. Zoe shifted her weight, and a tinkling melody played when she broke one of the leaves.

Simon rested his hands just above her breasts. He heard her quick, indrawn breath. In some part of her, she must be resisting, knowing he was motivated by anger, not caring, otherwise his *ma-at* would not work, but she made no move to stop him. Instead she watched him with wide eyes.

His hands stroked across her serviceable cotton blouse, circling and teasing, before halting atop the breasts he'd longed to touch. He gently thumbed her nipples and felt them harden. When he caressed the outsides of the soft mounds and whispered ancient words, the fabric changed beneath his hands.

Zoe did not protest. Her chest moved in rapid motion, sending waves of pleasure through him. Her breathing was a light rasp in the room, still except for the sounds of the vines. She watched him beneath lids made heavy with passion. Her head tilted back, opening her vulnerable throat to him. One vein pulsed. He took advantage, gave her a tiny nip, then a kiss.

Blowing sands, the taste of her was like sweet nectar.

Meanwhile, his hands moved lower.

"Touch me," he commanded. He needed the feel as well as the taste of her.

Her hands crept to his shoulders, catching him as firmly as he caught her. Snaring him in a feminine determination that both surrendered and conquered. He spanned her waist, cupped her hips, smoothed her thighs. With each stroke the clothing changed. His hands lifted to run their magic across her hair, and then bracketed her face.

At last, he kissed her as he had longed to do for days. When she moaned in response, he knew her acquiescence precluded further *ma-at*.

Nothing further must he do.

Nothing further did he want to do. The need to dominate had become a need to share and delight.

Nothing further could he do. The weakness shot bolts of agony through his limbs, but the arousal in his groin was a deeper pain. Before he returned to Kaf, he must have her.

"Now you look like the wanton woman of passion I know you can be." Ripping pains made his voice hoarse.

His deep, masculine groan tore through Zoe.

There had been a need in Simon, a need she'd never seen before, a need that had frightened her until she'd almost run from him. It had been a very male need to dominate.

Yet she hadn't run. For she'd seen something else, a vulnerability that tugged at her and made her yearn to satisfy the longing she'd seen in his eyes.

Sparks and crackling energy surrounded her. Intense djinn emotions, he'd called them once.

Simon's breath was warm against her bare skin while his tongue traced the edge of the vest she wore, its glittery fabric a beacon beside his soft, dark hair. At her hip, one of his hands bunched the loose, gauzy fabric of her trousers and rubbed against her, sending a shower of embers through her.

Loose, gauzy trouser. Glittery vest. Zoe looked down. Aw hell, he'd been watching *I Dream of Jeannie* reruns.

He unbuttoned the top button of her vest with a jerk. Startled, she stepped back and bumped against something.

It was a bed. A lush bed made of a radiant cloud. Fingers of mist twined around it, reached out for her ankles, begged her to lose herself in its decadence.

Simon tumbled her onto it. She drifted through softness delicate as a strand of cotton until she felt satin, puffy pillows, and warm cashmere. It was a bed that made a woman think of sinking into its depths with an ardent lover.

That lover had followed her down and was undoing the remaining few buttons on the vest with haste. A nimbus of glittering silver enclosed him. "Five minutes. Solomon's beard, grant me five minutes." He looked not at Zoe, but at his trembling hand. Perspiration shone across his face.

"I think it might take more than five minutes." Zoe trembled, unsettled in the face of such need.

Simon took her hand past the folds of his robe and held it against his erection. Of their own volition, Zoe's fingers curled around him.

"I don't think so," he said. "Five minutes is more time than I have right now." He stared, as if awaiting an answer.

From a distant part of the house, Zoe heard Mary's clear laughter. She tried to remove her hand, but Simon's grip tightened around her wrist.

"I . . . we can't," she stuttered. "Mary . . . I'm afraid . . ."

With an oath, Simon flung her hand away. He pressed his fists against his temples. "Always afraid,

Zoe. So be it." His whole body started shaking. "I can no longer delay."

Simon departed in a violent wind. The bed disappeared, sending Zoe to the floor with a thump. Her clothes changed back to normal.

Bless the saints, what was he going to do?

Simon stumbled across the sand, but the pains would not allow him to reach his house. He knelt on the hot sands of Kaf, opened his arms, and turned his face to the sun above, soaking up the heat and life. Like a puddle of water on a desert, the pains receded to nothingness, leaving fatigue in their wake. The knife edge of desire waned but did not leave. That he could deal with later, as he always had.

With infinite care, he wove tight the bonds to Kaf, revitalizing his spirit and his body.

Kafian night had almost fallen before he moved. He struggled to his feet and took a breath of cleansing air. Looking skyward, he saw a glow reflected in the distant sky.

The first fire of Baharshan had been lit. It would be tended for the next thirty-two days, and each day a new fire would be lit until the final sacred feast day, when the blazes would fuse in a fierce conflagration.

And just a short time ago, he had dreamed of being free to attend.

As he strode toward his home, Simon kicked up the hot sands. The ties of his homeland had strengthened and infused him with energy.

He had waited too long before returning, but he hadn't expected the pains. Always before it had been weakness that signaled the need to return, and it had never been so severe or progressed so rapidly. Come what may, he would have his way tonight, though he would take care not to spoil the Terran picnic for the others.

What she did not realize was that as long as he was bound to Zoe, she was bound to him. She was not free to act without his acquiescence, just as he was not free to refuse her wishes.

Simon stayed outside and moved to the far side of his house, away from the evening glow and into the cold shadow of the mountains. He divested himself of his robe, and then closed his eyes, slowing his breathing to the rhythm of Kaf.

He had never sought the sinister trails of *ma-at*. The poison fog that stole the breath, the eternal prison of blinding light, the knife of a thousand deadly cuts, these and more he had never pursued, had never wanted to employ. Now he searched for them in the depths of Kaf. Evil did exist, for without evil there could be no goodness.

Brilliant, blood-red light filled his vision. It beckoned him, whispered of powers unfathomable. If he pulled it into him, let it become part of him, used it as it begged to be used, he could do what he must. He could find the means to turn against Zoe, to get what he wanted from her. Simon gave a cold laugh.

A sandy wind told him he was no longer alone.

"What do you do?" Darius spat each word in fury. "Cease, Simon." Darius sliced through the connections Simon was forming.

Simon looked at him through glazed eyes. "I must."

Darius grabbed him by the shoulders, using physical touch to reach his friend. "Nay, you mustn't. Simon, throughout all, you have retained your goodness. You have not allowed the taint of darkness here." Darius struck Simon's chest with a fist.

"She will not wish," Simon answered.

"Did you ever tell her? Tell this Zoe about the

conditions of your binding? Tell her you are near the end? Tell her about the weakness?"

For a moment Simon faltered. He'd seen the way Zoe helped people, sometimes at cost to herself. Perhaps if he explained his exile, she'd be sympathetic, be willing to use her wishes. Then he shook his head.

"Did I ever tell you about one of my early summoners, Darius?" he asked in a distant voice. "He, too, was a teacher, friendly, with a voice that invited confidences. I was not as experienced then."

"Not as hurt, you mean."

Simon shrugged. "I told him about my turquoise tablet, thinking a gentle, learned man could help me retrieve it. Instead, he took perverse pleasure in delaying his wishes. He taunted me about being forever bound to him."

Darius's hand tightened on his shoulder.

Simon ignored the sympathy. "He did wish, eventually. They all do."

"What did he wish for?"

"A painful wasting illness for a rival, possession of an evil book of arcane magic, and a chest of silver coins. I watched, invisible, while he poisoned himself with the potions in the book and spent all the silver coins in vain attempts at healing. I knew then, I could never trust another human." Simon tried to reach for the dark *ma-at*.

Darius spun him around and transported them both into the house. "Do not do this to yourself."

The rhythm he had tried to find was gone, shattered by Darius's insistent intervention. "Are you going to keep stopping me?"

Darius's jaw tightened. "If I have to. Why not give the woman another chance?"

Simon looked at his friend. "For you, for your loyalty, I will give her that chance. Now leave me."

160

Chapter Ten

Zoe's West Bank neighborhood met in the school-yard every July as part of the Neighborhood Watch "Get to Know Your Neighbor" Campaign. It provided the perfect excuse for neighbors who had lived beside each other for years to party, not that anyone in New Orleans needed an excuse.

Aaron Somerset, the school principal, cooked an immense pot of chicken and sausage jambalaya. The owners of the houses across the street joined to boil hundred-pound sacks of crawfish, together with potatoes and half ears of corn, until the potent scent of boiling cayenne pepper set mouths watering a block away. Everyone else brought their specialities, chosen by the popular method of scraping dishes clean of every morsel in previous years. Zoe always brought the iced tea.

"Race you to the swings, Joey," Mary called. The dragon she'd painted on her fuchsia and emerald skirt rippled in the wind, as though its wings carried it. She took off, her ballet slippers skimming the concrete, Joey close behind. Soon Mary was swinging high, her blond hair a stream behind her.

Just ahead, Elvina, her long Madras skirt swinging, her blouse—half yellow, half white—slipping from one shoulder, talked animatedly to Lucky. His pug face nodded while he righted Elvina's blouse with a proprietary touch.

"They've been seeing a lot of each other," Zoe said in a quiet voice to Simon, beside her.

"You noticed?"

Zoe ignored the mocking tone. "I'd never have picked him for her. If I'd met him on a dark street, I'd have discreetly backed away." Lucky's scarred hands and rough exterior were unsettling, but there must be a depth there if he recognized the treasure he had in Elvina.

And Zoe would bet her last Snickers candy bar that Lucky was the friend with the connections to forge license plates.

Lucky glanced over his shoulder at Simon, and then shifted his attention to Zoe. Ghost fingers sent a quiver up her spine at the touch of his gray eyes, eyes that seemed to know too much.

Zoe shifted the dessert to her left hand and rubbed a tingling spot on her scalp. Ever since that recent scene with Simon—when they'd almost made love on a magical bed in front of the television—it had felt as though she'd bumped her head on a door. She rubbed again and wiped her forehead on her sleeve.

"Blast, it's hot," she complained. The earlier storm hadn't cooled the air, only shoved up the humidity and heat index. She wiped eyes stinging from dripping sweat and rubbed her head again.

Simon didn't answer her.

Assorted members of the neighborhood had

banded together to provide music for the fete. When they swung into an enthusiastic, if not altogether synchronized version of "They All 'Ax' for You," Lucky deposited Elvina's bowl of homebaked, whole-wheat rolls on the serving table and swung her into a two-step. Elvina laughed, and her Birkenstock sandals danced across the grass.

Zoe angled a glance at the silent djinni walking beside her and carrying the enormous cooler of tea with effortless ease. Tall, dark, and handsome were not clichés when applied to Simon, for he gave the words new definition, but Zoe didn't trust the dangerous glitter in his eyes. The hard edge was back on Simon, more brilliant than before.

Which made the feeling she owed him an apology even stronger.

She set Simon's dessert on the table. He'd thrust it into her hands when he'd reappeared, then hefted the tea and stalked out the door. No kiss, no acknowledgment of what they'd almost shared.

"What's in your dessert?" she asked, squinting at the deep narrow dish, not seeing anything recognizable.

"It will not harm," Simon replied as he surveyed the milling crowd, "but I doubt *you* will want to taste it. It was assembled with *ma-at*."

Zoe took another look at the dessert. It smelled delicious, like almonds and figs, and, strangely, she did trust Simon about it. Besides, leaving it behind would have been an exercise in futility. The mood he was in, neither Simon nor his dessert would have stayed "left."

If she'd seen the T-shirt he'd donned as they'd left, she might have made the attempt anyway.

Most men couldn't, or wouldn't, wear bright colors, but Simon looked at ease and devastatingly masculine in denims and an iridescent blue T-shirt.

A shirt emblazoned with tiny, flashing white lights that spelled out, "Watch the magic."

No one would realize he meant that as a warning. No one would suspect he didn't have a battery hidden in the seam. Ribbons of tension unfurled in her stomach, reaching lower and spreading to her overheated skin.

She'd thought his leather sandals were ordinary until he'd seen the direction of her gaze and whispered in her ear, "They're made from the hide of a basilisk, an evil creature that slays with one look."

Zoe refused to admit she saw scales imbedded in the leather.

When Simon returned to her side after depositing the tea container, Zoe took a deep breath. "I want to apologize."

His swift glance told her she'd surprised him. "What for?"

"The things I said before you left about how easy it is for you. You're right, I don't know much about your life, about djinn life. You've abilities I don't understand, can't even comprehend. I'm sorry."

"Does that mean you're ready to wish?" His voice was flat.

"Ah—" Zoe stumbled for an answer. She had thought she could risk wishing, but this icy Simon frightened her. What had she done to cause the cold change in him? Old insecurities and self-doubts, long since buried under hard-won accomplishments, resurfaced.

Was it the way she'd responded, the way she'd kissed back? Dustyn had called her clumsy. He'd criticized her attempts to direct their lovemaking. Instead, he'd instructed her where to touch and how to stroke until he reached his satisfaction. Until Simon, she hadn't wanted to risk finding out if satisfaction was possible for her, too.

Was it because she refused at the last minute?

Or was it something else, some djinn thing she had no knowledge of?

Was it something dangerous?

Suddenly feeling cold, Zoe rubbed one arm. Was her fragile trust misplaced?

Simon read her answer in her silence. "I thought not," he said.

"Hey, Ms. Calderone." Chris sauntered up, wolfing down a handful of taco chips. "I didn't know you were a Shaq fan, Simon." When Simon looked at him, puzzled, Chris nodded to the T-shirt. "Shaquille O'Neal. Orlando Magic. Don't they have basketball, either, where you're from?"

"No," Simon returned.

Chris shrugged, apparently unable to comprehend a place where the Shaq Attack was unknown. "Did you ever get a chance to check out the Web?"

"Not yet."

Zoe started to move away. Simon laid a heavy hand on her shoulder, stopping her.

"You should. I bet you can find those books of magic somewhere," Chris said. He looked at Zoe. "Remember how I found those books about laser holography in the Library of Congress, Ms. Calderone?" His glance went back to Simon. "It's a maze at first, but you'll catch on pretty quick. Even Grandma tried it the other day."

"What did I try?" Abby came up and added her baked beans to the table.

"Searching through the Web," Chris answered.

"Which reminds me, Chris, last month's on-line bill was much too high. You're going to have to cut down on the chats."

While the two argued, Zoe started to edge away. Simon's hand tightened on her shoulder. She looked up at him.

165

One corner of his mouth lifted in mocking challenge. "Running away?"

Zoe could not look away, but she refused to cower. "If you want, I'll show you how to get started with the Web browser."

"Oh," he said softly, his eyes darkening, "that's not what I want."

His quiet menace sent a shiver through her, despite the steamy weather. Zoe drew in a ragged breath, blinked, and pulled her glance from his.

Apparently Abby and Chris had finished their argument to neither's satisfaction, for Chris was stomping away and Abby was frowning.

"When you were a boy, did you get into a lot of trouble?" Abby asked Simon.

"Don't all youths? Perhaps you should stop thinking of Chris as a boy. In my culture he is a man, responsible for his actions and their results."

"Here, he's not considered an adult until eighteen," Zoe said.

"Maybe I have been holding the reins too tight," Abby mused.

Zoe looked over at Chris. He was kicking one sneakered toe against the cement and gazing in the distance while a girl, another fifteen-year-old, talked to him, her hands moving in animated punctuation, her entire body flirting. "Are you sure this is the best time to loosen up?" Zoe asked.

Abby followed her glance. "Oh, no. Please say you're going to put him to work soon."

Zoe shifted uneasily. "I meant to tell you, I won't need Chris to scan those records."

"Why?"

"I didn't get the contract."

"Did they give you a reason?"

Zoe shrugged. "No, just said they weren't ready."

Abby frowned. "ZEVA could have used the

money. You won't be able to hire Chris now, will you?"

"I promised him," Zoe answered. "I'll think of something."

"Perhaps you should discuss this with Chris," Simon interjected.

"I'll handle it," Zoe answered, more sharply than she'd intended.

Abby glanced from one to the other. "You know, you don't look much like Elvina, Simon. I'd never guess you were cousins."

"It is a distant relationship."

"She never mentioned you before. How long did she say you were staying?"

"That depends upon Zoe." His cheek brushed across the top of her hair.

Zoe tried to move away, but his hand remained clamped on her shoulder.

Abby glanced from one to the other and smiled. "I see."

"Yoo-hoo, Simon, Zoe." Vivian fluttered up and put her dish on the table.

Simon trailed his finger along Zoe's shoulder, from her neck to beneath the strap of her tank top, an erotic, possessive gesture. Suddenly, the day turned even hotter. Sweat rolled between her shoulder blades.

Vivian watched the telltale gesture, exchanged a glance with Abby, and sighed.

Great; all she needed was for her partners to start matchmaking.

Zoe contented herself with taking a step away from Simon. Unfortunately, he shadowed her, his finger still tracing tingling whorls on her skin. She shrugged her shoulder, trying to dislodge his hand.

You know, I like the feel of your skin.

Aw hell, he was back to the voices trick. And his

hand was delving further beneath her top.

Zoe gazed up at him, a smile of false adoration plastered on her face, grabbed the offending finger, and twisted it.

Ouch! His hand dropped.

So why did it seem as if she could still feel the hot pressure of it on her neck? Zoe sighed. It was going to be a very long evening.

Vivian looked at the table. "I thought you were bringing cookies, Zoe."

Zoe gestured to the casserole dish containing whatever it was Simon had made. "Simon—"

"Simon is anxious to taste your contribution," he interrupted and began winding a strand of her hair about his fingertip. The slight tug restarted the tingling in her scalp and told her he hadn't forgotten that twist to his finger.

"What's it made of?" Vivian peered at the dish.

"Ask Simon. He made it."

Simon laughed. "Do I look like someone who could make a confection like that?" Zoe rolled her eyes at his blatant chauvinism. "Zoe's just too modest to take credit."

"So what's in it, Zoe?" Apparently Vivian was more prepared to believe that Zoe, who'd never exhibited a culinary skill worth mentioning, had made the dish rather than Simon.

Zoe gave up. "Let's see, there's sugar and flour and eggs." She tried to think of something else that might go into a dessert.

Cardamom. Simon's voice again.

"Cardamom."

Yogurt.

"Yogurt."

Ants.

"Ants."

Thigh of goat.

"Thigh of goat."

"What?" Vivian exclaimed.

"What?" Abby echoed.

"Thigh of . . ." Zoe began, then smiled weakly. "Just kidding. Had you going there for a minute, didn't I?"

Vivian and Abby gave her matching surprised looks. She glared up at Simon, who was still winding one of her curls around his finger.

One of her curls? She didn't have curly hair.

"I love what you've done with your hair," Vivian said, "but I never thought you'd go for color and perm all at once. Who did it? It's very becoming."

Color and perm? Zoe batted Simon's hand from her hair, and then rubbed the rioting tingling in her scalp. Her hair sprang beneath her touch. "Excuse us," Zoe said between clenched teeth, "I just remembered something." She headed for the far side of the school building, tugging Simon along in her wake. He made no protest.

Around the building, away from prying eyes, she pulled a mirror from her purse. No longer one length, her hair was a mass of layers and colored a darker brown, more like sable than rabbit. It also had more waves than a flag in a hurricane.

"What have you done to my hair? Put it back the way it was."

"Only if you wish it. Do you like it?"

It was attractive, but she'd eat raw crawfish before she admitted it. "No. It's too frivolous. It's not me."

"I knew you would think that. That's why the ritual worked."

"How long is it going to stay this way?"

"Forever. Unless you wish it otherwise."

Zoe glared into the mirror. Now she'd have to get used to curls. Had she really been thinking of caving in, of using her wishes? Not now. Not until she thought of a suitable revenge. "When hell freezes over," she muttered and stalked back to the picnic.

Simon was at her side in an instant. He spun her around to face him. Zoe shook her arm from his grasp. "Hell?" he asked bitterly and gave her a harsh, mocking smile. "When you've spent a thousand years catering to the wishes of cruel idiots, you can speak to me of hell."

He had her so tied up in knots, she couldn't think straight. Compassion mutated to desire that warred with frustration. Insecurities replaced plans of vengeance. The loss of control over her life and her emotions buffeted her, until she was afraid to turn, afraid to decide.

Zoe lifted her fists to her temples. "Just leave me alone, Simon, leave me alone!"

The picnic went downhill from then on.

Zoe watched Simon charm and enthrall her neighbors, those that he hadn't met already. From the number of greetings he got, Simon had been making himself a known presence in the neighborhood.

She shouldn't be surprised. He was outrageously charming, flamboyantly confident, and heart-stoppingly male.

A few people gave her arch looks, when they saw how Simon hovered around her, for she'd never brought a man to one of these affairs before. Zoe almost choked. She still hadn't brought a man. She'd brought a djinni, but if she tried to tell them that, even Abby and Vivian, they'd be measuring her for a jacket with sleeves long enough to wrap around and tie.

Simon knelt and retied the laces on a three-year-old's shoes. No one—no one except Zoe—noticed when the shoes became a shade brighter under his touch. The toddler gave him a big grin.

Even at that age, they weren't immune.

Zoe took a step away, feeling closed in. Simon rose. The muscles of his back rippled from the movement and his derriere tightened. A shaft of desire slammed into her.

Why didn't biology class teach you that raging hormones dried your tongue so you couldn't answer a simple question? Why did the child's mother look at Simon as if he was a serving of rich bread pudding?

He was being too charming, too effusive. He planned some trouble tonight, Zoe knew.

Mary's laughter rang across the playground as she did a cartwheel on her way to the merry-go-round. She glanced back and gave Zoe and Simon a wave.

The heat, the crowd, the noise pressed upon Zoe, giving her a raging headache. Her churning thoughts confused her. She couldn't handle the speculative looks and arched brows any longer. Maybe if she could just get away from the sultry night, find a cool spot to rest a few minutes . . .

"I have to go to the washroom," she muttered to Simon, hoping he wouldn't follow her. Then she rushed into the school, which had been left partially unlocked for just that purpose. She wandered deeper inside, seeking solitude, halting when she saw a light on in the office.

No one should be in there. The office was always locked during the picnic.

She pushed open the door and saw Isaiah Knox seated at the computer, his hands racing over the keys.

Zoe moved closer and looked over his shoulder. "What are you doing?"

He spun around, then jumped up and cursed at her.

171

Zoe, however, had her eyes on the computer screen. "That's a purchase order, but I've never heard of that company." She punched the page-down symbol. "And so's that." She turned to Knox, unable to accept the inevitable conclusion. Dull shadows hid his gaunt face except for the fervid eyes. "You're authorizing payment, using the automatic funds transfer," she breathed. "Finishing what your son started."

Knox thrust a sheaf of papers at her. "Isaiah Junior wrote down what to do. And you're not going to stop me."

His bony fingers clamped around her wrist. With a swift movement, he dragged her toward the supply closet. Zoe tugged, but could not free her arm. The years of manual labor had made Knox strong. She tried to drag her feet, but they moved along the floor as though pushed from behind. When she shouted to alert the others, her words dried to a thin croak.

"No noise," Knox warned. "I don't want to get rough."

His grip was cold, and an aura of supernatural darkness spread from him to envelope her.

"I'll put you in here 'til I'm finished," he muttered, fumbling with the mass of keys at his waist. "If you keep quiet, I might even let you out when I'm done."

Wish, Zoe. A haunting, incorporeal voice enticed her.

Zoe shook her head, refusing to give in to the temptation, refusing to acknowledge the blackness that dimmed the room. She'd get out of this herself.

She couldn't just wait in the closet; she had to stop Knox before he did further damage. Knox's grip loosened on her while he worked at opening the closet. What could she use to get away?

Wish, Zoe.

The broom. Knox had left his long-handled broom beside the closet. Zoe grabbed it and swung it to the side, catching Knox on the side of the face with the handle. Knox shouted with anger and pain and let go of Zoe.

Hearing voices, she ran to the door. A security guard was coming down the hall with Aaron Somerset, the principal.

"I wondered if you wanted these doors locked," the guard was saying.

"What's going on?" Aaron asked, catching sight of her.

"It's Knox," she gasped. "The computers."

Aaron hurried down to the office, the security guard coming up behind him. Zoe leaned over the keyboard and punched the keys to intercept the funds transfer. The guard grabbed Knox.

Knox's attempt at revenge was over. His shoulders slumped as he braced himself with one hand against the desk. When he looked at her, his eyes were blank, defeated. "You think you got all the answers," he said with hatred.

Zoe reached out for him, then clenched her hand and drew back. He wouldn't want her comfort. Instead, she watched, a tear trickling down her cheek, while the guard took the defeated man into custody.

"Will you prosecute?" she asked Aaron.

"I have to," he replied, and then glanced at the monitor. "Did he do any damage?"

Zoe wiped the moisture from her face and studied the papers Knox had left. There had been more in Isaiah Junior's instructions than simple funds transfers. He'd wanted to sabotage the whole system. "He might have."

"Can you repair it?"

"I'll see what I can do." Zoe sat down at the computer and began to work. "You don't have to stay, Aaron. They need you outside."

When the guard added that he needed a complaint signed, Aaron thanked her and left.

After about a half an hour, Elvina poked her head in the door. "Zoe? Aaron said I might find you here. What are you doing?"

Zoe rubbed the back of her neck. "It's a long story." At least, Isaiah hadn't gotten too far with his sabotage. She'd been able to reverse everything except one fund transfer. Work accomplished, she turned off the computer. "I think I'm going home. Will you watch Mary?"

"That's why I came to find you. Dustyn is here. Said he stopped by the house first, then came over."

Zoe closed her eyes and pinched the bridge of her nose. She wasn't up to dealing with her ex-husband just now. He could only make a bad evening worse. "I don't want to see him."

"He wants Mary to spend the night at his place," Elvina continued.

Damn, he kept pushing, wanting more. "That wasn't part of the visitation agreement," she said tersely. Her headache grabbed her scalp in its pulsing grip. Zoe rotated her head and reached into the desk drawer for the aspirin she knew was there. She swallowed two, dry, and pushed wearily to her feet. "I'll go talk to him."

As she left, she wondered if, during the confrontation with Knox, she had really heard Simon's voice demanding her wishes.

Elvina leaned against the doorjamb to the office and crossed her arms, while she watched Zoe trudge down the hall. When Zoe was out of sight, Elvina called, "Simon."

Simon materialized in front of her. His eyes

burned, and she could see the glow about his hair. The planes of his face were harsh in the evening darkness.

The uneasy feeling she'd had since seeing him with Zoe tonight came back with a vengeance.

"I don't know what you're planning, Simon, but don't do it. For your sake, as much as Zoe's."

He crossed his arms. "Do not expect to see Zoe for a while."

Frightened, she laid a hand on his arm. "No, Simon." She rummaged in the pouch at her waist and held out a small book. When he refused to take it, she tucked it into the crook of his elbow. "I shouldn't do this, but I know you're frustrated because Zoe won't wish. Read that first before you do anything. It will help you understand. This is her diary from when she was twenty. Please, read it."

Simon took it from her but said nothing. He disappeared.

Lucky came up beside her. "I never before seen anyone on earth disappear like that."

Elvina cast him a wary look. Did he know? "What do you mean?"

Lucky scratched his cheek. "That was a right pretty story you wrote for class. About the genie and all. So detailed, I felt like I was seeing it happen."

Elvina could barely breathe.

"And I never seen a car like the one I got those plates for. For one thing, it's got no engine. How do you suppose that happened?"

He knew! She felt a curious lightness that she didn't have to keep this secret from him, but unanswered questions remained. What would he do with the knowledge? Would he want Simon to perform some magic feat?

"Will you say anything?" Elvina asked. "We don't

want Simon hounded by people pestering him for magic."

"I reckon I can handle that." Lucky scratched his cheek again. "Who would I tell?"

"Thank you." Elvina looked out the door, where Zoe had just left. "Oh, Lucky, I'm so worried about them. Simon and Zoe."

He peered at her. "You really care about them, don't you?"

"Zoe's the daughter I never had. I know you think she takes advantage of me, but I get so much from her."

His jaw tightened, and he ran a hand through his graying hair. "Yeah, I've been watching. Zoe Calderone is different than I expected." His hand dropped. "If I can help—"

"I don't think there's anything we can do. Except pray."

Simon gazed at the book in his hand.

He had tried. He had done as Darius suggested and given her one last chance to wish. Several chances, in fact, even going so far as to intensify the threat from Knox. She had failed. The woman was more obstinate than a *hamad-el-halad*.

He transported the diary into his room, not wanting anything to sway him from his purpose, now that he had made his decision. He didn't want to feel compassion or need. He couldn't, and do what he planned to do. Instead, he fed his anger and determination by recalling his life before Minau and every base thing he'd been obliged to do since then.

Darkest night was fit for a darkening soul. It was time.

Chapter Eleven

Simon shed the trappings of Terra for black robes and transported into Zoe's home, where he found her gazing out the window at the night, sipping a soda. She staggered back a step from the whirlwind of his entrance.

Her eyes widened as sparks of fury crackled around him. The can clattered to the floor. One hand lifted, though that gesture could do nothing to stop him.

Not giving her time to speak, not giving himself time to change his mind, Simon grabbed her wrist with unyielding fingers and transported them from Terra. Wind buffeted them, whipping Simon's robes around his legs, plastering Zoe's shirt against her. The fiery red light surrounding them flickered eerily.

Zoe covered her eyes with her free hand. "Simon?"

He heard her, though they were where thoughts and feelings ruled, not words.

He heard her fear.

Simon opened a rift on the edge of the plane, freeing a stab of light so brilliant it froze the blood. Only the other, the twisted forces of *ma-at*, could force the rift wider.

He would put Zoe in that place between planes, a place of unending light and moaning winds, a place of chaotic confusion where the will would snap and she would have no choices.

His breath came in short pants as he concentrated. The *ma-at* fought him, rebelled against this wrenching perversion. Aching tension shook his body. He jerked, tried to open the rift.

Voices, memories whirled about him.

Do not. Darius.

Do not. Elvina.

Please, Simon. Mary

I'm afraid. Zoe.

Simon stretched out his hands. Zoe drifted from him, almost imperceptibly, moving toward the cold, glittering light of the rift. Around him, the red quivered and pulsed. Only his mind anchored her. All he need do was pull in the darker forces, give them sway over him, and the slender bond would snap.

She would be yanked into the rift. There she would stay until he chose to free her, until she used her wishes.

His soul sucked inward, shriveling from the abuse.

Zoe gazed at him with wide, unblinking eyes. A tear formed in the corner of her eye and rolled down her cheek, glistening a moment in the brilliant light until the wind dried it.

It was only the second tear he'd seen her shed,

both of them tonight. One because of Isaiah Knox.
One because of him.

He reached for the dark forces. Cold, he was so cold. A fine trembling overtook him.

"Why?" he heard her ask. Then, "Mary."

He could not! By Solomon, though he might remain endlessly bound, though the weakness might overtake him, he could not do this! He could not turn from the rightness of *ma-at* he had always believed in.

"Nooo!" he shouted soundlessly.

He could not do this to Zoe.

Simon thrust away the perverted forces. In fury, they howled and swirled, tugging at Zoe, trying to drag her from him. Loosening his grip. Opening the rift. Claiming him.

She began falling into the chaos. Simon reached deep into his soul and reconnected with the goodness of Kaf that resided there.

It was not enough! He needed more!

Terra! He grabbed onto the strengths of Terra and pulled them inside. He lunged forward with his mind, snagged Zoe, and slammed shut the rift.

The thwarted forces evaporated on a moan.

Simon pulled Zoe with him, back to Terra, back to her home.

Pain, agonizing and endless, brought him to his knees. An unconscious Zoe in his arms, Simon struggled to his feet. He could not see, the pain blinded him, but he knew her house well now. He staggered to her bedroom and laid her on her bed. She tensed, thrashed wildly.

He shook his head, willing the pain away from his vision for brief moments. "Shhh," he whispered. "You're home, safe, Zoe Calderone. Sleep now." He repeated the words until she relaxed and slept. Simon wrapped his arms around himself, holding himself together against the pain. He had one more task to do. Keeping himself invisible, he found Elvina coming home with Lucky and Mary.

Zoe is at home, he told Elvina. *She is asleep, well and safe, and will be fine on the morrow. Do not call for me until I return.*

With his last conscious thought, his very last bit of energy, Simon transported to Kaf.

Zoe shot upright. Damn, that had been one dilly of a dream. Aftershocks of terror still coursed through her. Damp curls stuck to the nape of her neck. Her arms wrapped around her waist, and she rocked on her bed.

She had been so helpless, sucked toward the light that reminded her of the spotlights at her second-grade Christmas play, the year she'd gotten the magic set. In the play, she'd been the star of Bethlehem, proud until her drunken father had destroyed the pleasure with his loud, sneering comments from the audience. She'd frozen then, unable to speak her lines, humiliated beyond a seven-year-old's ability to bear. In the dream last night, she'd also been unable to speak, to move, to escape.

Simon had been there, too, a changed Simon, who channeled bitter, blinding, cold. He was going to leave her, she'd realized, in that place of unending, maddening light until she wished.

At the last moment, as her vision faded from the savage brilliance and her blood congealed with cold, he had pulled her away.

For an instant in the dream, she'd felt blinding agony and knew it had not come from her. Simon had made a wrenching choice. He'd brought her home and cared for her until the terror passed and she slept.

Zoe yawned and stretched, wincing at the ache in her muscles. She blinked at the bedside clock. Two o'clock? The hot sunshine streaming through her windows and the sun catcher's rainbow patterns on her pillowcase were ample evidence that it wasn't two in the morning. She ruffled her hair and frowned. The curls were still there. Zoe paused in the middle of another stretch and looked down. She still wore the clothes she'd had on at the picnic yesterday, shoes and all.

Frowning, she swung her feet to the floor; she staggered as the weakness in her legs made her knees buckle. She grabbed onto the headboard, braced herself.

Dream? The hell it was.

Sore muscles or no, she was out the bedroom door in one minute. Furious, she searched the house.

"Simon!" she yelled.

She stormed into Elvina's half of the double and into Simon's room, flinging the door open with a bang that didn't fulfill her need for release.

The room was immaculate, the futon rolled neatly in one corner, a mound of pillows piled beside it, a crystal sitting on a table next to a pitcher of water and a plastic Mardi Gras cup. There were no clothes strewn about. It was immaculate and empty.

"Simon!" she shouted again, but the echoing silence made a mockery of her anger. She kicked the futon in frustration. Blast him.

Zoe sank down on the pillows. Simon was gone. Where? Why?

What had he almost done to her last night?

She shivered and wrapped her arms about her waist, rocking in the soft cushions.

What would she do when he came back?

181

* * *

Three days later, she still didn't know what she would do, because Simon had not returned. Her initial fury had abated, to be replaced by an edgy wariness. She had started to trust Simon. Now she didn't know what to think. She wanted to see him again, to understand what had happened, but she found she was afraid.

Not liking her fear, Zoe buried herself in her work, giving the proposal to Crescent City Curios, working on the tutorials, seeking new business, supervising a project for Chris. Now that Isaiah Knox was behind bars, she hoped the sabotage of ZEVA would halt, ignoring the uneasy feeling that Knox didn't have the necessary skills to undermine her company.

And, in filling her hours with work, she found something else beneath the fear.

Zoe stared blindly at the computer screen, shocked by the sudden revelation.

She missed Simon with an ache that wouldn't go away. Despite the way he had shattered her trust, she still missed him.

Aw hell, no way was she going to fall in love with a genie.

She blinked, saw her blank computer screen, and realized the machine had gone into sleep mode, because she hadn't hit a key in fifteen minutes. She saved her work, then exited and turned off the computer.

Time to say good night to Mary.

Mary was sitting at a desk in her bedroom, painting, her tongue held between her teeth as she made a tiny addition to the picture with the tip of her brush.

"What are you drawing?"

When Mary lifted her head, there were tears dotting her cheeks. Zoe knelt beside her and brushed one off with her thumb. "Hey, honey, what's wrong?"

"Did you wish? Did you wish and send Simon away and not tell me?"

Zoe took Mary's hands. "No, I didn't. I don't know where Simon is."

"Do you suppose he's all right? I tried calling to him, but he didn't answer. He's never done that before."

Zoe remembered the flash of pain. What *had* happened to Simon? He had been on the verge of something terrible, something unforgivable, and he had stopped. He had stopped, and she was beginning to fear the cost might have been quite high. She smoothed a hand down Mary's hair. "Maybe he had something else to do."

Mary shook her head. "What else would he do? He's a djinni. He grants wishes. Promise you won't wish without telling me."

It hurt to see Mary so attached to a djinni. That attachment could break her heart, for he would never stay.

Would it break your heart, too? asked the brutally honest voice inside her.

Meanwhile, Mary waited for the promise, watching with expectant eyes.

"I promise I won't wish without giving you a chance for a proper good-bye first. At least," Zoe added drily, "not deliberately. I sometimes let my tongue get the better of me when I'm angry."

Mary gave her a lopsided grin. "You don't get that from me." She reached out, arms wide. "Thanks, Mom."

It had been days since she'd hugged Mary like this, Zoe realized. She had been working such long hours, she'd failed to spend time with her daughter, except to scold and remind her to study her math. Shame filled Zoe.

"Now, how about you get ready for bed, and I'll read you a chapter of *Anne of Green Gables*?"

Mary gave a big smile, warming Zoe to her toes. "I'd like that. First, though, what do you think about my picture? I thought I might use it in the show Dad and I are going to have."

Zoe's mother-warning-signals started clanging. Mary was a very talented artist, but she *was* only nine, a long way from the polish needed for commercial exhibits. "What show?"

"Some guy in California wants us to display together. Dad said he'd talk to you about it."

California? Dustyn had some explaining to do.

Mary slid the painting in front of her. "What do you see?"

The painting was an excellent representation of Simon . . . and more. Mary had captured an elusive quality, a sense that he wasn't like other men. "This is wonderful!" Zoe exclaimed.

"But what do you see?" Mary insisted.

Zoe looked again. "I see magic."

She saw magic!

Dawn was a couple of hours away when Simon materialized in Zoe's workroom. He'd arrived earlier, invisible, and overheard Zoe and Mary talking.

Zoe had seen magic. Hearing that had given him pause. He'd come to take one last look, to tell Mary good-bye; then he had planned to retire to Kaf, away from Terra and the disturbing humans. If, because of his absence, Zoe never wished, then so be it, he had decided, though his exile would be prolonged.

Learning she had seen magic had given him the

tiniest amount of hope. Hope that he could rebuild the trust he'd destroyed.

Simon studied the array of computer equipment. Despite his criticisms that Zoe never relaxed, he had found, during these past hours of soul-searching, that he admired her for that. His previous summoners had liked the idea of having something given to them, something of value that they had to do nothing to earn. Zoe had fought it from the start.

Zoe was different. He'd said it before, but he hadn't believed it. He had treated her according to the tricks and attitudes he'd learned over vast years of exile. Even after the interlude at Brechtel Park, he'd still been trying to manipulate her.

Now he wanted a different relationship with Zoe. He wanted to be friends. Intimate friends, to be sure, but friends, nonetheless. The idea appealed to him on a very basic level.

He just wasn't sure how to accomplish that, and Simon could not tolerate feeling unsure. Why else would his emotions be so erratic?

When he held up his hand, the diary Elvina had given him appeared in his palm. Stretching out on the sofa, he opened the book and began to read.

An hour later, he snapped it shut and frowned. A tightness in his gut told him how badly he'd misjudged Zoe. It was a wonder her second wish hadn't been to turn him into a slug.

Simon clenched one fist. The diary was part a recounting of events in Zoe's life, part barely fictionalized stories, all intensely personal. He'd grown uncomfortable with the invasion of her privacy and stopped reading. Those entries, though, had given him troubling insight into Zoe Calderone and her deep-seated mistrust of dreams and wishes.

She'd given him hints before, offhand comments

she'd made about her father. She hadn't talked about Dustyn, however.

She'd been seventeen when she'd married, fresh out of high school and a home life that had done nothing to build her self-esteem. Marriage to Dustyn Calderone only eroded her confidence. Simon had read between the lines to the disparaging words disguised as help, the subtle cruelties, the endless undermining of her sense of worth. Zoe hadn't been trained with any marketable skill, yet she'd sought job after job to support an artist husband who couldn't be bothered to put food on the table. Even though she'd been their most reliable source of income, Dustyn had sabotaged her every effort, preferring her to stay home where she could devote her full attention to his comfort. It was a tribute to her determination that she had taken so long to give in.

The turning point in her life had been her twentieth birthday. Dustyn had received a commission and, flush with money, had promised his wife anything she'd wanted.

"Wish for the stars," Zoe had written in her journal. "He told me to wish and it would be mine."

Zoe had requested a trip to Disney World, and the plans were made. Until Dustyn bought himself a motorcycle with the money.

"He told me, 'Next year, babe,'" Zoe had written. "When he said that, the radio was on, playing an old song about the day the music died. I still hate that song. My music died that day. I got pregnant a month later. When I told Dustyn, he left. With his motorcycle and most of our bank account."

It was Mary, Simon realized, who had made the difference to Zoe. For Mary, she had gone to school and gotten a job. She worked hard, fought insecurities and hardships for Mary. Her dreams were all for Mary.

Until recently. Solomon, what courage it must have taken for Zoe to admit that one dream hadn't died, to reach for that dream. No wonder she worked so hard at ZEVA. Especially since she also considered herself responsible for the well-being of Elvina, Vivian, Abby and, by extension, Chris and Joey.

Simon stretched out and rested his head on his hands. Not that Zoe would ever admit it, but she needed wishes, and magic, in her life, too. He had to find a way to show her that *ma-at* could enrich her life. Since he couldn't use his talents to benefit her, she'd have to learn to trust him and thus trust the magic. That wasn't going to be easy.

Simon shifted uneasily on the sofa. As long as he was delving into Zoe's psyche, he might as well be honest about himself. He wanted her trust, not just for the sake of getting her to wish, but because he wanted to feel that fierce caring she showered on Mary and the others. After lonely centuries, he wanted someone to care about him, someone he cared about in return.

He wanted it with a depth that frightened him.

"You're back."

His eyes flew open at the wary voice.

Zoe moved inside and shut the door behind her. "Mary was worried."

"Were you?"

Her lips tightened. "I thought you might be hurt. I felt pain that night." Zoe sank into her desk chair and eyed him with the look of an abused puppy.

Simon sat up. "I'm sorry." He was sorry, and he knew the words were necessary, but he had enough djinn pride that they did not come easily.

"Can you tell me what that night meant?"

Simon rubbed a hand on the back of his neck. "What happened that night should not have happened. It was wrong, soul wrong, and I am not proud of my actions. I promise you, it will not happen again. Ever. I will never try to coerce you."

She lifted her brows but said nothing, just sighed.

"Please, believe me."

"You know, I think that's the first time you've ever said 'please' to me."

He grinned at her. "Djinn are not a humble people."

Her faint, fleeting smile gave him hope.

"I've been thinking of wishes—" she began, serious again.

He held a hand up to stop her. "Do not wish yet."

"Why not?"

"Give me a month, Zoe. No tricks, no wishes. Just a month for you to trust me enough to wish for something you really want. Then I'll help you fashion your wishes."

He waited, watching every nuance of her expression.

"One month?"

He nodded.

"No tricks?"

"No tricks," he agreed.

"That place. You won't—" She shuddered.

"Never." He wanted to reach out, wanted to take her in his arms and offer comfort and assurance, but he could not. He could only wait while she studied him.

At last, she nodded. "All right. One month."

Simon hesitated, then moved to her side and pulled her to her feet. He had to know. Had he killed the tender feelings she'd had for him?

"Shall we seal the bargain with a kiss?" he suggested, and held his breath, awaiting her answer.

"Ah, yes, there is that between us."

"Do you still feel it, too?"

One side of her mouth tilted up. "You already have enough arrogance that I shouldn't admit it, but, yes, I feel it, too." She lifted one hand, though he still had his wrapped around it. "Let's take it slowly. You're a bit overwhelming to a woman's senses, Simon."

"Do you not realize you have a similar effect on me?" Simon took a step backward, prepared to tamp down his desire in deference to her wants; his spirit was lighter than it had been in days.

Her half smile grew to full size. "I said slow, not stop."

He shifted their entwined hands to her chin and tilted her head. Her eyes shut with a languid sweep when his lips dipped down to meet hers. It was a sweet kiss he gave her, not propelled by open-mouthed passion or ragged emotions. Only her minty breath mingling with his, her soft lips giving beneath his, her warmth binding to his, gave power to the embrace. It was a power he had thought never to feel. He touched her with only his lips on hers and his hands holding hers, yet he felt as if her entire being burned into him. The air around them shimmered with a rich golden glow.

He ended the kiss. "Slowly doesn't mean short or infrequent, either."

"No, it doesn't," she agreed.

"Does this mean you will spend some time with me?"

She gave a tiny frown. "I still have a lot of work."

"And I shall not interfere. I can use that—" he motioned to her second computer—"while you work, if you show me how to 'surf the net.'"

She laughed. "Oh, Simon, I don't know if cyberspace is ready for you."

* * *

To her surprise, Zoe became accustomed to Simon working beside her. She set up his e-mail address, showed him how to use the web browser, and wondered why all her students couldn't learn at Simon's pace. Within half an hour, he had impatiently waved her away to begin his independent negotiation of cyberspace. Before week's end, when Zoe did her daily log-on to scan the NewsNet and retrieve e-mail, most of the messages were for "Djinni," not "ZoeC."

Her work on the school tutorials continued smoothly until one day when she had too much information to fit one screen. Yet it all needed to be there. Frustrated, Zoe threw off her headphones and swore at the computer screen.

Simon looked up from his work. "You have a problem?"

Zoe gestured toward her monitor. "You need reading glasses to see the type."

Simon got up and looked over her shoulder. "You're right." He sat back down at his computer.

She waited a moment, but, when he said nothing more, she cleared her throat. "You have any ideas?"

He ran a heated, lingering glance over her. "Lots of them."

Zoe flushed. He hadn't made any sexual overtures since he had returned and given her that kiss four days ago. Was he waiting for her to indicate willingness? Simon exercising restraint; now there was a thought!

She got up and stood behind his chair. Wrapping her arms around his shoulders, she rested her chin on his soft, thick hair. "Ideas about what I might do with the screen."

He leaned his head back between her breasts but made no other move, his eyes still staring straight ahead at his computer screen. "When I studied *ma-at* and had trouble understanding a concept, my teacher would do this." He lifted his hands and bracketed her face with unerring accuracy, though he still looked at the screen instead of her.

For an instant, instead of his computer screen, she saw—and felt, and smelled, and tasted—a vision of the two of them naked, kissing and sinking into the depths of that cloud bed. Though it lasted a brief moment in her mind, the image lingered in her more primitive senses. His forefingers traced her temples. The sensations exploded within her.

"Whatever you just did, it makes an indelible impression," she said in a ragged breath, "but I don't think multimedia can duplicate it yet."

"No? But you can use imagery to make your point." He lowered his hands.

"Perhaps." A glimmer of an idea came to Zoe, a twist on what he was trying to demonstrate. She didn't force it, knowing it would bloom better with a bit of neglect. Instead, she reached across Simon's shoulder and stroked a piece of velvet cloth he had draped around the keyboard. "Why did you put this here?"

He didn't answer with words. Instead, he took her hands from his shoulders and put them on the keys, making her stretch across him. The firm strength of his back pressed into her breasts and belly. Her cheek touched the line of golden balls at his nape. Her wrists rested on the velvet. His arms enclosed hers so she could feel the faint rasp of his hairs, feel the muscles bunch as he crossed his arms, reached for the edges of the velvet, and drew them across her arms. "Pleasurable stimulation of the senses can inspire the mind and the soul." His touch whispered across the top of the cloth, creating tingling waves of warmth before he unwrapped it. "Type something, anything, without thought."

Zoe typed a word, two, deleted the nonsense, typed and deleted again. The velvet beneath her wrists rubbed against her pulse points. His skin created a pleasurable friction against hers. She typed, and the solution to her problem burst into life in her thoughts. Her hands jerked back. "That's not a magic cloth, is it?"

"Nay, just one Elvina found for me. You supply your own answers." She felt him shrug. "Although, perhaps, a tiny bit of me has woven into the fibers."

Zoe found her fingers were trembling. She straightened away from him and rubbed her hands together for warmth and steadiness. She looked at the screen where she'd been typing below his work.

"What's a grimoire?" she asked.

"It's an ancient manuscript of Terran magic."

"I thought you knew all about magic."

"There are elements of Terran magic that are different from djinn *ma-at*. Different roots. I seek to learn more about it, to find the old writings and the older practices."

"Can't you just snap your fingers and find what you need? Why do you need a computer?"

"Most knowledge I can easily absorb. Magic is different. Magic of Terran origin remains elusive."

"Have you found what you want?"

"I make progress."

"Did you look at the book we used to summon you?"

Simon leaned back in his chair. "You still have it?"

"Elvina does." Zoe paused. "That is, she did. She said it was lost."

"Lost? That is not wise." He disappeared.

Zoe caught a paper disturbed by his departure before it could fall to the floor. And that, she decided, was as much as she was going to get from him. She went back to work, using the insight she'd gotten to create scenes that showed the information, rather than simply telling it to the student.

This tutorial was going to be good.

Zoe stared at the notes she'd jotted down during the earlier phone call: fascinating technology, not unique, difficult choice, sorry. At the bottom of the paper she'd written, in bold print, Roger Broussard. That call had come in three hours ago, at the close of business, and she still couldn't accept it.

She ripped the paper from the small pad and tore it in half, then in half again. Methodically, she tore and wadded each piece until it was the size of a fake pearl on a Mardi Gras necklace.

How could she have lost the Triple C contract to her creep of an ex-husband? Her product was polished, businesslike, Leo had told her, and he loved the high-tech concept of multimedia. He just hadn't felt "moved"—his word, not hers—by her presentation. Roger's presentation, and thus Dustyn's, had more magic, was Leo's final excuse.

Magic. She had lost a contract because she didn't have enough magic. Wasn't that ironic?

Moreover, there had been a reserve in Leo she had never heard before. Always he had at least two new jokes to tell her before they got down to business, always he asked her if she couldn't come up with just one riddle. Not this time. It had been "just the facts, ma'am." Perhaps he'd been uncomfortable telling her about his choice, but Zoe suspected something else had factored into his decision, something she couldn't get him to admit.

Zoe didn't like the feeling that things were slipping from her control again. Restless, edgy, she emerged from her workroom to the living room where Elvina, Vivian, and Abby were playing a game of three-handed cribbage.

"Hello, Zoe, dear," Vivian greeted her. "Fifteen two." She laid a five onto Elvina's ten, then pegged two points. "I've been mulling over that section of the tutorial you're working on. What do you think about this for the music behind it?" She hummed a vigorous tune, waving her hand as though she were directing an orchestra. "Put it in a vibrato string, then build to a crescendo of brass for a rousing finish."

"Do you want vibrato string?" Abby asked. "Won't that sound a little harsh?"

"Now, Abby, dear, you know you have a tin ear," Vivian admonished.

"I may not be able to sing a tune, but I do know what I enjoy."

"We agreed, Abby," Elvina said, "that Vivian would have final say over the sound. You wouldn't appreciate it if she checked your books."

Abby settled down with a grumble.

"It's a catchy tune," Zoe said. "I think it will sound nice." She paced to the window, then back again to watch Vivian gleefully peg eight points.

Elvina handed her cards to Abby to shuffle. "What's wrong, Zoe?"

Zoe rubbed a hand down her thigh. "I lost the Triple C commission. I'm sorry. It was my fault. They just didn't think my project had enough . . . pizzazz. They gave it to Roger Broussard."

It surprised Zoe when, instead of showing their disappointment in her, her three partners began clucking and sympathizing. Vivian patted her shoulder. Abby murmured platitudes.

Elvina rubbed two thumbs together, her forehead creased in thought. "How are our books?" she asked Abby.

"We're in the black, but it's more gray than ebony," Abby replied. "This is a bit of a setback, but I think we can weather it as long as nothing more happens."

Zoe started guiltily, aware that she hadn't mentioned her suspicions of sabotage. First she had to figure out what was going wrong, how they could handle it. She paced back to the window and stared out, playing with the edge of the curtain, while her partners talked.

"I'll look at our expenses," Abby continued, "and see where we might be able to economize."

"Zoe, do you think Leo might give you a second chance? And, if he did, could you meet expectations?" Elvina asked.

Zoe thought about the little salamander she'd taken out of the program. She turned back to Elvina. "Maybe. Possibly. But they've already awarded the contract. I won't get a second chance."

Elvina didn't say anything. She just started stroking her crystal pendant.

"Well, you could always wish for it," Vivian suggested.

"Vivian!" Abby said. "Remember, we agreed."

Zoe stared at a shamefaced Vivian. "What do you mean?"

Vivian coughed and looked about the room for deliverance.

"Well, the cat's out of the bag," Abby said with a snort. "Might as well tell her all."

"I just thought you might want to use one of the wishes Simon granted you. After all, he seems like such a nice young man, er, djinni."

"Who told you—Elvina!"

Elvina shrugged. "Abby didn't believe he was my cousin."

"I thought you and Simon were living in sin together, Zoe," Vivian added, not sounding at all shocked at the prospect.

"Do you all think I should wish for this?" Zoe whispered.

"No," said Abby. "We know you want the business to succeed, or fail, on our merits, and we respect that. If you wished for this, what would we do the next time a crisis came along and there were no wishes? We have to learn to solve our problems using our God-given talents."

"Do you think that, too?" Zoe asked Elvina and Vivian.

Vivian nodded. "We have faith in you, dear."

"I want you to use the wishes for something personal," Elvina added.

Zoe pressed her fist against her mouth to still her trembling lips, afraid if she gave in to the weakness, she'd break down and cry. They didn't know how good their support made her feel. "I'll find something to replace this contract."

"We know you made these jobs for us because you wanted to help us," Elvina said. "But I think we've proved we can handle them."

"You can," Zoe hastened to assure her.

"Then, it's up to each of us to look for a solution."

Elvina looked at the other three women when Zoe left the room. "Something's wrong," she said. "She's worried about more than just this one loss."

Abby nodded. "She's been tense all week."

"Do you think it's because of Simon?" Vivian suggested.

"Simon makes her tense, all right," Elvina said with a laugh, "but that's nothing to worry about."

This problem was unlike the night of the neighborhood picnic when she had been worried, sensing forces at work that should not be loosened. Had someone found the lost book and tried one of the incantations? Had Simon done something? Elvina still didn't know what had happened that night, but at least the disturbing powers had quieted. Now, all she could see was that Simon was unusually diffident and Zoe was unusually hesitant.

She didn't expect either to tolerate that situation long.

"Maybe she needs a short vacation," said Abby.

Elvina smiled. "And maybe she needs a little privacy. I think I'll have a talk with Simon."

Vivian gave a small, romantic sigh.

Chapter Twelve

"What's wrong, little one?"

Simon sat at the kitchen table beside Mary. Her cereal bowl was pushed to the middle of the table beside her sketchbook. Before her were a piece of lined paper and a math workbook. She slumped in her chair, staring at the papers, her lips turned down, a pencil dangling limply between her fingers. The perfect picture of nine-year-old dejection.

"It's this blasted math. I work and work, but I just don't remember it." She cast a longing look at the unopened sketchbook. "I woke up with these pictures so clear in my mind, I've just got to get them out and onto paper. They are too awesome."

"Why not draw first?"

She shook her head. "You heard Mom last night." Mary put her hands on her waist and bobbed her head back and forth. " 'Mary,' " she mimicked, " 'do your math first thing tomorrow. No drawing, no play until you finish.' I got up early, but I can't do the problems. I'll never get it." She shoved the papers away. Resting her elbows on the table, she braced her chin in her palms and heaved a giant sigh. After a moment of silence, she cocked one brow at him. "Could you help me?"

"How?"

She sat up straight. "Could you do some magic so I understood the math, so I can remember the stupid times tables?"

"Yes," Simon answered without hesitation. This might be a chance to show Zoe the benefits of *ma-at*.

"Would you? I'll do something for you, whatever you want." Her face fell. "Oh, but what could I do for a djinni?"

Simon ruffled her hair and laughed. "There is something you could do. Stay with Miss Elvina this weekend." He poured himself a glass of orange juice.

She tilted her head and eyed him with an adult gleam in her eye. "You want to spend time with Mom?"

He nodded.

"You like her, don't you?"

"Yes, I do."

Mary continued to regard him with unblinking scrutiny. Wondering what thoughts fueled that knowing gaze, Simon took a drink of juice.

"Are you two gonna *do it?*" she asked.

Simon choked, spitting the orange juice back in his cup. " 'Do it'?" he asked when his breath returned, not believing he understood her.

She gave him a disgusted look. "You know what I mean."

He was afraid he did. "How do you know about . . . ?"

She rolled her eyes. "This is the 1990s, Simon.

Kids know all about where babies come from and how they got there. There're books and videos and my mom's good about answering questions." She gave him a sharp look, as though propelled by a sudden thought. "Djinn can do it, can't they?"

"Of course," Simon answered without thinking, and then gave her a warning glance before she could delve further.

Mary rolled her pencil back and forth on the table. "One of the books said when two people love each other, they want to get really close."

Simon decided to redirect the conversation. He didn't want Mary dreaming impossible dreams. "Your mother and I aren't in love," he said gently. "I just want to spend time with her. What we do during that time is of no concern to anyone else."

Mary nodded in agreement. "Men shouldn't kiss and tell. It's not nice. You know, I'm glad Mom's being stingy about using her wishes. I like having you here. She likes you, too. I can tell. She laughs a lot more these days, even though she's stressing out. Okay, I'll stay with Miss Elvina. Now, will you help me with the math? Do I have to wish?"

Simon, relieved to have gotten away so lightly, confused by the jumps in nine-year-old logic, didn't stop to think. He placed one hand on each side of Mary's head, his forefingers pressing against her temples.

"This is not a wish," he said. "This boon I grant thee by my choice. Repeat these words: I call on the powers of Terra; send to me that which I seek."

"I call on the powers of Terra. Send to me that which I seek," Mary repeated.

With the link to the human child, the energies of Terra and the powers of Kaf melded, then unfurled throughout Simon, bathing him in their might. He spoke the Ritual of Learning, and the knowledge of Terra enveloped him, energized him.

"State what you seek," he said.

"I want to understand math, to be able to do the problems."

Pricks of light encircled him. Simon chose what he needed, and let it flow into him, through him, into Mary. With the proper words, he sealed the knowledge tight within her, and then lifted his hands.

Mary blinked. "That's it?"

He gestured toward the workbook. "Try it and see."

She scratched out an answer, then two, then moved faster, working down the page in a flurry of movement. Finished, she held the paper up. "I did it, and I understood it. This is *easy*." Mary flung her arms around him. "Oh, thank you, Simon."

Elvina opened the back door and shuffled into the room, coming from her half of the duplex via the back porch. She wore a claret-and-gold caftan and pink fuzzy slippers. Her blond hair stood in jagged spikes. She headed straight for the sink and filled a tea kettle.

"Tea, I'm out of tea," she mumbled in a gravelly voice and turned on the burner beneath the kettle; then she rummaged through the cabinets until she found a box of tea bags. Leaning against the counter, she asked, "What did Simon do to elicit such enthusiasm at this hour?"

Mary gave him a kiss on the cheek. "He used his magic to make me smart in math." She picked up her sketchbook and dashed to the door. "I'll give you one of the pictures, Simon. They are going to be so bad."

"Bad?" Simon's brows knit as he gazed at the vacated door. "I thought she wanted to make attractive pictures."

"In her vernacular, bad is good." Elvina said nothing more. When steam escaped the kettle, she poured the boiling water into a mug with a tea bag, filling the room with the scent of tea and lemon.

Simon had the strange, uncomfortable feeling he'd made a mistake. "Pour me a cup?" he asked to break the silence.

Elvina complied, handed him the mug, and started stirring her tea. Her spoon clanked against the china. "That may not have been a wise thing to do, Simon. Zoe's a strong believer in the work ethic and doing things yourself."

"It will show her that *ma-at* can be useful." Simon shrugged, shaking off unaccustomed guilt. "It's done. Zoe can do nothing now."

Elvina raised her brows but changed the subject, "Have you thought about what I said a couple of days ago?"

"I have." When Elvina had mentioned how tense Zoe seemed, Simon recalled his earlier idea of taking her to Kaf. It would be one more chance for her to get to know, and trust, him.

In truth, though, he had another, baser motive. When he thought about leaving Terra after Zoe wished, the idea left him feeling bereft and frustrated, feelings Simon didn't enjoy any more than he did guilt. He needed to find out why she stirred him so, and why he enjoyed kissing her so. He wanted to experience all the pleasures of the erotic with her, to explore the taste and smell and feel of her. An impossible task in a double with a bright nine-year-old, a too-wise friend, and neighbors that watched their every move.

He also had a curious yearning to have her see his home, to see if she found it as beautiful as he did. Last night he had begun the proper rituals.

"Will you watch Mary for the weekend?" Simon asked. "I would like to show Zoe my home on Kaf."

Elvina set her spoon on the counter and took a sip of the steaming tea, blowing on it first. She scrutinized him over the edge of her cup. "How will you manage? Your magic doesn't work if she's willing."

Simon waved a hand. "A little trick. Nothing that will harm."

"How will you get back?"

"I can return to Terra any time after the point when I last left."

"You can't travel to the past, then?"

"No. A few hours in Kaf, however, and a day has passed here. We can return at the second after we left, but it would be easier on Zoe to return in the equivalent time. I shall weave my spell so we return automatically on Sunday evening."

Elvina nodded. "All right. I'll keep Mary."

At least she hadn't asked if they were going to "do it." Simon got up and gave her a kiss on the cheek. "Thank you."

"I hope we don't regret this," he heard her mutter as he transported from the kitchen. Simon had the distinct impression that Elvina had gotten exactly what she'd intended from the first.

Zoe was asleep, sprawled on her back, the sheet flung to the floor and her nightshirt wound around her hips. The prism in her window caught the morning light and spread a rainbow across her face. Trust prim, practical Zoe to arrange to wake with a rainbow in her eyes.

She stirred, shoving her nightshirt further up and exposing her silk panties. Simon swallowed to moisten a suddenly dry throat and began reciting the twelve Mantras of Unity, the most boring thing he could think of. Anything to resist the urge to lie down beside her and awaken her with hungry kisses, a plundering tongue, and eager hands.

On second thought, why should he resist?

On third thought, because this was not the place or the time. He had a spell to cast and a world to visit. He started searching her closet for something for her to wear.

A discordant click, click, click roused Zoe. She listened, but failed to identify the sound. She opened one eye and squinted through it. Simon stood at her closet, moving hangers, studying each article of clothing. He picked out her shortest pair of shorts, and then burrowed to the back for the red tube top Elvina had reelasticized for her but that Zoe had never worn.

"What are you doing?" she asked, her voice and mind still fogged with sleep.

Simon spun around and gave her a brilliant smile. Zoe's insides turned to warm oatmeal. "You're awake," he said cheerfully.

"If you say so." In Zoe's mind, mornings barely ranked above getting shots and forcing Oz into his cat carrier for a trip to the vet. She blinked, and he was sitting beside her, the mattress sagging under his weight. He captured her hand on her pillow, lacing his fingers with hers.

"Come with me to Kaf."

"Right now? No. I'm not even dressed."

"Good." His smile warmed her toes and started fairies dancing in her stomach. She saw his lips move and felt a tingling spread down her arm from their clasped hands.

"I've got a million things to do today," she protested.

The room faded. A hot vortex of wind and light surrounded her. Too late, Zoe remembered that his magic always worked against her, unless she wished. She tried to shout, to say yes she did want to go so he had to take her back, but her throat closed on the words.

White light surrounded them like a gauzy veil. Through the veil she could distinguish shadows, stars, worlds unknown and unimagined. The vortex turned, and the spinning became a rushing corridor, a mad ride through an endless, enclosed slide.

Hold tight, Zoe, you are safe.

Zoe heard Simon's voice. His hand, firm and warm, surrounded hers. Its strength gave her courage and assurance. Though neither of them had substance in this place of between, she clutched his hand anyway, and clutched his words with her mind.

The spinning returned and everything around her was caught in the vortex of wind and light. The vortex closed in on her, bringing solidity in a rising swirl. With a sudden thud, she stopped moving.

Zoe took a breath, then another. Okay, she was still alive and still connected to her body. Nothing hurt. In fact, she felt wonderful, invigorated and alert. Hot sun burned through her closed lids. She was lying on something grainy but soft. Zoe rubbed her palm against it. Fine sand. So, she hadn't returned to her bed. A light breeze cooled the sweat gathering on her face and brought the pleasing scents of sandalwood and oranges and heat. "That's what is known as sweeping a lady off her feet," she grumbled.

"Open your eyes."

Intrigued by the eagerness in Simon's voice, she opened her eyes and sat up. Desert, its white sand gleaming under a yellow sun, spread before her. To her right, a grove of date palms was carpeted with vines that curled up the tree trunks. When the

205

breeze gusted, the leaves vibrated and emitted a pleasant tinkling, like tiny glass bells.

Zoe stared in awe. "I guess Scotty beamed me up."

Simon, who was kneeling at her side, laid his hand on her forehead. "Who's Scotty? It's just us here. Are you all right, Zoe? The trip didn't scramble you?"

Zoe struggled to her feet and tugged down the hem of her nightshirt. Simon brushed sand from her back, his hand lingering as he skimmed off the sparse grains.

"I meant I wasn't in New Orleans," she explained. A gust of dry wind emphasized her comment.

"You're in Kaf."

"I figured that." She took a longer look around. Beyond the desert she saw a smudge of gray that seemed to be mountains. Now she noticed strips and patches of green as well. "Oh, Simon, it is lovely. Stark, but majestic."

He smiled, as though pleased with her appreciation.

"But what about Mary? I can't leave her alone. And Elvina, Abby, Vivian—they'll worry. My work— I had so much work to do."

Simon lifted her hand and blew away the few grains of sand clinging to her fingers. The touch of his breath sent twists of excitement through her. Her hand and arm tingled as though they'd been under the hot desert sun too long.

"I have spoken to Elvina and Mary," Simon said. "Elvina agreed to watch your daughter for the weekend. We will spend a few hours here and when we return to Terra it will be Sunday. I am sorry about the suddenness, but if I asked you and you said yes—" He lifted one shoulder.

"—then your magic wouldn't work," Zoe finished.

"Sort of a Catch-22, wasn't it? Never mind," she added at Simon's puzzled look.

"Elvina, Abby, and Vivian were worried about you. They thought you needed a vacation."

"Those three want to mother me."

"They care about you," Simon corrected gently. "Bringing you to Kaf was my idea, the one place where your work cannot reach you. Although mothering you was not what I had in mind."

His throaty words sent waves of heat and longing throughout her body. When he ran his fingers through her hair, unknotting the curls tangled from sleep, Zoe rested a hand on his broad shoulders, needing the support his solid body offered.

"Do you forgive me for the deception?" he asked.

Zoe cleared her throat. "There's nothing to forgive."

"Good," he breathed. A tiny smile tugged at the corners of his mouth. His hands outlined the curve of her jaw, the column of her neck, the slope of her shoulders, before dropping to his sides. His lids half lowered in seductive promise. "I cannot take you back before our allotted time is completed. It shall be your choice, Zoe, how we spend it. If you want, I will leave you alone. You will be safe in my home." He moved back a step and crossed his arms, waiting.

Zoe's breath lodged in her throat. Simon was telling her, in no uncertain terms, that he wanted an intimate, physical relationship with her, that he had arranged this time for that purpose. He was also giving her the opportunity to back out, a rare concession from Simon.

Did she want to spend her time alone? Did she want to play tourist and ask Simon to show her the sights of Kaf?

No, Zoe realized in an instant.

She didn't expect a forever with Simon. She was no simpering virgin who thought a night with a man entitled her to claim him. And Simon . . . well, Simon was a djinni who had told her outright he could only live in Kaf. That she would never forget.

But she hadn't been with a man since her husband left her, unwilling to settle for emotionless sex and too busy to develop anything more. With Simon, however, there was something between them, some enduring tug of attachment. She wasn't ready to name it, but she found she wanted to explore the attraction; she suspected that if she said "no," she might not get another chance.

How to answer when everything she said meant he could only do the opposite? Let her actions speak.

She held out her hand. "I think you brought something for me to change into."

"I have some other things there, if you prefer." Simon nodded toward the trees, and then bent to pick up her shorts and top.

Zoe followed the direction of his movement. Through the grove of palms she could detect a white building, although the trees prevented her from seeing details of size or architecture. "What's that?"

"My current home. Would you like to see it?"

Zoe thought carefully. "No."

The smile faded from Simon's face. He gripped her clothes until his knuckles turned white. "Are you so angry you can't even accept my hospitality? You said there was nothing to forgive. Did you mean my actions were unforgivable?"

Zoe shook her head, confused. "I thought if I said no, then you'd take me, because your magic doesn't work for things I want."

Simon laughed. "It's not far. I planned on walking." His hand moved from her cheek to trail along her neck and collarbone. "While we are here, we will be simply a djinni and a woman enjoying one another. All differences, all goals forgotten."

He was offering companionship as well as sex. It wasn't an offer she could refuse. "I would love to see your home."

A breathtaking smile broke across his face. Zoe answered with one of her own.

They crossed the grove of palms, the vines chiming without discernible melody in mellow greeting. Simon's house was made of large white stones of a coarser grain than marble, finer than brick, set in an interlocking pattern. It was two stories, although the bottom rooms were twice the height of the upper ones, judging by the position of the balcony that encircled the house.

Zoe looked up at the beautiful structure. "This is exquisite, Simon. It's a wonder you ever leave."

His hand at the small of her back tightened into a fist, and he looked up toward the distant mountains for a moment. "I'm glad you like it," he said, but his voice was faint.

They stopped in front of a massive front door made of multicolored glass cubes. Through the rainbow, Zoe could see a narrow hall, empty of furniture.

Simon said a few foreign words and passed his hand in a semicircle before the door. The center of the glass bricks became milky, concealing the glimpse she'd gotten of the interior. "When the door cannot be seen through," he explained, "it means the djinni is at home and the protocols of privacy must be observed."

The door opened at a touch from Simon, and Zoe entered, eager to see his home. Opulent rooms opened to the left and right of the short hall and segued into further space with the simple division of a column or a low divider. Straight ahead she could see the blaze of sunlight.

Simon urged her forward with a light touch at her back.

The hall spilled into a courtyard surrounded on four sides by the walls of the house. Zoe squinted in the bright sunshine. A bead of sweat trickled between her breasts. It was hot here, particularly after the darker coolness inside, yet the small fountain in the center and the bright splashes of greenery created the illusion of comfort. She circled, taking in the beauty.

"No wonder you get angry when people think you live in a lamp," she said. "How did that notion get started, anyway?"

Simon's shoulders shook with laughter. "One time, and we're stereotyped for eternity."

She tilted her head and raised a questioning brow.

"One time, when a spellbound djinni was summoned, he decided to play a little trick. The human had a bottle he had cleaned until it sparkled, planning to fill it with oil and sell it as a magic lamp. So, out comes the djinni from the bottle. The human, Aladdin, was so shocked, his mouth grew this long and his eyes this wide." Simon made a face. "He actually believed the tale the djinn spun, about being held for eternity by a wicked vizier, not that Aladdin did anything to free the djinni. Instead, he told so many people the story that somehow that one incident had you humans believing we live in the blasted things."

Zoe lifted her chin. "Are you telling me that the whole story of 'Aladdin and the Lamp' is a fake?"

"Not a fake, for the wishes were true, but Aladdin did have a vivid imagination."

"From such small incidents, legends are born."

Simon laughed. "You may change there." He pointed to a door in a small alcove. "Some other clothes are there, should you wish a different choice." He handed her the shorts and top.

Zoe tilted her head. "You keep women's clothing here?"

"Women's clothing. I do not keep women. They were for a female I once thought to make my *zaniya*. My wife."

A wife! She'd never thought of Simon as belonging to someone else. She had never thought of the djinn as having lives separate from their service to humans. "You were married?"

"We never spoke the words of binding. It was many centuries ago, and my feelings for her withered. She never wore the clothes; they have no memories for me." Zoe heard an undertone of bitterness in his words, but before she could reply, he smiled at her. "In fact, I think I should like to see them enjoyed by you."

Beyond the door Simon had indicated, Zoe found a room whose purpose she couldn't quite define. Long panels lined the room, each one depicting a scene from Kaf, Zoe guessed. The scenes were formed by marquetry, tiny pieces of wood carved, polished, and placed so their grains blended to create a work of complex beauty. Zoe ran a hand across the stunning art, reveling in the cool, smooth surfaces. She peered behind one panel and found it shielded shelves lined with books, scrolls, jars, and bottles.

Two tables stood in one corner of the room. One was low, carved, and polished to a shine, whereas the other, tall enough to be stood at, was scarred and stained. A sybaritic couch invited her to recline. When she touched it, it swayed, as though fastened like a swing, but Zoe could see no chains. Peering around a door at the back, she found a tiled room that seemed to be the djinn equivalent of a bathroom. She washed the sand from her face, neck, and feet, then returned to the first room.

When she found the clothing, the idea of donning her shorts disappeared. Never had she seen such beautiful colors and fabrics. They were draped from pegs and hung on specially designed stands. She fingered first one, then another, drawn by cloth that slipped through her hands like soft silk, yet resisted tearing or snagging when her watch caught on a seam. How Simon must have loved the woman for whom these clothes had been intended. A stab of jealousy pierced Zoe.

"Well, you're here now, and she's not," she told herself. "You'll never get another chance like this, so pick something."

There were dresses, tunics and pants, and long wrap cloths. Zoe chose an above-the-knee-length skirt made of layers of sheer fabric, each a different color, that tied at the waist, and a loose, guava-pink top that set her skin tingling when she pulled it over her head. She debated about sandals but decided she liked the feel of the tile floor beneath her feet.

She found Simon in the courtyard, setting a tray filled with cups and dishes onto a small table between two chaises.

"Could you have offered anything more appealing to wear?" Zoe called. The skirt brushed against her legs with every step, and she could not resist running a hand down the soft length.

"You did not find an outfit that pleased you?"

The hurt look that settled on Simon's face surprised Zoe. She'd never thought of him as vulnerable. He felt, she realized, felt deeply, and she had the power to wound. It was not a power she wanted, or enjoyed. "I'm sorry, that didn't come out as I intended. I meant that everything in that closet was so beautiful, I had a hard time choosing. Thank you for offering them to me." She held out her arms and made a slow revolution. "This seemed to fit my rounded figure best."

Having finished setting out his tray, Simon crossed his arms and tilted his head, studying her. His lazy gaze trailed from her head to her toes and back to her face. "I happen to enjoy rounded figures. I like to know I'm touching a woman, not a date palm trunk."

Zoe returned the gesture. He appeared both foreign and familiar in an unbuttoned, waist-length vest and loose, red trousers gathered at her ankles. Give him a scimitar and he'd look like the pictures from the Arabian Nights. Here, in Kaf, he was relaxed, yet there was an edge to him, a demeanor that reenforced the fact that he was djinn, not man.

"You truly are a djinni," she whispered.

"Yes, I am."

His husky voice drew her gaze on a slow pass back up his body. The soft fabric of his pants did not conceal his obvious arousal, and Simon made no gesture to hide it.

She gulped. Her gaze shot back to his face. He was smiling. Determined not to allow this blatantly exotic Simon to fluster her, she smiled back. "We have something in common. I, too, enjoy things round. Although I might argue about the date palm trunk." She briefly lowered her eyes.

Simon let out a hearty laugh. He took a step forward, and then stopped. "Anticipation is a pleasure all its own," he said in a low tone, and made a sweeping gesture toward the tray. "I took you away without your breakfast—"

"And my coffee."

"—and your coffee. Would you care to eat?"

Zoe settled onto one of the chaises, and Simon reclined on the other. On the tray were yeasty rolls fragrant with cinnamon and honey and two cups of steaming coffee with a pot between them. She took a sip of the dark brew. It was robust and flavored with almond. "When you set out to seduce, you do it up right, Simon," she observed.

"Is that what you think I'm doing?" His voice sounded strange, not angry, but more bleak or pensive.

She looked up from the roll she was tearing into bite-sized pieces. "Aren't you?"

"Is it because of the exotic trappings that you agreed to stay? Or do you think I coerced you?"

Zoe shook her head. "I'm responsible for my decisions. I'm not going to be swept off my feet unless it's something I truly want. I'm not a spontaneous person; I deliberate."

"Of course the right setting doesn't hurt."

She tapped her chin. "Even a pragmatist like *moi* can appreciate a magical time and place like here and this day."

He gave an exaggerated sigh. "And I was hoping it was me you liked. How devastating to find it's my *ma-at.*"

Zoe started to give a flip retort, but then stopped, caught by a note of longing in his voice. She reached across the table and stroked the lean lines of his cheek. "Have you ever known anyone less likely to be impressed with your magic, Simon? I'm here, with you, in spite of it, not because of it." She paused. "Well, to be honest, I'm in *Kaf* because of your magic, but that's all I'll concede."

He captured her wrist in his hand. "Did the trip here frighten you?"

"No, because I was with you."

"That is good."

His slow smile worked its usual magic on her insides. When he cupped his palm across hers, then blew a light breath into the small space he'd created, Zoe felt as though she held champagne.

The sensation tickled and fizzed up her arm, changing the surrounding air to a gleaming blue. Just as it reached her lips, Simon popped a piece of roll in her mouth. Cinnamon, sweetness, yeast, the tastes burst inside her, richer and more complex than she'd ever tasted. Simon's brief, hard kiss, following close behind, melded into the explosion of sensation.

Zoe stared, wide-eyed, as Simon leaned back and gave her a smug smile.

"*That*," he said, "was seduction. Enjoy your breakfast."

They ate heartily, then reclined and soaked up sun like two engorged lizards. Zoe's hand dangled over the side of the chaise. A moment later Simon laced his fingers through hers. They lay, hands entwined, listening to the whisper of the breeze, the music of the vines, and the bubbling of the fountain. Contentment seeped into her bones. Her eyes drooped shut.

Random thoughts drifted through her, and she gave voice to one. "How did the djinn come to be in the wish granting business?"

Simon dropped her hand in an instant. The hairs on her arms rose, as though the air had become charged with electricity.

Blast! Not a question she should have asked. With just a few words, she'd destroyed the illusion of companionship, and she found she missed it with a depth that frightened her. Zoe rolled to her side.

Simon's eyes had grown dark. The lock of hair falling across his forehead took on a familiar glow. Saying nothing, he sprang from his chaise and stalked to the fountain. He crossed his arms and stared into the spray of water.

Zoe rose to stand beside him. The pain in him sliced at her. Anger and frustration drew his lips into a tight frown, narrowed his eyes, radiated from him in a surrounding, swirling, pearl-gray mist. She laid a hand on his warm, bare arm. The muscles beneath her palm were knotted. "What did I say? What did I do wrong? I thought we'd progressed beyond unreasonable anger, Simon."

"Unreasonable? No, not unreasonable."

"Then explain it to me. I think I deserve that."

Simon did not want to talk, did not want to remember. Not now, when anger shifted to desire with her mere touch. He pivoted to face her. "Later. Maybe later I shall explain."

Now was the time to assuage the hunger he felt for Zoe. Simon took her hand. It wasn't soft and dainty, but strong and capable. He bent his elbow, drawing her closer. "Now, however, I want you."

She flushed at his bald statement of need.

Already he was aroused. Ah, but would Zoe need more wooing? He trapped her hand against his chest and wrapped his free arm around her shoulders to pull her closer. Zoe melted against him, reached around and began kneading his behind, rocking him against her.

Perhaps a slow seduction would be unnecessary.

Perversely, he found he wanted to draw out the moment. "Let's move slowly. We have time, here and on Terra."

"No, we have only these hours," she murmured against his neck.

Confusion and the beginnings of anger warred

with desire in Simon. Desire, strong and sweet, made his hand stroke up and down her spine, while the other emotions sparked inside him as he raised his head and questioned, "What do you mean?"

"I'm not going to conduct an affair in the house with my daughter and my best friend living there."

It was the reason he'd brought her to Kaf, but Simon didn't like hearing it.

"You're angry again." She speared her hands through his hair. "I've always wondered what your hair felt like when it's glowing. It's soft, but it sends tingles through me."

Simon rotated his head, relishing the feel of her fingers on his scalp. He lowered the edge of her gauze shirt and started to play with her breast. But she was changing the subject, and he would not be deterred. "There are ways to arrange matters."

"We can talk later, Simon. Let's take our now, and let the future wait." She lowered one hand and petted his length through the flimsy fabric of his trousers.

Simon groaned and returned to teasing her breasts, dallying with first one, then the other. Her nipples were tight nubs that he drew into his mouth and suckled.

When she gave a soft sigh, he wrapped both arms around her and drew her up on tiptoe, so that, with each shuddering breath, those lovely breasts rubbed against the sensitive skin on his chest.

He bent his head to nibble on her earlobe.

Hello, Simon. The presence of another impinged on his senses, cutting through the incandescence around them. Someone, not Zoe, coughed.

Simon opened his eyes. Darius was sprawled on a lounge, eating a roll and staring at them with avid interest.

The djinni waved the sweet in the air when he

saw Simon's glare. "Don't stop on my account. I'm learning a few things."

Zoe gasped and stiffened in Simon's arms. "I thought you said that change in the blocks was some kind of privacy guarantee."

"Oh, Simon and I have never needed ceremony between the two of us," Darius replied airily.

Zoe fumbled with her blouse. Simon settled it into place with a quick tug. If she had not had her back to Darius, he might have taken more serious steps.

Simon frowned, startled by the unaccustomed possessiveness of his thought. Djinn were faithful to their chosen mates, but before the vows were exchanged, jealousy was inappropriate.

Darius stared at Simon for a moment, raising his brows in silent question, before finishing his filched snack. Solomon's robes, he'd momentarily forgotten Darius's telepathic talents. Simon scowled in answer.

"Well, aren't you going to introduce us, Simon, my friend?"

Darius, apparently, was not going to leave.

Chapter Thirteen

Zoe turned to look at the owner of the melodious, mesmerizing voice. He had to be one of the most beautiful men she'd ever laid eyes on—black eyes surrounded by long, curly lashes; jet hair with curls tighter than fleece; a sculpted face with golden skin.

Sinuous, midnight blue robes outlined his lean body as he rose in a fluid movement and, before she could blink, stood beside her. A heavy, square amulet made of turquoise dangled from a black cord in the vee of his robes.

The man, or djinni, lifted her hand while giving her a sexy, half-lidded stare. He pressed a lingering, warm kiss in her palm, the tip of his tongue making brief contact. No, not *one* of the most beautiful, *the* most beautiful man she'd ever seen, and he did absolutely nothing for her pulse rate or her hormones. She glanced sideways and saw Simon glaring at her captured hand.

Oh, blast, Simon's hair was starting to spark. Zoe

turned back to the djinni who still held her hand, though he no longer kissed it. He was looking at her as a chocoholic might gaze at Elvina's Chocolate Decadence Cake.

Zoe tugged her hand from his grasp. "When Simon does that, his kiss sort of zings me. I must be getting used to this magic stuff. That didn't do a thing to me."

The djinni straightened. His lids dropped in that concentrating look she'd seen on Simon's face when he was working an intense bit of magic. Zoe could feel something plucking at her, like invisible hands trying to capture her thoughts. She frowned. "Are you doing some spell?"

The djinni blinked. "You felt that?"

Simon was grinning. "He's using an attraction spell."

Now Zoe was annoyed. "Stop it!" she told the stranger. "I'm not interested. One djinni is more than enough."

The stranger eyed her speculatively. "Introduce us, Simon," he suggested a second time.

"Zoe, this is my friend—and I'm using that term loosely right now—Darius. Darius, Zoe. Darius was just leaving."

"Oh, I don't think so." Darius was stretched out on the chaise again. He reached for another cinnamon roll. "I have been keeping to Kaf and now I wonder what I've been missing on Terra. I must make a visit soon and sample the pleasures. Perhaps Zoe could give me some recommendations."

"Why don't you start that visit right now?" Simon suggested.

"Such poor hospitality," Darius scolded, but Zoe detected the undercurrent of affection between the two.

Simon leaned one hip against the back of the

other chaise and crossed his arms. "Why did you come, Darius?"

"The same reason as always." He cast a glance at Zoe. "King Taranushi was particularly interested this time in your return."

Zoe had the definite impression the djinn knew Simon had brought a human along on this trip home. Aw hell, how much else had they been privy to? She groaned softly, and both djinn turned questioning glances toward her.

"Are you ill?" asked Simon.

She waved her hand. "No, but I find I have a sudden interest in learning more about your world."

"Then I shall be happy to oblige." Darius had her hand in his. Really, he was persistent. And quick.

"I'd rather Simon—"

"Simon cannot," Darius interrupted smoothly.

In the next instant, Zoe found herself buffeted by chilling winds. Swiping errant curls from her face, she discovered they stood on a high, rocky mountain. Simon's home was a distant white cube. She stumbled, and Darius braced her with one hand. She shook him off, enjoying his low "umph" when her elbow grazed his rib.

"Take me back."

"Soon." His hand lifted, as though to touch her cheek.

Zoe gave him a glowering look, unable to step back because of the precipice. "If you're his friend, why were you hitting on me in front of Simon?"

"'Hitting' on you?"

"That attraction spell. Really, Darius, how crude."

He buffed one nail against his silky robe. The wind whipped the fabric against him, outlining his body. "Most women find me attractive." He looked up, those eyes wide with fake innocence.

"You are beautiful, and I think you well know it."

"But?"

She shrugged. "I prefer more masculine beauty." Black hair falling over a forehead. A sinful body. A grin that dissolved her insides. Anger that came and went, yet left a glow in its wake.

Darius studied her. "You should not have felt the attraction spell. You should have come to me."

"Your ego's just going to have to accept that I'm not attracted to you."

"The one cause of failure," he mused, as if she hadn't spoken, "is if the woman's attraction is fixed elsewhere."

"Nonsense. How could I be attracted to Simon when I know he'll leave as soon as I use my wishes?"

"I did not say your attraction was fixed to Simon," he said softly.

Zoe felt a wave of heat claim her cheeks despite the surrounding cold. Blast, she'd blushed more since meeting Simon than she had in years. She looked back at Darius. The wind blew back the edge of his robe, and she saw the turquoise amulet again. It was square, about two inches on a side and covered with strange symbols.

Zoe crossed her arms and edged toward the mountain's solid side. "Simon will be angry. I expect he'll be here soon."

"He will be angry, I know, but he won't come after me." Darius waved a hand. "He cannot go past the foot of the ring of mountains."

Ignoring her irritation, Zoe followed his gesture. She hadn't noticed before, but the gray smudge of mountains did surround the entire area at her feet. Simon's home was smack in the middle, the only sign of habitation among the sand and oases. Her insides twisted as she understood his isolation. "What do you mean?"

Darius lifted her hand in response. Though she tried to pull it from his grasp, he brought her hand to his chest and slid it under the heavy square of turquoise. "Each djinni is given a turquoise tablet at birth, a gift from Solomon, the great magician who brought us to Kaf. Our tablets define who we are. They give us freedom."

His fingers tightened around her wrist. "I suppose you believe that fiction about all *genies* granting wishes."

Zoe could only nod at his sarcasm, her stomach knotting, her fingers growing numb in his grip.

"Only a djinni who has had his turquoise tablet replaced by the wristbands of enslavement is required to grant wishes."

Zoe remembered the copper bands at Simon's wrists. Simon did not wear a turquoise tablet. The tangle in her stomach tightened. She stopped trying to extricate her hand.

"Any djinni who allows himself to become mastered by the copper bands is as one dead to his fellow djinn for the term of his enslavement," Darius continued relentlessly. "He can go nowhere on Kaf beyond his home circle and no djinni is allowed to enter the circle."

Oh, God, she hadn't known!

Her gaze flew to Simon's home. How lonely he must be. What would it be like to spend centuries apart from the ones you loved, cast off from all you held dear and everything that gave you definition? She stared at the isolated house and the ring of towering mountains, until the wind and sand made her eyes gritty and sore.

She'd been so selfish, thinking only of herself, of her damned independence; she'd never considered that he might have reasons for what he did.

Darius was now looking out at the single house

instead of at her. "Each enchantment, each enslavement is different, the length, the conditions."

"Like being unable to do beneficial magic for me?"

Darius nodded. "The skills and intent of the sorcerer are the deciding factors. The sorcerer who bound Simon was very powerful. And very vengeful. Simon's binding has been a long and harsh one. He has spent more time on Terra than any other djinni. I wanted to see the one who persists in prolonging his exile." He thrust her hand away from him.

Zoe wrapped her arms around her waist, trying to contain the spreading ache inside her. How would it be to be dependent upon people who commanded you with only greed in their hearts?

"I didn't know," she whispered. The words, no true defense, tasted like sand.

"After you, Simon needs seven more summoners to be free."

She had to do something! Had to help him. She would use her wishes. Use them now.

If she wished now, he would be free of her. Would he abandon her in Kaf, his responsibility to her done? The mere thought left her shaking as she remembered the cold light.

She wouldn't believe that.

But she was greedy, Zoe found. She wanted this brief interlude with him to store memories for when he left her, returning to his own land. During his time with her he had brought her joy and laughter. Frustration, too, but even that was a form of living.

"Do you know *any* honorable humans?" Darius interrupted her thoughts. "Have you friends you trust?"

Simon might have ample reason to dislike humans, but she didn't like Darius's scorn. "Yes, I have honorable friends."

Darius caught both her hands. "Do you care for Simon?"

"More than I like to admit," Zoe said.

"Use your wishes, then teach seven of your most honorable friends to call him. Let the final days of his exile be swift and easy."

"The attraction spell was a test, wasn't it? You wanted to be sure you could trust me."

"I also read your mind." His mouth tightened. "Djinn rarely trust humans, and we have good reason for our beliefs."

Zoe was getting pretty tired of being told what a miserable lot her race was. Let him stew a bit. "I'll think about what you've said."

"I guess that's all I can expect."

Zoe rolled her eyes and pulled her hands from his. "And I expect that's all the thanks I'll get. In your own way, you djinn are just as annoying as any human."

She stepped away until the sheer edge of the mountain halted her retreat. Unless Darius willed it, she was stuck here. Zoe rested her hands on her waist. "Are you going to take me back?"

A tiny shiver moved through him. In a low monotone he said, "If you should ever need me, Zoe Calderone, call me."

"What?"

Darius shook his head and gave a light laugh. "Sometimes I foolishly think I am precognitive." He circled her upper arm with his hand. "But what I said was true. Should you need me, just hold on to the bands on Simon's upper arms and call to me. Call with your mind, heart, and voice."

The last words faded, left in the winds of the

mountains. Zoe found herself back in the courtyard with Simon.

Darius had disappeared.

"What did Darius say?" Simon moved closer to Zoe and captured one hand in his.

"He told me to be nice to you." She laid her other hand on his cheek and gazed at him. Unshed tears made her eyes bright.

Simon would bet a basket of dates that wasn't all Darius had said. "I approve of that sentiment. Anything else?"

"He told me to call him if I needed him."

Simon's fingers tightened around hers. "Darius can be a troublemaker." Needing to touch her, to assure himself that she had not succumbed to his friend's practiced charm, Simon slipped his free hand beneath her blouse and cupped her breast. The soft weight filled his palm. He brushed his thumb across her nipple and delighted when it tightened in response.

"He's too beautiful for his own good." Zoe arched into his touch.

"Don't you like beauty?" Simon yielded to the craving to run his hand down her side. By Solomon, he loved having her like this, open, warm, and pliant.

"I like it in sunsets and paintings." Her words cheered him, until she added, "I'm wishing as soon as we get back."

"No, you aren't. You have promised me one month." He removed his hand from her breast. She sighed as though bereft. He tilted up her chin so she looked at him. A sparkling corona spread from his hands to encircle her face in a rainbow. "You will wish only after we have exhausted ourselves in numerous episodes of sweaty, vigorous sex," he commanded.

Ah ha, that excited her. He could tell by the widening of her eyes and the quickening of her breath. Her reaction shot a blaze of need through him, making him instantly hard, an erection that seemed to have developed a separate, and eternal, life.

He caught her behind and brought her to him. When she rubbed against him, Simon's lids drooped. That felt so good!

"You can't stop me from using the wishes," Zoe said.

"Oh, no? I have before."

She looked confused for a moment, and then he saw her eyes darken. "I knew it! I knew you were behind that tied tongue!"

Simon winced. "I was desperate at the time," he offered, but Zoe didn't seem to accept it as a defense.

A distraction; he needed a distraction. He kissed her, thoroughly, until the taste of her made him dizzy. "Did you know your skin flushes when you get aroused?" he mused. "It's as telltale as mine."

She sighed. "You erase my bad moods so easily. What are you? A djinni or something?"

"Sometimes I think you are the one with the magic."

"Did you know we have managed to reverse the argument we've been having all along?"

"Then we shall no longer argue. Instead, we shall continue from where we were interrupted."

Zoe tapped her chin with her forefinger. "And where was that?"

"Well," Simon drawled, "I remember your top was . . ." With the edge of his hand, he slowly pushed her top across her breasts to bunch at her waist. "And I was about to do this." Deftly he loosened the knot at her waist, pausing just before undoing it. The garment floated to rest on her hips. "I have figured out how zippers work, but djinn styles are less complicated, no?"

Zoe rested her hand at her waist, but Simon noted that she did nothing to arrange the skirt drooping on her hips. "I seem to remember your vest was lying on the chaise." She lifted her chin, as if to defy him to challenge the lie.

Simon was willing to play. He released her hand, shrugged out of the vest, and let it float over to the chaise.

"You're very good," Zoe said.

"Very good? I don't intend to be," Simon assured her, with a wicked grin. "What else do you remember?"

Her gaze skimmed across him, and a faint flush decorated her cheeks. She opened her mouth, then closed it and looked away. "That's all I remember."

"Ah, I do not think so." He circled until she faced him once again. "What's wrong?"

"We're so . . . open." She waved her hand around the courtyard. "And you're laughing at me."

"Laughing at you? No, Zoe, never. I had hoped you'd learn to laugh with me."

"Even about sex?"

"Especially about sex. There are no rules, except in here—" he tapped the top of her head—"that say two adults cannot play. As far as being in the open, I'm sure Darius explained that no one comes here."

"Except Darius."

"Trust me when I say he will not return."

She looked straight at him. "I trust you."

He smiled again. "What were you thinking before you turned away?"

"I was remembering the first time I saw you. You

were nude then, and I wanted to see you like that again."

"It shall be as you ask." He moved a step away and began to dissolve the trousers until he realized he wanted her to do it. Wanted her hands on him, wanted to feel her beneath his palms.

He stepped forward and drew her blouse down, catching her skirt and panties as he passed. He stroked and rubbed downward until she lifted first one foot, then the other, and finally stood before him gloriously naked. Her skin shone in the brilliant sun while the light breeze lifted and settled the strands of wavy hair.

"Your turn," he commanded and stepped away.

"No magic?"

"I find I want your touch."

The silk of his pants billowed around his legs, yet that faint contact seemed harsh in contrast to Zoe's light touch as she knelt before him. She lowered the silk with the heel of her hand, while she caressed his legs and studied every curve, every muscle, every sinew as it was revealed. Her fingers left trails of stardust in their wake.

Once, she stopped and ran the back of her hand along his inner thigh. Simon's breath caught, and then started faster. He widened his legs. "You're glowing," she whispered. "I like that." Then, when he was as naked as she, she leaned forward and kissed him, a lush, intimate kiss.

Simon groaned and reached down, pulling Zoe to her feet, unable to wait any longer. He snagged one arm beneath her knees and picked her up.

"I can walk." She squirmed, sending another shooting star through him.

"I know you can, but I like the feel of you here." He fondled the bare thigh within reach of his fingers.

She sucked in a quick breath. "Does this mean we get to play now?"

"We play now."

"What are we going to play? Gin rummy? Monopoly? Canasta? Cribbage?" she teased.

He turned and strode from the courtyard into the shadowed coolness of his home, Zoe planted against his chest, her arms around his neck. For, in spite of his assurances, he knew Zoe would be tense out in the open.

At least the first time.

"Cribbage—" He pretended to muse. "How do you play that?"

Zoe looked up at him, puzzled. "Elvina said you beat her regularly."

"Tell me anyway."

"Now?"

"Now."

"Well, you need a board and pegs to keep track of points."

"Points, hmmm?" He kissed her nose. "How do you score points?" He shifted the hand on her thigh until he could run his thumb along the juncture of her leg and hip.

"You, uh, keep cards that make fifteen or a run or a pair." Zoe's eyes widened. "Oh, my!"

"Ah yes, it's coming back to me now." He shifted her higher in his arms. "A pair of jacks and a five would be fifteen two." He kissed one breast as he counted out the cribbage scores, suckling twice. "Fifteen four." Four long tugs on the other breast. "And a pair makes six points." He sucked, first on one taut nipple, then the other.

Zoe inhaled with a sharp hiss. "Elvina better not have taught you that."

"I like to make my own variations." Simon paused before a wooden door. He muttered a few words, and the door disappeared, replaced by hanging strands of silver and gold beads that made a delicate tinkling sound as he shouldered through. His bed might seem strange to Zoe—not a mattress, but a pile of pillows, five thick—however, he believed she'd be comfortable there. He laid her down.

She twisted to look at the head of the bed, and then rose to her knees, admiring it. "Oh, Simon, it's beautiful!" she breathed.

Her praise delighted him. He had spent several years of his exile designing and making the marquetry on the wall that formed the headboard of his bed.

Zoe ran a hand along the wood. "I see sunshine and rain all intertwined."

"Those are the elements of nature, essentials of *ma-at*—fire, wind, rain, sand, and earth, growing plants, living animals."

"The patterns seem repeated, but they're not. Each is a little different; the design shifts in subtle ways."

She had a good eye for detail. Would she realize that when viewed as a whole, it was two naked figures, a man and a woman entwined? He had put a smile of male satisfaction on the man's lips, a smile of female welcome on the woman's.

The woman, he realized with a start, had soft curly hair and a rounded figure. Just like Zoe.

"My God, you're talented," she whispered. She leaned back, viewing it from a slight distance. Color rose in her cheeks. "And very wicked."

"Let me show you," he answered, need making his voice low and rough.

She wrapped her arms around him and pulled him down with her until he sprawled across her, the pillows mounding in heaps beside them.

Quickly he shifted, placing his legs between hers and stretching down her full length, keeping his weight on his arms.

By the powers of Solomon, she felt good against him. She was soft and giving and smelled like heaven. Forgetting for the moment his notion that they should play, he bent down and took advantage of her willing lips.

Their sweetness was his undoing. She opened to admit his plundering tongue, met him with the sure stroke of hers. Her hands roved up and down his back, scorching him with flames of desire.

He groaned. Trailing tiny kisses over her jaw, down her neck, across her collarbone, he whispered, "I can't wait, not this time. Later, later we'll play, we'll take our time. If I don't get inside you soon, if I don't feel you around me, I think I'll explode right now."

Zoe widened her legs. "There's no need to wait, Simon. I'm ready."

He tested her with his hand. She was wet and welcoming. His thumb circled, just above her opening. Zoe's hips arched, and she let out a moan. Distracted from his own urgency, Simon repeated the movement. Zoe arched again.

"I said I was ready, Simon!" Her words trailed into nothingness as he tried first a light stroke, then a firmer rub, enchanted by her avid responses. Zoe opened one eye.

Simon grinned at her. "Maybe I was a bit hasty when I said I didn't want to play." He bent down to kiss first her lips, then any other tempting square of skin within reach.

There was much about Zoe that tempted him.

He should have known Zoe would never passively submit to his ministrations. She bent forward and nipped the lobe of his ear, then soothed the inconsequential hurt with a gentle suck. Simon drew in his breath, almost forgetting what he was doing. She rubbed one foot up and down his calf, opening herself further. Then her magical hands came down from behind to cup him and push him toward her.

"I need you," she whispered. "Now."

Simon could think of no reason on Kaf or Terra to resist. He entered her with one smooth stroke. Zoe cried out and arched against him. Her muscles squeezed him with tiny flutters. He rested inside her, savoring the feel of her, until she subsided, and then he began to move with sure, even thrusts.

She was starbursts and moonglow. With her, he felt as if he had grabbed the tail of a comet. Simon moved faster and faster, higher and higher, Zoe matching him, until first he, then she, exploded in a nova of light and exquisite sensation.

His first thought, when conscious thought returned, was that never had he shared with anyone what he had just shared with Zoe.

His second thought was the shocking realization that living without Zoe could be as much an exile as the past thousand years.

Chapter Fourteen

Zoe sprawled supine on the chaise. She studied her cards, then languidly reached to the small table beside the chaise and laid a king of clubs on Simon's five of hearts. "Fifteen two." She kissed Simon's ear, running a lazy tongue along the edge, and then made a slow foray to the corner of his eye, which she also kissed.

Simon, stretched atop her, his head resting beside hers, reached across and matched her king. "Twenty-five and a pair for two points." He bent over and tugged the tip of one breast into his mouth. He caressed it with his tongue. "One." Then he repeated his loving on the other side. "Two."

Coherent thought fled, lost in a riot of sensations—the soft brush of his hair against her chin and the slide of his cheek across her skin. His muscles flexed as he moved, tiny pressures that massaged and stimulated. He drew back to blow softly across her breasts, moist and heated from his play. "Your turn," he murmured.

Zoe swallowed and looked from his cards to her hand, then back. That king seemed mighty convenient. "Are you cheating?"

Simon shook his head, his breath wafting across her damp breasts. "No." He held his hand for her to see. He had a jack and a queen left. "If I played the five, I knew you could not resist making a fifteen if you had the proper card." He nuzzled between her breasts. "And I had a three out of four chance of matching it," he added, his voice muffled. "That way we'd both get points. We both win." He returned to her breasts.

Zoe sighed as pleasure warmed her more than the sun overhead. This interlude in Kaf had been a time outside of her usual life, a time when she could play and enjoy and not think of rules or obligations. How else to explain the fact that she was still nude, hadn't felt the need to cover herself at all in the face of Simon's unabashed enjoyment of her, and was lying on a chaise longue in the middle of a courtyard, playing a very unusual game of cribbage.

"You're not supposed to let the other person score points," she informed him.

"Not according to the rules we're playing. I *like* it when you score points." To emphasize, he nudged her chin with his nose, inviting her to employ herself again. She complied by giving him a light kiss on the top of his head. She felt his smile against her neck.

"What would you have done if I'd laid down a ten? You didn't have one to match."

"Then I would have cheated."

She laughed softly, not remembering the last time she'd felt so happy and contented.

"It's a count of twenty-five to you," Simon prodded.

Zoe looked at her cards. She had a seven, eight, and nine. Since cards could be played only if they didn't go over a count of thirty-one, and her lowest, the seven, would make thirty-two, she couldn't play. "Go," she said faintly.

"Go?" Simon repeated, giving her a devilish smile.

Unable to say more, Zoe just nodded. When they'd first started playing, oh so long ago, and she'd told Simon to cut the cards, he had, instead, entered her with one gentle thrust. And there he'd stayed, growing harder, thicker, longer, with each point scored, but not moving, not letting her move, unless one of them called, "Go," and then only making tiny, controlled motions that brought them both to exquisite readiness, but stopped shy of pushing them to the climax.

Zoe was ready to shatter.

Simon's legs between hers tensed and he moved, pulling out until he almost left her, then surging back in. He repeated the motions, again, again, and again. Zoe lifted herself to him, hovering on the edge. Around them, glitter dusted the air.

Suddenly he groaned and stilled. Beads of sweat ringed his face. His hips gave two more involuntary thrusts, and then he stopped, staying hard inside her, not allowing either of them to slake their need. His hand cupped her neck. Bright points of red, orange, and purple light flashed down his sleek back and across her arms.

So, he was having more trouble with control than she was.

Zoe laid one hand on his tense buttocks, her fingers stroking him. "We need to finish the game, Simon," she said primly.

His response was short and pithy.

She laid down a card. "Seven."

Simon raised his head. Zoe swallowed hard at the bright luster in his eyes, starlight caught in obsidian. His chest, heaving with the deep breaths he took, brushed against her sensitive skin. Her breath caught in a sharp gasp. One corner of his mouth lifted. The queen floated from his hand to the pile on the table. "Seventeen," he purred and ran seventeen kisses down her breast bone, his hips pulsing with each kiss.

Zoe looked uncomprehendingly at the cards in her hand, her whole attention caught by the maelstrom inside her.

The eight shot from her hand.

"Twenty-five," said Simon, "and a go." He started his motions before he even got the word out. "Ten." His jack fluttered to the tile. The last card fell from Zoe's hand.

"Nineteen," she managed to say. "Last card. My point." Zoe bracketed his face and kissed him, even as her hips moved in concert with his.

"I've got nine points," Simon murmured. "You've got five in your hand and four in the crib," he continued, without bothering to pick up any cards or look at them. "Game over."

"I won." She rotated against him. "I had one hundred thirty-two points and you had one hundred nineteen."

He stilled a moment, startled. "We don't have a pegboard. You've been keeping score?"

"In my head."

He stared, and for a moment she thought he might be angry, but the twitch in her lips must have given away the lie.

Simon's laugh was, rich and full. "Ah, Zoe, you have a wicked sense of humor."

His rocking began again, first gentle, then fierce. His gaze stayed on hers, though, and he combed his fingers through her hair. "I think we both won."

"I think you're right." Zoe arched her neck, loving the way he touched her, making her feel loved and cherished.

Making her realize how much she loved him.

And all was silence except for the wind, the chimes, and the soft moans and whispered words of endearment from the lovers.

The time neared, however, when they would be pulled back to the Terran plane. The few hours, so quickly passed in Kaf, had been a weekend on earth. They dressed in quiet, but not in solitude, each assisting the other, straightening a seam, fastening a button, as though knowing this time had been magical and reality would be a far different thing.

Hand in hand, they walked to the open sands. Zoe squeezed Simon's hand. "Hug me, Simon. Just once more."

Simon complied. He felt so good to her, warm and smooth and strong. Zoe closed her eyes, forcing back tears. When they got home, she would let Mary and Elvina say their good-byes; then she'd use her wishes.

She knew what she would wish for. His freedom.

I wish, I wish. Mentally she practiced the words she'd tried so hard to avoid the past three weeks. *I wish.*

Soon after she said those words, Simon would be back with his own people.

From the beginning she'd known there could be no future between them. What she hadn't counted on was how hard it would be to face that future. During these brief hours, she'd discovered that she loved Simon. Loved his quick anger and quicker laughter, his djinni tricks, his kindness.

She didn't regret a thing. Simon had brought laughter back into her life. For that she would always be grateful, but she would miss him always, with an ache that would never die.

She stepped from his embrace and gave him a watery smile. "Time to go back."

As if sensing her perilous feelings, he gave her one quick, hard kiss. "Time to go forward."

They held hands as the vortex descended and swept them away.

Zoe stumbled when solidity returned to her feet. Simon braced her with a hand to her arm. Did one ever get used to that dizzying feeling? she wondered and shook her head to clear the momentary confusion. They were in her kitchen. Zoe looked out the window. It was dark out.

"Sunday night," Simon said.

Mary and Elvina were sitting at the table having a before-bed snack of lemonade. At the sound of his voice, they both whirled in their chairs. Mary leaped up to hug her mother. "Mom, you're home. What was Kaf like? What did you see? Was it pretty? Gee, maybe I can go, too, sometime."

"Maybe, baby," Zoe murmured, stroking her daughter's fair hair. She exchanged a knowing glance with Elvina.

Mary looked up. "Tell me all about it."

"Simon was a very entertaining host."

"Yeah," said Mary. She gave the djinni a big grin. "Isn't he the greatest? Just before you left he made me smart in math. Now I don't have to study anymore."

Zoe's hand stilled on her daughter's hair. Elvina groaned. Simon busied himself loading ice cubes into a glass. "What did you say, sweetheart?"

Mary looked up, her face beaming. "He used his magic to make it so I understood math. I can even do calculus. Isn't that great? It was so easy."

So easy. "Great," Zoe echoed faintly. Desolation invaded her like the seep of a spreading swamp. How could he have done that? Was he so casual about human feelings? Didn't he give a damn? Did he hate them all that much?

Because of all they'd just shared, because of the love she had just admitted to herself, the betrayal struck deep. Oh, God, how could he?

"Why don't you go get your pajamas on, Mary?" Zoe said, her voice no more than a thread. "I'll come tuck you in and tell you all about Kaf, about the beauty of it, about one of Simon's friends I met, a djinni named Darius."

"Okay. 'Night, Simon." Mary gave him a big hug, too, and then skipped from the room.

"I'll help her." Elvina pushed back her chair with a scrape.

Unseeing, unknowing, Zoe shuffled the mail that waited on the kitchen counter, gaining time until they were gone. God, she wished she didn't hurt like this. She wished she hadn't just relearned what it felt like to hope and then know those hopes for the dross they were.

After all they'd shared, all the pleasures and laughter, she had thought Simon had some feelings for her. But he couldn't, not if he could ignore something so important to her.

She had to face facts.

He was scornful of humans.

He'd been without a woman for a long time.

Her defiance had intrigued him.

If you had to be on Terra awaiting wishes, why not dally with the summoner? Why not wind her around your little finger, or some other appendage, until she did exactly as you wanted?

"How could you?" She threw down the mail.

Simon put the glass to his mouth, but, realizing it held only ice cubes, slammed it to the counter. "Mary was having trouble. I helped her. What was so wrong with what I did?"

"You *know* how I feel about independence." Her voice was harsh. "She's not always going to have a djinni to help her out. She can depend only on herself. For that she needs to be strong. She has to know she can do anything she puts her mind to. She has to accomplish things on her own."

"She's only nine years old."

"Self-confidence starts early. I want her to know she can do whatever she wants."

"You're putting too much of yourself on her, Zoe. Mary is not you." He braced himself against the tabletop. Sparks shot from him, setting the air in the shadowed kitchen ablaze with harsh silver. "Your ex-husband really warped your self-confidence."

"Warped!" The word came out on a ragged moan. He nodded. "I read your journal."

"My God, you read my journal, too?" She clenched a fist, loosened it. "Don't the djinn have a sense of privacy? Of right and wrong?"

"Of course we do." His voice reverberated through her.

"Warped," she repeated, barely able to speak for the choking anger and tears. "Is that what you think of me? After the time we just spent?"

"And after the time we just spent, you still think my *ma-at*, the very essence of me, is abhorrent. Your precious Mary will be fine. It is not a crime to ask for help."

"You're so damn smug, so sure you're always right!"

"And you are afraid to accept anything beyond what your senses can detect. Humans!" He whirled around and stalked away. Wind slapped at her.

He wasn't going to end this by disappearing, not this time. Zoe raced after him and grabbed his arm. "Don't you dare insult my people again. Dammit, Simon, I wish you had to spend two weeks as a human, without the use of magic! Then you'd understand!"

As soon as the words left her lips, Zoe clamped her hand over her mouth. Dear Lord, what had she said? No, no, no, she didn't mean it, that wasn't what she'd intended to wish.

Simon staggered back against the counter. His glass crashed to the floor. He grew until he overwhelmed the kitchen. Sparks shot from his fingers and the ends of his hair. The air around his glowed red, the scalding color of an unbanked fire. She had thought she had seen him angry before, but that was nothing compared to the fury that buffeted her now.

"No, wait," she stammered. "I didn't mean . . . I'll wish something else."

"It is too late." His voice reverberated around the room. "You said you would use your wishes, Zoe Calderone. Now I see how you will have your revenge."

The red glow encompassed him, until he was a wavering shadow in its depths. Simon called out, in a deep, agonized keen. The glow faded.

Simon slumped to the floor.

Chapter Fifteen

Simon levered himself up on the mattress. Solomon's robes, he felt heavier than wet sand, and about as fluid. He swung his legs to the floor and took a deep breath. Breathing was easier than it had been the past few hours, when it had seemed a camel sat upon his chest. Prodded by a grumbling in his stomach, he closed his eyes and sought to transport to the kitchen.

Nothing happened.

He dug further into his mind, then into his soul, seeking some word of *ma-at*, some vestige of knowledge. His only reward was a headache that obliterated all desire to think.

Frustration caught him in its hard grip.

Nothing had changed. Zoe had wished him human. Here he would stay for the next two weeks, in the room Elvina had prepared for him, in the Terran city of New Orleans.

He flung a plastic Mardi Gras cup across the

room, where it bounced instead of shattering, a very unsatisfying result. He hefted the pitcher of water, thought better of it, and gulped down the lukewarm liquid instead.

Zoe would pay for what she had done. Simon entertained himself with visions of revenge. He could make everything she ate taste like salt. He could encircle her computers with a thicket of thorns. He could bring thunder and lightning, wind and rain crashing about her.

Simon groaned. He could do nothing for two weeks.

Maybe if he concentrated, he could find a word, a ritual he needed.

The blinding headache threw him back on the mattress as he fought waves of nausea. When both subsided, he opened his eyes. His revenge would have to wait for two weeks. Unless—Simon eyed the glass prism in his window.

Could he find the rhythms of Terra? Could he use those for his *ma-at*? It might be possible for him. After all, he had straddled two worlds, Kaf and Terra, for longer than any djinni.

Filled with hope that he would not have to spend his time bereft of his *ma-at*, Simon stared into the prism and into the rainbow caught in its depths. His eyes were open, but the room faded from his consciousness, leaving only colors of red, blue, and green. His breathing slowed as he tuned himself to Terra. His awareness of her subtle depths grew. He heard the sound of the wind and waves, smelled the fertile richness of damp earth, felt the flare of volcanic fires.

The pulsating heart of Terra echoed around him, but he could not grab its energies. It remained as elusive as silk in the wind. He must still have his ties to Kaf. He turned deep within him. Still there, buried deep, was the yearning for Kaf. The bonds to his homeland could not be severed by a wish. Although his body had become human, his essence was still djinn.

The soft breath Simon expelled was as much relief as cleansing. *He was still djinn.*

Djinn and human.

An unpleasant thought gripped him. For fourteen days, he would be without his *ma-at*, unable to transport to Kaf. Unable to revitalize. The weakness had been coming sooner than normal. Could he endure for the fourteen days?

He could only hope he was human enough that the time could be extended, for he had no other options.

Simon rose to his feet and stumbled to the dresser, the unexpectedly heavy feel of his body making him clumsy. The old adage that djinn were air and fire, while humans were earth and water, had become a literal truth for him.

Still dressed in the denim shorts and tank top he'd had on when he returned from Kaf, Simon braced his hands on the dresser and peered into the mirror. Other than eyes reddened by fatigue and tangled hair, he looked the same. He found a comb and ran it through the strands, wincing as the comb pulled on his scalp and caught in the gold beads at his nape. Scowling at his reflection, Simon made a note to remember to wash his hair, for djinn did not need artificial grooming aids.

His closet was empty except for his sandals and the dark blue robe he'd brought with him from Kaf, thinking Mary might enjoy seeing it. He had no other clothes here. First thing, Zoe must remedy that.

Zoe was going to have to remedy a lot of things.

Zoe was going to be very sorry she had chosen that wish.

What would he do to her? This time, however, when Simon tried to envision a suitable reprisal, the only image of Zoe he could summon was the way she had looked when she had found her release, how she had gazed at him in contentment and joy afterward, as though he had given her a precious gift.

The vision made him stir with desire and groan with frustration. Simon leaned against the closet door and swore, trying out the new words he'd learned during this summoning.

The hours they had spent on Kaf had not slaked his need for her. Instead, they had intensified the longing, for now he knew, from experience, the passion behind her proper exterior.

She owed him amends for what she had done to him. She helped everyone else. Why not him? She could give him two weeks of pleasurable service in his bed.

Simon pressed a fist to his forehead.

No, he didn't want her with him out of a sense of guilt. He wanted her to be as crazy with wanting as he was. Crazy enough that she came to him because she could not keep away.

Thinking of Zoe, though, where was she? Why wasn't she here, tenderly nursing him, watching anxiously for him to awaken? Out of habit, Simon tried to hone in on her presence as he strode for the hallway. Since she had first summoned him, he had always known where to find her.

The nauseating headache made him moan and rest his burning brow against the cool wood of the bedroom door. "Zoe!" he shouted. No answer. He straightened, and then stamped down the hall, bumping once against the doorjamb and once against a small table. He caught Elvina's bust of Elvis before it toppled to the ground, replaced it, and shouted for Zoe again.

Maybe she had those bedamned headphones on and couldn't hear him. Simon banged open the door of Zoe's workroom. She wasn't there, but Abby was.

Abby looked away from the spreadsheet on the computer screen. "Simon, you're up. I was about to check on you. How are you feeling?"

"Where's Zoe?" Simon dropped to the sofa.

"She said she had some errands to run."

Simon snorted. "So, she did not care if I would feel pain or confusion or loss when I awoke."

"You told her to leave you alone, that you never wanted to see her again."

Now that Abby mentioned it, Simon did remember spitting out those words in a rare moment of consciousness when Zoe had been restoring the covers he'd thrown off during the throes of adjustment. He remembered ministering hands after that, but none with the soothing power of Zoe's touch. He remembered wanting her to comfort him and feeling bereft when she didn't.

"You mean, she took the excuse to leave me," he muttered, settling his hands across his chest and propping his feet on the sofa arm.

"I mean, she thought you were serious." When he didn't say anything more, Abby asked, "How are you feeling?"

"Angry. Weighted. Deprived. As if I am missing something here." He thumped his chest with one fist. "Something so much a part of me that I don't know how to function without it."

"Sometimes, when humans have lost an arm or a leg, they still feel its presence," Abby said. "It itches or aches, but when they try to scratch or rub, the limb is no longer there, just the empty space. Is that how it feels?"

It was an apt description, but Simon wasn't about to admit that humans could experience anything akin to what he felt.

In the silence that followed, Simon heard a jaunty tune playing. The ice cream truck, he'd learned. A hot breeze from the window carried in the sound of Mary and Joey laughing, then the deeper tones of Chris. He could smell gumbo simmering—Elvina had cooked him some once—the fragrance of okra and cayenne so thick he could almost taste it. New sensations bombarded him. On Kaf, he'd always revelled in tastes, scents, and sounds, but he'd never realized his sojourns on Terra had had a thin veil covering the richness. Surreptitiously, he rubbed the soft, worn fabric on the sofa, not willing to admit any advantages gained.

"Are there any lingering effects?" Abby asked. "Pain?"

"No," Simon admitted, for the clumsiness had begun to lessen. He heard a small rustle at the door and knew, with an instinct born of intimacy, that Zoe stood there, listening. "Just an intolerable headache when I search for *ma-at*."

"Zoe is truly sorry she made that wish."

"Is she? She has made it abundantly clear she rejects and fears anything to do with *ma-at*. She must, then, reject and fear me, as the source. Was this not her way of revenge for the powers she can neither understand nor control?"

"No, Simon, it wasn't." Zoe hurried into the room, Wal-Mart bags in hand, and knelt beside the sofa, her face level with his. "Are you all right? You weren't hurt by . . . by what happened?" She laid a hand on his shoulder.

Even now, he wanted to reach over and kiss her,

wondering if the passions would be as intense. Instead, Simon sat up, dislodging her hand, and stared at her. "I thought you had come to trust me, Zoe, trust that I would do no harm to Mary or you."

He touched the cotton shirt above her heart. "Here, you do not trust." The urge to shift his hand a few inches, to cup her breast, to feel its soft weight again, caused him to clench a tight fist. "Perhaps you never will."

"You don't understand! I am so sorry I wished that. I never intended—I didn't think you'd harm her; I know you wouldn't." She took a deep breath. "But I still think you sent the wrong message to Mary. She can't wish and have her problems solved. Our life isn't like that. It's not that easy."

"*Ma-at* is not easy. Did you know djinn children must study for many years before they are allowed to perform even the simplest of rituals? The elders do not wish to risk upsetting the balances in nature with an ill-thought act."

Zoe shook her head. "You never told me that. Did you tell Mary?"

Her question brought him up short. Had he never mentioned the costs, the potential risks, while sharing the wonders?

"I'd like to know more," Zoe continued softly, "and perhaps you will find things to learn as a human."

Human. The word sent a cold shudder through Simon. Zoe, with a few simple words, had cut him off from his people more thoroughly than his exile ever had.

He shoved himself to a sitting position, and then rose to pace toward the window. "On Terra? There is nothing of possible interest to me here," he sneered, his back to her.

He heard her gasp. Good, he thought. Let her

scramble to convince me otherwise. Let her beg to show me I am wrong.

One of the shopping bags hit him in the back. "You officious oaf. I said I was sorry and I meant it, even though I had good reasons for my anger." Another bag hit him in the head. "I went and bought you some clothes. I hope you choke on them."

She stomped from the room.

Abby's stern mouth softened with a hint of amusement. "You always did get her dander up, young man."

Rubbing his sore head, Simon scowled at her. "I'm hungry."

Abby pushed back her chair. "I'll dip you up some of Elvina's gumbo." She inclined her head toward the shopping bags. "Unless you'd prefer to choke down those."

Zoe watched the unexpected rain lash against the windowpanes. Why had she thrown the clothes at Simon? She pressed her fingers to the bridge of her nose. Had she expected a puny act of contrition, buying him new clothes, would earn forgiveness for what she'd done to him? He'd been unconscious for so many hours, she'd been afraid she'd done him permanent harm until she'd seen him with Abby and been reassured by his arrogance.

The sparks in his hair and the tunnel voice were gone, though. Zoe leaned her head back. What had she done?

Thunder rattled the windows of the quiet house. Mary was playing at Joey's. Abby, Vivian, and Elvina were all at work. She didn't know where Simon was. She was alone with her thoughts.

The outside door crashed open. Zoe raced to the hallway, and then skidded to a halt when she saw Simon. His hair was plastered to his head. Rain dripped in his eyes, down his neck, off the hem of his shorts. Mud streaked his arms and legs.

"Simon, you're soaked!"

"I know that!"

"Let me get you a towel, some dry clothes. Take off those muddy shoes. Do you want something hot to drink?"

"Cease, woman! I'll handle it myself."

He toed off his shoes, then began stripping, leaving everything in a sodden heap on the floor. And he didn't stop at his briefs.

Zoe backed up the hall. "I, uh, I'll make some hot chocolate." She glanced down, then up at his face, feeling a blush stain her cheeks.

Hands on bare hips, he glared at her. "Did you want something?"

Yes, she wanted something. She still wanted him.

But he was still madder than hell at her.

Zoe beat a strategic retreat.

All he'd wanted was a simple walk to settle his thoughts. He'd never been caught in a storm when he didn't want to be, never been splashed with mud from passing cars. Simon shoved one foot and then the other into a dry pair of shorts.

He'd never paid attention to New Orleans's daily summer showers. If he was out and one started, he just surrounded himself with a protective aura that kept him dry.

How did humans tolerate such chaos, such disasters? He scratched at a red welt on his arm. Even the mosquitoes dared to bite him now.

This was not going to be a pleasant two weeks.

Zoe, wisely, was nowhere to be seen when he came into the kitchen, but there was a steaming cup of cocoa on the counter, with a bag of marshmallows to the side. Simon heard the washing machine running. Since his clothes had not been in the hall, he assumed Zoe had started to clean them.

He shook his head as he sipped the hot drink. Such petty details to attend to.

Abby came in the back door. "Oh, good, I was hoping I'd find you, Simon." She held up a key.

Simon raised his brows in question.

"Before he ran off with the floozy," Abby began, "my ex fancied himself quite a carpenter. When he asked for his tools back, I told him I'd taken them to the dump." She flashed him a quick, satisfied grin. "You should have seen him scrambling around in the muck. Actually, I buried them under a pile of boxes and old clothes. You're welcome to use them if you want. This is the key to the garage. He had a workbench set up there."

"Why would I want to use his tools?"

There was a pause before she said, "To give yourself something to do besides pout?"

Simon scowled at her.

"Go on," she urged, more gently. "I'd like to see those old tools put to good use."

Working with wood had always been pleasurable. Simon took the key and a final sip of his cocoa. "I'll look at them." He headed toward the door.

"Don't forget an umbrella," Abby called. "Unless you want to get soaked."

Simon had a succinct answer, another of his new words.

By the next day Simon had figured out how to use the electric drill and how not to catch his thumb with the bit. Once he became used to it, the compact tool felt good in his hand. He was sitting, trying to figure out how much pressure the plane needed, when Vivian came in, carrying a child-sized dresser. She hoisted it to the workbench.

"This was mine when I was a child," she said without preamble, running a hand over the scratched, stained surface, her voice dreamy. "I used it to store my treasures." She opened the biggest drawer, the bottom one. "When I would hear some tune or measure I liked, I would open this drawer and hum into it, thinking it would store all that beautiful music for me." She gave a tiny laugh. "Whenever I open it, I still hear those snatches of tunes running through my mind.

"I'd like to give this to Mary for Christmas," she continued. "Could you help me? Make the finish look like new? Just tell me what supplies you need, and I'll get them."

Simon looked from her wide eyes to the tiny piece of furniture and sighed. "I'll help."

"I didn't think you could tolerate discord for long. Neither can Zoe." Vivian gave him a kiss on the cheek, the feathers in her hair tickling his temple, and then left.

The next day, as he sanded the top, Abby clomped into the garage. Simon wiped a hand across his brow—removing sweat, leaving grit.

"How do the tools work?" she asked.

"Fine."

"That'll be a pretty dresser when you finish."

"I hope so." Simon continued his work and smiled to himself as Abby chattered about inconsequential matters. Abby was not a chatterer. She had something she wanted to say, but she couldn't quite come out with it.

"Well," she said, "I'm glad those tools are getting some use."

Though she made as if to leave, Simon figured she wasn't done yet.

He was right. Abby paused in the doorway. "What

you tried to do to Zoe was pretty nasty, too, but she forgave you," she said in a rush.

Was nothing secret from these women? "I did not complete the ritual."

"Doesn't mean she wasn't hurt by it."

She left, letting in a beam of sunshine.

The beam inched across the floor of the garage while Simon labored. He grew more comfortable in his human body, found his dexterity returning while his muscles loosened with the motions of sanding, washing, and filling imperfections.

He was almost ready to quit for the day, the lowering light making his eyes ache with the close work, when Elvina came in.

"I was wondering when you'd visit," he said, wiping off his tools and returning them to their proper place. "Vivian and Abby have already given their pleas. Why do you think I should forgive Zoe?" He lifted a sheet to cover, and hide, the dresser.

"I don't think she needs forgiveness."

Startled, Simon dropped the sheet. It billowed over the dresser like a parachute. "What do you think?"

Elvina plopped down on a stool. "She was doing what she thought best for her daughter; no one should apologize for that. What she does need is understanding."

Simon perched on the edge of the other stool, stretched his legs out in front of him, crossed his arms, and waited.

Elvina traced a finger through a small pile of sawdust. "You know Dustyn's been pushing to see more of Mary. I think he has some reason beyond fatherly affection. After all, he went ten years without contact."

"What do you believe he wants?"

"To win back Zoe, perhaps."

This he did not like, not at all. Zoe was *his*, at least until she wished. He gave a mental shake, to ease his sudden tension. "Do you think he has a chance?"

"About as much as me finding snow in a New Orleans July," Elvina said, casting him an intent sidelong glance. "He hasn't changed that much, and Zoe sees right through him. But she's worried, and not just about Dustyn. Her wastebasket is filled with empty taco chip bags and candy wrappers, a sure sign."

Simon frowned, drawn out of his troubles. "Do you know what is wrong?"

"Something with the business. Zoe refuses to say anything, still thinks she has to take all responsibility for ZEVA, but when I make my sales calls, suddenly doors are closed to me, customers are too busy with meetings. Put that with her frantic pace— the only time she stops is to spend time with Mary—and how tired she looks . . ." Elvina lifted one shoulder. "You were working next to her. Did you see or hear anything?"

"No." He'd been so focused on searching for the grimoires, he had not paid close attention to Zoe's troubles. His self-absorption left a bitter taste in his mouth.

"There's something I wish you'd do for me," Elvina said.

"I can do nothing," he snapped. "My abilities have been wished away."

"I'm sorry, that was a poor choice of words, but you have more abilities than you credit yourself with." Elvina eyed him. "However, that's for you to figure out. What concerns me is this rift between you and Zoe. It's an added stress she doesn't need. Even though she threw the clothes at you, she is feeling guilty. Relieve her of that burden at least, Simon."

"I will think about what you have said."

"That's all I can ask." Elvina got up and brushed sawdust from her shorts.

"Elvina," Simon called, remembering something Zoe had told him. "What happened to the book containing the ritual you used to summon me?"

She stilled, and then pivoted to face him. "I don't know."

A sudden chill spread through him. Magic in the hands of the untutored could be dangerous. "You need to find it."

"I know," she said and left.

Warm darkness had descended before Simon returned to the comfort of home. He took a quick shower and dressed in a T-shirt and a pair of gym shorts, another fashion of which he heartily approved. Hair still damp and curling from the steam, he went into Zoe's half of the duplex to say good night to Mary, a pleasing ritual they'd established soon after his arrival.

Low sobs and Zoe's murmuring, soothing tones halted him at Mary's door.

"He promised, Mom." Mary's words came out jerky.

"I know he did. Sometimes things happen, things we don't expect, and we can't keep a promise."

"Dad's a bad man."

"No, he isn't, sweetie, but he can be . . . thoughtless."

"You never break a promise. I never want to see him again!"

There was a pause. "Don't cut yourself off from him. None of us could show you how to use your charcoals to shade for effect like Dustyn did last week."

Simon stepped inside and, resting an arm against the jamb, watched Zoe run a hand down Mary's fair hair. A potent yearning came over him: that Mary was also his child, that he had the right to sit beside Zoe and offer comfort.

Mary sniffed. "Every time I saw that glass unicorn with the diamond eyes, I wished I could get it and he promised he would, with his next paycheck. He held his hand over . . . his . . . heart . . . and promised." The final words were broken by sobs and shuddering breaths.

Simon's heart twisted. He thought about the lost trip to Disney World and about Mary's dreams shattering as thoroughly as Zoe's. His fist clenched. He should have done more than frighten Dustyn Calderone with a fiery salamander.

"Today he said he spent the money on some stereo equipment," Mary said. "Stereo equipment! You're right, Mom, wishing does no good."

"Ah, baby, don't say that."

"Why not? You always do." Mary spied Simon in the doorway. "Even *he* can't do magic anymore, and what did it get us when he could?"

Hurting children could be so cruel.

Hurting adults, human and djinn, could be, too.

"I came to say good night." Simon moved into the room and stood at the foot of the bed.

Mary twisted her covers. "Will you stay and tell me a story? Even if you aren't a djinni, we still want you."

Simon flinched, pierced with pain and pleasure by her words. *You're not a djinni.*

But, I am still djinn, he wanted to shout, deep inside.

We still want you.

It had been so long, so long he couldn't remember, since someone had wanted him for something beside his magic.

"I'll stay, little one. Perhaps I will tell you the story of Noureddin."

Zoe spared him a quick glance, and then turned back to Mary. "Simon's magic is gone because of a stupid wish of mine, not because it doesn't exist. Maybe the purpose of magic isn't to get us things. That's up to us."

Mary swiped a hand across her tear-streaked face. "What's magic good for, then?"

"Do you remember when we went to Brechtel Park with Simon and Miss Elvina? Simon tried to show me the magic."

Simon listened as intently as Mary.

"There weren't any fairies, but I felt the presence of the wood elves." Mary bounced up, the bed shaking under her enthusiasm. "Did you, too?"

"I can't say I did, but maybe that's because I'm not as experienced at it as you."

Mary nodded as she settled back into bed. "Adults have trouble with those things. Except for Miss Elvina."

"During that time, I saw and heard more than I ever had in the times we'd visited. I saw the water rippling across hidden rocks. I heard a frog croak. I saw an intricate spiderweb. I felt the touch of a snake and the brush of the wind." Zoe gazed past Mary for a moment, then looked down and smiled. "There was a shimmering brightness to the land."

Though she might be reluctant to admit it, Zoe's words told Simon that she did understand. *Ma-at* wasn't about gold or gems. It was about peace, oneness, fulfillment, empowerment.

Apparently Mary agreed. "That's a start, Mom."

"Don't ever lose your wishes and your dreams, Mary. Go after them. But instead of wishing for someone to *give* you the unicorn, wish for the courage to save for it or the inspiration to paint a beautiful picture you can sell to raise the money." Zoe rearranged the mangled covers, then leaned over and kissed Mary. "I'll leave you to your story. Sleep well."

It was a thoughtful djinni who went into the kitchen thirty minutes later. If Zoe could make the effort to see the beauty in his world, perhaps he could find the treasures in hers.

Zoe was stacking dishes beside the sink. She glanced over her shoulder and ran her tongue over her lips when she saw him in the doorway. "Story finished? How's Mary?"

"Sound asleep with a smile on her face, probably dreaming about a kind vizier and rainbow-hued gems."

"Good. She's so young to be so disappointed. Thank you, Simon." She jerked her head toward the refrigerator. "I had some ice cream. I'll scoop you some if you like."

Desire jolted him anew, brushing aside the remnants of his anger. Between his need for her, the little acts of caring she and her partners had shown him, and his sudden awareness of the problems humans dealt with daily, anger had little hope of remaining.

How much he still wanted her!

He gave her his most anticipatory smile. "I had another treat in mind," he said in a low voice. Zoe's gaze shifted to the sink, and a faint blush tinged her cheeks. Satisfaction coursed through Simon. She was going to invite him to come to her this night.

She held out a dishtowel. "Then how about drying?"

He crossed his arms. "That is not djinn work."

Her chin came up. "Like it or not, you're a member of this family now. Everyone pulls her, or his, weight."

Simon felt a curious shifting inside at her casual inclusion of him in her family. For so long he'd been alone. He wasn't ready to admit it, however. This woman already had too much power over his unruly body.

With difficulty, he transformed a smile to a scowl and refused to take the dishtowel. "I don't do dishes."

She draped the towel over his forearm. "You do now."

Without looking at him, she drew hot water into the sink and squirted soap to create a foam of bubbles. When she picked up a spoon, it slipped from her fingers and splashed into the water. A soap bubble flew up and landed on her nose.

He moved behind her, his steps loud in the sudden quiet. "Look at me, Zoe."

She didn't turn around. "I'm sorry. I don't know any other way to say it."

"Look at me, Zoe."

She whirled. Soapsuds hit him in the forehead and dripped onto his eyelids. "Oh, sorry." She dabbed at his face with the dishtowel. "About the soap." She stopped dabbing and bit her lower lip, staring at his chest. "About the wish." She worried her lip a bit more. "I want to make up for it somehow. I guess wishing is out of the question."

"For two weeks."

"That's what I thought."

"You can make up for it in other ways."

That got her attention. "How?" she asked, tilting her head a little, wariness in every nuance.

"You can stop dripping water on my foot to start." Water from her wet hands had dripped in a warm stream to his bare feet.

"Oh." She stuck her hands in the dishwater again.

"You could join me on my pillows for the next two weeks," Simon suggested.

Zoe flushed to the roots of her magic-curled hair. "I can't do that."

He crossed his arms. Since he was without his djinn talents, did she no longer want him? Had she had her brush with excitement and now found him lacking? If she thought to dismiss him, she was going to be surprised.

He moved forward, crowding her against the counter.

She laid a hand on his forearm, the hand still holding the wet dishcloth. When she pulled it back, she showered him with soapsuds.

Simon wiped off his arm and face. "You wash. I'll dry."

Her fleeting grin faded as she bent to her task. She washed a glass and handed it to him. When he grabbed the slippery surface, it broke beneath his grip. Glass sliced his flesh. Blood oozed from his cut finger.

Could he do nothing right in this human body?

"Oh no, you cut yourself. We need to dry off your hand." Zoe fussed over him, blotting the small cut with his towel. She held up his hand, examining the cut. "Are there any slivers left?"

Her concern washed over him, warming him. "I think it's clean," he said gruffly.

Zoe reached into a drawer for a bandage and wrapped it around his finger. When she finished, though, she didn't release his hand. Instead, she gave him a half-lidded sidelong glance. "Humans have a belief that if you kiss a hurt, it makes it better." She brought his finger to her lips and brushed against it. "Does that help?"

She did still want him!

Simon smiled. The tiny pulse in her neck started a wild fluttering. He took the dishtowel and looped it around her waist, using the ends to draw her close to him. He twisted his wrists and wrapped another layer of towel about his hands so there was no slack, no place she could move away. Only then did he lower his mouth to her lips.

Gaining a human body did nothing to detract from the impact kissing Zoe had on him. If anything, he found their contact richer, full of new textures and sensations. The subtle scent of her soap. The way the ends of her hair tickled his cheek. The way she fit into his stance. He slid down the towel with a gentle sawing motion, moving her hips across his until he was ready to explode. He cupped her behind with the cloth and gave her a nudge until she stood on tiptoe, pressed against him, every curve of her filling every hollow of him.

She felt good. She tasted good, too, her mouth cool with chocolate and caramel.

When she put her hands behind her, he felt her smile against his lips.

"Triple C has this book," she said, "called *101 Erotic Things You Can Do with Kitchen Utensils*. I always wanted to try number thirty-eight. Hold tight to that towel, Simon."

She drew her hands, filled with soapsuds, forward. Beneath the cotton shirt, she rubbed his belly, sending molten rivers flowing through him. She moved around his waist, to his back and lower, disregarding the thin barrier of his shorts. Blessed sands, her hands were nimble, warm from dishwater, slick from soapsuds. Slowly and tenderly and thoroughly she caressed him.

"You hold on tight," he commanded in a growl.

"All right." She moved her hands to his front and circled him.

"Not there! Around my neck."

She obligingly lifted one arm to his neck.

Using the dishtowel, he picked her up, giving her a boost with a shift of his hips, until she was perched on the edge of the counter. He leaned forward.

His hands fell into the sink. One into hot soapsuds, the other into steaming rinse water. He jerked his hands back.

Unfortunately he still held the towel.

Zoe crashed into him. Simon staggered backward, then slipped on the wet, soapy floor. Zoe came down on top of him.

Simon cast a baleful eye at her. "Is this sort of experience common for humans?"

"No, Simon, being with you is unique."

Simon closed his eyes and let his head drop back. It seemed he had a bit more adjusting to do.

Chapter Sixteen

The next morning, Zoe ambled into her workroom but didn't turn on her computer. She didn't have to demonstrate the finished tutorial until this afternoon, and other projects could wait a moment or two. Instead, she sat back in her chair and steepled her fingers.

Bless the saints, Simon had recovered from the blow she had dealt him when she'd wished him human. His collapse had ripped a hole inside her, a raw wound that began healing only as he adapted successfully to the loss of his magic. Daily he regained the masculine grace that had characterized his movements. Last night in the kitchen had given her hope that he would forgive her.

She had yet to forgive herself for hurting the man, djinni, she loved.

Zoe leaned forward and snapped on her computer. Loving him didn't make her blind to his arrogance, however. Perhaps these two weeks—

without his magic to smooth his path—would help Simon view humans with respect, not disdain.

After all, it was painful to love someone whose only reaction toward your humanity was haughty scorn.

The computer beeped at her. When she looked up, it took a moment for her to switch from her ruminations to the message on her screen:

"Attempted password violation."

Ice formed deep in her veins as she assimilated the meaning.

Someone had been trying to hack into her computer.

Adrenaline spurted through her, melting the ice in a furious blaze. Her hands raced across the keys. Had the hacker done any damage?

Only when she realized her protection program was still secure did her typing slow. The intruder hadn't been able to get past her security measures. Whether the unknown hacker didn't know she would discover the breach, or didn't care, she couldn't tell.

What had he been after? A few key strokes, and she leaned back in her chair, stunned.

Whoever it was, he'd tried to access accounts receivable, not knowing the active records were on Abby's computer. To what purpose? To mess them up so she wouldn't be able to bill for outstanding balances, or to obtain a detailed client listing? Either scenario would be disastrous for ZEVA.

The sabotage hadn't stopped; it had entered a new level.

Zoe clutched the handle on her laptop and knocked on the door to the principal's office. Her sweaty palm slipped on the doorknob when Aaron Somerset bade her come in. Get a grip, Zoe, she ordered and shrugged the strap of her work satchel higher on her shoulder.

She'd taught here for years. Although they hadn't been friends—he had been her boss and the school principal—she'd always worked amiably with Somerset. He'd been impressed with the work she'd done so far. This meeting was a mere formality to demonstrate the finished tutorial and to contract for the next.

Somerset came from around his desk to give her a quick handshake. His perfunctory gaze slid across her, not making contact beyond what was necessary for obligatory politeness. He motioned her to a seat, and then trotted back behind his desk.

Not this contract. Don't let anything happen with this one.

Acid burned in her stomach. Schooling her features, Zoe sat with back straight, knees together, ankles crossed. She snapped open her laptop. "The tutorial is complete. I'll burn the final CD with your approval."

Somerset leaned forward. "I'm anxious to see the finished product. We were impressed with the sample."

The tutorial contained some of her best work, she knew. The knot in her stomach loosened. Still, she fumbled starting the program. Only when the ZEVA logo came on did she relax.

Somerset began moving through the tutorial, smiling when a virtual experiment foamed across the top of the lab desk, showing the students, in amusing and dramatic pictures, what happened when they mixed acetic acid and sodium bicarbonate. His rapid pace slowed, though, when the program flickered and stalled. At his puzzled look, Zoe clicked the mouse on the page forward and the program continued. Somerset, bouncing a pencil by its eraser up and down on his desk, said nothing.

Zoe sat back and laced her cold fingers in her lap, thumbs pressing down hard to stop their involuntary trembling. That should not have happened. After discovering the unauthorized access, she'd checked her hard drive for viruses and opened the program on this disk to make sure everything was running smooth. There had been no problems like this.

The tutorial froze again. The burning in her stomach intensified. It spread, coating her mouth with a bitter taste.

Somerset looked up. "What's wrong with the program, Zoe?"

"I don't know, sir. It never happened before. Maybe I can—" A big white system failure warning box flashed onto the screen. Zoe spun the keyboard toward her and tried to reverse the disaster, but she was too late.

Her tutorial had just crashed her hard drive.

Her tutorial was a flaming disaster.

The pencil bounced faster. Zoe watched from the corner of her eye, her abdominal muscles twisting with each bounce.

"What went wrong?"

"I don't know," Zoe had to admit. She couldn't tell him that someone had sabotaged her. Without proof, it sounded like a pitiful excuse. "It worked fine earlier." Even that sounded whiny. Her throat closed on further explanation.

"Is the program going to run?"

"Not today."

Somerset cleared his throat. "I went out a limb for you, Zoe. ZEVA is a small company, and the project committee wanted to go with someone more established. I convinced them that you could do the job." He waved a hand toward the laptop. "What am I going to tell them now?"

"I'm sure I can fix it with a little time."

"I don't know . . ." Somerset shook his head. "We've been hearing rumors, undercurrents about ZEVA's financial stability. We'll honor this contract, but the committee is getting antsy. Despite what I say, they might look elsewhere for further work."

Somebody was doing a thorough job of destroying her. Zoe's nails dug into her palms. She dragged in a breath of thick air, fighting against numbing despair, letting anger win. She would not let them succeed!

"One month. Can you give me that, Aaron? That tutorial is good, and you know it." The pencil bobbed up and down again. "I've always come through for you. You owe me this chance."

The pencil stilled. "All right, one month."

She had one month to find out who was behind all this, one month to fix the tutorial. "Thank you." Zoe closed the laptop.

Aaron Somerset continued to watch her. When she caught his gaze, a dull flush crept up his neck and his eyes skittered to the wall calendar.

Zoe stared at him. "There's more, isn't there?"

The pencil bounced again, then stopped. Somerset gave a tiny nod of agreement. He retrieved a manila folder from his desk and edged forward the contents, a white envelope penciled with crudely formed letters and numbers. "I received this in the mail last week."

"From whom?"

"I don't know," he admitted.

Zoe almost gagged when she read the anonymous note. Her hand trembled, rustling the paper and blurring the words. The writer had accused her of lewd behavior, base acts she hadn't even known were possible. The paper fluttered to the desk.

"Do you believe this filth?"

"Of course not!" He looked shocked. "I haven't shown it to anyone else. It has no bearing on your work, but I thought you should know." He folded the paper back into the envelope. "It's why I'm giving you a second chance. I think someone is out to get you, Zoe."

Zoe stomped up the sidewalk. Details about the tutorial, loose ends she needed to finish on current projects, all that faded behind one burning question: What was she going to do about the sabotage of ZEVA?

No ideas came to her; her thoughts were like a tangled mass of wires. She couldn't think, couldn't plan. Her head pounded with confusion.

Inside the house, Zoe flopped into her desk chair and flipped on the computer. Just thinking about the tutorial, about the anonymous accusations, made her frustrated enough to spit. She dragged open the top button of her blouse. A strand of hair slipped from its barrette and flopped into her face. Undoing the barrette, she let the wavy strands drop. "Damn hair has a mind of its own," she muttered. "Used to be, when it didn't have curls, I knew what to do with it."

She slid off her shoes and, wiggling her toes in their nylon prison, turned her scowl on the run in her stockings. One more thing gone wrong on a day that was already below the pits.

Mary poked her head around the door. "Can I have supper and spend the night with Miss Vivian? She said she'd teach me the words to 'Bon Temp La Lousiane' and let me play her synthesizer."

"Sure, honey."

Mary skipped in to give her a kiss. "Thanks. Oh, by the way, Dad stopped by while you were gone. Said he wanted to talk to you about something. He asked me if I wanted to go with him to an art gallery in the Quarter this weekend. I thought about what you said, about not shutting him out, so I said yes. I hope that's okay."

"That'll be fine." She cleared her throat. "Mary, when Dustyn came by, did he come into the computer room?"

"Nope. Why?"

"Just wondered. Have a good time with Miss Vivian."

"I'll see you tomorrow." Mary skipped back out.

Zoe gave her an idle good-bye, mulling over who could have gotten into her computers.

The hacker could have been anyone with access to a modem. He'd hidden his tracks so she hadn't been able to trace him. The bug in her disk today, however, needed someone with physical access to her computers. Someone who'd been to the house, copied her disk, added the virus, and then switched disks.

Someone like Dustyn? The sneakiness of the program argued against Dustyn. She didn't think he had the computer skills. Until she figured it out, though, she'd better tighten the security on her and Abby's computers and keep an eye on who came and went.

Leaving Abby's after installing new safeguards on the computer, Zoe heard a tapping from the garage. Inside, she saw Simon, hammer in hand, driving a nail into a small dresser. The tiny, controlled motion made the muscles in his bare arm bunch and flex. Bits of yellow wood dotted his dark hair. His face was shadowed, the chiseled planes and hol-

ows rendered mysterious by the indoor shadows.
His attention focused on his work, he hadn't heard
er come in.

She remembered how it had been in Kaf and in
er kitchen, when that intense concentration had
een focused on her, and a wave of warmth en-
ulfed her. Despite the allegations of the crude let-
er, what she felt for Simon was nothing she need
e ashamed of.

She would not let a coward who hid behind anon-
mous letters dictate her actions.

The hammer dropped. Simon gripped the edge
f the bench, his knuckles whitening.

"Simon, are you all right?" Zoe rushed to his side.

His head whipped around. "I didn't know you
vere there."

"I just came in. Are you all right? Your face is
vhite."

"I am fine." He shook his head like a dog coming
ut of the water. "I have just been standing in one
pot too long." He rotated his shoulders and picked
p another nail.

"What are you doing?"

"Refinishing this dresser."

The child-sized piece of furniture was beautiful
nd Zoe told him so. "Can I touch it?" she asked. At
is nod, she stroked the smooth, silky surface, its
rain enhanced by a thin layer of varnish. "It's mag-
cal what you can do."

Zoe could have bitten her tongue as soon as the
vords were out.

"No, it's hard work," he replied with an edge of
itterness and drove in the nail with a single flick
f his wrist. "This is to be a surprise from Vivian to
Mary."

His face was still ashen. Zoe laid a hand on his
houlder. "Something's wrong. What?"

"Nothing." He looked down at her. His eyes were dark, mesmerizing. "Nothing you can fix, my Zoe," he whispered, so faintly she wondered if she'd heard the words right.

He lifted his hand and stroked her cheek with the back of his fingers. "You look troubled."

Tempted to blurt out everything, she shook her head and stepped away. "Just a lot going on."

He stiffened at the rebuff and, from his steady gaze, she knew she hadn't fooled him, but he didn't call her on it. "As you prefer." He turned his back and began hammering.

It was near supper when Elvina came through the open workroom door. "I'm going out tonight, Zoe. I've got some leftover spaghetti you can share with Simon."

Zoe looked up from her monitor. She had the distinct impression that Elvina already knew about Mary's planned evening with Vivian. "Thanks. You and Lucky have a hot date tonight?" she teased.

"We're going to Mudbugs."

Zoe raised a brow at her friend. "You plan on being home anytime tonight?"

Elvina flushed and gave her a grin. "Probably not."

"Then enjoy yourself."

"You, too."

Whereas solitude normally spurred Zoe to greater concentration, she found that tonight each small sound was amplified in the stillness, setting her on edge. She started when Mary left with Vivian, the door slamming behind them. She found herself listening to the rough edges of Lucky's voice when he said something that made Elvina laugh. His car backfired once when they left.

The true break in her concentration came, however, when she heard Elvina's back door open and shut and knew Simon had come in. The walls were too sturdy for her to hear his footsteps, but her imagination filled in each motion and step. When the pipes in the old house creaked and groaned, indicating that he was showering, her imagination kicked her into virtual reality.

Water sluicing down smooth skin. The clean scent of soap and shampoo. Steam blurring strong features. Washing, soaping, rubbing.

Zoe shook her head and shifted uneasily on her chair. If Simon had still had his djinni abilities she would have sworn he was inserting those vivid images in her mind, as he did his voice. As it was, she had no one but herself to blame for the warmth invading her.

When the pipes stopped moaning and she found herself imagining she could hear the rasp of his shorts pulled over strong legs, Zoe realized that getting further work done was a dream. In the sudden silence when she turned off all her equipment, she heard the faint rustle of footsteps. She stopped stretching her arms overhead and rotated her chair.

Simon, carrying a tool kit, stood in the doorway. "Abby said one of the chair legs in here needed fixing," he said.

"Chair leg? Ah, yeah, that one." Zoe gestured to a chair, annoyed with her bumbling response.

With a lithe grace, he moved to the floor beside her. He ran his hands over the chair leg, studying the problem by feel rather than eye. Zoe started massaging her calves, her legs aching from hours spent sitting.

As she watched Simon work, a familiar yearning rose somewhere in the vicinity of her stomach and spread with disarming rapidity down to her sex and up to her brain, two organs that seemed to be acting

273

in riotous concert. Zoe groaned and leaned back her head, keeping Simon in view beneath half-lowered lids.

No one should look that good in shorts and shirt from a Wal-Mart rack. No one should caress wood like he was caressing a woman. Especially when the woman watching was undergoing touch-withdrawal.

His hands traced the ridges of the chair leg. At her intake of breath, he looked up. Keeping his gaze locked with hers, his grin widening, he fondled the wood.

Zoe's traitorous body silently screamed, "Me, me, touch me, too!" Simon's smile got a little more knowing. Blast the djinni, he was too observant. He shifted his touch from the table to her leg and rested her foot in his lap.

"It's different from what I've tried before," he said conversationally, "but I think I can fix the leg." He ran one hand down her outstretched leg, cupping her calf in his palm. He started kneading her tight muscles.

Zoe sighed with pleasure.

His massage reached her foot. His blunt finger-nails abraded her stockings with a slight scratching noise as he pressed against the bottom of her foot.

"Lift your hips," he said and reached beneath her skirt.

Zoe gave a token protest.

"Be just a little wicked, Zoe Calderone," he teased. "Besides, this will feel better on bare legs."

She did as he commanded, and he pulled down her stockings. Zoe relaxed against the back of the chair and abandoned herself to the rhythmic pressures of his hands.

"So, tell me of your day," Simon suggested.

The subtle tension returned. She looked down at

the man at her feet. Continuing to work his magic on her legs, he raised one brow. It occurred to her that Simon was learning entirely too much, entirely too fast, about the intricacies and tricks of human interaction and manipulation.

"Nothing worth sharing."

"Did you demonstrate the tutorial?"

"Yes." The growing relaxation smoothed her worry.

"Did they like it?"

"At first." His hands were doing magical things to the backs of her knees.

"What happened then?" He moved to her thighs.

She tensed but said nothing, unwilling to discuss her failure.

"Still unable to share your troubles, hmmm?" He moved behind her. "Lean forward."

She complied. He began to work on her neck.

Zoe had never had a massage from anyone before, but she imagined this one would stand out in the annals of massagedom. He leaned her forward, stroking the tension from her neck and spine; then he leaned her back and replaced the tension with an electrical awareness as he massaged her shoulders. The soft fabric of her blouse caressed her skin as his hands stroked up and down her arms. Lean forward. Massage, soothe. Lean back. Stroke, electrify. The repetition both lulled and excited.

Once, she started when he pressed too hard on a tight back muscle. He smoothed and subdued it, coaxing out the tension, then crooned approval when she relaxed.

"You know," Simon said, "I still want to come together with you."

The words were soft, like the sighing wind, but Zoe had no trouble understanding them. They were an echo of her own thoughts, after all. Did Simon,

Kathleen Nance

too, wonder if those hours in Kaf had been a fig-
ment of magic? Real or magic, lasting or fleeting, it
changed nothing. She wanted him too.

They had a few more days, and nights, together,
to make their memories, and she needed something
good in her life right now.

"Will you come to me tonight?" he asked.

Zoe shook her head.

His hands tightened on her shoulders.

"You come to me," she said. "I've got the double
bed."

"So I shall."

Zoe's stomach took that inappropriate moment
to rumble.

Simon laughed and released her. "Perhaps we
should have sustenance first. I have many plans for
tonight and would not have you weakened." His
hand stroked across her curls, and he grinned at
her. "You shall not get much rest this night, Zoe,
and neither shall I."

Zoe almost said to hell with food.

Twenty minutes later, she wished she had.

Chris burst into the kitchen, the back door rattling with the exuberance of his entrance. "We got
it, Simon—access to the laser! You have to come.
Now we can make that hologram the way we want
it. Remember that fire trick? This is going to be so
fine."

"Thanks for knocking, Chris," Zoe said dryly.

Chris ran a knowing glance between the two of
them. "I didn't interrupt anything, did I?"

"Not yet," Simon muttered.

"Come on, Simon, we need you."

"Later."

"Later won't work." Chris rubbed the back of his
neck. "Tonight's the only time we could get." He

sent Zoe a beseeching look. "You understand, Ms. Calderone."

The siren call of technology; she understood it all too well. She bobbed her head toward the door. "Go ahead, Simon. I think I'll just head straight to bed."

Heat flared in his eyes. His chair scraped across the kitchen floor when he rose in an abrupt motion. "One hour, Chris."

Two hours later, Zoe lay on her back, the corners of the sheet wadded in her fists. Was he still coming? Should she put on some makeup? Had she brushed her teeth? Yes, she had. Maybe she should change? She'd first slipped into bed naked, but that had seemed too obvious, especially as the minutes passed, so she'd gotten up and put on her regular nightshirt.

Last time, in Kaf, had been fantasy. This . . . this was more real, somehow. More fraught with danger.

She let go of the sheet to smooth the shirt over her hips. *Sexy, Zoe, real sexy. That's just going to overwhelm him with passion.* Well, Simon never seemed to need much stimulation to fuel him.

She wasn't cut out for seduction, Zoe realized. She'd only been with one other man, and Dustyn's mattress endeavors hadn't relied much on seduction by either of them.

Just when she was ready to snap on the light and start reading—anything to avoid the agony of waiting—the door opened. For a moment, the hall light outlined Simon's tall figure; then the door shut with a faint click, bathing the room once more in moonlight and streetlight. Zoe swallowed, unable to say anything coherent, in greeting or in invitation.

Simon halted beside the bed and slipped off his shorts, leaving him nude and semi-aroused. "I'm sorry. Chris was so excited. I could not leave sooner."

"I understand." She did understand. His caring was important to Chris, who was starved for a man's guidance. She patted the bed, and he slid in beside her. When the mattress dipped beneath his weight, Zoe rolled toward him.

Simon wrapped his arms around her. "What an accommodating mattress you have."

"The better to touch you with, my dear."

"Isn't that supposed to be 'The better to eat you with, my dear'?" He nipped at her earlobe.

Zoe rubbed her cheek against the softness of his hair, his teasing transforming her earlier inhibitions into something more interesting. "So you've read 'Little Red Riding Hood'?"

"I have read most of your fairy tales."

"Even *Arabian Nights*?"

"Even that." Simon levered himself up, tugged off her nightshirt, and flung it across the room. "That's better," he muttered and started petting her in all the lonely places that had been begging for his touch. He bent down and trailed kisses between her breasts.

Simon's lovemaking had lost nothing of its power when he lost his magic.

Zoe remembered her hasty afternoon trip to the pharmacy. "Ah, Simon, there's one thing we have to talk about first."

"Talk?" He lifted his head and met her eyes. His lips were damp and parted.

Zoe ran a tongue across her mouth, unable to think for a moment what she wanted to say. "Birth control. We didn't use any in Kaf. I . . . I didn't think about it then. I can't ignore it here."

"Birth control?"

Zoe groaned to herself. "So we don't conceive a child."

"The djinn are not a very fertile lot."

"Just the same, I think we should use some protection." She jerked her head toward the beside table.

Simon's brows knit in puzzlement. "Protection?"

"You know, a condom."

"I have never heard of that."

Zoe flushed and cleared her throat. "They're in that drawer. The foil packets."

Simon reached across her and took one out. He turned it around in his hands, feeling the edges. "*This* prevents the bearing of a child?"

This was so embarrassing. "Open it."

Simon obliged and held the circle of thin latex in his palm. "What do you do with this?"

In her wildest dreams, she hadn't expected to have to explain to a man what a condom was for and how to use it. She shook it out and held it up, hoping the shape would be self-explanatory.

"It fits inside you?" he asked helpfully.

Give me strength. "No, it goes on you. You roll it on. Before you, ah . . ."

Understanding dawned in Simon's expression. "Will you help?"

He caught on fast. Zoe nodded. "Each time. You have to use a new one each time."

Simon leaned over her again and opened the drawer. "One, two, three . . ." he began counting. He looked over his shoulder and grinned wickedly. "You were planning on quite a night, weren't you?"

Then he was on top of her again and kissing her with fervor and abandon.

Zoe touched and was touched, stroked and was stroked. With restless hands, she explored Simon's body, while he uncovered sensitive areas she hadn't known existed. She discovered that he was ticklish on the bottoms of his feet when she kissed him there. He discovered that she arched and moaned when he used his lips and tongue and teeth on her.

Zoe demonstrated the practicalities of birth control.

Simon found erotic nuances to the technique she'd never dreamed possible.

Slowly, tenderly, together, they found passion and transformation. They joined and melded. As she cried out in release, as Simon groaned his climax, Zoe rejoiced in one more wonder, her love for Simon.

Her skin was soft and pleasingly scented. Simon buried his face in the curve of Zoe's neck and inhaled. He felt wonderful. Relaxed, satiated, drowsy. Zoe was tucked beneath him; her soft breath tickled his chin. Even the drying sheen of sweat over his body felt good and natural. Simon shifted a little, taking his weight off Zoe, except for the arm and leg that kept her bound to him.

Becoming human had done nothing to diminish his performance and his thorough enjoyment of Zoe, nor hers of him. Neither had that sheath she'd insisted he wear. They still had time, lots of time, before morning dawned. They would make love again. And again. And maybe again. Next time, it would be as hot and fast and furious as this time had been languorous and thorough.

Simon frowned. What they had shared had been special, unique. He felt as though he had exchanged pledges with Zoe, yet he knew that could never be.

Perhaps, after she wished, he could visit her. He couldn't live here, but he could spend time with her. Not permanently, never permanently, but he could come back whenever he wanted.

But what about what Zoe wanted? With sudden clarity, Simon realized that Zoe couldn't tolerate his dipping in and out of her life at will, coming for a few hours of pleasure but never staying. Never being around when she needed him. He would destroy her, or at least destroy the feelings between them.

For her sake, when they parted, it would have to be a final break. Even though it would feel like ripping out his gut, Zoe was too important, too special to treat any other way.

Until then, however, he would savor every moment.

And maybe, when she decided to tell him what her current dilemma was, he could help her with it.

That was for later, however.

He kissed her again, nipping and sucking her ear and jaw, and started to grow hard. Reaching into the bedside drawer, Simon, ever a swift learner, made quick work of the packet within.

Zoe stirred beneath him. "Simon, did you say you'd read *Arabian Nights*?"

"Uh-huh." Solomon's beard, she was so responsive to him. Already she moved to his rhythms, opening herself to him.

"There was something I was wondering—"

"Later, Zoe." He thrust into her.

She started convulsing around him. "Right. Later."

This time was frenzied and steamy, just as he'd predicted.

But he'd been wrong about one thing.

It wasn't quick.

Chapter Seventeen

The moon had long since set, leaving the room lit by the yellow glow of stars and streetlights, before Zoe remembered her question. Through the screened windows she could hear the occasional dog bark, the drone of distant cars, and the high-pitched clicks of insects. The circling fan above moved the air with languid ease.

Zoe raised herself on one elbow. Simon dozed beside her, his tousled hair and bare skin a dark contrast to the white pillowcase.

"Simon?" she whispered.

He opened one eye. "What?"

"*Arabian Nights*. Is there any truth to the stories? Do some of them depict the djinn accurately?"

He closed his eye, and Zoe thought he wasn't going to answer. She stretched out again. "Maybe you don't want to talk about it."

"The stories are accurate in spirit, for they tell what humans saw of djinn," he said at last. "However, like your times, only the disasters and scandals are considered worthy of recording, and those are colored by the views of the reporter."

He rolled to his side and turned Zoe to face him. He ran one hand up and down her arm. "Why do you ask?"

"I was a kid when I first read the stories, but I've always remembered Sinbad." His forefinger found a sensitive spot on the nape of her neck and traced a circle around it, sending a thrill through her. Zoe bent her head to allow him greater freedom. "Was Sinbad real?" she asked, her voice muffled against his chest, her fingers tangling in the dusting of hairs. "I always hoped those fabulous trips he took were truly possible."

"Yes, Zoe, Sinbad was real."

"I'm glad."

"Now I have a question." He tilted her chin until she looked at him. "Things did not go well for you today, did they?"

In the honesty of the night, Zoe could not temporize, nor avoid. She paused in her lazy exploration of his chest. "No. But I don't want to talk about it. Not tonight."

"Tomorrow, then. You have partners. You should allow them the honor of trusting them."

The honor of trusting them? She had never looked at it that way.

"You have given them jobs," Simon continued, "yet their pride wonders if it was only charity. Show your faith in their abilities by letting them solve the problems with you."

His dark eyes held her gaze. Zoe recalled that Elvina had once said something similar.

"It hadn't occurred to me that they might feel that way," she admitted. "I'll talk to them tomorrow."

Somehow, that decision didn't seem as difficult as it once would have.

She began toying with his chest again. "You know, Simon, for that good advice I could just kiss you."

"Then why don't you?"

"Why don't I, indeed." She strung kisses down his chest, then lower. "We still have the house to ourselves."

"And time to use at least two more foil packets. I wonder, have you ever . . . ?" Simon whispered in her ear.

"Simon!" Even in the darkness, Zoe flushed.

Simon just laughed and proceeded to demonstrate.

When the phone rang the next morning, they were still the only ones in the house, but at least they were dressed. Simon went to get the morning paper, while Zoe answered the phone.

"I have a tremendous opportunity for Mary," Dustyn began after a perfunctory greeting. "There's a gallery owner in Los Angeles who thinks it would be a marvelous draw to have a father-daughter showing of artworks. High concept, he calls it. We've been talking about it since I read that article about you in the *New Orleans* magazine where you mentioned Mary's art."

Zoe's hand tightened around the receiver. *High concept?* Was this the reason he'd come back? She'd bet her hard drive any deal he cut would be lucrative. For Dustyn.

Dustyn rushed ahead, filling the silence. "This is an opportunity she can't get anywhere else."

Hooks of unease clawed up her nerves, leaving her hands cold and her stomach tense. Whether Dustyn was doing this because he thought he'd make a lot of money or because he thought it would bring him fame, she didn't know and she didn't care. Mary was her only concern.

"What would the show entail?" She had to remain calm and find out all the details of his plan.

"It would be a showing of her best pieces along with my collection of work. The gallery owner wants to call it 'From the Branch Comes the Twig.' Isn't that a fascinating title?"

"When?"

"It's a fall theme. October."

"Mary's in school then. I suppose she could work on some things to give you before school starts."

There was a pause. "The owner thinks it important that she be there for the showing."

"For a weekend? He'd have to subsidize our plane fare." Going with Mary would not be easy, but Zoe would consider no other option.

Dustyn cleared his throat. "The showing is to run for eight weeks, and he wants Mary there the whole time. Without Mary, there will be no show."

"She can't do it, Dustyn."

"Don't ruin this for us, Zoe." His voice became sharp. "Chances like this don't come along too often."

Maybe not for Dustyn, but Mary would have a lifetime of opportunities. "She can display her pieces, and she can go out for a weekend, maybe even a week, but that's all. She can't afford to miss more school."

"I had hoped we could work this out amicably, but you're being very inflexible." Dustyn sighed into the telephone. "I'm sorry. I'm going to have to sue for custody of Mary."

Oh, God, no! Zoe's stomach churned. Her numb hands could barely grip the telephone. She braced herself against the wall and took a deep breath.

"You'll never win the case." Zoe strove to keep her response even. "You've been out of our lives for ten years. When you found out I was pregnant, you took off on your motorcycle. Cleaned out our bank balance, too. No judge will award you custody."

Dustyn gave a soft laugh. "Are you so sure? I have a steady job, while you're sinking all your funds into a floundering business. I share a common interest with our daughter. And, my dear Zoe, your moral reputation is suffering. Living with a man while our daughter's in the house . . ." He made a mocking *tsk*ing sound.

"I'm not living with anyone. Simon stays with Elvina. And ZEVA is sound."

"Tell it to the judge." Dustyn hung up.

Zoe unwrapped her stiff fingers from the receiver. He couldn't take Mary away. If she believed he could, even for an instant, she'd go crazy. Think. She needed to think and to plan. Zoe curled her arms around her waist, finding she was shivering and couldn't stop.

Simon came inside, took one look at her, and wrapped an arm around her. "Who was on the phone?"

"Dustyn." She picked up the phone, but it fell from her nerveless fingers. "Can you call? I need to talk to Elvina. And Abby and Vivian."

While he dialed, Zoe gazed at him with gritty eyes. If only Simon had his djinni powers back. She'd found something she would risk anything for, even wishing.

Within the hour, Zoe, Elvina, Abby, Vivian, and Simon were convened around the kitchen table, while Chris watched Mary and Joey at Abby's house. Zoe was glad to have Simon there, glad for his strength. At first, he had demurred at joining the "family council," but Abby had dismissed his protests.

"You're a member of this family," she insisted.

"Please, Simon," Zoe begged. "I want you here."

Simon had nodded and stayed.

His words last night had taken root. Zoe knew she could no longer hide ZEVA's problems, or hers. Her partners, if they were to be full partners, deserved to know everything that was going on, including Dustyn's threat.

"What did you want to tell us?" Abby asked.

Zoe took a deep breath, unsure where to begin.

"Is this about ZEVA's financial problems?" Vivian asked.

"Oh, hush," scolded Abby. "We were going to let her tell."

"You mean you knew?" Zoe asked.

"We knew something was wrong," Elvina replied.

Vivian patted Zoe's hand. "You were so tense, dear." She cast a quick look at Simon. "Most of the time."

Zoe blushed. Simon gave her a friendly wink.

"I do keep the books," Abby added. "I could see the revenues weren't coming in as expected."

"And I follow our accounts," Elvina said.

"Not in the conventional sense," Abby muttered.

"My methods work."

Zoe looked from one to the other. She didn't need to protect them. They'd simply been waiting for her to realize that. "I feel like such a fool."

"That's all right, dear," said Vivian. "You had a lot on your mind."

"Now, what's going on?" Abby asked. "After all, we are your partners." She stared at Zoe, daring her to challenge that fact.

Zoe smiled. "Yes, you are, and I need your help." She began to relate all the problems she'd encountered, ending with her phone call from Dustyn.

They soon formed a plan focusing on the financial problems at ZEVA. If they could prove ZEVA's solvency, then Dustyn's threat about custody would be toothless. Three people seemed the most likely source of the problems: Roger Broussard, Dustyn Calderone, and Isaiah Knox. Zoe wanted to dismiss Isaiah, since he was incarcerated, but Elvina insisted they couldn't. She volunteered to find out more about him. Simon suggested he question Roger Broussard, since Broussard had never met Simon. Vivian offered to investigate Dustyn, saying that she never had liked his condescending attitude. In the meantime, Abby would manage expenses and collect outstanding payments, while Zoe traced the computer sabotage.

Zoe sat back. "Then we're agreed?" Elvina, Vivian, and Abby nodded.

Abby stood, her hands resting on the table. "Then why are we sitting here? Let's get to work." Chairs scraped back. Abby laid a hand on Zoe's shoulder. "Dustyn won't get Mary."

Elvina fingered her crystal. "He won't."

"We'll make sure of it," Vivian added.

The three women left, purpose strengthening their strides.

Simon stood behind Zoe and wrapped his arms around her shoulders. "You did the right thing, Zoe."

She leaned back, savoring his warmth, his strength, his solidity. "I know. I had to."

Then she shivered, and Simon's arms tightened around her. "I'm worried, though. At first the problems were annoying, minor things. Somewhere along the line, when I lost the repair shop contract, it changed. The person who wrote those notes, who said those disgusting things about me, is a sick person." She looked at the empty doorway. "I hope I haven't put them in danger."

"What do you think you're going to learn about Isaiah Knox?" Lucky popped the top on a Dixie beer and took a long drag.

Elvina, sitting beside him on his living room sofa, sipped her iced tea. "What he's been doing in prison. If he's made some phone calls. Things like that."

"You gotta know the people to ask. If you haven't spent time on the street or in the joint, they won't be talking." Lucky took another pull on his long-neck.

That did not sound promising. Elvina sighed. She had hoped Lucky might know a prison guard or a policeman who'd be willing to talk to her once they understood the problem. Hanging out on Rampart Street wasn't her idea of a healthy activity, but if that's what it took to help Zoe, then she'd do it. "Maybe someone would talk to me," she mused, "for a price."

Lucky slammed his bottle on the scratched end table. "Don't try it. Nothing's worth your life." He looked at her, his eyes flat. "I told you I did time."

Elvina nodded.

"Does it bother you?"

"What were you in for?"

"Robbery."

Elvina knew Lucky was a hard man, could be a dangerous man. His aura showed a hint of darkness that would never go away, but it wasn't the muddy, dead black of an evil man. He'd always treated her with respect and gentleness.

"That's in the past," she said. "It's who you are now that's important."

He hooked his thumbs in his jeans pockets and

leaned his head back. She saw his Adam's apple bob, as though words caught there were fighting for freedom. "Who I am now is someone who cares for you, Elvina." He looked at her then, his rough features harsh. "All I want is for us to have a future together."

It was the first time he'd ever mentioned the future. Elvina's heart jumped. She stroked the crystal at her neck, startled to find it felt hot.

"What are you thinking?" Lucky placed his hand beneath hers, his knuckles resting on her chest. His thumb stroked the crystal with her. The crystal blazed. Lucky edged his fingers between hers and the crystal, and then pulled her hand down. He bent to kiss her neck. "Are you thinking of us?" Her hand in his, he stroked lower.

"Yes," breathed Elvina.

"Let me handle it. I'll find out what you need to know. That's a promise, Elvina."

It was the first time he'd given her a promise. "All right. When? Now?"

Lucky dropped her hand. "Let me go make a few phone calls, call in a few markers. You—" he gave her a quick, hard kiss "—wait right here."

While waiting for Lucky, Elvina wandered around the room tidying up: collecting cans and bottles to take to the recycling center, emptying wastebaskets, stacking newspapers. When she grabbed a haphazard pile of magazines, a book fell out from underneath. One look at the title immobilized her.

It was the ancient book of magic. The one she'd used to summon Simon. The one stolen from her. Elvina looked toward the door through which Lucky had disappeared. Why had he taken it? For what possible reason? The reasons she was coming up with, she didn't want to believe.

A piece of paper was stuck in the book. Elvina opened to the marked section but couldn't read it. There was a picture of two men on the crumbling page, however, and the primitive artist had been very talented. The look of horror on one subject's face and the look of satisfaction on the other's were clear, even across the centuries. Also vividly depicted were the oozing sores covering the horrified man's body. She didn't need the words to understand the intent of the spell.

Elvina swallowed hard against a wave of nausea. She opened the paper marking the page. It contained a name and address printed in ink. Beneath it were scrawled the words, "Does translations." The page had been torn from a memo pad. Elvina looked once toward the door, then back down. Preprinted at the top was, *From the desk of Roger Broussard.*

Clutching the book to her chest, Elvina fled home.

Simon watched Elvina hurry down the hall and disappear into her bedroom. Were those tears he had seen? He started to follow her but decided she would prefer solitude. Instead he studied the ancient tome she had thrust into his hands, saying "This is the book Zoe and I used to summon you. I entrust it to your care, Simon. Keep it safe."

He took the book with him when he went into the computer room. He had an e-mail message from an Egyptian museum curator with whom he'd been communicating. The woman had a fax to send but wanted to make sure it was seen by Simon alone. Simon put the fax machine on-line, and then propped his feet on the desk and thumbed through the book while waiting for the fax.

It didn't take him long to realize that none of the

rituals was the one he needed to obtain his freedom. Another dead end, as these humans would say. He hid the book in a drawer, and then picked up the fax and read the first words:

Thou who wouldst destroy the barakat *of the bound djinni by the power of this Ritual of Sovereignty do heed the words and warnings. With the authority of Nulush I do adjure thee.*

Nulush. Minau's father.

Blessed Solomon! His feet dropped to the floor. This was it! This was the Terran ritual he needed, the one that would tell him how to find his tablet.

The English translation fluttered to the desktop. Simon sent a quick e-mail thanking the woman who had found the ritual; then, his hands shaking, he picked up the faxed copy of the section from the old scroll. He could read the ancient language and did not need the Egyptian's translation.

This was not the original writing, of course, but a copy of a copy of a copy, carried down for centuries, and he wanted to read it in as original a form as possible. Holding his breath, Simon scanned the sheet.

A stone lodged in his stomach when he reached the end. His jaw tightened. He must have read it wrong. Surely this was not what was needed. He read it through again, then a third time.

There was no mistake. The ritual was as he had first thought. He threw the paper to the desk and slapped his palm down, the crack echoing in the silence. He shot to his feet, sending his chair rolling until it hit the edge of the sofa with a thud.

Simon paced the computer room. The ritual was impossible. Never would a summoner, unless foolish as well as selfless, agree to such conditions. Use the final wish to take them to the place of concealment, of magical boundaries? Speak the words of release using the djinni's true name?

The summoner would lose the final wish, would be placed in jeopardy, and Nulush had given ample warning against trusting a djinni. The djinni, also, would have to trust the human with absolute power.

No, it would not happen, just as Nulush had planned. Bitter though it would be, Simon would have to serve the 101 summons before he could be free.

Simon slammed a fist against the wall and swore. Just seven more summoners. A wave of fatigue washed across him. Seven more, that is, if he made it through the next week.

He flopped down into his chair, picked up the copy from the scroll, gave it one last long look, then crumpled it into a tiny ball and threw it in the wastebasket.

Zoe came in, greeted him, and turned on her computer. While it went through the batch commands, she swiveled in her chair to face him. Her eyes narrowed. "What's wrong?"

"Nothing."

"Something is. You're too . . . subdued."

He ignored her, the disappointment still too keen to talk about.

"And you said I needed to communicate," she muttered, then reached over and flicked off her machine. She strode to his side and tugged him to his feet. "C'mon."

"Where are we going?"

"We're going to get Mary, and then we're going to introduce you to a New Orleans treat—snowballs." She smacked her lips. "Cold, shaved ice. Sticky, sweet syrup of any color or flavor imaginable. Blackberry and wedding cake are my favorites."

He glanced at her computer. "Do you not have work to do?"

"You know," she said as she settled her arm in the crook of his elbow and hustled him out, "a very wise man once told me even a camel stops to drink in the desert. Some things are more important than work, like being with your family."

Family.

Zoe called him family. Mary missed him when he was gone. Abby invited him to a family council. Elvina entrusted him with the book.

Simon stared down at Zoe, bemused, the temporary weakness gone. *They thought of him as family.*

He was no longer alone.

Late that night, breathing deeply, Elvina emerged from the trance. Her gaze shifted from the candle flame to the shadowed room, and her hand tightened around the crystal. The guide had warned her, warned her of consequences, but had not told her what she needed to know. No matter.

Twelve years ago, Zoe had bullied Dustyn into renting Elvina the other half of the double and, though Zoe had needed the money, she'd charged Elvina a pittance. That act of kindness, and the many that had followed, had helped Elvina back on her feet after a nasty divorce. Zoe's determination had fueled Elvina's fierce independence. The sales job with ZEVA, started as repayment to Zoe, had turned into a delight, a perfect melding of Elvina's talents and dreams.

No one would bring down ZEVA, not while Elvina had a breath in her.

She had introduced Lucky to Zoe. It was up to her to find proof of the dirty tricks, of his collaboration. No one else need be involved. No one else need run the risks.

Elvina dressed in a pair of jeans and rummaged through her closet until she found a black shirt. She wrapped her blond hair in a dark silk scarf, turban-like.

Proof she needed. Proof she would find.

The ringing telephone pulled Zoe from a deep sleep.

She reached for Simon, wanting to cuddle and shut out the intrusive noise, but he wasn't there. Then she remembered. Even though Mary was spending the night with Vivian, Zoe had refused to let Simon come to her. She could not risk giving Dustyn fodder for his court case.

Zoe stumbled to the telephone, an appliance she'd come to dread. "Hello?"

"Zoe?" It was Elvina. She started coughing.

Zoe gripped the telephone. "What's wrong?"

The coughing slowed. "Could you come down to Charity Hospital?" Elvina's voice was husky. "There's been a fire at Roger Broussard's office, and I think the police are about to arrest me for arson."

Chapter Eighteen

The morning air shimmered with the promise of sultry heat. Already, sticky sweat coated Simon as he and Zoe returned from seeing Elvina. The miasma of the jail clung to him with its odors of wickedness and despair.

Zoe turned off the car, and then stared straight ahead, fingers drumming on the rainbow circle used to steer. "We'll get her a top-notch lawyer, get her out on bail at the arraignment. Maybe we should hire a private detective. The police are convinced she did it. They won't look any further."

"What if she did set the fire?" Simon interrupted.

Zoe whirled in her seat. "She didn't do it." Fierce protectiveness was stamped on her features.

"Roger Broussard swears he saw her coming from the building just before the flames started."

"Roger Broussard would swear cats could bark if he thought it might give him an advantage." Zoe got out, and then ducked her head to speak through the open door. "If Elvina says she didn't do it, then she didn't."

Simon followed her into the house, wondering if he would ignore the overwhelming evidence, if she would waver in her constancy to her friend. "ZEVA stands to gain a lot if Broussard is temporarily out of business."

"And Roger gains just as much, maybe more, if ZEVA is blamed and discredited." Zoe put her hands on her waist. "Elvina doesn't need to justify her actions to me. Whether she did or did not set the fire, she still has my support. I just needed the truth to know what to do next. She did not set that fire."

Her adamant defense, her unswerving belief, was a delight to hear, washing away the vestiges of Simon's cynicism toward humans. This was a woman who, once she gave her loyalty, would never betray.

"I'm going to let Abby and Vivian know we're home," Zoe said.

The doorbell rang. "I'll get it," Simon offered. Oz wove himself through his feet while he went to the front door.

Despite his concern about Elvina, Simon found a smile had taken possession of his mouth. Zoe made him believe in the goodness of the human spirit, and he'd forgotten how pleasurable that felt. His heart was lighter than it had been in many years.

Lucky stood on the porch, twisting a Saints cap in his hands. His clothes were wrinkled, and his eyes drooped with weariness. "Abby called me. I been waiting until you got back. How's Elvina?" He put the cap back on, picked up Oz, and began petting him under the chin. Oz lifted his head and purred.

"She's still in jail. Zoe thinks we can arrange bail today."

In the kitchen, Zoe, her back to them, spooned coffee grounds into the filter. "Vivian and Abby will be here soon."

She started the coffee brewing, and then spun around. Simon saw her freeze, her eyes fixed on Lucky.

"Elvina told me about the book."

Oz jumped from Lucky's arms, headed toward his food dish. Lucky cleared his throat and took off his hat. He began twisting it again. "I wondered if that was why she left and wouldn't take my calls. Hear me out first. That's all I ask."

Zoe crossed her arms. "You were behind the dirty tricks."

Simon leaned one hip against the counter. Lucky shot him a glance before returning his attention to Zoe. "At first."

Simon stepped forward. "Did you write the letter that dishonored her?" If Lucky had, no power on Terra would have stopped Simon's wrath against him.

Lucky shook his head. "I just made a couple of phone calls about delaying payments, bribed clerks to lose your orders. The rest of the stuff going on? I had nothing to do with that."

"Why?" Zoe sank onto a chair.

"I wanted some wishes. Elvina told me about *him*." Lucky jerked his head toward Simon. "Not in so many words, but enough that I put two and two together when I saw some things."

"You saw Zoe and me that night in her workroom, didn't you?" Simon said. "When we danced."

Lucky nodded. "You just disappeared. I watched and listened—I even stole that book of Elvina's, for all the good it did me—and figured out what was going on. One thing I realized—I couldn't get my wishes until Zoe used hers. I figured she'd use them to save ZEVA."

Simon watched Zoe's face whiten. Unlike him, she hadn't been exposed to the corrupting wanting, the sickness that would lead a human to any offense just to gain the power of three wishes. Yet he knew she had understood on a fundamental level. That was why she had resisted for so long.

Lucky sat beside Zoe. He reached out a hand but pulled back when she jerked away. "Elvina's the best thing that ever happened to me. For a while I told myself I did it because you took advantage of her, always having her watch your kid and not giving her credit for the work she brought in."

Simon heard Zoe's gasp of pain. A flush of anger, a need to protect, coursed through him. He stepped forward, but Zoe stopped him with a tiny shake of her head.

"Truth was—" Lucky clenched his fist atop the table—"I just wanted them wishes. As I got to know you, figured out you wasn't like that, I stopped."

"The sabotage didn't," Zoe said.

Lucky looked down, his thumb rubbing against a long white scar on his hand. "I made the mistake of going to Broussard, thinking he might help me. I never told him about the wishes, just said I wanted to pull a few practical jokes. Make Elvina spend less time with you and ZEVA. He listened, careful like, then refused." Lucky gave a bitter laugh. "All I got for my trouble was a memo pad. Later, I figured Broussard had to be behind the dirty stuff, but I didn't have proof. Who'd believe the word of an ex-con against an upstanding citizen like Broussard?"

"Roger couldn't have destroyed my tutorial," Zoe said. "He didn't have access."

"Do you have an idea who did?" Simon asked.

"I thought Dustyn. He was at the house and—" she made a face—"he still has a key. I'd asked Mary the other day if he'd been in the computer room, and she said, 'No,' thinking I meant that day. Later, she told me he had been in there once, to send an e-mail. I'm not sure his computer expertise is good enough to crash my tutorial, though."

"I talked to one of the guards," Lucky said, "and found out Dustyn sprung Knox—"

"Sprung Knox?" Simon asked.

"Paid his bail, got him out of jail. When I heard that, I figured the two of them were working together." Lucky cast a wary glance toward the door. "You've got a leak in your company, Zoe. It took insider information to plant that dirt. Do you trust Abby and Vivian?"

Zoe glared at him. "Implicitly."

"How about Chris? Teenagers are funny. They get ideas and don't think 'em through."

Zoe shook her head. "Not Chris."

That left Mary or Joey. Simon waited for her to reach the same conclusion he had.

She rubbed one finger against her chin. "Dustyn, that slug! I bet he pumped Mary for information when they were together."

"Everything keeps coming back to Dustyn," Simon said.

"Dustyn's an opportunist, not a strategist," Zoe said. "Told what to do, my devious ex could have copied the disk, given it to someone to infect, then replaced the good disk. He could have given information; that I could see him doing." She shook her head. "I think Roger Broussard's the brains. It would explain why he's lying and blaming Elvina for the fire. We need to focus on Roger."

Lucky looked up from his intent examination of his hands. "I'd like to help."

There was such a long silence, Simon thought Zoe wasn't going to answer. He saw Lucky's shoulders slump, heard his feet scrape against the tile floor.

"We need all the help we can get," Zoe said at last. She stuck out her hand. "Welcome to the team, Lucky."

Lucky gave her a wary glance before offering a firm shake. "Do you think Elvina'll forgive me?"

Zoe looked straight at him. "I don't know. That's for you two to work out. I need to figure out how to unmask Roger." She dusted her hands, as though the issue had been decided.

Simon had other plans. He had met Roger yesterday, pretending to need his services. The man was hard and slick as polished marble and treacherous as Oxus slime. Zoe might prefer to focus on Roger, but Simon knew who was the sand, who would crumble with pressure.

Dustyn Calderone.

Making him crumble was a very satisfying notion.

"So," Zoe mused to herself, "what's our next step?"

"Step to what?" Vivian asked as she and Abby bustled in. "I brought beignets for breakfast." She held up a white bag.

"Chris is watching Mary and Joey for an hour," Abby added.

When Zoe started to explain, Lucky caught Simon's attention and jerked his head toward the door. Simon's brows rose at the man's temerity, but, curious, he followed him nonetheless.

Outside, in the hall, Lucky planted his feet. "Why don't you use your magic to help her?"

"Because Zoe wished my powers away. I have to

spend two weeks as a human." Disgruntlement crept into Simon's voice.

Lucky cackled. "There's a story behind that, I bet. Look, like you said back there, all this leads to Dustyn Calderone. We need to convince him it's in his best interest to tell what he knows."

Simon glanced toward the kitchen and lowered his voice. "Would you like to help me this night?"

Lucky followed Simon's gaze. "Is this something the ladies shouldn't know about?"

"This is about djinn justice. It tends to be . . . fundamental. And I do not think Zoe would agree to it, even with her former husband."

"You think we should pay Dustyn a little visit?" Lucky clapped him on the back. "You know, Simon, this could be the start of a beautiful friendship."

Zoe had said the same thing once, in the same tone of voice.

Simon shook his head. Humans still confused him. "I have an idea, but we shall need to borrow some items from Chris."

Simon, Lucky, and Chris worked diligently throughout the day. Simon visited a Royal Street magic shop, bought the gimmicks they would need, and practiced with them. Chris assembled equipment and suggested some diabolical tricks Simon hadn't thought of. Lucky paid a visit to Dustyn's house, making certain adjustments while their quarry was out. They did as much preparation as possible, knowing they would have to be quick, and quiet, at night.

Finally, at one o'clock in the morning, the three loaded the final piece of equipment in the trunk of Lucky's car. Lucky had refused to take Zoe's red car, even though Simon persisted in suggesting it. "Too noticeable," he said.

While Lucky closed the trunk with a light snap, imon turned to Chris, to bid him to return home. 'he youth was standing with his arms crossed and is chin raised, a stance Simon recognized as an cho of his own.

"I'm going with you," Chris said.

Simon shook his head. "What we do is illegal in our world."

Chris gave a snort. "You mean it's legal in that *istant land* you come from? Cut rope, Simon. I now you're a genie. Joey told me. Mary told him vhen he showed her the flower you two planted."

Lucky leaned against the car, hands in pockets, vatching the whispered argument. Simon closed is eyes. *Was nothing secret with these people?* "I'm djinni," he said and opened his eyes.

Chris shrugged. "Whatever. Anyway, I figure ve've got to be pretty safe with you around."

"I do not have my djinn abilities."

"Why not?"

Simon chopped the air with his hand. "It is not mportant. For Abby's sake alone, I cannot let you :ome."

Chris glanced toward the house, then back. Look, Simon, it's this way." Still talking, Chris got n the car. "I'm the one who knows the equipment, letter than either of you. Lucky can't run all of it ly himself, not for the effects you want to create. Vho else you gonna get at this hour? Who else you ;onna trust?"

Listening, Simon sat in the front seat. Lucky tarted the car and pulled away from the curb.

"You told me," Chris continued, "in your culture was of an age to earn a man's status by undergoing trial of passage and accepting responsibility for he outcome of that trial."

"What's your point?" Lucky asked as he melded

into the sparse Westbank Expressway traffic.

"This is my passage. I want to do this for Ms Calderone. I'll stand behind my actions, regardless of what happens."

Simon gazed at Chris's determined face. The smooth features of a child were no more. In the darkness, he'd acquired the strong edges of a man willing to take responsibility to protect what was his.

"As you say, you know how to run the equipment." Simon glanced around and gave Lucky a quick look. "And we seem to be underway."

Chris did not give a juvenile, jubilant shriek. Instead, he stared back at Simon. "I'll do my best."

They pulled into an empty parking spot in front of Dustyn's rental house. Lucky had parked Elvina's car there earlier to be assured of a spot, but they didn't need it. The equipment was heavy, and the need for silence and stealth made the task difficult, but eventually they wrestled it to the door. Chris watched, mute and solemn, while Lucky picked the lock. Simon crossed his arms and waited, hating resorting to such crude methods.

The place smelled of alcohol and paint. The open kitchen to their left was immaculate, but the living room revealed the occupation of the owner. Tubes of oils, charcoals, and chalk littered every surface. Two easels, one taller than the other, stood angled to the window, half completed pictures on each. Simon strolled over and saw a picture of Zoe, kneeling down at the edge of a deep green pond, her arm outstretched, sparks coming from her palm. The depths of the water concealed an elfin face.

Mary's work.

A snore came from the other room. Lucky peered past the unlatched door. He lifted one thumb in what Simon assumed was a positive signal and mouthed, "He's alone."

While Chris and Lucky set up the equipment, Simon donned the hooded robe he'd brought from Kaf. The fabric, a dark blue shot deep with silver, molded to him and defined his presence by shadowy glints. His face alone would remain distinct, illuminated by a tiny flashlight clipped under his robe. When Chris nodded their readiness, Simon pulled up the hood.

Dustyn Calderone was about to encounter the unknown.

Simon took a step, and his knees buckled. He braced one hand against the wall and took a deep breath. *Not now!* The weakness could not be allowed to overcome him.

After another deep breath, Simon glided into the room. He gazed for a moment at the sleeping man, his lips curling in derision. A weak face, even in repose.

Simon clapped his hands. Outside the door, Chris made the sound they had recorded earlier reverberate and grow in intensity. Drawing on centuries of haughty djinn demeanor, Simon crossed his arms across his chest, stilled his shaking hands, and waited.

Dustyn shot upright in bed. He stared, rubbed his eyes, and stared again. "Simon? What do you mean by breaking in here? Get out before I call the police." He fumbled for the bedside phone, but, thanks to Lucky's visit, neither lights nor phone worked.

"I come for you to admit the truth, human," Simon boomed.

Dustyn's hand faltered. *"Human?* Like you're not? Man, you're insane. I knew it when Mary told me those crazy stories. Poor kid, surrounded by a bunch of old women, a mother who ignores her, and a man who thinks he's Mork."

Mork?

Dustyn swung out of bed and pulled on a pair of jogging shorts. "This trick won't stop me from taking Mary. She's an artist; she appreciates my work. We can exhibit together. The sales will be phenomenal."

The self-centeredness of a man who would use his daughter for his own aggrandizement disgusted Simon. "Is that why you destroy the reputation of her mother?" Simon reached forward. Eyes wide, Dustyn watched the robe, as the magical fabric grew and reformed to once more cover Simon's arms.

"I don't know what you're talking about, man." The weak words barely sounded above a low, insistent beat. Dustyn reached behind himself, toward the telephone.

Simon lifted his chin. Utter fatigue pierced him in radiating bursts. He gritted his teeth and scowled at Dustyn. From the corner of his eye, he saw glittering lights. Chris and Lucky must be projecting the glow of gold and the sparkle of diamond into the room, surrounding Simon in an unTerran aura. "Do not lie to me," Simon hissed and was gratified to see Dustyn pale. "Do not move!"

Dustyn stopped reaching for the phone.

Simon lifted his hands above his head, hating that he had to use a packaged trick, hoping he could do this without setting his hand on fire, and made the practiced motions. White flame blazed from his hand. He held it aloft, knowing it would look as if he held a magically lit fire in his palm. "Do you remember the salamander?" From his reaction, obviously Dustyn did. This might be a gimmick, but t appeared to be an effective one. "That was but a small sample of my powers."

"You're nuts. I'll see you're sent to DePaul Hospital."

"Who will be believed? You, who would claim I have magical powers, or me, who will remain silent and let their conclusions come?" Simon paused for a moment. "But you and I, we shall know the truth."

Solomon, he hoped Dustyn caved in soon. He closed his hand around the dying heat. Ouch! Despite the protective salve he'd smeared on his palm, that hurt. The hurt was minor, however, compared to the fatigue sapping his strength. Simon poked one finger into the flesh above Dustyn's heart. "Shall I stop this from beating?"

A faint drumming sound began.

Dustyn was panting, his fear working against him, making him believe. The room grew warmer, the drumming beat more insistent.

"No, no," Dustyn screamed. "It wasn't me. It was Roger. All Roger's ideas. I didn't want to destroy Zoe; I just wanted my daughter. Roger said he'd make sure I was named custodial parent. He planned everything."

Simon glared at him. The drumming slowed, its deep bass sounding ominous in the otherwise silent room. Simon slipped a thin, blunt-tipped wire from beneath his sleeve. In the darkness and glitter, the wire could not be seen. He traced it across Dustyn's throat. "Your breath grows short, for you tell me lies, human!"

Dustyn clutched his neck. "Stop it! I just gave him the information he needed. Contracts she had, stuff like that. That's all! I swear it, that's all. Roger Broussard told me what he wanted, and I found it out."

"The bail for Isaiah Knox was not information!

The damaged disk was not information!" The windows rattled with the slow pounding force of the bass.

"Roger said I had to be in as deep as him. He wasn't satisfied with the disk. Said if we got Knox out, we could make sure he was suspected, not us." Dustyn buried his face in his palms. "I don't want to do more. I just want to sell my art."

Simon waved his hand. The drumming quieted and resumed its normal rhythm. Dustyn took a deep breath.

"I will leave your judgment to the humans." Simon heard a rustle when Chris left, taking the evidence and extra equipment as planned. Simon covered the sound with words. "It is you who will be blamed, for it is you who *betrayed!*" A pain slashed through his gut, making his voice harsh and unyielding.

"No, no! I'll do anything."

"Go to the police. Tell them what you have told me. Absolve yourself." Simon lifted one hand. "But beware of treachery. My minions shall be watching you."

Simon inched backward. He was almost finished. A projected image of himself, the hologram Chris had been working on, stayed in the room, fooling the eye in the darkness. Silently counting, Simon timed his exit. Eight, nine, ten . . . On cue, the holographic flames surrounded his image. It appeared he stood in the room, engulfed in flames, but not consumed. Dustyn reached out a hand, but before he could touch the illusion, the image faded.

Simon and Lucky fled the apartment with the last of the equipment and met Chris outside.

"I'll keep an eye on him," Lucky said. "He'll go to the police station, never fear. We've got Roger Broussard nailed. You get the kid home, Simon."

Simon nodded, unable to speak. The need for re-vitalization overwhelmed him. He stumbled to the car. "Drive us home, Chris."

Chris leaped into the driver's seat, not realizing the distress behind the request. On the trip home, he relived every detail of the evening, enthusiastically describing how he had created the effects.

Simon leaned his head against the seat back. Solomon, he didn't think he could make it back to Zoe. Not that that would make any difference. They had frightened Dustyn with illusions and tricks, but illusions and tricks would not get him back to Kaf. Only true *ma-at* could do that.

He had no way of returning to Kaf. He had no way of fighting off the fatigue that enveloped him in endless waves. Without the vitalizing powers of Kaf, he would die.

He wanted to see Zoe.

At the house, Chris pulled into the driveway, and then whispered, "Thanks for taking me, Simon."

Simon barely heard the words. He opened the door, rolled out of the car, and struggled to his feet. Zoe. He wanted Zoe.

"Simon, what's wrong? You're hurt. What happened?"

"Zoe," Simon muttered.

Chris raced to his side and braced him as he walked haltingly to the house. The youth flung open the back door and shouted, "Ms. Calderone!"

A shout awoke Zoe. Deep in sleep, it took her a moment to realize that Chris was calling her. At three in the morning? She raced into the kitchen, fastening the belt on her robe.

Simon leaned against the counter, propped up by Chris.

"What's going on?" Zoe asked. "Do you know what time it is? *Where have you been?*"

Mary came in, rubbing sleepy eyes. "I heard some noise."

Chris glanced at her, then back at Zoe. "I'll explain later, Ms. Calderone. Right now, Simon needs help."

Zoe saw Simon's face whiten. A shudder went through him. He gripped the countertop and swallowed hard. She raced to his side and braced him against her. "Are you sick?"

He straightened. "I—" He swayed, and then caught himself.

Zoe wrapped an arm around his waist. "What's wrong? Are you bleeding?" She patted him, searching for sticky wetness.

"No blood. Must . . . lie . . . down."

"My room's closest. Chris, help me get him there. Mary, call 911 for an ambulance."

Simon gripped her arm. "No!"

"You need a hospital."

"No. I will not go. They cannot help. Swear you will not send me there. Swear it!"

Zoe swallowed and nodded. "Go get Elvina," she told Mary. Maybe Simon needed something beyond the understanding of modern medicine.

She and Chris struggled down the hall bearing Simon's weight. He shuffled his feet but did little more to help. Working together, they soon had him sprawled on Zoe's bed. Chris took off Simon's shoes and covered him with the spread. Not knowing what else to do, Zoe found a thermometer and stuck it under his tongue, while she took his pulse.

His temperature was higher than normal for a human. Was that typical for djinn? His pulse was weak, fluttery. He groaned, wrapped his arms around himself, and shivered. She didn't know what to do. She didn't know what was wrong. A raw sense of helplessness invaded her, leaving her cold and shaken.

Zoe clutched the spread beside Simon. "What were you doing tonight, Chris?"

He sketched at their midnight call on Dustyn. Zoe knew he'd left out a few pertinent details, but those were unimportant. Simon's illness was paramount.

"Nothing happened that might have caused this?"

"No."

Simon moaned, and Zoe's chest tightened in pain. When Chris handed her a damp cloth, she laid it across Simon's forehead. Elvina, followed by Mary, bustled into the room.

Mary paled when she saw the stricken djinni. "Wish, Mom. Make him better."

"I can't, baby." Zoe could barely push the words out. "He has to grant the wishes, and he can't right now." *Because of my stupid wish!*

"We've got to do something," Mary wailed.

Zoe leaned down and adjusted the covers. "What's wrong, Simon? Tell me. What can we do?"

"Nothing," Simon moaned. "Only Kaf will help. Must revitalize."

"What's he mean, Mom?"

Zoe grabbed Simon's hand. Tears blurred her vision. "You need to return to Kaf? For strength?"

Simon nodded weakly. "No *ma-at*. Can't find the way back."

Without his magic, he hadn't been able to return to Kaf. Now he was fading before her eyes.

Oh, God, I did this to him.

She ran a hand across his face, needing to touch him. His skin was coated with sweat. Her gut clenched in fear. They had to keep him alive until his magic returned. Five more days; they only needed five more days.

"We've gotta do something," Chris said, his voice cracking.

Simon opened his eyes. "Only Kaf. You swore, no hospital." His eyes drifted shut.

Zoe gripped Simon's hand tighter, willing her strength to him. "No," she said savagely. "I won't let you give up, Simon. Withdraw if you must, save your strength. Just don't leave us."

He took a shuddering breath. "I try, but I fear . . ." His eyes opened a slit, the thick lashes a heavy frame. "You restored . . . faith, Zoe. All of you. Faith in goodness." Simon swallowed once. "Tell him, *Man khaley dust darum.*"

"Tell who?"

"You were my strength, my friend." He sank deeper in the pillow. "Tell Darius." His eyes closed, and he became motionless.

Darius!

Darius had said to call him if she needed help.

Darius could take Simon to Kaf. If it wasn't too late.

Zoe gripped Simon's armbands. Her hands couldn't circle them entirely, for Simon was so muscled. The edge of the metal cut into her palms, but she didn't relinquish an ounce of pressure.

Darius, she called, trying to open her mind to the mysteries Elvina and Mary and Simon had attempted to show her. *Darius. Simon needs you. Come now, Darius. Come.*

Nothing. He wasn't listening or he wasn't responding.

Darius! she shouted in her mind.

Still, nothing.

"What's she doing?" Zoe heard Mary whisper.

"Shhh, child," Elvina replied in a thin voice. "She's working magic."

"Blast, you, Darius," she roared, flinging her head

312

back, sending the words skyward. "If you have any feeling for Simon, come here, now. I love him! Show me you love him as much as I do, as much as a mere human."

Simon moaned, low and weak.

"You promised me!" she screamed.

Behind her, she felt a rush of wind. The force staggered her, but she kept her hands wrapped around Simon's arms, unwilling to risk breaking contact.

Darius was at Zoe's side in an instant and just as quickly judged the problem. "The idiot," Darius snapped. "Why did he wait so long to return?"

"He couldn't," Zoe confessed. "I wished his powers away."

Darius glared at her. His dark eyes snapped with anger. "Then you are to blame."

"I know," Zoe whispered. "Can you help him?"

"Let go of him."

Painfully, Zoe opened her cramped fingers and stepped away.

Darius bent over and wrapped Simon's limp arm about his neck. He straightened, pulling Simon with him. "He will not return until he can do so on his own, for I shall never send him here."

"Is he going to be all right?" Zoe asked.

"I think the summons came in time." Darius took the side of his robe and pulled it across the two of them.

Zoe laid a hand on his arm. "Will you let me, us, know how he is?"

Darius stared at her, his face hard with emotion. Then his harsh look softened. "I shall let you know."

Zoe watched the two djinn disappear in a whirlwind.

Chapter Nineteen

The four days following Darius's departure with Simon were eventful ones for Zoe. After Simon's late-night visit, Dustyn went to the police. Though details of the resulting investigation were unconfirmed, bad news gossip has a way of seeping out, and Roger Broussard was well on his way to becoming persona non grata in the New Orleans business community.

The police had released Elvina. She showed no signs of forgiving Lucky for his part in the fiasco, though he had attempted to make amends. Isaiah Knox was home. Business at ZEVA was picking up again. Crescent City Curios had broken with Broussard and offered Zoe a chance to resubmit. Most important, Mary's custody was no longer an issue.

Now, Zoe stared at the colorful images on her computer screen, unmoved and unexcited by her creation except for the dancing salamander in one corner. The salamander grinned before disappearing from the screen, and Zoe pressed her fist against her lips, remembering. Work had always been her escape, her shield, but burying herself in it this time had not helped.

She picked up a bottle of cologne Leo had sent over. The scent was called Cinnamon Buns, and the bottle had a rearview picture of a man in a thong. When she opened the bottle and sniffed, cinnamon, pungent and sweet, teased her nostrils. She dabbed a drop on her wrists, delaying a return to the salamander.

Keeping busy had not eased her worry. Or her loneliness.

Worry about Simon remained foremost, worry that could only be alleviated by knowing he survived and was well. Why hadn't Darius returned? Had something gone wrong?

The loneliness would be a part of her forever.

Zoe pushed back her chair, stretched out her legs, and faced her emotions.

Would she have been better off never knowing Simon? The answer was immediate and emphatic. No.

He'd given her something that even her love for Mary and her satisfaction with ZEVA had not given her, a joy in life that had been missing for a long time, perhaps always. He'd given her completeness, filled the missing piece of her. From him, she'd learned to laugh and enjoy life: the ups and downs, the lost dreams, and the wishes fulfilled. She'd felt the love of a woman for a man.

Or for a djinni, she added ruefully.

A sudden wind propelled her chair forward. Her stomach hit the keyboard, forcing the breath from her. Zoe shoved her chair back and sprang from her seat. "Simon?"

The chair flew into a shin. The top of her head

hit a chin. Teeth clicked sharply together.

"Ouch. You're a walking disaster, human." The melodious voice had a distinct edge.

Zoe rubbed the top of her head, turned, and glared at the djinni, who'd moved a step back. "You've got a hard chin, Darius."

"No harder than your head."

"How's Simon?"

Darius rubbed his jaw. "I can't believe I didn't move out of the way fast enough."

Zoe grabbed the lapels of his burnt-orange robe. "How is Simon?" She spaced each word for emphasis.

"In Kaf," Darius replied, still rubbing his chin.

Zoe shook him slightly. "Not where. How?"

Darius raised his brow, and then cast a haughty glance at her fists, which were wrinkling his robe.

Zoe loosened her grip and smoothed the fabric. "Sorry. Please, how is he?"

"He is out of danger."

"Thank God," she whispered, and sank into her chair. The settled weight in her stomach lifted, and relief made her giddy.

"It is I you should thank."

Zoe looked at him. "I do, truly. Thank you, Darius, from the bottom of my heart."

"You are welcome."

"How does he feel?"

"He is tired, still needs to rest."

"He hasn't been alone, has he?"

Darius shook his head. "I have stayed with him."

"I'm glad. You're a good friend."

Darius gave her a curious look. "Simon is a very irritable patient. He says he wants to come back, to dance and play cribbage."

Zoe flushed with vivid memories.

"Oh, ho," Darius said with a knowing look, "I

wondered what he meant. Even without his *ma-at*, Simon can protect his thoughts, but you—you're so transparent."

"Save me from nosy, telepathic djinn," Zoe muttered.

Darius prowled around, reminding her of the first time Simon had been in this room, touching, sniffing, examining. Once or twice he glanced at her.

Zoe sighed. "Spit it out, Darius."

He looked at her, startled. " 'Spit it out'?"

"Clear your craw, vent your spleen, tell me what's bugging you." At his continued puzzlement, she took pity on him. "What do you want to say to me?"

Suddenly Darius stood next to Zoe. He grabbed her chin and tilted her head up. "Why does he have no anger toward you? What is your appeal? It's not as though you are a great beauty. You have no wealth, no magical talents to recommend you, no particular knowledge of our ways."

"You do wonders for a woman's ego." Amused, she mustered only small sarcasm in response to his insults. Besides, he'd told her Simon wasn't angry with her. That was a credit in her ledger book, but credits went just so far.

"I know you love him. You said so when you called to me."

"No secrets from you djinn."

"What does he see in you? Why did he send me back to tell you of his recovery as soon as we knew he would survive?" Darius persisted, ignoring her other comments.

"Ask Simon." She smiled sweetly.

Darius tilted her head to the side. "I did. He said you were kind and would be worried." He tilted her head to the other side.

"If you start checking my teeth," Zoe said amiably, "then I will get angry. Not a pretty sight, I warn you."

"Do you threaten me, human?" His hand dropped.

Aw hell, he was starting to grow and spark. At least he'd let go of her head first.

"Me? What could I possibly do to you?"

Darius stepped back and crossed his arms. "Are you laughing at me?"

Zoe held up her hand, her thumb and forefinger an inch apart. "Just a little. Simon taught me to have a sense of humor about you guys."

He perched on top of the small sofa and frowned. "Amazing, he still speaks well of you."

"You thought he'd hate me for what I'd done?"

Darius rested his chin in his hand and levitated a bit from the sofa. "I remember his fury over Minau."

"Minau? What's Minau?"

Darius sat straight. "He never told you?"

"Told me what?" Zoe's eyes narrowed.

"About Minau, the woman who pledged to be his *zaniya*."

Zoe remembered the clothes on Kaf. *My feelings for her withered.*

Still levitating, Darius cocked his head, studying her with djinn intensity. A hardness came into his eyes. "Simon loved her, passionately, but Minau betrayed him. Instead of joining with Simon, she returned to her sorcerer father and gave him Simon's true name. With this knowledge, her father created the spell that binds Simon to this day."

The words, deliberately spoken, killed any faint, unexpressed hope Zoe had had that Simon might love her back. She had known he had many years of distrust to overcome, but not the bone-deep, biting source. He'd been betrayed by a human, by a woman who had violated his trust in the worst possible way. How could she hope to erase such deep bitterness? A month with her wouldn't make a difference.

"I am surprised he did not entrust you with the story," Darius added with cruel nonchalance, landing back on the sofa.

Trust. Simon did not trust her. Why should he? The thought hurt more than she would have believed possible. She closed her eyes, squeezing them against the pain.

Zoe felt as though a fly were buzzing through her brain. Her eyes shot open to see Darius's intent gaze. Annoyance—welcomed, for it shrouded the pain—suffused her as she realized what he was doing. She scowled and shook a finger at him. "Get out of my thoughts, Darius."

Darius sucked in a breath. "I begin to see your appeal. You *do* love him, without conditions. For a djinni who's been fulfilling wishes so long, such devotion must be appealing."

"You make me sound like a dim-witted puppy dog."

Darius smiled.

Even Zoe, whose soul was filled with Simon, felt her breath catch for a beat. *He's so blasted beautiful, and he knows it. Whoever lands him will have her hands full.*

His smile widened. "I don't intend to ever be landed."

"Be careful. Such statements tempt the gods. Look what happened when I said I didn't believe in wishes."

Darius looked around and made a small movement with his hand, as though warding off encroaching spells. "This is something I need to think on. I shall tell Simon you are well. He won't be back until his powers return. Prepare to use your final wish then." He cinched his robe tighter, folded his arms, and disappeared. Papers flew around the room.

Smiling, Zoe shook her head. "One of these days, you're going to have to clean up the mess those exits leave."

Then her smile faded. Papers half gathered, she stared at the spot where Darius had disappeared. *Prepare to use your wish.*

Memories spun through her: Simon getting angry, his tricks to get her to wish, playing cribbage together.

The loneliness, the pain of Simon's lack of trust, would always be there, but she had work she liked, a daughter she loved, and solid partners as perceptive as they were eccentric. No more would she forget to appreciate, to laugh, or to share.

And she had memories of a loving most women would pay every last blessed red cent for.

Dropping the papers to the floor, Zoe smiled and scraped back her chair to the computer. Now that she knew Simon was healing, the urge to work and create filled her.

And, at last, she was prepared to use her final wish.

Simon stared at the ceiling above his bed. By Kaf time it had been but hours, yet he was heartily bored with the sight. He sat up, fought the dizziness, and made his way outside to the chaise.

He sank to the cushions, annoyed by the persistent weakness, and stretched out. The rising sun spread fingers of warmth across his face and chest. Simon closed his eyes and sighed. That felt good. He let his hands drop to rest on the tiled courtyard.

Strength returned, bringing vigor with it. His

breathing quickened. His muscles twitched, demanding recognition and activity, as though he were coming to life after a long hibernation. The strength of Kaf returned to him and awakened him. When he felt strong enough to sit up, he flexed his hands and rotated his head. His headache was gone, his neck no longer sore. Now that he had revitalized, Simon found he was starved.

He had no food in the house. The *ma-at* teased the edges of his mind, a word here, a motion there, but not enough to allow him to gather edibles. He strode over to the fountain, cupped his hands, and took a drink. The cool, refreshing water held the faint, sharp taste of his homeland. He drank deep, filling his belly and his soul.

Satiated, he started pacing. Where was Darius? Simon wanted to return to Terra, and he couldn't do it on his own, not yet. He stopped and grimaced. When had he come to yearn for Terra as well as Kaf?

Some of the weakness must be lingering, Simon decided, and resumed his pacing. When his *ma-at* returned, he would no longer feel torn.

The gust of wind told him of Darius's arrival.

"It's about time. Take me back," Simon told his friend, before the djinni took a first breath.

Darius matched his crossed-arm, wide-legged stance. "No. I won't risk your health again. You'll go back when your *ma-at* can take you."

Simon glared at him. Darius stared back impassively.

"Did you find Zoe?" Simon asked, tacitly giving in.

"Yes. I told her you had recovered and would return when your powers were restored."

"How was she?"

"Do you really care?"

That startled Simon. "Of course I care. Zoe and her family—they're special."

"You still don't trust her, though."

"What do you mean?"

"You refused to tell her how weak you were. You haven't even trusted her with the knowledge of Minau. You didn't tell her Simon was not your true name. Do you believe she would seek out your real name, to use it against you?"

"No." The answer came quickly, without thought.

"Then why not tell her?"

Why not? Why haven't I told her?

"Because you are djinn, and she is human." Darius answered the unspoken question. "You can never bring yourself to fully trust her. Or love her," he added. "Let her go. Let her find a mate among the humans, as you will do with the djinn."

Simon did not like that suggestion, not at all. He braced his hands on his hips. "Why do you care?"

Darius's lips twitched in a faint, rueful smile. "Sometimes my motives are obscure even to me." He gathered his robe and his power about him. "Your time of servitude is nearing its end, and you will soon regain your rightful place among the djinn. The next time we meet, I shall be overjoyed to welcome you home, Simon, my friend." The whirlwind of Darius's departure caught the last word and sent it spinning into the skies of Kaf.

Darius had left a plate of fruit, spiced meat, and cinnamon rolls. Biting into one of the rolls, Simon considered what Darius had said.

His friend had only put into words what Simon had already decided. So why, when stated so baldly, did it sound so wrong?

There was time before he could go back.

He had time to think.

* * *

She'd give him his freedom; that was what she'd do.

Zoe propped up her feet on the coffee table and flipped through her multimedia magazine. Simon had come so close to dying, damn his djinni pride, by refusing to tell her of his weakness. Her fingers drummed the slick pages of the magazine. No, *she* had brought him to that with her second wish. Her last wish would be to return his tablet.

Simon would return to Kaf, of that she had no doubt. He was not of earth, and he couldn't live here. She had to face that reality. She closed her eyes and leaned her head back against the sofa, her arms wrapped around her waist. It hurt to know he'd be gone forever, hurt deep inside.

Yet helping Simon was the right thing to do. She could do this for him, something no one else could, or would, do. That knowledge would comfort and sustain her.

She heard footsteps come into the room, pause, then shuffle forward. Zoe opened her eyes. Elvina and Oz had come in.

While Oz jumped onto the sofa to rub his soft fur against her leg, Elvina dropped two papers into her lap, and then plunked herself into a chair next to the sofa. "I found those in the computer room."

Absently petting Oz, Zoe eyed her friend's impassive features before she glanced at the papers. The crumpled one on top was mumbo-jumbo, but her attention snagged on the drawing in one corner—a face that bore a slight resemblance to Simon. Her eyes narrowed. Whoever had drawn this had seen the haughty arrogance of the djinn. The features were harsh, with a hint of cruelty about the mouth. Even though smudged by age and fax transmission, the eyes were chips of black ice. This djinni sent shivers through her veins.

Zoe looked up to see Elvina's worried look. Uh-oh. She wasn't going to like whatever was on her friend's mind.

"What are you going to do when Simon returns?" Elvina asked.

"Use my last wish."

Elvina nodded, as though she'd expected that answer. She rubbed her crystal. "Have you decided what you're going to wish for?"

Zoe took a deep breath. "I'm going to wish for Simon's freedom. He has a turquoise tablet that must be returned for him to be unbound. I'm going to wish for that." There—she'd said it. For her, that made it real and irrevocable. She shifted her feet to the sofa. Laying her magazine and the papers to the side, she wrapped her arms around her legs and rested her cheek on her knees. Within her, a deep sense of cold loss warred with the warm satisfaction that told her that she was doing the right thing. She pressed her lips together against the surge of feelings and hugged her legs tighter.

"You always give so unstintingly to those you love." Elvina's words were soft, but Zoe heard them.

Yes, I do love Simon, and I'm not ashamed to admit it.

Elvina cleared her throat and looked at Zoe. "When did you decide about the wish?"

"When I was in Kaf and talked to Darius. You know, that's the first time I *really* realized that not all djinn grant wishes. Simon is spellbound, exiled from his own people. No one, not even an arrogant djinni, deserves that. Then we came back, and I let my temper get the best of me. You know the rest. I decided not to say anything until Simon returned to normal." She rubbed her hands on her legs. "To tell him my plans before he could do anything about granting my wish seemed so self-serving."

"And you wanted him to experience being human?"

Zoe gave her friend a rueful smile. "There was that, too."

"I know you better than you think." Elvina returned to stroking the crystal at her neck.

Zoe shot a worried glance at the papers. Whenever Elvina faced a difficult decision or an unpleasant task, she rubbed her crystal for calm and strength. Something was bothering her, and those papers were involved.

"Why didn't you wish while you were on Kaf?"

Zoe shifted uneasily. "I was afraid wishes wouldn't work there. I wanted to think about how I should phrase them, what little thing I could ask for. I thought Mary might want to say good-bye."

"All valid reasons."

A knot formed in Zoe's stomach. Elvina wanted something more from her, an admission of hidden feelings she didn't want to examine or explain. She turned her face away.

"Were you scared, Zoe?" Elvina asked very softly. "Did you think that, once he had what he wanted, Simon would abandon you on Kaf? Did you still not fully trust? Were you unable to give total control to another?"

Zoe didn't answer.

Elvina sighed. "Read the translation on the other paper before you make that wish. It's not going to be as easy as you expect."

What could she mean? Zoe heard Elvina get to her feet.

"If you decide you can't go through with it, we can find people to summon Simon and finish his binding. If only wishes weren't so tempting. . . ."

Zoe knew Elvina was thinking of Lucky.

After Elvina left, Zoe stared at the papers, afraid

to find out what they contained. Finally, she unfolded herself and reached for them. Oz meowed at being disturbed.

Even in a fax, the dark strokes of the writing radiated power, although the words—indeed, even the lines, slashes, and dots of individual letters—were undecipherable to Zoe. She laid the first page aside and picked up the second paper. For a moment, she couldn't decipher the bold, elaborate script. She glanced away, took a deep breath, and gathered the determination to read whatever it said.

She read it twice to make sure she understood the strange sentences; then she reached out to pet Oz, his soft, rumbling purr a needed comfort.

"I can't wish him back his tablet, Oz."

All the verbiage couldn't hide that one fact.

A simple wish for the tablet would be useless; it was under an enchantment, as well as hidden. In order to return the tablet to its djinni owner before the conditions of the spellbinding were met, the summoner must wish himself, along with the djinni, to the hidden location of the tablet.

"Where would a magician hide a djinni's tablet so it would remain concealed for a thousand years?" she asked Oz.

Oz didn't have an answer, but Zoe did. Horrific visions—of the fiery interior of a volcano, of the ocean depths where no sunlight penetrated, of a mountaintop with no air—answered her frightened question. She would be expected to wish herself and Simon there? It was beyond belief.

"Even if I did go, I wouldn't know what to do. What do you suppose this means?" She pointed to one stanza. " 'Thrice must thou harken to the true name of the djinni, for thrice must thou be blessed. Bless thrice more and the power shall be envisited to thee, power beyond all imagining. Heed the call of eternity and the song of the siren bound.' " Zoe gave Oz a wry grin. "It's all like that, clear as mud to someone who speaks modern English. There's also a nasty, stark warning, Oz."

She read the words again, aloud this time.

" 'I call to thee, foolish heart, to beware fulfilling the time of the djinni. I implore thee be wary of the djinni, unbound and unfettered by the control of the rituals, for he is a creature not of earth, nor of man. I tell thee be wary of the place of magick, from which escape comes not with the powers of the eye, but with the powers of the mind and the strengths of the mage. Heed these warnings well, at the cost of thy soul.' "

The paper fluttered to the sofa. Zoe leaned back her head. In other words, once she handed over the tablet, she'd be at the mercy of a djinni in a place she had no prayer of escaping alone.

She remembered the night of the neighborhood picnic. Even now, the memories held power over her. The terror closed her throat. The helplessness made her hands shake. The loneliness knotted her stomach.

Her hand stroked Oz's back, willing calm to return. "I love Simon, Oz, I really do."

She did love Simon, Zoe knew.

She just didn't know if she had that much trust.

Chapter Twenty

The next night, pulling into her driveway after teaching a one-day seminar, Zoe still worried about the problem. She glanced at her watch for the twentieth time. The moment when Simon regained his djinn abilities was at hand, fifteen minutes until the hour she'd wished him human two weeks ago.

Choose. After using her wish, she could arrange for others to call Simon and complete the terms of his binding. Elvina, Abby, Vivian, she trusted. To whom else could she entrust the unlimited power of three wishes? Look what had happened with Lucky, what he'd done.

Decide. What if the location were uninhabitable? She could be burned to a crisp or implode from unbearable pressures or suffocate within seconds of transporting.

What if Simon left her? What would she do? What would happen to Mary? To ZEVA?

She gripped the door handle but didn't get out, still deep in thought.

Choose. Security and safety, or a man's life.

Decide. Did she trust Simon with her life?

The car door jerked open, pulling her sideways from her seat. Before she hit the concrete, Zoe found herself yanked upward. She cried out as her arm was wrenched behind her back.

"Quiet," Roger Broussard snarled, the yellow light from the streetlights giving a demonic cast to his contorted face. Zoe rammed her elbow back, but from its twisted angle the blow didn't command enough force to do any damage. She stomped her foot down, hard. Roger grunted but didn't release her. Damn, why hadn't she worn heels?

Something jabbed her side.

"Careful now. You wouldn't want this to go off."

Zoe stilled. Something hard and blunt was jammed against her ribs. A gun? What did the barrel of a gun feel like? She couldn't struggle or call out. What if Mary came outside? What if he wasn't bluffing? The risks were too high. She remained motionless.

"That's better."

"Why are you doing this?"

"Because your friend sounded the alarm, the fire didn't destroy my records as intended, and the investigation has discovered certain, ah—irregularities in my business. I'm finished, Zoe, destroyed. If I'm going down, I'm not going alone; I'm taking you with me."

Zoe took another look at him. His normally immaculate hair was disheveled, and she'd never seen him without a tie.

The polished facade had cracked.

"We're going inside, where you will load this into

your operating systems." He held up a disk.

Zoe swallowed. "What's on it?"

"A particularly nasty virus. One that will corrupt every program and every file. Irretrievably."

"No!" With damage like that, ZEVA would be finished. Reconstructing all her records would be a nightmare, and she couldn't afford to replace all her software. He would destroy her and everything she'd worked for.

Roger shoved her forward. Pain shot between her shoulder and side. Fear made breathing a near impossibility.

"Remember, I've got a gun. I'll use it."

From the corner of her eye, Zoe saw dull metal. He did have the gun. He wasn't bluffing. She stumbled forward in silence, fearful of bringing Mary into this.

The computer room was dark, lit only by the moonlight streaming in the window. Neither Zoe nor Roger bothered with a lamp. Roger wiped the sweat from his face.

"Turn on the computer." He emphasized his command by hiking her arm higher. Her muscles burning from the abuse, Zoe complied. Stark light from the monitor screen blinked into eerie brilliance in the shadowy room. Roger's hand shook as he inserted the disk in the drive. "Execute the program," he said, his eyes bright with malice.

A whirlwind tangled her hair. Zoe and Roger stumbled away from the computer. The wind, the tightening in her stomach, the awareness stiffening her spine told Zoe all she needed to know.

Simon had returned.

He looked different. There was an aura of power, of danger, of alienness about him. While she watched, his short, loose robe of silky red shifted to denims and T-shirt. She felt Roger recoil and then shake his head. Apparently he decided not to believe his eyes, for he jabbed the gun harder against her. Zoe winced.

Simon's gaze ran over her, then to Roger. His eyes narrowed, and Zoe saw the silver sparks gathering around his hair. He looked back at her, his gaze more heated than before.

"What happens here?" The words reverberated in the deep night.

"So, it seems your interest in my services was a sham, Mr. James." Roger's words sounded shrill above the computer's hum.

Simon ignored him. "Will you use your last wish, Zoe? I cannot help you otherwise."

Zoe's gaze caught on the thin disk nestled in the drive. A couple of keystrokes and ZEVA would be destroyed. She couldn't think of any way to prevent it.

She looked back at Simon, and all doubts and indecision vanished, leaving the calm of trust. She trusted him and his magic. If she wished, he would set everything right.

But regardless of the consequences, her third wish was for Simon, for his freedom. Zoe shook her head.

Simon jerked back, as though she'd struck him.

"Some noble lover you've got, Zoe," Roger said. He waved the gun toward the computer. "Execute the program."

In one of his impossibly quick moves, Simon got between them and the computer. "Let her go. Cease this folly."

"No, Simon," Zoe shouted. "He's got a gun."

Roger swung the gun from Zoe toward Simon. Simon raised his hands, fingers outstretched and pointing forward. At the movement, Roger dropped her arm and braced his gun with both hands. Zoe, standing next to him, felt his muscles bunch.

She could wish to spare Simon. Her dry throat tightened, blocking the words with fear. Instead, she rammed her shoulder into Roger.

The gun did not fire. She heard Roger scream, a bloodcurdling sound.

His gun had turned to a snake that wrapped itself around his arm and buried its fangs in his flesh. Roger's scream turned to a high-pitched shriek of pain. He let go of the snake's tail. It fell to the ground and turned back into a gun. Zoe kicked it away from Roger, but she needn't have bothered.

Roger backed away from the gun, his face filled with horror. He turned, ready to flee. Zoe stuck out her foot, and he tumbled to the floor. His fingers clawed on the hardwood surface as he scrambled toward the door.

"Do not!" Simon was blocking his path.

Zoe reached over and pushed the eject button, removing the dangerous disk from her system.

Roger halted and stared at Simon in terror, his hand clutching his injured arm. "What are you?" he hissed.

Simon looked at him innocently. "Whatever do you mean?"

"The gun. The *snake.*" Revulsion filled his voice.

"The gun is there." Simon nodded once at the floor. "The snake? Somebody's pet that got loose and has slithered home."

"Is its bite poisonous?" Zoe asked and moved to Simon's side.

"No. Do you wish it to be?"

Zoe rubbed her sore shoulder and then shook her head. She leaned against his arm. "Thank you, Simon. I could not have stopped him by myself."

His lids were half-lowered, veiling his dark eyes

as he looked into her face. She saw no warmth, no welcome.

"Are you all right?" she asked. "You are recovered?"

"Yes."

Her hand lifted to his cheek but fluttered down when he flinched. "How did you do that?" she asked. "Your magic doesn't work for me." She grabbed the lapels of his robe. "You might have been killed!"

Simon shrugged, dislodging her hand. "Once he turned the gun on me, you were no longer in danger. *Ma-at* will protect me. Since you did not trust me enough to wish, it was my only option."

He had done what he did, pulled Roger's attention to himself so he could use his magic, even though he believed she trusted him so little, she wouldn't wish to save her life. Zoe reached toward him, treasuring the knowledge that he cared, even if he did not love.

The computer-room door crashed open, making them jump apart, and Elvina raced in. "I was in the kitchen and heard him say he had a gun. I called the police." A distant siren emphasized her words.

The next hour was chaotic. The police asked questions and took statements, discounting Roger's claim that Simon James had attacked him with a snake. Mary, Abby, Joey, and Chris milled around, full of questions.

After the police left with Roger in tow, Zoe took Mary, Chris, and Joey aside. "If you want to say good-bye to Simon, you should do it now."

None of them needed further explanation.

Simon looked puzzled when Mary came up, gave him a big hug, and then burst into tears.

"The danger is over, little one," he said.

"I know. I just wanted you to know, I love you, Simon." She held him tighter.

"I love you, too." Simon said the words as though they were a revelation.

She stepped back. "Maybe you'll come see me sometime."

Before Simon could reply, Chris said, "Thanks for the help you gave me on that special project." He glanced at Abby, then leaned over and whispered in Simon's ear. Simon clapped him on the back, and the two shared a very masculine laugh.

While Joey said his good-byes, Zoe knelt down before Mary, and spoke in a private voice. "I'm going to be away for a little bit, honey. You listen to Miss Elvina while I'm gone. She'll take care of you. She and Miss Vivian and Miss Abby." Eyes filled with tears, Zoe reached out and pulled her daughter into her arms. "I love you, baby. I always will."

"I love you, too, Mom."

Zoe went inside to get the two papers with the ritual, while her partners hovered around Simon. She read through the translation, and then shoved it into her pocket. Simon transported to her side and laid a hand on her shoulder. The warm touch helped banish any lingering soreness from Roger's rough handling.

"You are not injured?" he asked.

Zoe shook her head. She licked dry lips and watched Simon's gaze turn hungry. "Simon, kiss me," she commanded, needing his touch one last time.

His mouth snapped shut in surprise. Then, in a heartbeat, it was covering hers and very deftly opening again. His tongue tangled with hers. His arms pulled her against him, molded her against his hard body. He tugged at her blouse, pulling it from the waistband of her skirt; his hand burrowed eneath the cotton, sliding up her back in soft, warm, kneading circles.

The whirlwind that heralded his arrival was now nside her, leaving her breathless, aching, and wanting.

"You still want me," she whispered.

He nibbled his way from her mouth to her ear. "Shall I demonstrate further?" he breathed against er, and then moved lower, until his cheek rested gainst her chest. "We are alone."

She was selfish enough to want one more night, o want endless nights. No, one more night would nly intensify the loneliness to come. One more ight would only prolong Simon's bondage.

"I want to make my final wish," Zoe said, the low vords rough with need.

His head slowly lifted, but he didn't loosen his mbrace. "I thought you would not."

Zoe stared into his dark eyes. She took a deep reath and patted her pocket. "I'm ready now."

His arms tensed, the muscles becoming iron opes at her waist. He swallowed once and stepped way. His gaze roamed from her toes to her throat, ingering at all parts in between, before settling on er face.

Then, his expression closed. He crossed his arms cross his chest. The denims and T-shirt trans-ormed back into a robe. "What is your wish, Sum-noner?"

Zoe took his hand. "I wish to be taken with thee, he djinni I know as Simon, to the place of enchant-ment, wherein lies thy turquoise tablet. *Dar Solo-non ghavi.*"

Her words buffeted Simon, the roaring in his ears o strong he wondered if he'd heard right. Then, suddenly, he knew! He knew where his tablet lay. Where it had lain hidden all these long years. By Solomon's beard, he could see it! He could feel it!

He laced his fingers through Zoe's and said the necessary words. The wind swirled around them, obliterating the ordinary surroundings of Terra. Simon felt the familiar sensations of exhilaration and of nothingness, heard the howl of the wind, tasted the rawness at the butting edges of the dimensions.

Then, there was cold. Bone-deep cold. And quiet. Deathly quiet.

Somehow, Zoe had moved into his embrace. He felt her shiver. "That has to be the most unsettling way to travel," she whispered.

Simon, gazing around the ancient cave, didn't answer. A sheen of ice covered the ragged rock walls. His breath formed a white cloud in front of him, a cloud that drifted in slow motion in the unmoving air. A faint blue glow filled the room, illuminating expanses but hiding details. He took a deep breath. The cold burned his lungs.

"Where are we?" she asked.

"At the end of Terra, beneath the endless glacier." He tilted his head, searching the room.

There it was!

The woman in his arms shivered again with a fine trembling that continued unabated. Simon let the cold seep inside him, and then protected himself with a jacket of suede and lamb's wool. Welcome though the covering was, he took it off and wrapped it around her.

His attention remained on the source of that faint blue glow. He glided to the small niche in the gray, glistening rocks. The blue light made him squint as he knelt and peered into the opening.

His turquoise tablet! Simon reached out a hand to touch it, to touch and possess it. To be free. After centuries, to be free!

A tingling pain started at his fingertips and spread up his arm, numbing all in its path. He jerked back his hand and shook his arm, ridding it of the shards of ice that had begun crystallizing in his blood.

"Solomon's beard," he hissed. "'Tis still enchanted. Is there no end to your fiendish curse, ancient mage?" His hand clenched in impotent fury.

"I think you need this."

Startled, he looked up at the woman standing beside him. For one moment, entranced by the lure of his tablet, he'd forgotten that Zoe had come with him. Though her face and her toes in her sandals were white with the cold, she stared at him with a steady, warming gaze. The jacket sleeves were too long for her, and they bunched on her arms where she'd shoved them back to free her hands. Only the quiver in her pale fingers betrayed her when she held out a paper.

He took it from her, recognizing the spell of unbinding.

"Oh, wait, I have the translation."

Simon, knowing the ancient words, shook his head. How could he have forgotten? Only a summoner using his rightful name could return the tablet to him. Could he come so close and yet still not attain his tablet? He could feel the power emanating from the niche. His soul called out to it with the longing of the many solitary years, until he trembled with the yearning to hold it.

How could he trust someone else to hold his tablet, to feel the swirling powers of the djinn, of *maat*? How could he trust her not to want to possess and control? The call, the temptation would be strong.

How could he trust any summoner with the knowledge of his true name? Only with his name could he be enslaved again. He had trusted once. He could not survive a second betrayal, a second enslaving.

He could not do it.

"What do I do? I'm not sure I understood all the instructions." The voice beside him was soft. He heard a rustling paper. "I have to say your name three times—Simon, Simon, Simon—then repeat some words."

He turned and looked. Zoe crouched beside him, studying a piece of paper, speaking under her breath as she sounded out the words. His chest tightened with undefined emotion.

He put his hand over the paper. "You need speak my true name."

She shot him an astonished look. "You name isn't Simon?"

"It is not my full, true name."

"Then what is it? Let's finish this, Simon." She wet her lips; the moisture dried instantly in the cold. "Then you'll take me home?"

The note of questioning he heard surprised him. Her brown eyes were wide and bright. The curls he'd created surrounded her head in a soft, dark cloud. One hand clutched the lapels of the jacket together, while the other wrinkled the paper it held. An erratic pulse beat in her throat. He touched it. Her skin was cold beneath his fingers.

"Did you doubt I'd take you home?"

She swallowed. "I can't get out myself; there are no doors. I cannot survive here long." Her breath frosted before her, adding credence to her words.

She glanced at the paper, and then returned her steady gaze to him. "I trust you."

"You knew the conditions the spell set down? And the warnings?"

She nodded.

By Solomon, when all she valued had been threatened, she had not used her wish for herself, but had saved it for him, knowing the cost. She had brought herself to a place of magic, of no escape, going against her every instinct to trust him.

Blessed Solomon, what a woman! The cold receded, replaced by an inner glow. He tried to speak but could not find the needed words. One shaking hand caressed her white cheek.

She had trusted him. He could do no less for her.

Simon drew in a tumultuous breath. "You must pick up the tablet."

Zoe reached into the niche and pulled out the tablet with no difficulty. It sung to Simon, echoing the long years of loneliness. He steeled himself against reaching for it. He could do nothing to coerce or convince. The tablet must be freely transferred.

Simon looked into Zoe's eyes, saw her loyalty and steadfastness, understood he would never know another like her. Capturing her gaze, he said, "My full, true name is Simeon be Darvant-Kaveh, Asha-Kafi, Virahl-Mindar el Shabauh."

Zoe listened intently to the list. *No wonder they preferred nicknames.*

"Say it three times, adding 'I bless this to thee,' after each."

Zoe repeated his name, stumbling once, but Simon corrected her gently before she added the blessing.

The turquoise tablet began to hum. Her hands, where they touched the stone, tingled. The thick gold chain strung through the top dangled across her arm, and an electrical, or magical, charge rushed across it. Strange vibrations spun through her, a surge of power such as she'd never experienced.

Again she repeated his name and the blessing.

New words, words of *ma-at*, began to swirl through her. *I can be anything, do anything,* she realized. Her breath quickened.

A third time, she said the words.

"Say those words on the page." Simon's command was faint.

She looked at the words that would transfer the tablet to Simon. She now knew other words, words that would make her *ma-at* equal to his. Words that would keep him at her side forever.

The promise of the spell came back to her. *Bless thrice more and the power shall be envisited to thee, power beyond all imagining. Heed the call of eternity and the song of the siren bound.*

He had given her the power to rebind him. He had given her the power that Minau had perverted.

Zoe gazed at the djinni crouched before her. His dark eyes were filled with trust, and worry. In the blue light his hair shone with the rich, deep tones of midnight. The skin on his bare arms had tightened with the cold. Dear God, she loved him.

Zoe didn't need the paper. She had the words memorized. Without looking away, she repeated three times, "*Rejan bev alla-Shehan.* I give thee freedom."

She held out the tablet. It glowed a rich, vibrant blue.

He took it, stared at it, turned it around, and then draped the chain over his head. His hand clutched the tablet, convulsing until his knuckles turned white. He rose, and a beatific look came over him.

"I'm free," he whispered. "Finally free."

The tears at the corner of her eyes spilled out. They froze on her cheeks and mouth as she smiled. She wanted to laugh even as she cried with joy.

Before her eyes, he changed again. An inner glow came shining through, surrounding him in a lustrous, golden aura. The power she'd seen in him before had been muted, she realized, for now he radiated it.

He held up his hands, lifted them toward the heavens. The copper wristbands dissolved.

Simeon be Darvant-Kaveh, Asha-Kafi, Virahl-Mindar el Shabauh, known to her as Simon, was free.

Chapter Twenty-one

Before his stunned gaze, the copper wristbands disappeared, taking with them the invisible chains that had surrounded him. Simon moved his arms experimentally, reveling in the passage of air across his wrists. He felt buoyant, no longer bound to the ground but filled with the rush of the wind and the heart of the fire. The ties to Terra fell off, like unwanted ribbons loosened on a package.

He held the tablet in his palm and rubbed his fingers against words of empowerment. The raised edges of the glyphs filled him with the vitality of *maat*, gave him choices and determination. He could once more walk and live among his people. He was free!

Simon looked down at Zoe, still crouched at his feet. Her wide eyes glistened with unshed tears. He saw her swallow and clutch the jacket about her. He helped her rise. Lifting her hand, he kissed the backs of her fingers. *"Motashakker,* Zoe Calderone of Terra." he said, the rasp in his voice making the words barely audible. "Thank you. Now I must take you home."

Her breath exhaled in a tiny cloud of white.

Simon surrounded her two hands with his, feeling her cold skin warm at his touch. In a blink, he transported through the vortex and landed on the sidewalk before Zoe's home.

Zoe's home, no longer his.

"I must leave." The words were true, yet he held her hands, unwilling to let go.

Zoe's gaze roamed across his face, as if memorizing the details. "You have made my life richer for your presence, Simon of Kaf." She leaned forward and gave him a delicate kiss that was over too soon. "Now return to your home and your people." She took a step back and slid her hands from his grip. Her chin lifted and her jaw clenched.

Simon reached forward, but then dropped his hand. Never letting his eyes stray from her face, he transformed his attire to the celebratory red robe and trousers of the djinn. Kaf beckoned. He was going home. Softly, he intoned the words of transporting.

His last sight of Terra was of Zoe, wrapped in the oversized jacket, her eyes bright, her lips pressed tightly together.

Home. Kaf. Landing outside the main city, he looked at the blaze of lights before him. The plaintive sounds of flute and harp, the irregular beat of the drum filled him. It was the final day of Baharshan, an all-day, all-night revelry of sharing and revitalization. For the first time in so many years, he could partake of the feast, perform the dances, touch the altars. Thrills of anticipation wound through him, speeding up the beat of his heart and making his breath uneven.

Simon picked up a fistful of sand. His fingers tightened around the hot grains as he closed his eyes and let go of conscious thought, let only emotion and the essence of being remain. Kaf seeped into him. The bonds that connected him to his homeland grew strong. His djinn power soared.

He opened his fist and let the sand trickle through his fingers, enjoying the sun glinting off the tiny scattered crystals. He lifted his face to draw in the warmth and stood rooted, watching distant figures in their bright robes. At the far side of the city, he could see the shining spires of the schools where he had learned to call and control the *ma-at*. He turned to point out the landmark to Zoe and remembered that he was alone.

Alone. Now that the reality of his return was at hand, he found the exhilaration diminished because she wasn't at his side to share it.

A spray of sand stung his face and arms. Suddenly, he was engulfed in an embrace. "Simon, my friend, you have returned to us." Darius squeezed tighter before letting go and stepping back to eye Simon. "It is so good to have you here."

To greet his friend, not in subterfuge nor in isolation, but freely as equals, was a true treasure to be savored. Simon clapped him on the shoulder. "It is good to be here, Darius."

"So, the woman finally wished? What did she wish for? Did her friends also call you? Their wishes must have been simple if you are back so soon. Come, tell me all. King Taranushi and the court will want to hear your stories." Darius wrapped a companionable arm about Simon's shoulder.

"Her final wish was for my tablet," Simon told him.

Darius stopped and stared. "I thought you could not be wished free."

"She took me to the place of enchantment and gifted me freely with the tablet."

Darius gave a low whistle. "So, the human did not choose the easy path given her. She risked much, for the more difficult, righteous way. Your Zoe is a remarkable woman."

His Zoe. Those words warmed him more than the sands of Kaf.

Darius eyed him for a moment, and then, without a word, transported the two of them to the center of the feast.

The tumult of a hundred voices embraced Simon. The aromas of sizzling meat, sliced oranges, and steeping rose tea made his mouth water. He was surrounded by shades of red; the djinn were dressed in their finest for the celebration.

The mélange of color, sound, and scent was both achingly familiar and curiously strange.

A roar sounded from the front of the room, piercing the clamor. Simon looked toward the source. An immense djinni rose from the distant table. Behind him, a painting of sand and fire shifted from symbols of ritual to those of welcome. King Taranushi had spotted him.

"Simeon el Shabauh!" The king beckoned him forward.

Simon transported to the king's side and made a bow of allegiance. The king grasped his elbow. "It is good to have you back with us. Tomorrow, we shall talk about your return and hear your tales. For tonight, my friend, celebrate, pay homage to our past, eat, and enjoy." He raised his voice. "Friends, tonight we rejoice in the return of Simeon el Shabauh."

Simon blinked. The enthusiastic acceptance

should have delighted him. He found it did not, that he could not so easily dismiss the past.

"Join me at my table," Darius urged. When Simon nodded, he transported them to the edge of the room. Darius waved a hand, and another pillow appeared beside the low table. Simon lowered himself and began to eat. The food was delicious, the tea perfection, but he ate mechanically, ignoring Darius's chatter.

Where was the elation, the feeling of belonging? All this was home, many of the faces familiar. He looked around. Many were not. There had been changes.

Simon found himself wondering what Zoe and Mary and the others were doing. Did they miss him? Wouldn't Mary be thrilled if she could see this?

At the end of the feast, the djinn transported outside the city to the endless sands of the desert. The bonfires grew to a conflagration that burned but did not consume. Simon stood on the edge, watching, responding to the sallies of acquaintances who stopped to welcome him.

"You do not join in, Simon. Is something wrong?" Darius laid a companionable hand on his shoulder.

"I was wishing Zoe were here to share this with me."

Darius tilted his head to look at Simon. "Something is different about you."

Something different? Yes, he did feel different. Puzzled, Simon's mind traced his links to Kaf. They were there, powerful, surging. But . . . something foreign was forged with them.

Terra, he realized. Although Kaf was his home, although he would live here, a part of Terra would always be with him. He took a step toward the fires and stopped.

Zoe was his bond to Terra. In an utterly unselfish act, she had used her final wish to obtain his tablet and his freedom.

Nobody had ever sacrificed for him, had put his needs first.

Zoe was a giver, always willing to support and help. Was that why she had done this? It became urgent that he find out.

Simon grabbed Darius's hand. "I must go back. There are things I must know." He gestured toward the king, rising from the center of the blaze. "Tell them I shall return, but now I must go to Terra."

Darius looked at him with a penetrating gaze. After a moment, he nodded. "You are right. You must go back."

Simon transported to Terra, to the time just after he had left.

Zoe, head bent, shoulders slumped, was going inside. She spun around before the whirlwind subsided. "Simon!" Pleasure leaped into her face, then diminished. "I thought you'd stay in Kaf. That's where you went, didn't you?"

"You didn't expect me ever to return?"

She shook her head, and touched one finger to the tablet. "You had your tablet."

Simon watched her slow strokes. She had made her wish expecting never to see him again. His gaze shifted from the tablet to her.

"Why?" he asked.

"Why what?"

"Why, with all you need, did you wish this?" He held up the tablet.

She turned away from him. "Because it was the right thing to do. Because you deserve to be free."

"You could have found seven summoners and still retained your last wish, for Mary's custody or for ZEVA, if not for yourself."

She shook her head. "You were growing weak. You might not have survived."

Simon frowned. The idea that she had dared so much, that she had sacrificed so much, out of pity for him rankled. It also did not seem entirely true. "Was that the only reason?"

"What other reason could there be?"

"You tell me, Zoe." He drew one finger from the pulse at her neck up to her chin. With a delicate pressure, he turned her face toward his. "Look at me, Zoe," he whispered. Her eyes captured his. "Tell me," he breathed, his thumb caressing her lips in an airy stroke.

She drew in a deep, shuddering breath, but her eyes didn't waver from his. "Because I love you."

Because I love you. With those four simple words, Simon's world shifted and rearranged itself.

Because I love you. The words echoed inside him, filling him with their sweet melody.

The bonds with Terra had started with his exile, with his many hours spent in this land, with his recent experiences as a human.

Because I love you. It had been Zoe's love that had made those bonds so strong and lasting.

Zoe's love for him.

And his love for her.

"You love me?" he repeated. "You never said that before."

She smiled. "I did once, but you weren't conscious at the time, and it doesn't change the fact that your home is Kaf."

He slid between her and the screen door and bracketed her face in his palms. Using the slightest pressure of his thumbs, he tilted her head to face him. "I have never known a female, human or djinn, like you, Zoe."

"I'll take that as a compliment." She gave a tiny laugh.

"Most assuredly." Her hair, the back of her neck were soft against his fingers. He breathed deep, drawing in her clean scent, as sweet as a fresh pear. Awe and love filled him. "I did not realize, until just this moment, how very much I love you, Zoe Calderone."

She sucked in a breath, let it out in a slow sigh. Then she smiled, wide and unrestrained.

The warmth of that smile heated him more than the sun and winds and sand of Kaf. He bent to her lips. She lifted on tiptoe to meet him halfway. Simon kissed the woman who was *janam*, his soul. The darkness of deep night about them crackled and sparked with the shining nimbus of djinn, and human, love.

Slowly, reluctantly, he ended the kiss. "Will you wait for me?" he asked in voice harsh with need.

"Wait for you?"

"I shall be back, to stay, but it will take time."

Her hands gripped the djinn bands around his upper arms. "What are you going to do?"

"Strengthen my ties to Terra."

"Strengthen—?" She shook him. "Is this that crazy thing you were telling me about at Brechtel? Severing the bonds to Kaf and forming new ones to earth?"

He didn't answer. Instead he gave in to the need to kiss her again. Her lips parted beneath his, yielding and giving. Her tongue met his in a fierce battle for possession.

"Where's Mary?" he whispered against her lips.

"With Elvina. Before we left, she asked if she could spend the remainder of the night in your old room."

Wrapping his arms around her, he transported

the two of them to her bedroom. In a moment, he had her tumbled on the bed.

"Where—?" Zoe exclaimed, looking around.

Simon swallowed the question with another kiss as he nudged her legs apart with his knee.

"You aren't going to distract me with sex," Zoe insisted, her voice muffled against his neck. Her words lost all power, however, as her hips moved against his.

He didn't answer, merely ran his hand down the front of her blouse, opening it. He snapped his fingers once and the front clasp of her bra opened. His hand slipped across her silky skin; he needed to feel her. No, he needed more. With a few muttered words, the jacket and her blouse and bra were gone. Simon sighed and laid a kiss on the tip of each breast.

"Well, maybe you could distract me for five minutes," Zoe said. She trailed tiny kisses up the throbbing vein in his neck, along his jaw, to his cheek.

"Five minutes? What I have in mind, I have never done in five minutes."

Oz leaped from his perch on the dresser to land on the pillow. Simon opened his eyes and glared into the whiskered face. Green eyes stared back impassively. Simon jerked his head once toward the door. Oz jumped to the floor and, tail held high, paced out of the room. The door swung shut behind him, and the lock turned with a click.

"Neat trick." Zoe kissed Simon's other cheek. "Five minutes is over," she announced in a ragged voice. Her hands rested on his chest with fingers digging lightly into the skin. She straightened at the elbows.

Simon allowed himself to be lifted a few inches, but only because it settled him more firmly between her thighs.

"You're going to try to switch your ties from Kaf to Terra, aren't you? You told me no djinni had done that before." She scowled. "It's too dangerous. I won't let you do it."

"You can't stop me."

She lifted her chin. "I won't wait for you."

Simon studied her and then kissed the tip of her nose. "Never lie to a djinni." His teasing mood faded. "Don't you see, Zoe? My future is on Terra. Kaf is no longer home. Home is where *you* are."

Her lids shuttered her eyes for a moment. "Blast you, Simon," she whispered.

"Now, what were we doing?"

He had only to say the words of *ma-at* in his mind. In a heartbeat, they were skin to skin, entwined under cool, smooth sheets. He circled his hand in the air, and the sounds of piano, harp, and desert breeze surrounded them in a melody formed by the rhythm of their loving.

Zoe was deeply asleep when Simon got out of bed. He gazed down at her, sending her one last, tender, mental kiss. *I love you, Zoe.* He gave her his thoughts, hoping they would become a part of her dreams.

He had two stops to make. At each, he found Roger and Dustyn sound asleep. He waited until they entered the dream state, then pressed his forefingers against their temples and entered their dreams with his thoughts. When he had finished, he knew both would doubt their memories of his djinn attributes. Instead, Roger would believe a neighbor's snake had bitten him, while Dustyn would ascribe his attack of conscience to a bad dream.

The first morning bird raised a lazy chirp at Simon's final stop, to bid a silent good-bye to Mary.

He remained invisible so as not to disturb her. She stirred, but didn't awaken, at the brief wind accompanying his arrival. A paper fluttered to the floor.

Simon picked it up. It was a companion sketch to the painting he'd seen at Dustyn's apartment, only this was a drawing of a troll sitting in the weeds at the edge of a pond. She'd caught the habitual troll scowl perfectly, Simon thought. In the background, a woman with an expression of surprised delight on her face peered into the weeds at a sparkling light. He turned it over. Mary had written a title on this one. "Mom Finds Magic."

Simon took the picture when he left.

Chapter Twenty-two

The room was Simon's favorite in his home. The walls were of lustrous blue and red except for the frame of white around Mary's painting. The thick floor covering was of scented moss. Chiming vines wound around the single window, which looked out to the distant mountains. A small brazier stood in the center. There was no furniture except the mounds of pillows. It was to this room that Simon retired for the daily meditations and training necessary to transfer the bonds of *ma-at*.

His time of preparation was ended.

As if on cue, he heard Darius's voice in his thoughts.

Simon, I am outside. May I come in?

You need ask? Enter, my friend.

Before Simon finished the thought, Darius had joined him. "You never stood on ceremony before, Darius. Why now?"

"I didn't want to disturb you. You will need every

bit of training and preparation." Darius sat cross-legged on the opposite side of the brazier from Simon. He stared into the glowing coals until they flared into yellow brilliance, and then sprinkled blue crystals on the flames. The resultant thin stream of smoke filled the room with the scent of sandalwood and rosemary, the djinn wishes for luck.

"Thank you," Simon said simply.

Darius looked at him. "Your time is near."

Simon nodded, though it hadn't been a question.

"Are you sure you want to do this? It's been tried before, never successfully."

"None of the other djinn had spent as much time on Terra as I. None had such strong ties calling to them."

"You will follow the time lines of Terra and will age as they do."

"I know." He would grow older with the woman he loved.

"Even if you survive, there is a chance you will lose the *ma-at*."

Simon nodded once, unable to speak. He knew the dangers, the possibilities, and they frightened him, but being with Zoe was more important.

"It will have been six months since you left. You won't be able to shift in time. Do you think she still waits?"

"Yes, I'm sure she does."

Darius stared at the smoke. "Humans expect one to work. What will you do?"

"I've found I have a talent for carpentry. Part of my time has been spent accumulating the knowledge I will need."

"You are determined? I can say nothing to change your mind?"

"I am determined."

Darius held up his hands and a bulging leather satchel materialized in them. "Then I have a gift for you. I have been studying Terran customs, and they place great store in these documents." He handed Simon the satchel.

Inside, Simon discovered, were a driver's license, a passport, naturalized citizenship papers, a birth certificate, a Social Security card, and a bank book with a healthy balance. All in the name of Simon James and carrying a likeness of him where needed. He held up a gold and blue plastic rectangle. "A Visa card?"

Darius shrugged. "Humans seem to find them important."

Simon inclined his head. "Thank you. I appreciate your efforts and your gift. I have something for you." He handed Darius the ancient book of Terran magic, knowing his friend's interest in the unique. "Zoe used this book to call me. It led to my freedom."

Darius bowed. "I shall remember whenever I look at it. I'm going to miss you, Simon."

"You can still visit me. That has not changed." Simon held out his hand. The two djinn clasped each other just below the elbow.

"May the earth and water of Terra grant you strength and joy."

"May the winds of Kaf blow you good fortune."

They squeezed tight for a moment, then unclasped by unspoken accord.

"Do you want me to leave?"

Simon shook his head. "Your presence gives me strength."

With a glance, Simon set the vines singing in a light breeze. He cast oily droplets on the brazier. The fire roared up in a foot-tall column. Resting his wrists on his knees, Simon closed his eyes.

He had been thinning the bonds to Kaf, pulling closer the bonds to Terra, during this time of preparation. In this final step, he had to cut the binding to Kaf before he could gather in and seal the binding to Terra. There would be an instant when he would be untethered to any *ma-at* or magic. If he could not complete the connection to Terra, he would be severed forever from *ma-at*, or he would dissolve into the cosmos.

Simon pulled the bonds of Kaf tight, thinning them until the barest of touches connected him to his home. Then, with a snap, he severed them.

Immediately, he felt himself tumbling, over and over, and with each spin, spreading into a thin, vaporous film. He heard a screaming and knew the agony was within him. Where were the welcoming bonds to Terra? He had lost them. He could not find his way.

He was fading. Zoe! Where was Zoe?

Singing; he heard singing. Sweet voices raised in tune.

"Dashing through the snow, in a one-horse open sleigh."

Dogs barking?

He turned toward the music accompanying the barking dogs.

"Arf, arf, arf, arf-arf."

"Bells on bobtails ring, making spirits bright."

He reached out. His mind grabbed onto the words. His soul captured the voices.

"Arf arf arf."

"Jingle bells, jingle bells, jingle all the way."

"Oh, what fun it is to ride in a one-horse open sleigh."

Mary and Zoe clamored out the words in merry

356

harmony above the dogs barking "Jingle Bells" on the radio.

"It's two days before Christmas," said the announcer before the dogs' howls faded. "With temperatures in the 70s expected for Christmas Eve day, WNOE is getting you in the mood with our all-day, all-zany Christmas hits. We may not have a white Christmas, but we've got the Christmas spirit. Next up? Patsy and Elmo singing 'Grandma Got Run Over by a Reindeer.'"

Laughing, Zoe collapsed on the living room sofa beside Elvina and sent an admiring glance toward the tree. It was more of a bush than a tree, but Elvina had bought it, claiming it was lonely and no one else would take it.

That had probably been an accurate prediction, Zoe agreed, for the bush was full on one side, barren on the other, and broadest in the middle. But when they had set it up, they found it had a straight, sturdy trunk and an abandoned bird's nest hidden in it. As they all decked the tree with their collections of home-made ornaments, it began to look pretty.

Mary claimed it would be a lucky tree, and Zoe knew who she was wishing for.

Although it had been six months since Simon had left, they all believed he would one day return. Mary had reasoned that Darius would have told them if it were otherwise. Zoe had no such logical reason. She simply knew he still lived, and that he had promised to return.

They had lived full lives, however, during the time of his absence.

ZEVA was doing better than ever, thanks to Leo's gushing praise of her sales catalog and Aaron Somerset's solid appreciation of her tutorials. Isaiah Knox had given them no further trouble; his brief jail time, trial, and subsequent fine had deflated his need for vengeance.

She looked over at Abby and Vivian, who were arguing about the best way to place tinsel. Once she'd started asking for, and listening to their advice, her partners had come up with some creative suggestions for improving ZEVA and increasing their own roles in the operation of the business. They were even thinking of hiring another multimedia designer.

"Do you want to put this up, Zoe?" Lucky held out the treetop angel.

Zoe shook her head. "You do it. You're the tallest."

Lucky nodded once, and then glanced toward Elvina. "You want to help?"

Elvina rummaged in the box at her feet and held up a chain made of colorful scraps of fabric. "Let's wrap this around the tree just beneath it."

It had taken some weeks, but Elvina had begun to see Lucky again. The fact that he had testified in Roger's trial had helped. For their testimony, both Lucky and Dustyn had received suspended sentences. After Roger went to jail, Dustyn had returned to California. He still kept in touch with Mary, but the question of custody was never raised. Zoe had kept much of her father's involvement in the sabotage concealed from Mary.

Zoe was pleased to note Elvina's blush when Lucky's hand brushed hers as they wound the fabric around the tree. Lucky was a rough man, but at heart he was a good one.

Zoe turned her attention to Mary, who was helping Joey set up the nativity scene. Mary had astounded her teachers by acing the accelerated math program this semester. Her explanation? "Mom made me study flash cards all summer."

Chris came into the room, carrying a small box. "Wait'll you see this!" He set the box on the floor, studied the tree a moment, and then adjusted the angle of the box. He flipped a switch on the side.

A sparkling glow of silver enveloped the tree.

Zoe drew in a sharp breath. It was the aura that surrounded Simon when he was angry. "It's beautiful," she whispered.

"Where did you get the idea for that?" Abby asked.

Chris cast a sidelong glance at Lucky, who was suddenly busy rearranging ornaments. Chris shrugged. "I, uh, experimented with it a few months ago. Saw a picture somewhere."

Zoe gazed at the tree, fighting back unwanted tears, unwilling to dim the celebration. Most of the time, she handled things very well, was happy and productive. Every once in a while, though, she'd see something, hear something, taste something, and memory would pierce her with keen longing.

There was still a gap in the center of her, a yearning for a missing part that she buried beneath good times, fellowship, and hard work. And she longed for magic. Not more spells, but the magic of love and laughter.

Mary stared at the tree for a moment, and then slipped out of the room. She came back carrying a rectangular package, which she tucked beneath the tree, at the back. She sat beside Zoe and rested her head on her mother's shoulder.

"It's for Simon," she whispered. "I painted a picture of Darius. Did you get Simon something?"

Zoe flushed. "Just a game," she muttered. She'd found a local artist who specialized in handmade games, toys, and puzzles and had commissioned him to make a one-of-a-kind cribbage board with a goose painted in the middle. "How about some popcorn? You can eat some and string some."

The doorbell rang.

Seven pairs of eyes turned to Zoe. She swallowed once and pressed her hand against the sudden fluttering in her stomach.

"You get it, Zoe," Elvina said.

It couldn't be Simon, Zoe told herself. Simon would materialize within their midst. It was the mailman or UPS or a neighbor.

A tall, muscular man stood on the porch examining the neighborhood, his back to her, a leather jacket snagged over his shoulder by one finger. He wore new tennis shoes, a lemon yellow sweatshirt, and a pair of faded jeans that hugged a butt she would recognize in the dark. As she would the tiny row of gold balls braided in the hair at his nape.

"Simon?" she whispered.

He whirled around.

"Simon." she repeated.

He still had the same wave in his hair, the same dark eyes, the same bronzed skin. The sunglasses were new, however. He looked gaunter, and, when he hooked the sunglasses in his shirt neckline, she realized there were faint lines about his eyes. She could see the gold of a chain about his neck.

He looked wonderful.

"Zoe?" Simon answered.

She looked wonderful.

She was still rounded and soft. The waves he'd put in her hair were there, but she'd had them cut and styled until they fell about her face in a cloud that had him longing to touch and caress. Her eyes were wide and lustrous and a smile played at the edges of her lips.

"Zoe," he repeated when she didn't move. Suddenly he was unsure, wondering if his confidence had been misplaced.

She smiled and flung herself against him.

His arms came about her.

She wrapped her arms around his head and pulled it down for a welcoming kiss that burned away all his doubts.

They were married as soon as the law allowed. Mary served as flower girl, Joey as ring bearer, Elina as matron of honor, and Darius as best man. Abby, Vivian, Chris, and Lucky were enthusiastic witnesses. Remembering Zoe's long-ago wish, Simon planned a honeymoon at Disney World.

Simon had studied human rites, ancient and modern. He found, now that he was of Terra, that these rituals fed his soul, bringing peace, endurance, and strength. On their wedding night, in a French Quarter bed-and-breakfast, he insisted on carrying his new bride over the threshold. Zoe complied with a delicate laugh.

Inside the spacious bedroom, Simon kicked the door shut with one foot, and then lowered her slowly to her feet, enjoying the feel of her curves sliding along him. Before her toes reached the ground, he couldn't resist stopping to kiss her neck, dislodging the sprig of orange blossom pinned in her hair. Only then did he set her down and step an arm's length back.

"You are so beautiful," he murmured, and then he gathered her back close. She readily came to him. "The management has left champagne. Do you want some?"

She shook her head, her soft hair tickling the bottom of his chin. "I'm giddy enough already."

He swelled, inside with pride, lower with desire, that he could make her feel so. "I love you, Zoe." He started undoing the buttons at her back.

"I love you, too, Simon."

One djinn ritual he had followed, asking Zoe to wear red for the ceremony. She had complied with a dress that shimmered and flowed every time she moved. At his first sight of her today, before the altar, he had felt keenly his insistence that they follow the human tradition of celibacy before the wedding.

They need wait no longer.

His hands lingered on her arms before sliding to her back and circling down to her hips. The red dress pooled around her feet, leaving her in a froth of lacy underwear, sheer stockings, garter belt, and a satin ribbon around her arm, the ribbon he had tied during the ceremony as a symbol of their unity. His blood pounded through him, intensifying the ache of desire and love.

He captured her hands between his, needing to perform one last ritual. "I desire now to be made one with thee." He kissed the tips of her fingers then the ring he'd given her. The ancient runes engraved in the hammered gold caught the evening light.

Zoe slid out her hands, laid them on his, and kissed his matching ring. "I desire now to be made one with thee."

"My *zaniya*." She belonged to him, and he to her by the laws of Terra, the custom of the djinn, and the words of the ancients. Simon gathered her close with one arm, capturing her mouth in a kiss that seared him to his bones, while he tore at his shirt studs with the other arm. He pressed her to him basking in the feel of her skin against his. In two quick movements, he had her where he wanted her naked in his arms.

He didn't intend to wait any longer.

Zoe pulled off his red cummerbund and tie, unfastened his belt.

Neither, apparently, did she.

Later, temporarily sated by the hot, quick explosion, Zoe sprawled on top of Simon, who ran a lazy hand up and down her spine. She rested her chin on her stacked hands and looked at him.

"You know, Simon, I wondered if the minister got part of the ceremony right."

"Which part?"

"The part that pronounced us man and wife."

He lifted his hips against hers and parted her legs until they rested on either side of his. "Do you doubt I am a man, my woman? Do you need more proof?"

Zoe laughed. "I meant, should he have said djinni and human?"

His hand, now cupping her bottom, stilled. "Would it make a difference to you?"

"I'd still love you, no matter what." She waited. When he didn't answer, she nudged him with her foot. "That's your cue to say, 'I love you, too, Zoe,' and then answer my question."

"I love you, too, Zoe," he dutifully parroted.

"And? I haven't seen you work any magic. You said you would age with me. So, I wondered. Should I be prepared for any djinni surprises?"

"Was there a specific reason you wanted to know right now?"

"Well, remember that one night? With the cloud bed? I've been having this fantasy. . . ." Her voice trailed off when his hand resumed its gentle explorations.

"When I substituted the bonds to Terra," Simon began, "I realized right away that something was different."

He's going to tell me he's lost his powers. Nice go-

ing, Zoe James, telling him about a djinni fantasy. "I
doesn't matter, Simon. It's you that I love."

He laid a finger to her lips, silencing her. "I am
enjoying all the rituals of Terra because they give
me power. On Kaf, the *ma-at* is more . . . ethereal
is the best word I can think of. On Terra, magic is
more rooted, temporal. It is as strong, just different.
I thought I would give you time to get used to me
again, before springing any surprises on you."

While he spoke, his hands slid down her back and
across her bottom, then caressed up her sides, trailing stardust in his wake. He touched the wall above
his head, and then gave an expansive wave before
settling his hands at her waist to hold her tightly to
him. Though Simon lay quietly beneath her, Zoe
saw his eyes blaze with heat and felt kisses on her
nose, her chin, her neck, lower, then lower still, until she blushed.

"So, you're still a djinni?" she asked breathlessly

"What do you think? Look around."

Zoe blinked, realizing that the room had taken
on a soft rosy hue. She shifted for a better look and
felt the rustle of silk on her skin. She looked down
her front, but from her position on Simon, with his
arm clamped about her waist, she couldn't see too
much. But even that small peek was enough to see
the top of the glittery vest she now wore and the
purple robe about his shoulders.

Delighted, she gazed around the room. Soft
chimes came from the walls, where vines entwined
the room, their shiny leaves swinging in a barely
felt breeze. Tendrils of sweet-smelling smoke
wafted along the floor.

"Hold me," he whispered, and Zoe complied, encircling his smooth, strong shoulders beneath the
purple silk. Simon rolled over. His weight pressed
her into a mound of pillows that billowed around

them. Fragrant flowers drifted down from above, so wherever she moved delicate scents of orange blossom and lavender surrounded her. Gauzy veils of pink, rose, and white encircled them.

Zoe ran her hands along the delicate fabric of his purple cloth robe. The fabric shimmered with changing patterns of lights and clouds where she moved it.

"You see," Simon whispered, "whatever you wish is mine to make true."

"All I want is your love."

"And that you have. Forever." He bent to her lips. The air surrounding them began to spark and shimmer.

Zoe laughed. Simon joined her, in body, in joy, in love.

Heart's Magic

Flora Speer

Bestselling author of *ROSE RED*

In the year 1122, Mirielle senses change is coming to Wroxley Castle. Then, from out of the fog, two strangers ride into Lincolnshire. Mirielle believes the first man to be honest. But the second, Giles, is hiding something–even as he stirs her heart and awakens her deepest desires. And as Mirielle seeks the truth about her mysterious guest, she uncovers the castle's secrets and learns she must stop a treachery which threatens all she holds dear. Only then can she be in the arms of her only love, the man who has awakened her own heart's magic.

___52204-7 $5.99 US/$6.99 CAN